RELIC

By Douglas Preston
Jennie
Cities of Gold
Dinosaurs in the Attic

Edited by Lincoln Child
Dark Company
Dark Banquet
Tales of the Dark 1–3

RELIC

DOUGLAS PRESTON

LINCOLN CHILD

A TOM DOHERTY ASSOCIATES BOOK
NEW YORK

RELIC

Copyright © 1995 by Douglas Preston and Lincoln Child

This book is printed on acid-free paper.

A Forge Book
Published by Tom Doherty Associates, Inc.
175 Fifth Avenue
New York, N.Y. 10010

ISBN 0-312-85630-X

First edition: February 1995

Printed in the United States of America

0 9 8 7 6 5 4 3 2 1

To Charles Crumly.
   —D. P.

To Luchie, who came along for the ride.
And in memory of Nora and Gaga.
   —L. C.

ACKNOWLEDGMENTS

The authors wish to express their thanks to the following persons, who generously lent their time and/or expertise in helping to make *Relic* the book it is: Ken Goddard, Tom Doherty, Bob Gleason, Harvey Klinger, Anna Magee, Camille Cline, Denis Kelly, Georgette Piligian, Michael O'Connor, Carina Deleon, Fred Ziegler, Bob Wincott, Lou Perretti, and Harry Trumbore.

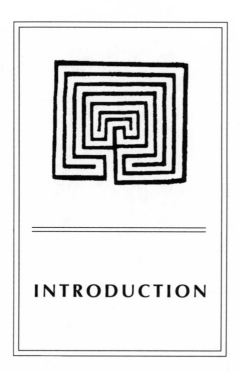

INTRODUCTION

= 1 =

The Amazon Basin, September 1987

At noon, the clouds clinging to the top of Cerro Gordo broke free and scattered. Far above, in the upper reaches of the forest canopy, Whittlesey could see golden tints of sunlight. Animals—probably spider monkeys—thrashed and hooted above his head and a macaw swooped low, squawking obscenely.

Whittlesey stopped next to a fallen jacaranda tree and watched Carlos, his sweating camp assistant, catch up.

"We will stop here," he said in Spanish. "*Baja la caja*. Put down the box."

Whittlesey sat down on the fallen tree and pulled off his right boot and sock. Lighting a cigarette, he applied its tip to the forest of ticks on his shin and ankle.

Carlos unshouldered an old army packboard, on which a wooden crate was awkwardly lashed.

"Open it, please," said Whittlesey.

Carlos removed the ropes, unsnapped a series of small brass clasps, and pulled off the top.

The contents were packed tightly with the fibers of an indigenous plant. Whittlesey pulled aside the fibers, exposing some artifacts, a small wooden plant press, and a stained leather journal. He hesitated a moment, then drew a small but exquisitely carved figurine of a beast from the shirt pocket of his field jacket. He hefted the artifact in his hand, admiring again its workmanship, its unnatural heaviness. Then he placed it reluctantly in the crate, covered everything with the fibers, and reattached the lid.

From his rucksack, Whittlesey took out a folded sheet of blank paper, which he opened on his knee. He brought a battered gold pen out of his shirt pocket and began writing:

> Upper Xingú
> Sept. 17, 1987
>
> Montague,
> I've decided to send Carlos back with the last crate and go on alone in search of Crocker. Carlos is trustworthy, and I can't risk losing the crate should anything happen to me. Take note of the shaman's rattle and other ritual objects. They seem unique. But the figurine I've enclosed, which we found in a deserted hut at this site, is the proof I've been looking for. Note the exaggerated claws, the reptilian attributes, the hints at *bipedalia*. The Kothoga exist, and the Mbwun legend is not mere fabrication.
> All my field notes are in this notebook. It also contains a complete account of the breakup of the expedition, which you will of course know about by the time this reaches you.

Whittlesey shook his head, remembering the scene that had played itself out the day before. That idiotic bastard, Maxwell. All he'd cared about was getting those specimens he'd stumbled on back to the Museum undamaged. Whittlesey laughed silently to himself. Ancient eggs. As if they were anything more than worthless seed pods. Maxwell should have been a paleobiologist instead of a physical anthropologist. How ironic they'd packed up and left a mere thousand yards from his *own* discovery.

In any case, Maxwell was gone now, and the others with him. Only Carlos and Crocker, and two guides, had stayed. Now there was just Carlos. Whittlesey returned to the note.

> Use my notebook and the artifacts, as you see fit, to help restore my good standing with the Museum. But above all else, take care of this figurine. I am convinced that its worth to anthropology is incalculable. We discovered it yesterday by accident. It seems to be the centerpiece of the Mbwun cult. However, there is no other trace of habitation nearby. This strikes me as odd.

Whittlesey paused. He hadn't described the discovery of the figurine in his field notes. Even now, his mind resisted the memory.

Crocker had wandered off the trail for a better look at a jacamar; otherwise they'd never have found the hidden path, slanting down steeply between moss-slick walls. Then, that crude hut, half-buried among ancient trees, in the wet vale where daylight barely penetrated . . . The two Botocudo guides, normally chattering nonstop to each other in Tupian, shut up immediately. When questioned by Carlos, one of them just muttered something about a guardian of the hut, and a curse on anybody who violated its secrets. Then, for the first time, Whittlesey had heard them speak the word *Kothoga*. Kothoga. The shadow people.

Whittlesey was skeptical. He'd heard talk of curses before—usually, right before a request for higher wages. But when he emerged from the hut, the guides were gone.

. . . Then that old woman, blundering out of the forest. She was probably Yanomamo, obviously not Kothoga. But she knew of them. *She had seen them.* The curses she'd hinted at . . . And the way she'd just melted back into the forest, more like a jaguar yearling than a septuagenarian.

Then, they turned their attention to the hut.

The hut . . . Gingerly, Whittlesey allowed himself to remember. It was flanked by two stone tablets with identical carvings of a beast sitting on its haunches. Its claw held something weathered and indistinguishable. Behind the hut lay an overgrown garden, a bizarre oasis of bright color amid the green fastness.

The floor of the hut was sunken several feet, and Crocker almost broke his neck on the way in. Whittlesey followed him more carefully, while Carlos simply knelt in the entranceway. The air inside was dark and cool and smelt of decaying earth. Switching on his flashlight, Whittlesey saw the figurine sitting on a tall earthen mound in the middle of the hut. Around its base lay a number of strangely carved discs. Then the flashlight reached the walls.

The hut had been lined with human skulls. Examining a few of the closest, Whittlesey noticed deep scratch marks he could not immediately understand. Ragged holes yawned through the tops. In many cases, the occipital bone at the base of the skull was also smashed and broken off, the heavy squamosal bones completely gone.

His hand shook, and the flashlight failed. Before he switched it on again, he saw dim light filtering through thousands of eye sockets, dust motes swimming sluggishly in the heavy air.

Afterward, Crocker decided he needed a short walk—to be alone for a while, he'd told Whittlesey. But he hadn't come back.

The vegetation here is very unusual. The cycads and ferns look almost primordial. Too bad there isn't time for more careful study. We've used a particularly resilient variety as packing material for the crates; feel free to let Jörgensen take a look, if he's interested.

I fully expect to be with you at the Explorer's Club a month from now, celebrating our success with a brace of dry martinis and a good Macanudo. Until then, I know I can entrust this material and my reputation to you.
Your colleague,

Whittlesey

He inserted the letter beneath the lid of the crate.

"Carlos," he said, "I want you to take this crate back to Pôrto de Mós, and wait for me there. If I'm not back in two weeks, talk to Colonel Soto. Tell him to ship it back with the rest of the crates by air to the Museum, as agreed. He will draw your wages."

Carlos looked at him. "I do not understand," he said. "You will stay here alone?"

Whittlesey smiled, lit a second cigarette, and resumed killing ticks. "Someone has to bring the crate out. You should be able to catch up with Maxwell before the river. I want a couple of days to search for Crocker."

Carlos slapped his knee. "*Es loco!* I can't leave you alone. *Si te dejo atrás, te morirías.* You will die here in the forest, *Señor,* and your bones will be left to the howler monkeys. We must go back together, that is best."

Whittlesey shook his head impatiently. "Give me the Mercurochrome and the quinine, and the dried beef from your pack," he said, pulling the filthy sock back on and lacing his boot.

Carlos started unpacking, still protesting. Whittlesey ignored him, absently scratching insect bites on the back of his neck and staring up toward Cerro Gordo.

"They will wonder, *Señor.* They will think I left you. It will be very bad for me," Carlos said rapidly, placing the items in Whittlesey's pack. "The cabouri flies will eat you alive," he continued, moving over to the crate and lashing it shut. "You will catch malaria again, and die this time. I will stay with you."

Whittlesey stared at the shock of snow-white hair plastered to Carlos's sweaty forehead. That hair had been pure black yesterday, before Carlos looked into the hut. Carlos met his gaze for a moment, then lowered his eyes.

Whittlesey stood up. *"Adiós,"* he said, and disappeared into the bush.

By late afternoon, Whittlesey noticed that the thick, low clouds had returned to shroud Cerro Gordo. For the last several miles, he had been following an ancient trail of unknown origin, barely a narrow alley in the brush. The trail cleverly worked its way through the black-water swamps surrounding the base of the *tepui,* the soggy, jungle-clotted plateau that lay ahead. The trail had the logic of a human trail, Whittlesey thought. It moved with obvious purpose; animal tracks often wandered. And it was heading for a steep ravine in the shoulder of the approaching *tepui.* Crocker must have come this way.

He stopped to consider, unconsciously fingering the talisman—a gold arrow overlaid by another of silver—that had hung around his neck since childhood. Besides the hut, they'd seen no sign of human habitation for the last several days except a long-deserted root-gatherer village. Only the Kothoga could have created this path.

As he approached the plateau, he could see a few braids of water cascading down its steep flanks. He would camp at the bottom tonight, and make the thousand-meter ascent in the morning. It would be steep, muddy, and possibly dangerous. If he met the Kothoga—well, he would be trapped.

But he had no reason to think the Kothoga tribe was savage. After all, it was this other creature, Mbwun, to which local myth cycles ascribed all the killing and savagery. Strange—an unknown creature, supposedly controlled by a tribe nobody had seen. *Could Mbwun actually exist?* he wondered. Conceivably, a small remnant could be alive in this vast rain forest; the area was virtually unexplored by biologists. Not for the first time, he wished that Crocker hadn't taken his own Mannlicher .30 06 when he'd left camp.

But first, Whittlesey realized, he had to locate Crocker. Then he could search for the Kothoga, prove they hadn't died out centuries before. He'd be famous—the discoverer of an ancient people, living in a kind of Stone Age purity deep in the Amazon, on a plateau that floated above the jungle like Arthur Conan Doyle's *The Lost World.*

There was no reason to fear the Kothoga. *Except that hut . . .*

Suddenly, a sharp sickly smell assailed his nostrils, and he stopped.

There was no mistaking it—a dead animal, and a big one. He took a dozen steps as the smell intensified. His heart quickened with anticipation: perhaps the Kothoga had butchered an animal nearby. There might be artifacts left at the site—tools, weapons, perhaps even something ceremonial in nature.

He crept forward. The sweet nauseating reek grew stronger. He could see sunlight in a patch of canopy high above his head—the sure sign of a nearby clearing. He stopped and tightened his pack, not wanting to be hampered in case he had to move fast.

The narrow trail, walled in by brush, leveled off and took a sudden turn into the head of the small clearing. There, on the opposite side, was the carcass of the animal. The base of the tree it lay against had been ritually carved with a spiral, and a bundle of bright green parrot feathers lay on top of the gaping, greasy brown rib cage.

But as he walked closer, he saw that the carcass was wearing a khaki shirt.

A cloud of fat flies roared and swarmed about the open rib cage. Whittlesey noticed that a severed left arm was lashed to the tree trunk with a fibrous rope, the palm sliced open. A number of spent cartridge casings lay around the body. Then he saw the head. It lay face up under the corpse's armpit, the back of the skull torn away, the cloudy eyes staring upward, the cheeks bulging.

Whittlesey had found Crocker.

Instinctively, Whittlesey began stumbling backward. He saw how rows of claws had flayed the body with obscene, inhuman strength. The corpse looked stiff. Perhaps—if God was merciful—the Kothoga had already departed.

Assuming it was the Kothoga.

Then he noticed that the rain forest, normally overflowing with the sounds of life, was silent. With a start, he turned to face the jungle. Something was moving in the towering brush at the edge of the clearing, and two slitted eyes the color of liquid fire took shape between the leaves. With a sob and a curse, he drew his sleeve across his face and looked again. The eyes had vanished.

There was no time to lose—he had to get back down the trail, away from this place. His path back into the forest lay directly ahead. He'd have to make a run for it.

Just then he saw something on the ground he hadn't noticed before, and he heard movement, ponderous yet horrifyingly stealthy, through the brush in front of him.

= **2** =

Belém, Brazil, July 1988

This time, Ven was pretty sure the dock foreman was onto him.

He stood well back in the shadows of the warehouse alley, watching. Light rain obscured the bulky outlines of the tethered freighters and narrowed the dock lights into pinpoints. Steam rose as the rain hit the hot deckboards, bringing with it the faint odor of creosote. From behind him came the nocturnal sounds of the port: the staccato bark of a dog; faint laughter leavened with Portuguese phrases; calypso music from the waterfront bars on the avenida.

It had been such a sweet deal. He'd come down when Miami got too hot, taking the long route. Here, it was mostly light trade, small freighters bound up and down the coast. The dock crew always needed stevedores, and he'd loaded boats before. He'd said his name was Ven Stevens, and no one questioned it. They wouldn't have believed a first name of Stevenson, anyway.

The setup here had all the right ingredients. He'd had plenty of practice in Miami, plenty of time to sharpen his instincts. Those instincts paid off down here. Deliberately, he spoke Portuguese badly, haltingly, so he could read eyes and gauge responses. Ricon, junior assistant to the harbormaster, was the last link Ven had needed.

Ven was alerted when a shipment was coming in from upriver. Usually he'd just be given two names: incoming and outgoing. He always knew what to look for, the boxes were always the same. He'd see that they were safely off-loaded and stowed in the warehouse. Then, he just made sure they were the last cargo loaded onto the designated freighter headed for the States.

Ven was naturally cautious. He'd kept a close eye on the dock foreman. Once or twice he'd had a feeling, like a warning bell in his brain, that the foreman suspected something. But each time Ven had eased up a little, and in a few days the warning bell had gone away.

Now he checked his watch. Eleven o'clock. He heard a door opening, then closing, from around the corner. Ven drew himself up against the wall. Heavy footfalls sounded against wooden planking, then the familiar form passed under a streetlight. When the footsteps receded, Ven peered around the corner. The office was dark, deserted, as he knew it would be. With a last glance, he edged around the corner of the building, onto the docks.

An empty backpack slapped damply against his shoulders with each step. As he walked, Ven reached into a pocket, withdrew a key, and clenched it tightly. That key was his lifeline. Before he'd spent two days on the docks, he'd had an impression made of it.

Ven passed a small freighter berthed along the wharf, its heavy hawsers dripping black water onto rusted bitts. The ship seemed deserted, not even a harbor watch on deck. He slowed. The warehouse door lay directly ahead, near the end of the main pier. Ven glanced quickly over his shoulder. Then, with a quick turn of his hand, he unlocked the metal door and slipped inside.

Pulling the door closed, he let his eyes grow accustomed to the darkness. Halfway home. He just had to finish up in here and get the hell out.

As soon as possible. Because Ricon was growing greedy, cruzeiros running through his hands like water. Last time, he'd made a crack about the size of his cut. Just that morning, Ricon and the foreman had been talking fast and low, the foreman looking over at Ven. Now, Ven's instincts told him to get away.

Inside, he saw the darkened warehouse resolve itself into a vague landscape of cargo containers and packing crates. He couldn't chance a flashlight, but it didn't matter: he knew the layout well enough to walk it in his dreams. He moved forward carefully, threading a path through the vast mountains of cargo.

At last, he saw the landmark he'd been waiting for: a battered-looking stack of crates, six large and one small, stacked in a forlorn corner. Two of the larger crates were stenciled MNH, NEW YORK.

Months before, Ven had asked about these crates. The quartermaster's boy had told him the story. Seemed the crates had come downriver from Pôrto de Mós the previous fall. They'd been scheduled for air shipment to a New York museum, but something had happened to the people who'd made the arrangements—the apprentice couldn't say exactly what. But payment hadn't come through in time, and now the crates were snarled in a mass of red tape, seemingly forgotten.

Except by Ven. There was just enough room behind the forgotten crates for him to stash his shipments until the outgoing freighters were loading.

The warm night breeze came in from a broken window high in the wall, stirring the sweat on Ven's forehead. He smiled in the darkness. Just the other week, he'd learned that soon the crates would finally be shipped back to the States. But he'd be long gone by then.

Now, he checked his own cache. Just a single box this time, whose contents would fit nicely into the corners of his backpack. He knew where the markets were and what to do. And he'd be doing it—somewhere far away—very soon.

As he was about to squeeze behind the large crates, Ven stopped abruptly. There was a strange odor here: something earthy, goatish, decaying. A lot of odd cargoes had come through the port, but none smelling quite like this.

His instincts were going off five-alarm, yet he couldn't detect anything wrong or out of place. He slid forward, between the Museum cargo and the wall.

He stopped again. Something wasn't right back here. Something wasn't right at all.

He heard, rather than saw, something moving in the cramped space. The pungent odor welled forward, blanketing him with its rotten stench. Suddenly, he was slammed against the wall with terrific force. Pain exploded in his chest and gut. He opened his mouth to scream, but something was boiling in his throat, and then a stab like lightning tore through his skull, leaving only darkness behind.

MUSEUM OF
UNNATURAL
MYSTERY

PART ONE

= 3 =

New York, Present Day

The red-haired kid was clambering onto the platform, calling his younger brother a chicken, reaching toward the elephant's foot. Juan eyed him silently, easing himself forward just as the kid's hand touched the exhibit.

"Yo!" Juan yelled, breaking into a trot. "Hey, no touching the elephants." The boy looked scared and snatched back his hand; he was still at an age where a uniform impressed him. Older ones—fifteen, sixteen—would give Juan the finger sometimes. They knew he was only a museum guard. Lousy fucking job. One of these days he was going to finish that equivalency shit and take the police exam.

He watched suspiciously as red-hair and little brother walked around the cases in the darkened hall, looking at the stuffed lions. At the case full of chimps, the boy started hooting and scratching under his arms, showing off for junior's benefit. Where the hell were the parents?

Now Billy, the redhead, tugged his little brother into a chamber filled with African artifacts. A row of masks with flat wooden teeth leered at them from a showcase. "Wow!" exclaimed Billy's kid brother.

"That's *dumb*," said Billy. "We're going to see the dinosaurs."

"Where's Mommy?" said the kid, screwing his head around.

"Aw, she got lost," said Billy. "Come on."

They began to move through a vast, echoing hall filled with totem poles. At the far end, a woman holding a red flag was leading the final tour group of the day, her voice shrill. To Billy's younger brother, the hall smelled faintly spooky, like smoke and old tree roots. When the group disappeared around a corner, the hall fell silent.

The last time they had been there, Billy remembered, they had seen the biggest brontosaurus in the world, and a tyrannosaurus and a trachydent. At least, that's what he thought it was called, a trachydent. The teeth on the tyrannosaurus must have been ten feet long. That was just about the greatest thing Billy had ever seen. But he didn't remember seeing these totem poles. Maybe the dinosaurs were through the next door. But that led only to the boring Hall of Pacific Peoples, full of jades and ivories and silks and bronze statues.

"Now look what you did," said Billy.

"What?"

"You made me get lost, that's what," said Billy.

"Mommy's gonna be *real* mad," the kid said.

Billy snorted. They weren't supposed to meet his parents until closing time, on the big front steps. He'd find his way out, no problem.

They wound through several more dusty rooms, down a narrow flight of stairs, and into a long dim hall. Thousands of little stuffed birds lined the walls from floor to ceiling, white cotton poking out of sightless eyes. The hall was empty and smelled of mothballs.

"I know where we are," said Billy, hopefully, peering into the dimness.

The kid started to snuffle.

"Shut up," said Billy. The snuffling stopped.

The hall took a sharp dogleg, ending in a darkened cul-de-sac full of dust and empty display cases. There were no visible exits except back through the hall of dead birds. The footfalls of the children echoed hollowly, far from the other Sunday tourists. Against the far side of the chamber stood a rolling barricade of canvas and wood, pretending unsuccessfully to be a wall. Letting go of his brother's hand, Billy walked up and peered behind the barricade.

"I been here before," he said confidently. "They've closed this place off, but it was open last time. I bet we're right below the dinosaurs. Lemme just see if there's a way up."

"You're not supposed to go back there," the kid brother warned.

"Listen, stupid, I'm going. And you'd better wait." Billy ducked behind the barricade, and a few moments later the kid heard the squeal of metal as a door was pulled open.

"Hey!" came Billy's voice. "There's a spiral staircase here. It only goes down, but it's cool. I'm gonna try it out."

"Don't! Billy!" the kid cried, but the only answer was retreating footsteps.

The kid started to bawl, his thin voice rising in the gloom of the hall. After a few minutes he fell to hiccupping, sniffed loudly, and sat down on the floor. He started pulling on a little flap of rubber that was coming off the toe of his sneaker, working it loose.

Suddenly, he looked up. The hall was silent and airless. The lights in the cases threw black shadows on the floor. A forced-air duct thumped and began to rumble somewhere. Billy was gone for real now. The kid started to cry again, louder this time.

Maybe it would be okay if he followed Billy. Maybe it wasn't such a scary thing after all. Maybe Billy had gone ahead and found his parents, and they were waiting for him, there on the other side. But he had to hurry. The Museum was probably closed by now.

He stood up and slipped behind the partition. The hall continued on, the cases filled with the dust and mold of long-neglected exhibits. An ancient metal door on one side of the hall was slightly ajar.

The kid walked up to it and peered in. Behind the door was the top landing of a narrow spiral staircase that circled downward out of sight. It was even dustier here, and there was a strange smell in the air that made his nose wrinkle. He didn't want to stand on those steps, at all. But Billy was down there.

"Billy!" he called. "Billy, come up! *Please!*"

In the cavernous gloom, his echoes were the only answer. The child sniffled, then gripped the railing and began walking slowly down into darkness.

= 4 =

Monday

As Margo Green rounded the corner of West Seventy-second Street, the early morning sun struck her square in the face. She looked down a minute, blinking; then, tossing her brown hair back, she crossed the street. The New York Museum of Natural History loomed before her like an ancient fortress, its vast Beaux Arts facade climbing ponderously above a row of copper benches.

Margo turned down the cobbled driveway that led to the staff entrance. She walked past a loading dock and headed for the granite tunnel leading to the interior courtyards of the Museum. Then she slowed, wary. Flickering stripes of red light were painting the mouth of the tunnel in front of her. At the far end, she could see ambulances, police cars, and an Emergency Services vehicle, all parked at random.

Margo entered the tunnel and walked toward a glass pillbox. Normally, old Curly the guard would be dozing in his chair at this time of the morning, propped up against the pillbox corner, a blackened calabash pipe resting on his ample front. But today he was awake and standing. He slid the door open. "Morning, Doctor," he said. He called everyone 'doctor,' from graduate students to the Museum Director, whether they owned that title or not.

"What's up?" Margo asked.

"Don't know," Curly said. "They just got here two minutes ago. But I guess I'd better see your ID this time."

Margo rummaged in her carryall, wondering if she even had her ID. It had been months since someone had asked to see it. "I'm not sure I've got it with me," she said, annoyed that she hadn't cleaned her bag of last winter's detritus. Her carryall had recently won 'messiest bag in the Museum' status from her friends in the Anthro Department.

The pillbox telephone rang, and Curly reached for it. Margo found her ID and held it up to the window, but Curly ignored her, his eyes wide as he listened to the receiver.

He put it down without saying a word, his whole body rigidly at attention.

"Well?" Margo asked. "What's happened?"

Curly removed his pipe. "You don't want to know," he said.

The phone rang again and Curly grabbed it.

Margo had never seen the guard move so quickly. She shrugged, dropped the ID back in her bag, and walked on. The next chapter of her dissertation was coming due, and she couldn't afford to lose a single day. The week before had been a write-off—the service for her father, the formalities, the phone calls. Now, she couldn't lose any more time.

Crossing the courtyard, she entered the Museum through the staff door, turned right, and hurried down a long basement corridor toward the Anthropology Department. The various staff offices were dark, as they always were until nine-thirty or ten o'clock.

The corridor took an abrupt right angle, and she stopped. A band of yellow plastic tape was stretched across the corridor. Margo could make out the printing: NYPD CRIME SCENE—DO NOT CROSS. Jimmy, a guard usually assigned to the Peruvian Gold Hall, was standing in front of the tape with Gregory Kawakita, a young Assistant Curator in the Evolutionary Biology Department.

"What's going on here?" Margo asked.

"Typical Museum efficiency," Kawakita said with a wry smile. "We've been locked out."

"Nobody's told me nothing, except to keep everyone out," the guard said nervously.

"Look," Kawakita said, "I'm giving a presentation to the NSF tomorrow, and this day's going to be a long one. Now, if you'll let me—"

Jimmy looked uncomfortable. "I'm just doing my job, okay?"

"Come on," Margo said to Kawakita. "Let's get some coffee up in the lounge. Maybe someone there will know what's going on."

"First I want to hunt down a men's room, if I can find one that isn't sealed off," Kawakita responded irritably. "I'll meet you there."

* * *

The door to the staff lounge, which was never closed, was closed today. Margo put her hand on the knob, wondering if she should wait for Kawakita. Then she opened the door. It would be a cold day in hell when she needed *him* as backup.

Inside, two policemen were talking, their backs turned to her. One sniggered. "What was that, number six?" he said.

"Lost count," the other replied. "But he can't have any more break-fast to bring up." As the officers moved apart, Margo got a look at the lounge behind them.

The large room was deserted. In the kitchen area at the far end, someone was leaning over the sink. He spat, wiped his mouth, and turned around. Margo recognized Charlie Prine, the new conservation expert in the Anthro Department, hired on a temporary grant six months before to restore objects for the new exhibition. His face was ashen and expressionless.

Moving to Prine's side, the officers propelled him gently forward.

Margo stood aside to let the group pass. Prine walked stiffly, like a robot. Instinctively, Margo's eyes traveled downward.

Prine's shoes were soaked in blood.

Watching her vacantly, Prine registered the change of expression. His eyes followed hers; then he stopped so suddenly that the cop behind plowed into his back.

Prine's eyes grew large and white. The policemen grabbed his arms and he resisted, neighing in panic. Quickly, they moved him out of the room.

Margo leaned against the wall, willing her heart to slow down as Kawakita came in, followed by several others. "Half this Museum must be sealed off," he said, shaking his head and pouring himself a cup of coffee. "Nobody can get into their offices."

As if on cue, the Museum's ancient PA system wheezed into operation. "*Attention please. All nonsupport personnel currently on the premises please report to the staff lounge.*"

As they sat down, more staffers entered in twos and threes. Lab technicians, for the most part, and assistant curators without tenure; too early for the really important people. Margo watched them detachedly. Kawakita was talking but she couldn't hear him.

Within ten minutes, the room was packed. Everyone was talking at once: expressing outrage that their offices were off-limits, complaining about how no one was telling them anything, discussing each new rumor in shocked tones. Clearly, in a museum where nothing exciting ever seemed to happen, they were having the time of their lives.

Kawakita gulped his coffee, made a face. "Will you look at that sediment?" He turned toward her. "Been struck dumb, Margo? You haven't said a word since we sat down."

Haltingly, she told him about Prine. Kawakita's handsome features narrowed. "My God," he finally said. "What do you suppose happened?"

As his baritone voice boomed, Margo realized that the conversation in the lounge had died away. A heavyset, balding man in a brown suit was standing in the doorway, a police radio shoved into one pocket of his ill-fitting jacket, an unlit cigar protruding from his mouth. Now he strode through, followed by two uniformed policemen.

He centered himself at the front of the room, hiked up his pants, removed his cigar, picked a piece of tobacco off his tongue, and cleared his throat. "May I have your attention, please," he said. "A situation has arisen that's going to require you to bear with us for a while."

Suddenly, a voice rang out accusingly from the back of the room. "Ex-*cuse* me, Mister? . . ."

Margo craned her neck over the crowd. "Freed," Kawakita whispered. Margo had heard of Frank Freed, a testy Ichthyology curator.

The man in brown turned to look at Freed. "Lieutenant D'Agosta," he rapped out. "New York City Police Department."

It was a reply that would have shut most people up. Freed, an emaciated man with long gray hair, was undaunted. "Perhaps," he said sarcastically, "we may be informed of what exactly is going on around here? I think we have a right . . ."

"I'd *like* to brief you on what happened," D'Agosta resumed. "But at this point, all we can say is that a body has been found on the premises, under circumstances we are currently investigating. If—"

At the explosion of talk, D'Agosta wearily held up his hand.

"I can only tell you that a homicide squad is on the scene and that an investigation is in progress," he continued. "Effective immediately, the Museum is closed. For the time being, no one may enter, and no one may leave. We expect this to be a very temporary condition."

He paused. "If a homicide has occurred, there is a possibility, a *possibility*, that the killer is still inside the Museum. We would merely ask you to remain here an hour or two while a sweep is conducted. A police officer will be around to take your names and titles."

In the stunned silence that followed, he left the room, closing the door behind him. One of the remaining policemen dragged a chair over to the door and sat down heavily in it. Slowly, the conversations began to resume. "We're being locked in here?" Freed cried out. "This is outrageous."

"Jesus," Margo breathed. "You don't suppose Prine is a murderer?"

"Scary thought, isn't it?" Kawakita said. He stood up and went to the coffee machine, beating the last drops out of the urn with a savage blow. "But not as scary as the thought of being unprepared for my presentation tomorrow."

Margo knew Kawakita, young fast-track scientist that he was, would never be unprepared for anything.

"Image is everything today," Kawakita went on. "Pure science alone doesn't get the grants anymore."

Margo nodded again. She heard him, and she heard the swirl of voices around them, but none of it seemed important. Except for the blood on Prine's shoes.

= 5 =

"Listen up," the policeman said an hour later. "You're free to go now. Just be sure to stay out of the areas behind the yellow tape."

Margo raised her head from her arms with a start as a hand landed on her shoulder. Tall, lanky Bill Smithback clutched two spiral notebooks in the other hand, and his brown hair looked, as usual, as if he'd just gotten out of bed. A chewed pencil was tucked behind one ear, his collar was unbuttoned and his grimy tie knot pulled down. The perfect caricature of a hard-driving journalist, and Margo suspected he cultivated the look. Smithback had been commissioned to write a book about the Museum, focusing on the *Superstition* exhibition that would open next week.

"Unnatural doings at the Natural History Museum," Smithback muttered darkly in her ear as he folded himself into a chair beside her. He slapped his notebooks on the table, and a flood of handwritten papers, unlabeled computer diskettes, and xeroxed articles covered with yellow highlighting spilled across the Formica surface.

"Hello, Kawakita!" Smithback said jovially, slapping him on the shoulder. "Seen any tigers lately?"

"Only the paper variety," Kawakita replied dryly.

Smithback turned to Margo. "I suppose you must know all the gory details by now. Pretty nasty, huh?"

"They didn't tell us anything," Margo said. "All we've heard is some talk about a killing. I guess Prine must have done it."

Smithback laughed. "Charlie Prine? That guy couldn't kill a six-pack, let alone a biped. No, Prine just found the body. Or should I say, *them*."

"Them? What are you talking about?"

Smithback sighed. "You really *don't* know anything, do you? I was hoping you'd heard something, sitting in here for hours." He sprang up and went over to the coffee urn. He tipped and rattled and cursed it and came back empty handed. "They found the Director's wife, stuffed, in a glass case in the Primate Hall," he said after settling himself in the chair again. "Been there twenty years before anyone noticed."

Margo groaned. "Let's hear the real story, Smithback," she said.

"All right, all right," he sighed. "Around seven-thirty this morning, the bodies of two young boys were found dead in the Old Building basement."

Margo pressed a hand to her mouth.

"How did you learn all this?" Kawakita demanded.

"While you two were cooling your heels in here, the rest of the world was stuck outside on Seventy-second Street," Smithback went on. "They'd shut the gates on us. The press was out there, too. Quite a few, in fact. The upshot is, Wright's going to give a press conference in the Great Rotunda at ten to quell the rumors. All that zoo talk. We've got ten minutes."

"Zoo talk?" Margo pressed.

"It's a zoo around *here*. Oh, God. What a mess." Smithback was savoring not telling what he knew. "Seems the murders were pretty savage. And you know the press: They've always assumed you've got all sorts of animals locked up in here."

"I think you're actually enjoying this," Kawakita smiled.

"A story like this would add a whole new dimension to my book," Smithback went on. "The shocking true account of the grisly Museum killings, by William Smithback, Junior. Wild, voracious beasts roaming deserted corridors. It could be a best-seller."

"This isn't funny," Margo snapped. She was thinking that Prine's laboratory wasn't far from her own office in the Old Building basement.

"I know, I know," Smithback said good-humoredly. "It *is* terrible. The poor kids. But I'm still not sure I believe it. It's probably some gimmick of Cuthbert's to boost publicity for the exhibition." He sighed, then started guiltily. "Hey, Margo—I was really sorry to hear about your father. I meant to tell you earlier."

"Thanks." Margo's smile held little warmth.

"Listen, you two," Kawakita said, rising, "I really have to—"

"I heard you were thinking of leaving," Smithback continued to Margo. "Dropping your dissertation to work at your father's company, or something." He looked at her curiously. "Is that true? I thought your research was finally getting somewhere."

"Well," Margo said, "yes and no. Dissertation's dragging a bit these days. I've got my weekly eleven o'clock with Frock today. He'll probably forget, as usual, and schedule something else, especially with this tragedy. But I hope I do get in to see him. I found an interesting monograph on the Kiribitu classification of medicinal plants."

She realized that Smithback's eyes had already started to wander, and reminded herself once again that most people had no interest in plant genetics and ethnopharmacology. "Well, I've got to get ready." Margo stood up.

"Hold on a minute!" Smithback said, scrambling to gather up his papers. "Don't you want to see the press conference?"

As they left the staff lounge, Freed was still complaining to anyone who would listen. Kawakita, already trotting down the hall ahead of them, waved over his shoulder as he rounded a bend and disappeared from sight.

They arrived in the Great Rotunda to find the press conference already in progress. Reporters surrounded Winston Wright, Director of the Museum, poking microphones and cameras in his direction, voices echoing crazily in the cavernous space. Ippolito, the Museum's Security Director, stood at the Director's side. Clustered around the periphery were other Museum employees and a few curious school groups.

Wright stood angrily in the quartz lights, fielding shouted questions. His usually impeccable Savile Row suit was rumpled, and his thin hair was drooping over one ear. His pale skin was gray, and his eyes looked bloodshot.

"No," Wright was saying, "apparently they thought their children had already left the Museum. We had no prior warning. . . . No, we do *not* keep live animals in the Museum. Well, of course, we have some mice and snakes for research purposes, but no lions or tigers or anything of that sort. . . . No, I haven't seen the bodies. . . . I don't know what kind of mutilation there was, if any. . . . I don't have the expertise to address that subject, you'll have to wait for the autopsies. . . . I want to emphasize that there's been no official statement made by the police. . . . Until you stop shouting I won't answer any more questions. . . . No, I said we do *not* have wild animals in the Museum. . . . Yes, that includes bears. . . . No, I'm not going to give any names. . . . How could I possibly answer that question? . . . This press conference is over. . . . I said this press conference is *over*. . . . Yes, of course we are cooperating in every way with the police. . . . No, I don't see any reason why this should delay the opening of the new exhibition. Let me emphasize that the opening of *Superstition* is right on schedule. . . . We have *stuffed* lions, yes, but if you're trying to imply. . . . They were shot in Africa seventy-five years ago, for Heaven's sake! The zoo? We have no affiliation with the zoo. . . . I'm simply not going to respond to any more outrageous suggestions along those lines. . . . Will the gentleman from the *Post* please stop shouting? . . . The police are interviewing the scientist who found the bodies, but I have no information on that. . . . No, I don't have anything more to add, except that we're doing everything we can. . . . Yes it was tragic, of course it was. . . ."

The press began to fan out, heading past Wright into the Museum proper.

Wright turned angrily toward the security director. "Where the hell were the police?" Margo heard him snap. As he turned, he said over his shoulder, "if you see Mrs. Rickman, tell her to come to my office immediately." And he stalked out of the Great Rotunda.

= 6 =

Margo moved deeper into the Museum, away from the public areas, until she reached the corridor called 'Broadway.' Stretching the entire length of the Museum—six city blocks—it was said to be the longest single hallway in New York City. Old oaken cabinets lined the walls, punctuated every thirty feet by frosted-glass doors. Most of these doors had curators' names in gold leaf edged in black.

Margo, as a graduate student, had only a metal desk and a bookshelf in one of the basement labs. *At least I have an office,* she thought, turning off from the corridor and starting down a narrow flight of iron stairs. One of her graduate-student acquaintances had only a tiny battered school desk, wedged between two massive freezers in the Mammalogy Department. The woman had to wear heavy sweaters to work, even at the height of August.

A security guard at the bottom of the stairwell waved her on, and she moved down a dim tunnel, flanked on both sides by mounted horse skeletons in ancient glass cases. No police tape was in sight.

In her office, Margo dropped her carryall beside her desk and sat down. Most of the lab was actually storage for South Seas artifacts: Maori shields, war canoes, and cane arrows stuffed into green metal cabinets that stretched from floor to ceiling. A hundred-gallon fish tank, a simulated swamp belonging to the Animal Behavior Department, perched on an iron frame underneath a battery of lights. It was so overpopulated with algae and weeds that Margo had only rarely been able to catch sight of a fish peering out through the murk.

Next to her desk was a long worktable with a row of dusty masks.

The conservator, a sour young woman, worked in angry silence, spending what seemed barely three hours each day at her task. Margo figured it took her about two weeks to conserve each mask, judging by the slow turnover. The particular mask collection she was assigned to contained five thousand such masks, but it didn't seem to concern anyone that, at the rate she was going, the project would take close to two centuries to complete.

Margo logged onto her computer terminal. A message in green letters appeared, swimming into focus out of the depths of the CRT:

HELLO MARGO GREEN@BIOTECH@STF
WELCOME BACK TO MUSENET
DISTRIBUTED NETWORKING SYSTEM,
RELEASE 15-5
COPYRIGHT © 1989–1995 NYMNH AND CEREBRAL
SYSTEMS INC.
CONNECTING AT 10:24:06 03-27-95
PRINT SERVICE ROUTED TO LJ56

YOU HAVE NO MESSAGE(S) WAITING

She went into word-processing mode and called up her notes, preparing to review them before her meeting with Frock. Her adviser often seemed preoccupied during these weekly meetings, and Margo was constantly scrambling to give him something new. The problem was, there usually wasn't anything new—just more articles read, dissected, and stuffed into the computer; more lab work; and maybe . . . *maybe* . . . another three or four pages of her dissertation. She understood how somebody could end up a permanent rider on the government-grant gravy train, or what the scientists derisively referred to as an ABD— All But Dissertation.

When Frock had first agreed to act as her adviser two years before, she half suspected some mistake had been made. Frock—intellect behind the Callisto Effect, occupier of the Cadwalader Chair in Statistical Paleontology at Columbia University, Chairman of the Evolutionary Biology Department at the Museum—had chosen her as a research student, an honor awarded to only a handful each year.

Frock started his career as a physical anthropologist. Confined to a wheelchair by childhood polio, he had nonetheless done pioneering fieldwork that was still the basis of many textbooks. After several severe bouts with malaria made further field research impossible, Frock diverted his ferocious energy to evolutionary theory. In the mid 1980s, he had started a firestorm of controversy with a radical new proposal. Combining chaos theory and Darwinian evolution, Frock's hypothesis disputed the commonly held belief that life evolved gradually. Instead, he postulated that evolution was sometimes much less gradual; he held that short-lived aberrations—"monster species"—were sometimes an offshoot of evolution. Frock argued that evolution wasn't always caused by random selection, that the environment itself could cause sudden, grotesque changes in a species.

Although Frock's theory was backed by a brilliant series of articles and papers, much of the scientific world remained dubious. If bizarre forms of life exist, they asked, where are they hiding? Frock replied that his theory predicted rapid demise of genera as well as rapid development.

The more the experts called Frock misguided, even crazy, the more the popular press embraced his idea. The theory became known as the Callisto Effect, after the Greek myth in which a young woman is suddenly transformed into a wild creature. Although Frock deplored the widespread misconceptions of his work, he shrewdly used his celebrity to further his academic efforts. Like many brilliant curators, Frock was consumed by his research; sometimes, Margo suspected, everything else, including her work, bored him.

Across the room, the conservator got up and—without a word—left for lunch, a sure sign that it was approaching eleven o'clock. Margo scribbled a few sentences on a sheet of paper, cleared the screen, and scooped up her notebook. She had some new data about Kiribitu plant classification that might intrigue Frock.

Frock's office was in the southwest tower, at the end of an elegant, Edwardian fifth-floor corridor; an oasis far from the labs and computer workstations that characterized much of the behind-the-scene Museum. The heavy oak door of the inner office read simply, DR. FROCK.

Margo knocked.

She heard a great clearing of the throat and the low rumble of a wheelchair. The door opened slowly and the familiar ruddy-complexioned face appeared, bushy eyebrows knitted in surprise. Then his gaze brightened.

"Of course, it's Monday. Come in." He spoke in a low voice, touching her wrist with a plump hand and motioning her to an overstuffed chair. Frock was dressed, as usual, in a somber suit, white shirt, and loud paisley tie. His thick brush of white hair looked ruffled.

The walls of his office were lined with old, glass-fronted bookcases, many of the shelves filled with relics and oddities from his early years in the field. Books were piled in enormous, tottering stacks against a wall. Two large bow windows looked out over the Hudson River. Upholstered Victorian chairs sat on the faded Persian carpet, and on Frock's desk lay several copies of his latest book, *Fractal Evolution*.

Next to the books, Margo recognized a large chunk of gray sandstone. Embedded in its flat surface was a deep depression, oddly smudged and elongated along one end with three large indentations at the other. According to Frock, this was a fossil footprint of a creature unknown to science: the single piece of physical evidence to support his theory of aberrant evolution. Other scientists differed: Many didn't believe it was a fossil at all, calling it "Frock's folly." Most of them had never seen it.

"Clear away that stuff and sit down," Frock said, wheeling back to his favorite spot under one of the bow windows. "Sherry? No, of course, you never do. Silly of me to forget."

On the indicated chair lay several back issues of *Nature* and the typescript of an unfinished article titled "Phyletic Transformation and the Tertiary 'Fern Spike.'" Margo moved them to a nearby table and sat down, wondering if Dr. Frock would mention something about the deaths of the two little boys.

He looked at her for a moment, motionless. Then he blinked, and sighed. "Well, Miss Green," he said. "Shall we begin?"

Disappointed, Margo flipped open her notebook. She skimmed her notes, then began explaining her analysis of Kiribitu plant classification and how it related to her next dissertation chapter. As she spoke, Frock's head gradually dropped to his chest and his eyes closed. A stranger might think him asleep, but Margo knew Frock was listening with intense concentration.

When she finished, he roused himself slowly. "Classification of medicinal plants by use, rather than appearance," he murmured at last. "Interesting. That article reminds me of an experience I had among the Ki tribe of Bechuanaland." Margo waited patiently for the reminiscence that was sure to follow.

"The Ki, as you know"—Frock always assumed his listener was as familiar with a subject as he was—"at one time used the bark of a certain bush as a headache remedy. Charrière studied them in 1869 and noted their use of this bush in his field journals. When I showed up three quarters of a century later, they had stopped using the remedy. They believed instead that headaches were caused by sorcery." He shifted in his wheelchair.

"The accepted remedy was now for the kinfolk of the headache victim to identify the sorcerer and, naturally, go off and murder him. Of course, the kin of the dead sorcerer were then required to avenge this death, so they often went right back and killed the person with the headache. You can imagine what eventually happened."

"What?" Margo asked, assuming Frock was about to explain how all of this fit into her dissertation.

"Why," Frock said, spreading his hands, "it was a medical miracle. People stopped getting headaches."

His generous shirtfront shook with laughter. Margo laughed too—for the first time that day, she realized.

"Well, so much for primitive medicine," Frock said a little wistfully. "Back then, fieldwork was still fun." He paused for a minute. "There will be a whole section on the Ki tribe in the new *Superstition* exhibition, you know," he went on. "Of course, it will be terribly played up for mass consumption. They've brought in some young fellow fresh from Harvard to curate the show. Knows more about computers and mass-marketing than pure science, I'm told."

Frock shifted again in his wheelchair. "In any case, Miss Green, I think what you've described will make a fine addition to your work. I suggest you obtain some samples of the Kiribitu plants from the herbarium and proceed from there."

Margo was gathering her papers when Frock suddenly spoke again. "Bad business this morning."

Margo nodded.

Frock remained silent for a moment. "I fear for the Museum," he said finally.

Surprised, Margo said, "They were brothers. It's a tragedy for the family. But things will die down soon—they always do."

"I think not," Frock said. "I've heard something about the condition of the bodies. The force used was . . . of a nonnormal nature."

"Surely *you* don't think it was a wild animal?" Margo asked. Perhaps Frock was as crazy as everyone said.

Frock smiled. "My dear, I make no assumptions. I will await further evidence. For the moment, I simply hope this unpleasantness will not influence your decision on whether to remain with the Museum. Oh, yes, I've heard about it, and I was very sorry to get the news of your father's death. But you've displayed three gifts that are indispensable to a first-class researcher: a sense of what to look for, a sense of where to look for it, and the zeal to see your theories through." He moved the wheelchair closer to her. "Academic zeal is just as important as zeal in the field, Miss Green. Always remember that. Your technical training, your lab work, has been excellent. It would be a shame if our profession were to lose someone of your talents."

Margo felt a mix of gratitude and resentment. "Thank you, Dr. Frock," she replied. "I appreciate the kind words—and your concern."

The scientist waved his hand, and Margo said good-bye. But at the door, she heard Frock speak again.

"Miss Green?" he asked.

"Yes?"

"Please be watchful."

= 7 =

Outside she nearly collided with Smithback. He leaned toward her, winking roguishly. "How about lunch?"

"No," said Margo. "Too busy." Twice in one day—she wasn't sure she could stand such a full dose of Smithback.

"Come on," he urged. "I've got some more grisly details about the murders."

"It figures." She quickened her pace down the hall, irritated that her curiosity was aroused.

Smithback grabbed her arm. "I hear they're serving a delicious aged and oven-dried lasagna in the cafeteria." He steered her toward the elevator.

The lunchroom was filled with the usual crowd of curators, beefy guards talking loudly, and assorted technicians and preparators in white lab coats. One curator was passing specimens around to a table of fellow scientists, who were murmuring in admiration and interest. Margo took a closer look. The specimens were pickled parasitic worms, coiled in jars of cloudy formaldehyde.

They sat down and Margo tried to saw through the crust of her lasagna.

"Just like I promised," Smithback said, picking up a piece in his hand and biting off a corner with a crunch. "Been on the steam table since nine o'clock this morning, at least."

He chewed noisily. "Well, the police finally made it official. There were two murders here last night. Brilliant to have figured it out! And you remember all those questions the reporters asked about wild animals? Well, there's also a chance they *were* mauled to death by a wild animal."

"Not while I'm eating," Margo said.

"That's right. Literally shredded, by the sound of it."

Margo looked up. *"Please."*

"I kid you not," Smithback continued. "And the heat is on to get this thing *solved*, particularly with the big exhibition coming up. I hear the cops have even enlisted a special coroner. Someone who reads gaping claw wounds like Helen Keller reads braille."

"Damn it, Smithback," Margo said and dropped her fork. "I'm sick of this—your cavalier attitude and your gory particulars while I'm having lunch. Can't I eat first and hear about this stuff later?"

"As I was saying," Smithback continued, ignoring the outburst, "she's supposedly an expert on big cats. Dr. Matilda Ziewicz. Some name, huh. Sounds fat."

Despite her annoyance, Margo suppressed a smile. Smithback might be a jerk, but at least he was a funny jerk. She shoved her tray away. "Where'd you hear all this?" she asked.

Smithback grinned. "I have my sources." He shoveled another piece of lasagna into his mouth. "Actually, I ran into a friend who writes for the *News*. Somebody got the story from a contact in the NYPD. It's going to be all over the afternoon papers. Can you imagine Wright's face when he sees that? Oh, God."

Smithback cackled for a moment before filling his mouth again. He'd finished his own and was starting on Margo's. For a thin guy, he ate like a beast.

"But how could there be a wild animal loose in the Museum?" Margo asked. "That's absurd."

"Yeah? Well, get this: They've got someone in here with a blood-hound, trying to track the son of a bitch."

"Now you're joking."

"Hey, not me. Ask any of the security guards. There's a million square feet in this joint where a big cat or something could be roaming, including five miles of forced-air ducts big enough for a *man* to crawl around in. And under the Museum is a warren of abandoned tunnels. They're taking it seriously."

"Tunnels?"

"Yup. Didn't you read my article in last month's magazine? The first Museum was built on an artesian swamp that couldn't be permanently drained. So they built all these tunnels to divert the water. Then, when the original Museum burned down in 1911, they built the present Museum on top of the old Museum's basement. The subbasement is huge, multileveled . . . much of it isn't even electrified. I doubt if there's anybody still alive who really knows their way around down there."

Smithback munched the last piece of lasagna and pushed the tray aside. "And then, there're the usual rumors about the Museum Beast."

Anybody who worked in the Museum had heard that story. Maintenance men working late-night shifts saw it out of the corners of their eyes. Assistant curators wandering down dimly lit corridors on their way to specimen vaults saw it moving in the shadows. Nobody knew what it was, or where it had come from, but some claimed the beast had killed a man several years before.

Margo decided to change the subject. "Is Rickman still giving you trouble?" she asked.

At the mention of the name, Smithback grimaced. Margo knew that Lavinia Rickman, the Chief of Public Relations for the Museum, had hired Smithback to write his book. She had also worked out the Museum's cut of the advance and royalties. Although Smithback wasn't happy about the contractual details, the exhibition promised to be such a blockbuster that book sales, riding on the success of the exhibit, could easily climb into six figures. It hadn't been a bad deal for Smithback at all, Margo thought, given the only modest success of his previous book on the Boston Aquarium.

"Rickman? Trouble?" Smithback snorted. "Oh, God. She's the definition of trouble. Listen, I want to read you something." He pulled a sheaf of papers out of a notebook.

" 'When Dr. Cuthbert pitched the idea for an exhibition on Superstition to the Museum Director, Wright was very impressed. It had all the makings of a blockbuster exhibition, something on the level of *The Treasures of King Tut* or *The Seven Levels of Troy*. That meant big money for the Museum, Wright knew, and an unparalleled opportunity to raise funds from corporate and government sponsorship. But some older curators were unconvinced; they thought the exhibit smacked of sensationalism.' "

Smithback stopped. "Look what Rickman did." He pushed the paper over to her. A big line sliced across the paragraph and a marginal note in fat red marker read: OUT!

Margo giggled.

"What's so funny?" Smithback demanded. "She's butchering my manuscript. Look at this." He jabbed his finger at another page.

Margo shook her head. "What Rickman wants is a snow job for the Museum. You two won't ever see eye to eye."

"She's driving me crazy. She's taking out everything that's the slightest bit controversial. She wants me to spend all my time talking to that nerd who's curating the exhibition. She knows that he'll only say what his boss Cuthbert tells him to." He leaned forward conspiratorially. "You've never seen such a company man in your life." He looked up, and groaned. "Oh, God, here he comes now."

A young, slightly overweight man with horn-rimmed glasses materialized at their table, holding a tray balanced on a shiny leather briefcase. "May I join you?" he asked shyly. "I'm afraid this is practically the only seat left in the house."

"Sure," said Smithback. "Have a seat. We were just talking about you, anyway. Margo, meet George Moriarty. He's the guy who's curating the *Superstition* exhibition."

Smithback shook the papers at Moriarty. "Look what Rickman did to my manuscript. The only things she didn't touch were *your* quotations."

Moriarty scanned the pages and looked at Smithback with almost childlike gravity. "I'm not surprised," he said. "Why air the Museum's dirty linen, anyway?"

"Come on, George. This is what makes for an interesting story!"

Moriarty turned to Margo. "You're the graduate student working on ethnopharmacology, aren't you?" he asked.

"That's right," she said, flattered. "How did you know?"

"I'm interested in the subject." He smiled and looked at her briefly. "The exhibition has several cases devoted to pharmacology and medicine. I wanted to talk to you about one of them, actually."

"Sure. What did you have in mind?" She looked at Moriarty more closely. He was about as average a Museum character as she could imagine: average height, a little pudgy, hair an average brown. His rumpled tweed jacket sported the heather tones that were regulation Museum-issue. The only things unusual about him were his large wristwatch, shaped like a sundial, and his eyes: an unusually clear hazel, shining with intelligence from behind his horn-rims.

Smithback sat forward, shifted irritably in his chair, and stared at the two. "Well," he said, "I'd like to stay on and witness this charming scene, but I'm interviewing someone in the Bug Room on Wednesday, and I need to finish my current chapter. George, don't sign any movie contracts for that exhibition of yours without talking to me first." He stood up with a snort and made for the door, threading a complex path between tables as he went.

= 8 =

Jonathan Hamm peered down the basement corridor through a thick pair of glasses that badly needed cleaning. Leather leashes were wrapped around his black-gloved hands, and two hounds sat obediently at his feet. His assistant tracker stood beside him. Next to the assistant was Lieutenant D'Agosta, holding soiled, heavily creased blueprints, his two deputies leaning against the wall behind him. Police-issue pump-action Remington 12-gauges hung off their shoulders.

D'Agosta rustled through the blueprints. "Can't the dogs smell which way to go?" he asked irritably.

Hamm let out a long breath. "*Hounds.* They're hounds. And they're not on a scent. They haven't been on a good scent since we began. Or rather, they've been on too many scents."

D'Agosta grunted, withdrew a sodden cigar from his jacket pocket, and began to raise it toward his mouth. Hamm caught his eye.

"Oh yeah," said D'Agosta. He pushed the cigar back into his pocket.

Hamm sniffed the air. It was damp, which was good. But that was the only good thing about this little picnic. First, there was the usual stupidity of the police. *What kind of dogs are these?* they'd asked. *We wanted bloodhounds.* These *were* hounds, he'd explained, a bluetick hound and a black-and-tan coonhound. Given the right conditions, these hounds could track a lost hiker after a three-foot blizzard. *But these,* thought Hamm, *aren't exactly the right conditions.*

As usual, the crime scene had been fouled up. Chemicals, spray paint, chalk, a thousand people tramping in and out. Besides, the area around the base of the staircase had been literally bathed in blood;

even now, eighteen hours or so after the crime, the smell hung heavily in the air, agitating the hounds.

They first tried to follow the scent from the crime scene itself. When that failed, Hamm suggested they "cut for scent," making a perimeter loop around the crime scene, hoping to pick up the trail as it exited.

The hounds had never been trained to work indoors. Naturally, they were confused. But it wasn't his fault. The police wouldn't even tell him if they were looking for a human or an animal. Perhaps they didn't know themselves.

"Let's go this way," said D'Agosta.

Hamm passed the leashes to his assistant, who started walking ahead, the hounds nosing the ground.

Next, the hounds had bayed up a storage room full of mastodon bones, and the paradichlorobenzene preservative that poured out when they opened the door had caused a half-hour delay while the hounds recovered their sense of smell. And that was just the first of a series of storage rooms full of animal pelts, gorillas in formaldehyde, a freezer full of dead zoo specimens, a whole vault full of human skeletons.

They came to an archway with an open metal door leading onto a descending stone stairway. The walls were covered with a crust of lime, and the stairway was dark.

"That must be the dungeon," one of the policemen said, with a guffaw.

"This goes to the subbasement," D'Agosta said, consulting the blueprints. He motioned to one of the officers, who handed him a long flashlight.

The shallow stairs ended in a tunnel made of herringbone brickwork, its arched ceiling barely the height of a man. The tracker moved forward with the dogs, D'Agosta and Hamm behind. The two policemen came last.

"There's water on the floor," said Hamm.

"So what?" D'Agosta said.

"If there's been any water flowing through here there won't be any scent."

"I was told to expect puddles of water down here," D'Agosta replied. "It only floods when it rains, and it hasn't rained."

"That's reassuring," said Hamm.

They reached a place where four tunnels came together, and D'Agosta halted to consult the blueprints.

"Somehow I thought you'd need to look at that," Hamm said.

"Oh, yeah?" D'Agosta said. "Well, I've got a surprise for you. These blueprints don't cover the subbasement."

When one of the dogs whined and began furiously sniffing, Hamm came suddenly to attention. "This way. Quick."

The dogs whined again. "They've got something!" said Hamm. "It's a clear scent, it must be. Look at their hackles rise! Keep the light up here, I can't see a blessed thing."

The dogs were straining, pulling forward, noses up and sniffing the air ahead.

"You see, you see!" Hamm said. "It's an air scent. Feel the fresh air on your cheek? I should have brought the spaniels. They're unbeatable with an air scent!"

The policemen slid past the dogs, one beaming his flashlight, the other carrying his shotgun at the ready. Ahead the tunnel forked again, and the dogs lunged to the right, breaking into a trot.

"Hold it, Mr. Hamm, there might be a killer out there," D'Agosta said.

The dogs suddenly broke into a deafening baying. "Sit!" cried the assistant. "Heel! Castor! Pollux! *Heel,* damn you!" The dogs lunged forward, paying no attention. "Hamm, I need a hand here!"

"What's gotten into you?" cried Hamm, wading into the frantic dogs, trying to grab their collars. "Castor, *heel!*"

"Shut them up!" snapped D'Agosta.

"He's loose!" cried the assistant, as one of the dogs bolted into the darkness. They rushed after the retreating sound of the dog.

"You smell it?" Hamm said, stopping short. "Christ Jesus, you *smell* it?"

A pungent, goatish odor suddenly enveloped them. The other dog was frantic with excitement, leaping and twisting and suddenly breaking free.

"Pollux! *Pollux!*"

"Wait!" said D'Agosta. "Forget the fucking dogs for a second. Let's proceed with a little order here. You two, get in front again. Safeties off."

The two men pumped their shotguns.

In the echoing darkness ahead of them, the barking faltered, then stopped. There was a moment of silence. Then a terrible, unearthly shriek, like the screeching of tires, leapt from the inky tunnel. The two police officers looked at each other. The sound ended as suddenly as it began.

"Castor!" Hamm cried. "Oh, my God! He's been hurt!"

"Get back, Hamm, goddammit!" barked D'Agosta.

At that moment a shape suddenly hurtled at them from the darkness, and there were two stunning blasts from the shotguns, two flashes of light accompanied by deafening roars. The rumble echoed and died in the tunnel, and there was an intense silence.

"You fucking idiot, you just shot my hound," said Hamm quietly. Pollux lay five feet from them, blood pouring freely from his ruined head.

"He was coming right at me . . ." began one of the officers.

"Jesus Christ," said D'Agosta, "Stow that shit. There's still something out there."

They found the other dog a hundred yards down the tunnel. He was torn nearly in half, guts strung out in crazy patterns.

"Jesus, will you look at that," said D'Agosta.

Hamm said nothing.

Just beyond the body the tunnel branched. D'Agosta continued to stare at the dog. "Without the dogs, there's no way of knowing which way it went," he said at last. "Let's get the hell out of here and let forensics deal with this mess."

Hamm said nothing.

= 9 =

Moriarty, suddenly alone with Margo in the cafeteria, seemed even more uncomfortable. "So?" Margo prompted, after a brief silence.

"Actually, I really *did* want to talk to you about your work." He paused.

"You did?" Margo was unused to anyone showing interest in her project.

"Well, indirectly. The primitive medicine cases for the exhibition are complete, except one. We've got this terrific collection of shamanistic plants and artifacts from the Cameroons we want to display in the last case, but they're badly documented. If you'd be willing to take a look . . . ?"

"I'd love to," Margo said.

"Great! When?"

"Why not now? I've got some time."

They left the staff cafeteria and moved down a long basement hall lined with rumbling steam pipes and padlocked doors. One of the doors bore the label DINOSAUR STOREROOM 4—UPPER JURASSIC. Most of the Museum's dinosaur bone and other fossil collections were stored here in the basement, since—she had heard—the great weight of petrified bone would cause the upper floors to collapse.

"The collection's in one of the sixth-floor vaults," Moriarty said apologetically as they entered a service elevator. "I hope I can find it again. You know what a warren of storage rooms they've got up there."

"Have you heard anything more about Charlie Prine?" Margo asked quietly.

"Not much. Apparently he's not a suspect. But I don't think we'll see him back here for quite a while. Dr. Cuthbert told me before lunch that he was severely traumatized." Moriarty shook his head. "What an awful thing."

On the fifth floor, Margo followed Moriarty along a wide passageway and up a flight of metal stairs. The narrow, labyrinthine catwalks that made up this section of the sixth floor had been built directly underneath the Museum's long pitched roofs. On either side were rows of low metal doors, behind which lay the hermetically sealed vaults of the perishable anthropology collections. In earlier times, a poisonous cyanic compound had periodically been pumped into the vaults to kill vermin and bacteria; now, artifact preservation was handled with subtler methods.

As the two threaded their way along the catwalks, they passed a number of objects stacked against the walls: a carved war canoe, several totems, a row of slitted log drums. Even with one million square feet of storage space, every square inch had been utilized, including stairwells, corridors, and the offices of junior curators. Of fifty million artifacts and specimens, only about 5 percent was on exhibition; the rest was available only to scientists and researchers.

The New York Museum of Natural History consisted not of a single building, but several large buildings, connected over the years to form one sprawling, rambling structure. As Margo and Moriarty passed from one of the buildings into another, the ceiling ascended, and the catwalk became a branching corridor. A dim light filtered down from a row of dirty skylights, illuminating shelves filled with plaster casts of aboriginal faces.

"God, this place is huge," said Margo, feeling a sudden cold thrust of fear, glad that she was seven stories above the dark spaces where the little boys had met their deaths.

"Largest in the world," Moriarty said, unlocking a door stenciled CEN. AFRICA, D-2.

He switched on a naked, 25-watt bulb. Peering in, Margo could see a tiny room stuffed with masks, shaman's rattles, painted and beaded skins, and a group of long sticks topped by grimacing heads. Along one wall was a row of wooden cabinets. Moriarty nodded toward them.

"The plants are in there. This other stuff is the shaman paraphernalia. It's a great collection, but Eastman, the guy who assembled the Cameroon stuff, wasn't exactly the most careful anthropologist when it came to documentation."

"This is incredible," said Margo. "I had no idea—"

"Listen," Moriarty interrupted, "when we began researching this exhibition, you wouldn't *believe* the things we found. There are close to a hundred anthropology vaults in this section alone, and I swear some of them haven't been opened in forty years."

Moriarty was suddenly more confident and animated. Margo decided that if he dumped the tweed jacket, shed a few pounds, and swapped the horn-rims for contacts, he could almost be cute.

But Moriarty was still talking. "Just last week, we found one of only a couple of existing examples of Yukaghir pictograph writing—right next door! As soon as I get time, I'll be writing a note for the *JAA*."

Margo smiled. He was so excited, he could have been talking about discovering an unknown Shakespeare play. She was sure that only a dozen readers of the *Journal of American Anthropology* would be interested. But Moriarty's enthusiasm was refreshing.

"Anyway," Moriarty said, pushing his glasses up his nose, "I just need someone to help me make sense of this Cameroon stuff for the display case write-up."

"What do you want me to do?" Margo asked, temporarily forgetting the next chapter of her dissertation. His enthusiasm was infectious.

"That's easy," said Moriarty. "I've got the rough script for the case right here."

He extracted a document from his briefcase. "See," he said, running a finger down the covering sheet, "this sets out what, ideally, we want the case to say. We call it the story line. All you have to do is flesh this out, plugging in a few of the artifacts and some of the plants."

Margo scanned the document. It was starting to sound a little more time-consuming than she'd anticipated. "How long do you think this will take, by the way?"

"Oh, ten to fifteen hours, max. I've got the accession listings and some descriptive notes right here. But we've got to hurry. The opening is just a few days away."

Back came the memory of her next chapter. "Now wait a minute," she said. "This is a big job, and I've got a dissertation to write."

The dismay on Moriarty's face was almost comical. It hadn't even occurred to him that she might have other things to do. "You mean you can't help?"

"Maybe I can squeeze it in," she murmured.

His face brightened. "Great! Listen, while we're on the sixth floor, let me show you some of the other stuff up here."

He led her to another vault and inserted a key. The door rasped open to a dazzling display of painted buffalo skulls, rattles, feather bundles, and even a row of what she recognized as raven skeletons tied up with rawhide.

"Jesus," Margo breathed.

"There's a whole religion in here," Moriarty said. "Wait till you see what we're putting on display. This is just the stuff left behind. We've got one of the best Sun Dance shirts anywhere. And look at this!" He pulled open a drawer. "Original wax cylinder recordings of the Sun Dance cycle songs, every one. Recorded in 1901. We've put them on tape, and we're going to play them in the Sioux room. What do you think? *Great* exhibition, huh?"

"It's certainly caused a fuss in the Museum," Margo replied cautiously.

"Actually, there isn't as much controversy as people seem to make out," Moriarty said. "There's no reason why science and entertainment can't meet as friends."

Margo couldn't resist. "I'll bet your boss Cuthbert put you up to *that* line."

"He's always felt that exhibitions should be more accessible to the general public. People may attend this because they expect ghosts and goblins and a spooky show—and they'll get them. But they'll go away with more than you might expect. Besides, the show's going to generate a lot of cash for the Museum. What's wrong with that?"

"Nothing," Margo smiled. She'd leave the baiting to Smithback.

But Moriarty wasn't finished. "I know the word *superstition* has a bad connotation in some people's minds," he said. "It smacks of exploitation. And it's true that some of the effects we're putting together for the show are . . . well . . . a bit sensational. But an exhibit called *Aboriginal Religion* just wouldn't sell, would it?" He looked at her with mute appeal.

"I don't think anyone objects to the title," Margo said. "I guess there are a few people who don't feel your ends are truly scientific."

He shook his head. "Just the crusty old curators and the crackpots. Like Frock, for example. They chose the *Superstition* exhibition over his proposal for one on evolution. So of course he doesn't have a good word to say about it."

Margo's smile faded. "Dr. Frock is a pretty brilliant anthropologist," she said.

"Frock? Dr. Cuthbert says he's gone off the deep end. 'The man's bloody daft,' he says." Moriarty imitated Cuthbert's Scottish accent. The sound echoed unpleasantly down the dim corridors.

"I don't think Cuthbert is half the genius *you* feel he is," Margo said.

"Now please, Margo. He's top rate."

"Not compared to Dr. Frock, he isn't. What about the Callisto Effect?" Margo asked. "That's some of the most cutting-edge work being done today."

"Does he have a single speck of proof to back up his speculations? Have you seen evidence of any unknown, monstrous species roaming the earth?" Moriarty shook his head again, sending his glasses plunging dangerously down his nose. "Theoretical hype. I mean, theory has its place, but it has to be backed up with fieldwork. And that sidekick of his, Greg Kawakita, just encourages Frock with that extrapolation program he's developing. I suppose Kawakita's got his own reasons. But it's pretty sad, really, to see a great mind take such a bad detour. I mean, just look at Frock's new book. *Fractal Evolution?* Even the title sounds more like a kid's computer game than science."

Margo listened with rising indignation. Perhaps Smithback had been right about Moriarty, after all. "Well," she said, "considering my affiliations to Dr. Frock, I don't suppose you'd want me messing with your exhibit. I might add too much hype to the script." She turned and walked briskly out the door and down the corridor.

Moriarty looked shocked. Too late, he remembered that Frock was her major advisor. He danced after her.

"Oh, no, no, I didn't mean—" he stammered. "Please, I was just . . . You know that Frock and Cuthbert don't get along. I guess I've picked up some of that."

He looked so horrified that Margo felt her anger fade.

"I didn't know they had *that* much of a problem with each other," she said, allowing Moriarty to stop her.

"Oh, yes. From way back. You know that ever since Frock came forward with this Callisto Effect, his star has been falling in the Museum. Now he's a department head in name only, and Cuthbert pulls the strings. Of course, I've just heard one side of the story. I'm very sorry, really. You *will* do the case for me, right?"

"On the condition," Margo countered, "that you get me out of this maze. I've got to get back to work."

"Oh, sure. Sorry," Moriarty said. The gaffe had brought back all of his shyness, and as they began retracing their way to the fifth floor, he was silent.

"So tell me more about your exhibition." Margo tried to put him at ease. "I've heard a little about some fabulously rare artifacts that will be on display."

"I guess you must mean the Kothoga tribe material," Moriarty said. "Only one expedition has ever found any traces of them. The figurine of their mythical beast Mbwun is—well, it's one of the centerpieces of the show." He hesitated. "Or I should say, it *will* be one of the centerpieces. It's not on display yet."

"Really?" Margo asked. "Isn't that waiting till the last minute?"

"The situation is kind of unusual," Moriarty replied. "But listen, Margo, this isn't for public consumption." They had returned to the catwalks, and Moriarty led her down the long corridors, speaking low. "There's been a lot of high-level interest in the Kothoga artifacts recently. People like Rickman, Dr. Cuthbert . . . even Wright, apparently. There's been controversy over whether the material should be included in the exhibition. Surely you've heard the stories of a curse on the figurine, that sort of nonsense?"

"Not much," Margo said.

"The expedition that found the Kothoga material met with tragedy," Moriarty continued, "and nobody's been near the stuff since. It's still in the original crates. Just last week, all the crates were taken from the basement area where they'd sat all these years and moved to the Secure Area. Nobody's had access to them since, and I haven't been able to prepare the final displays."

"But why were they moved?" Margo pressed.

They entered the elevator. Moriarty waited until the door had closed before answering. "Apparently, the crates had been recently tampered with."

"What? You mean somebody had broken in?"

Moriarty stared at Margo, his owlish face wearing its look of perpetual surprise. "I didn't say that," he replied.

He turned the key, and the elevator lurched downward.

= 10 =

D'Agosta wished with all his heart that the double-chili-cheeseburger in his stomach would disappear. Not that it was bothering him—yet—but it was an unwelcome presence.

The place smelled like they all did. In fact it stank. All the disinfectants in the world couldn't cover up the smell of death. And the vomit-green walls in the Medical Examiner's Office didn't help things any. Nor did the large gurney, currently empty, sitting like an uninvited guest under the bright lights of the autopsy suite.

His thoughts were interrupted as a large woman entered, two men following close behind. D'Agosta noticed stylish glasses, blonde hair escaping from under a surgeon's cap. The woman strode over and held out her hand, her red lipstick creased in a professional smile.

"Dr. Ziewicz," she said, with a crushing grip. "You must be D'Agosta. This is my assistant, Dr. Fred Gross." Ziewicz indicated a short, skinny man. "And this is our photographer, Delbert Smith." Delbert nodded, clutching a 4×5 Deardorff to his chest.

"So, Dr. Ziewicz, you come here often?" D'Agosta asked, suddenly eager to say something, anything, to stall the inevitable.

"NYME's my home away from home," Ziewicz replied with the same smile. "My field is—how shall I put it—special forensics. For just about everybody. We do our thing and ship them back out. Then I read about what it all means in the papers." She looked at him speculatively. "You've, ah, seen this kind of thing before, right?"

"Oh yeah," said D'Agosta. "All the time." The burger in his gut felt like a lead ingot. Why didn't he think ahead, remember what his afternoon schedule was before chowing down like a damned hog?

"That's good." Ziewicz consulted her clipboard. "Let's see, parental consent? Good. Looks like everything's in order. Fred, start with 5-B."

She began slipping on latex gloves, three pairs, a mask, goggles, and a plastic apron. D'Agosta did likewise.

Gross wheeled the gurney over to the morgue bank and slid out 5-B. The indistinct shape under the plastic looked strangely short to D'Agosta, with an odd bulge at one end. Gross slid the cadaver and its tray onto the gurney, wheeled the cart under the lights, checked the toe tag, and locked down the wheels. He placed a stainless-steel bucket under the gurney's outlet pipe.

Ziewicz was fiddling with the microphone hanging above the body. "Testing, one two three . . . Fred, this mike is totally dead."

Fred bent over the reel-to-reel. "I can't understand it, everything's turned on."

D'Agosta cleared his throat. "It's unplugged," he said.

There was a short silence.

"Well," said Ziewicz, "I'm glad there's someone here who's not a scientist. If you have any questions or comments, Mr. D'Agosta, please state your name and speak clearly toward the microphone. Okay? Everything goes on the tape. I'm just going to describe the state of the body first, and then we'll start cutting."

"Got it," D'Agosta replied tonelessly. *Cutting.* It was one thing when a dead body was just lying there at the scene. But when they started cutting into it, peeling the layers away—he'd never gotten used to that.

"Are we up and running? Good. This is Dr. Matilda Ziewicz and Dr. Frederick Gross, and the date is Monday, March 27, at two-fifteen in the afternoon. We are joined by Detective Sergeant—?"

"Lieutenant Vincent."

"Lieutenant Vincent D'Agosta, of the NYPD. We have here—"

Fred read off the tag. "William Howard Bridgeman, number 33-A45."

"I am now removing the covering." The thick plastic crackled.

There was a short silence. D'Agosta had a sudden flash of the gutted dog he'd seen that morning. *The trick is not to think too much. Don't think about your own Vinnie, eighth birthday just next week.*

Dr. Ziewicz took a deep breath. "We have here a Caucasian male, a boy, age about, ah, ten to twelve years, height, well, I can't give a height for this one because it's decapitated. Maybe four feet ten inches, maybe five feet? Weight, about ninety pounds. This is very approximate. The state of the body is such that I can see no other identifying marks. Eye color and facial features indeterminate due to massive head trauma."

"No anterior wounds or marks on the feet, legs, or genitals. Fred, please sponge off the abdominal area . . . thank you. There are an un-determined number of large lacerations proceeding from the left an-terior pectoral region at a hundred and ninety degree angle downward through the costals, sternum, and terminating at the right anterior abdominal region. This is a massive wound, perhaps two feet long and a foot wide. It appears that the pectoralis minor and pectoralis major are separated from the external thoracic cavity, the external and in-ternal intercostals are separated, and the body is eviscerated to a great degree. The sternal process has been split and the rib cage exposed. Massive hemorrhaging in the aortal—it's hard to see before cleaning and exploration.

"Fred, clean the edge of the thoracic cavity. The viscera that are clearly exposed and fully protuberant are the stomach, small and large intestines. The retroperitoneal organs appear to be in situ.

"Sponge the neck off, Fred. The neck area shows signs of trauma, some bruising, perhaps indicative of extravasation, possible spinal dis-location.

"Now for the head . . . dear God."

In the silence, Fred cleared his throat.

"The head is decapitated between the axial process and the atlas. The entire occipital portion of the calvarium and half the parietal process have been crushed, or rather seemingly punched through and removed, by means unknown, leaving a hole perhaps ten inches in diameter. The skull is empty. The entire brain appears to have fallen out or been extracted through this hole . . . The brain, or what is left of it, is in a pan here to the right of the head, but there is no indication of its original position vis-à-vis the body."

"It was found in pieces near the body," said D'Agosta.

"Thank you, Lieutenant. But where's the rest of it?"

"That's all there was."

"No. Something's missing. You got full scene-of-crime series for this?"

"Of course," said D'Agosta, trying not to show his annoyance.

"The brain is severely traumatized. Fred, bring me a number 2 scalpel and transverse speculum. The brain appears to have been severed at the medulla oblongata. The pons Varolii is intact, but separate. The cerebellum shows surface lacerations but is otherwise intact. There is little evidence of bleeding, indicating postmortem trauma. There's the body of fornix, attached. The cerebrum has been completely severed from the mesencephalon and the mesencephalon has been bisected and—look, Fred, there's no thalamoid region. And no pituitary. That's what's missing."

"What's that?" asked D'Agosta. He willed himself to look more closely. The brain, sitting in a stainless-steel pan, looked a hell of a lot more liquid than solid. He turned away. Baseball. Think about baseball. A pitch, the sound of a bat . . .

"The thalamus and the hypothalamus. The body's regulator."

"The body's regulator," repeated D'Agosta.

"The hypothalamus regulates body temperature, blood pressure, heartbeat, and the metabolism of fats and carbohydrates. Also the sleep-wake cycle. We think it holds the centers of pleasure and pain. It's a very complicated organ, Lieutenant." She looked fixedly at him, anticipating a question. D'Agosta mumbled dutifully, "How does it do all that?"

"Hormones. It secretes hundreds of regulatory hormones into the brain and bloodstream."

"Yeah," D'Agosta replied. He stepped back. The baseball soaring deep into center field, the center fielder dropping back, glove raised . . .

"Fred come over here and look at this," Ziewicz said sharply.

Fred bent over the pan. "It looks like . . . Well, I don't know . . ."

"Come on, Fred," Ziewicz coaxed.

"Well, it looks almost like—" Fred paused. "Like a bite was taken out."

"Exactly. Photographer!" Delbert rushed forward. "Get this. Looks just like when one of my kids takes a bite out of a cake."

D'Agosta leaned forward, but he could see nothing special in the gray, bloody mess.

"It's semicircular, like a human's, but it appears larger, more ragged than you'd expect. We'll take sections. Let's test for the presence of salivase enzymes, Fred, just in case. Take this to the lab, tell them to flash-freeze it and microsection here, here, and here. Five sections each. Stain at least one with eosinophil. Stain one with salivase activating enzyme. Anything else you or they can think of."

As Fred left, Ziewicz continued. "I am now bisecting the cerebrum. The posterior lobe is bruised, consistent with removal from the cranium. Photograph. The surface shows three parallel lacerations or incisions, approximately four millimeters apart, about half an inch deep. I am parting the first incision. Photograph. Lieutenant, see how these lacerations start wide and then converge? What do you think?"

"I don't know," D'Agosta said, peering a little closer. *It's just a dead brain,* he thought.

"Long fingernails, maybe? Sharpened fingernails? I mean, do we have a homicidal psychopath on our hands?"

Fred returned from the lab, and they continued working on the brain for what seemed an eternity to D'Agosta. Finally, Ziewicz told Fred to put it in the refrigerator.

"I will now examine the hands," she spoke into the microphone. She removed a plastic bag from the right hand and carefully resealed it. Then she lifted the hand, rotated it, examined the fingernails. "There is foreign matter under the thumb, index, and ring fingers. Fred, three well slides."

"He's just a kid," D'Agosta said. "You'd expect his fingernails to be dirty."

"Perhaps, Lieutenant," Ziewicz replied. She scraped the material into small depressions in the slides, one finger at a time. "Fred, the stereozoom? I want to look at this."

Ziewicz placed the slide on the stage, peered down, and adjusted the instrument.

"Normal fingernail dirt under the thumb, from the looks of it. Same with the others. Fred, full analysis, just in case."

There was nothing of interest on the left hand.

"I will now," Ziewicz continued, "examine the longitudinal trauma to the anterior portion of the body. Del, photographs, here, here, and here, and whatever else you think will show the wound best. Close-ups of the areas of penetration. It looks like the killer has done our Y-incision for us, wouldn't you say, Lieutenant?"

"Yeah," D'Agosta said, swallowing hard.

There were a series of rapid flashes.

"Forceps," Ziewicz continued. "Three ragged lacerations begin just above the left nipple in the greater pectoral, penetrating and eventually separating the muscle. I am opening and probing the first laceration at the point of entry. Clamp there, Fred.

"I am now probing the wound. There is unidentified foreign matter here. Fred, a glassine? It looks like clothing material, perhaps from the victim's shirt. Photograph."

The flash popped, and then she held up a small piece of what looked like bloody lint, dropping it into the glassine envelope. She continued probing in silence for a few moments.

"There is another piece of foreign material deep in the muscle, about four centimeters directly below the right nipple. It is lodged on a rib. It appears to be hard. Photograph. Stick a flag in there, Fred."

She extracted it and held it up, a bloody lump poised at the end of the long forceps.

D'Agosta ventured forward. "What is it? Rinse it off, maybe, and see?"

She glanced at him with a slight smile. "Fred, bring me a beaker of sterile water."

As she dipped the object in and stirred, the water turned brownish red.

"Keep the water, we'll see if there's anything else in it," she said, holding her find to the light.

"Jesus H. Christ," said D'Agosta. "It's a claw. A fucking claw."

Ziewicz turned to her assistant. "That will be a charming snippet of monologue for our tape, won't it, Fred?"

= 11 =

Margo dumped her books and papers on the sofa and glanced at the clock perched atop the television: ten-fifteen. She shook her head. What an unbelievable, horrible day. Staying all those extra hours had only netted three new paragraphs on her dissertation. And she still had to work on the display-case copy for Moriarty. She sighed, sorry she'd ever agreed to the project.

Reflected neon light from a liquor store across the avenue struggled through the lone window of Margo's living room, throwing the room into electric-blue chiaroscuro. She turned on the small overhead light and leaned against the door, scanning the disorder slowly. Normally, she was neat to excess. But now after just one week of neglect, textbooks, letters of sympathy, legal documents, shoes, and sweaters were scattered across the furniture. Empty cartons from the Chinese restaurant downstairs lay neglected in the sink. Her old Royal typewriter and a fan of research papers were spread out on the hardwood floor.

The shabby neighborhood—not-yet-gentrified upper Amsterdam Avenue—had given her father another reason why she should return home to Boston. "This is no place for a girl like you to live, Midge," he had said, using her childhood nickname. "And that Museum is no place to work. Cooped up day after day with all those dead, stuffed creatures, things in jars. What kind of a life is that? Come back and work for me. We'd get you a house in Beverly, Marblehead. You'll be happier there, Midge, I know you will."

When she noticed her answering machine was blinking, Margo pressed the message button.

"It's Jan," the first message began. "I got back into town today, and I just heard. Listen, I'm really, really sorry to hear about your father's death. I'll call back later, okay? I want to talk to you. Bye."

She waited. Another voice came on. "Margo, this is your mother." And then a click.

She squeezed her eyes tightly for a moment, then took a deep breath. She wouldn't call Jan, not just yet. And she wouldn't return her mother's call, either; not until tomorrow, at least. She knew what her mother would say: *You have to come home to your father's business. It's what he would have wanted. You owe it to both of us.*

Turning away, she settled herself cross-legged in front of the typewriter, and stared at the curators' notes, catalogue data, and accession listings Moriarty had given her. It was due the day after tomorrow, he'd said, and the next chapter of her dissertation was due the following Monday.

She glanced at the papers for another minute or two, collecting her thoughts. Then she began to type. A few moments later, she stopped and stared into the dusk. She remembered how her father used to make omelettes—the only thing he knew how to cook—on Sunday mornings. "Hey, Midge," he would always say. "Not bad for an old ex-bachelor, huh?"

Several of the lights outside had been shut off as the shops closed. Margo looked out at the graffiti, the boarded-up windows. Maybe her father was right: Poverty wasn't much fun.

Poverty. She shook her head, remembering the last time she'd heard that word, remembering the expression on her mother's face as she'd pronounced it. The two of them had been sitting in the cool, dark office of her father's executor, listening to all the complex reasons why her father's debt-to-equity ratio and lack of estate planning was forcing liquidation—unless some family member were to step in to keep his business afloat.

She wondered about the parents of the two little boys. *They must have had high hopes for their children, too,* she thought. Now, they'll never know disappointment. Or happiness. Then her thoughts moved to Prine. And the blood on his shoes.

She got up and turned on more lights. Time to start dinner. Tomorrow, she'd lock herself in her office, get that chapter finished. Work on the Cameroon write-up for Moriarty. And put off making a decision—for one more day, at least. By next week's meeting with Frock, she promised herself, she'd have made up her mind.

The telephone rang. Automatically, she picked it up.

"Hello," she said. She listened for a moment. "Oh. Hello, Mother."

= 12 =

Night came early to the Museum of Natural History. As five o'clock neared, the early spring sun was already setting. Inside, the crowds began to thin. Tourists, schoolchildren, and harried parents streamed down the marble staircases toward the exits. Soon the echoes and shouts and clatter of footsteps in the vaulted halls died away. One by one, the exhibit cases went dark, and as the night wore on, the remaining lights threw crazed shadows across the marble floors.

A lone guard wandered along a hall, making his rounds, swinging a long key chain and humming. It was the beginning of his shift, and he was dressed in the standard Museum-issue blue-and-black guard uniform. Long ago the novelty of the Museum had worn off.

The whole joint gives me the creeps, he thought. *Look at that son of a bitch in there. Goddamn native shit. Who the hell would pay to look at this stuff? Half of it's got curses on it, anyway.*

The mask leered at him out of a dark case. He hurried on to the next station, where he turned a key in a box. The box recorded the time: 10:23 P.M. As he moved into the next hall, he had the unsettling impression—as he had so often—that his echoing footfalls were being carefully duplicated by some unseen presence.

He came to the next station and turned the key. The box clicked, and registered 10:34 P.M.

It only took four minutes to get to the next station. That gave him six minutes for a toke.

He ducked into a stairwell, closing and locking the door behind him, and peered down toward the darkened basement, where another door opened to an interior courtyard. His hand went for the light switch at the top of the stairs, but then withdrew. No sense calling attention to himself. He gripped the metal handrail tightly as he crept downward. In the basement, he made his way along the wall until he felt a long horizontal handle. He pushed, and frigid night air streamed in. He wedged open the door and lit up a joint, inhaling the bitter smoke with pleasure as he leaned out into the courtyard. A thin light from the deserted cloister beyond gave a pale illumination to his movements. The faint hum of passing traffic, muffled by so many intervening walls, passages, and parapets, seemed to come from another planet. He felt, with relief, the warm rush of the cannabis—another long night made bearable. Smoke finished, he flicked the roach into the dark, ran his fingers through his crew cut, stretched.

Halfway up the stairs, he heard the door slam shut below. He stopped, feeling a sudden chill. Had he left the door open? No. Shit, what if someone had seen him toke up? But they couldn't have smelt the smoke, and in the dark, it would've looked just like a cigarette.

There was a strange, rotten odor in the air that had nothing to do with weed. But no light flicked on, no footstep sounded on the metal steps. He started up toward the landing above.

Just as he reached it, he sensed a swift movement on the stairs behind him. He spun around, and a hard jerk on his chest shoved him backward against the wall. The last thing he saw were his shadowy entrails rolling and slipping down the stairs. After a moment, he stopped wondering where all that gore had suddenly come from.

= 13 =

Tuesday

Bill Smithback sat in a heavy chair, watching the sharp, angular figure of Lavinia Rickman behind her birchwood veneer desk, reading his rumpled manuscript. Two bright red fingernails tapped on the glossy finish. Smithback knew that the fingernail ditty did not bode well. A very gray Tuesday morning sat outside the windows.

The room was not a typical Museum office. The untidy stacks of papers, journals, and books that seemed a fixture in other offices were missing. Instead, the shelves and desk were decorated with knicknacks from around the world: a storyteller doll from New Mexico, a brass Buddha from Tibet, several puppets from Indonesia. The walls were painted light institutional green, and the room smelled of pine air freshener.

Additional curios were arranged on both sides of her desk, as formal and symmetrical as shrubs in a French garden: an agate paperweight, a bone letter opener, a Japanese netsuke. And in the center of the motif hovered Rickman herself, bent primly over the manuscript. The swirled stiff orange hair, Smithback thought, didn't go well with the green walls.

The tapping speeded, then slowed as Rickman turned the pages. Finally she flicked over the last page, gathered the loose sheets together, and squared them in the precise center of the desk.

"Well," she said, looking up with a bright smile. "I have a few small suggestions."

"Oh," said Smithback.

"This section on Aztec human sacrifice, for example. It's much too controversial." She licked her finger daintily and found the page. "Here."

"Yes, but in the exhibition—"

"Mr. Smithback, the exhibition deals with the subject *tastefully*. This, on the other hand, is not tasteful. It's far too graphic." She zipped a Magic Marker across his work.

"But it's entirely accurate," Smithback said, wincing inwardly.

"I am concerned with *emphasis*, not accuracy. Something can be *entirely* accurate but have the wrong emphasis, and thus give the wrong impression. Allow me to remind you that we have a large Hispanic population here in New York."

"Yes, but how is this going to offend—"

"Moving on, this section on Gilborg simply must go." She zipped another line across another page.

"But why—?"

She leaned back in her chair. "Mr. Smithback, the Gilborg expedition was a grotesque failure. They were looking for an island that did not exist. One of them, as you are so zealous in pointing out, raped a native woman. We were careful to keep all mention of Gilborg *out* of the exhibition. Now, is it really necessary to document the Museum's failures?"

"But his collections were superb!" Smithback protested feebly.

"Mr. Smithback, I am not convinced that you understand the nature of this assignment." There was a long silence. The tapping began again. "Do you really think that the Museum hired you, and is *paying* you, to document failure and controversy?"

"But failure and controversy are part of science, and who's going to read a book that—"

"There are many corporations that give money to the Museum, corporations that might very well be disturbed by some of this," Mrs. Rickman interrupted. "And there are volatile ethnic groups out there, ready to attack, that might take *strong* exception."

"But we're talking about things that happened a hundred years ago, while—"

"Mr. Smithback!" Mrs. Rickman had only raised her voice a little, but the effect was startling. A silence fell.

"Mr. Smithback, I must tell you quite frankly . . ." She paused, then stood up briskly and walked around the desk until she was standing directly behind the writer.

"I must tell you," Mrs. Rickman continued, "that it seems to be taking you longer than I thought to come around to our point of view. You are not writing a book for a commercial publisher. To put it bluntly, we're looking for the kind of favorable treatment you gave the Boston Aquarium in your previous—ahem—assignment." She moved in front of Smithback, perching stiffly on the edge of the desk. "There are certain things we expect, and indeed, that we have a *right* to expect. They are—" she ticked them off on bony fingers.

"One: No controversy.

"Two: Nothing that might offend ethnic groups.

"Three: Nothing that might harm the Museum's reputation.

"Now, is that so unreasonable?" She lowered her voice and, leaning forward, squeezed Smithback's hand with her dry one.

"I . . . no." Smithback struggled with an almost overwhelming urge to withdraw his hand.

"Well, then, that's settled." She moved behind the desk, and slid the manuscript over to him.

"Now, there's one small matter we need to discuss." She enunciated very precisely. "There were a few spots in the manuscript where you quoted some interesting comments by people 'close to the exhibition,' but neglected to identify the exact sources. Nothing important, you understand, but I'd like a list of those sources—for my files, nothing more." She smiled expectantly.

Alarms rang in Smithback's head. "Well," he replied carefully, "I'd like to help you out, but the ethics of journalism won't let me." He shrugged his shoulders. "You know how it is."

Mrs. Rickman's smile faded quickly, and she opened her mouth to speak. Just then, to Smithback's relief, the phone rang. He got up to leave, gathering his manuscript together. As he was closing the door, he heard a sharp intake of breath.

"Not *another!*"

The door hissed shut.

= 14 =

D'Agosta just couldn't get used to the Hall of the Great Apes. All those big grinning chimps, stuffed, hanging out of the fake trees, with their hairy arms and hilarious realistic dicks and big human hands with real fingernails. He wondered why it had taken so long for scientists to figure out that man was descended from the apes. Should've been obvious the first time they clapped eyes on a chimp. And he'd heard somewhere that chimps were just like humans, violent, excitable, always beating hell out of each other, even murdering and eating each other. *Jesus,* he thought, *there must be some other way to get around the Museum without going through this hall.*

"This way," said the guard, "down this stairway. It's pretty awful, Lieutenant. I was coming in at—"

"I'll hear that later," said D'Agosta. After the kid, D'Agosta was ready for anything. "You say he's wearing a guard's uniform. You know him?"

"I don't know, sir. It's hard to tell."

The guard pointed down the dim stairs. The stairway opened onto some kind of courtyard. The body lay at the bottom, in shadow. Everything was streaked and splattered in black—the floor, the walls, the overhead light. D'Agosta knew what the black was.

"You," he said, turning to one of several policemen following him, "get some lights in here. I want the place dusted and swept for fibers pronto. Is the SOC unit on its way? The man's obviously dead, so keep the ambulance people out for a while. I don't want them messing things up."

D'Agosta looked down the stairs again. "Jesus H. Christ," he said, "whose footprints are those? Some jackass walked right through that pool of blood, it looks like. Or maybe our murderer decided to leave us a fat clue."

There was a silence.

"Are those yours?" He turned to the guard. "What's your name?"

"Norris. Eric Norris. As I was saying, I—"

"Yes or no?"

"Yes, but—"

"Shut up. Are those the shoes?"

"Yes. See, I was—"

"Take the shoes off. You're ruining the carpet." *Fucking doorshaker,* D'Agosta thought. "Take them to the forensics lab. Tell them to seal 'em in a crime bag, they'll know what to do. Wait for me there. No, don't wait for me there. I'll call you later. I'll have a few questions for you. No, take the fucking shoes off right here." He didn't want another Prine on his hands. What was it about this Museum, people liked to go around wading in blood? "You'll have to walk over there in your socks."

"Yes, sir."

One of the cops behind D'Agosta snickered.

D'Agosta looked at him. "You think it's funny? He tracked blood all over the place. It's not funny."

D'Agosta moved halfway down the stairwell. The head was lying in a far corner, face down. He couldn't see it all that well, but he knew that he'd find the top of the skull punched out, the brains floating around somewhere in all that gore. God, what a mess a body could be if it wanted to.

A step sounded on the stairway behind him. "SOC," said a short man, followed by a photographer and several other men in lab coats.

"Finally. I want lights there, there and there, and wherever else the photographer wants 'em. I want a perimeter set up, I want it set up five minutes *ago,* I want every speck of lint and grain of sand picked up. I want TraceChem used on everything. I want—well, what else do I want? I want every test known to man, and I want that perimeter observed by everyone, got it? No fuck-ups this time."

D'Agosta turned. "Is the Crime Lab team on the premises? And the coroner's investigator? Or are they out for coffee and croissants?" He patted the breast pocket of his jacket, looking for a cigar. "Put cardboard boxes over those footprints. And you guys, when you're done, squeegee a trail around the body so we can walk without tracking blood everywhere."

"Excellent." D'Agosta heard a low, mellifluous voice behind him.

"Who the hell are you?" he said, turning to see a tall, slender man, wearing a crisp black suit, leaning against the top of the stairwell. Hair so blond it was almost white was brushed straight back above pale blue eyes. "The undertaker?"

"Pendergast," the man said, stepping down and holding out his hand. The photographer, cradling his equipment, pushed past him.

"Well, Pendergast, you better have a good reason to be here, otherwise—"

Pendergast smiled. "Special Agent Pendergast."

"Oh. FBI? Funny, why aren't I surprised? Well, how-do, Pendergast. Why the hell don't you guys phone ahead? Listen, I got a headless, debrained stiff down there. Where're the rest of you, anyway?"

Pendergast withdrew his hand. "There's just me, I'm afraid."

"What? Don't kid me. You guys always travel around in packs."

The lights popped on, and the gore around them was bathed in brilliance. Everything that previously appeared black was suddenly illuminated, all the various shades of the body's secret workings made visible. Something D'Agosta suspected was Norris's breakfast was also visible, lying amidst a wash of body fluids. Involuntarily, D'Agosta's jaw started working. Then his eye caught a piece of skull with the dead guard's crew cut still on it, lying a good five feet from the body.

"Oh Jesus," said D'Agosta, stepping back, and then he lost it. Right in front of the FBI guy, in front of SOC, in front of the photographer, he blew his own breakfast. *I can't believe it,* he thought. *The first time in twenty-two years, and it's happening at the worst possible moment.*

The coroner's investigator appeared on the stairs, a young woman in a white coat and plastic apron. "Who's the officer in charge?" she asked, sliding on her gloves.

"I am," said D'Agosta, wiping his mouth. He looked at Pendergast. "For a few more minutes, anyway. Lieutenant D'Agosta."

"Dr. Collins," the investigator replied briskly.

Followed by an assistant, she walked down to an area near the body that was being squeegeed free of blood.

"Photographer," she said, "I'm turning the body over. Full series, please."

D'Agosta averted his gaze. "We got work to do, Pendergast," he said authoritatively. He pointed at the vomit. "Don't clean that up until the SOC has finished with these stairs. Got it?"

Everyone nodded.

"I wanna know ingress and egress as soon as possible. See if you can ID the body. If it's a guard, get Ippolito down here. Pendergast, let's go up to the command post, get coordinated, or liaised, or whatever the hell you call it, and then let's return when the team is done for a look-see."

"Capital," said Pendergast.

Capital? thought D'Agosta. The guy sounded deep South. He'd met types like this before, and they were hopeless in New York City.

Pendergast leaned forward and said quietly, "The blood splattered on the wall is rather interesting."

D'Agosta looked over. "You don't say."

"I'd be interested in the ballistics on that blood."

D'Agosta looked straight into Pendergast's pale eyes. "Good idea," he said finally. "Hey, photographer, get a close-up series of the blood on the wall. And you, you—"

"McHenry, sir."

"I want a ballistic analysis done on that blood. Looks like it was moving fast at a sharp angle. I want the source pinpointed, speed, force, a full report."

"Yes, sir."

"I want it on my desk in thirty minutes."

McHenry looked a little unhappy.

"Okay, Pendergast, any more ideas?"

"No, that was my only one."

"Let's go."

In the temporary command post, everything was in place. D'Agosta always saw to that. Not one piece of paper was loose, not one file was out, not one tape recorder sitting on a desk. It looked good, and now he was glad that it did. Everyone was busy, the phones were lit up, but things were under control.

Pendergast slipped his lean form into a chair. For a formal-looking guy, he moved like a cat. Briefly, D'Agosta gave him an overview of the investigation. "Okay, Pendergast," he concluded. "What's your jurisdiction here? Did we fuck up? Are we out?"

Pendergast smiled. "No, not at all. As far as I can tell, I would not have done anything differently myself. You see, Lieutenant, we've been in the case from the very beginning, only we didn't realize it."

"How so?"

"I'm from the New Orleans field office. We were working on a series of killings down there, some very odd killings. Not to get into specifics, but the victims had the backs of their skulls removed, and the brains extracted. Same modus operandi."

"No shit. When was this?"

"Several years ago."

"Several *years* ago? That—"

"Yes. They went unsolved. First it was ATF, because they thought drugs might have been involved, then it was FBI when ATF couldn't make any progress. But we couldn't do anything with it, the trail was cold. And then yesterday, I read a wire service report about the double murder here in New York. The MO is too, ah, too peculiar not to make an immediate connection, don't you think? So I flew up last night. I'm not even officially here. Although I will be tomorrow."

D'Agosta relaxed. "So you're from Louisiana. I thought you might be some new boy in the New York office."

"They'll be here," said Pendergast. "When I make my report tonight, they'll be in on it. But I will be in charge of the case."

"You? No way, not in New York City."

Pendergast smiled. "I will be in charge, Lieutenant. I've been pursuing this case for years and I am, frankly, interested in it." The way Pendergast said *interested* sent a strange sensation down D'Agosta's back. "But don't worry, Lieutenant, I am ready and willing to work with you, side by side, in perhaps a different way than the New York office might. If you'll meet me halfway, that is. This isn't my turf and I'm going to need your help. How about it?"

He stood up and held out his hand. *Christ,* D'Agosta thought, *the boys in the New York office will take him apart in two and a half hours and ship the pieces back to New Orleans.*

"Deal," said D'Agosta, grasping his hand. "I'll introduce you around, starting with the security director, Ippolito. Provided you answer one question. You said the MO of the New Orleans killings was the same. What about the bite marks we found in the brain of the older boy? The claw fragment?"

"From what you told me about the autopsy, Lieutenant, the ME was only speculating about the bite marks," Pendergast replied. "I'll be interested to hear the salivase results. Is the claw being tested?"

Later, D'Agosta would remember that his question had been only half answered. Now, he simply replied, "It's being done today."

Pendergast leaned back in his chair and made a tent of his fingers, his blond white hair hanging loosely over his forehead, his eyes looking off into space. "I'll have to pay a visit to Dr. Ziewicz when she examines today's unpleasantness."

"Say, Pendergast? You aren't by any chance related to Andy Warhol, are you?"

"I don't care much for modern art, Lieutenant."

The crime scene was packed but orderly, everyone moving swiftly and speaking in undertones, as if in deference to the dead man. The morgue crew had arrived but was standing out of the way, patiently observing the proceedings. Pendergast stood with D'Agosta and Ippolito, the Museum's Security Director.

"Indulge me if you will," Pendergast was saying to the photographer. "I'd like a shot from here, like this." Pendergast demonstrated briefly. "And I'd like a series from the top of the stairs, and a sequence coming down. Take your time, get a nice play of line, shadow and light going."

The photographer looked carefully at Pendergast, then moved off.

Pendergast turned to Ippolito. "Here's a question. Why was the guard—what did you say his name was, Mr. Ippolito, Jolley, Fred Jolley?—down here in the first place? This wasn't part of his rounds. Correct?"

"That's right," Ippolito said. He was standing in a dry spot near the entrance to the courtyard, his face a poisonous green.

D'Agosta shrugged. "Who knows?"

"Indeed," Pendergast said. He looked out into the courtyard beyond the stairwell, which was small and deep, brick walls rising on three sides. "And he locked the door behind himself, you say. We have to assume he went outside here, or was headed in that direction. Hmm. The Taurid meteor shower was peaking at about that time last night. Perhaps Jolley here is an aspiring astronomer. But I doubt it." He stood still for a minute, looking around. Then he turned back toward them. "I believe I can tell you why."

Christ, a real Sherlock Holmes, thought D'Agosta.

"He came down the stairwell to indulge a habit of his. Marijuana. This courtyard is an isolated and well-ventilated spot. A perfect place to, ah, smoke some weed."

"Marijuana? That's just a guess."

"I believe I see the roach," said Pendergast, pointing into the court-yard. "Just where the door meets the jamb."

"I can't see a thing," said D'Agosta. "Hey, Ed. Check out the base of the door. Right there. What is it?"

"A joint," said Ed.

"What's the matter with you guys, can't find a fucking joint? I told you to pick up every grain of sand, for Chrissake."

"We haven't done that grid yet."

"Right." He looked at Pendergast. *Lucky bastard. Probably wasn't the guard's joint anyway.*

"Mr. Ippolito," Pendergast drawled, "is it common for your staff to use illicit drugs while on duty?"

"Absolutely not, but I'm not convinced it was Fred Jolley that—"

Pendergast shut him up with a wave of the hand. "I assume you can account for all these footprints."

"Those belong to the guard who found the body," said D'Agosta.

Pendergast bent down. "These completely cover any local evidence that may remain," he said, frowning. "Really, Mr. Ippolito," he said, "you should have your men better trained in how to preserve a crime scene."

Ippolito opened his mouth, then closed it again. D'Agosta sup-pressed a smirk.

Pendergast was walking carefully back underneath the stairwell, where a large metal door stood partially open. "Orient me, Mr. Ippol-ito. This door under the stairwell goes where?"

"A hallway."

"Leading to—?"

"Well, there's the Secure Area down to the right. But the killer wouldn't have gone that way, because . . ."

"Excuse me for contradicting you, Mr. Ippolito, but I'm sure the killer *did* go that way," Pendergast replied. "Let me guess. Beyond the Secure Area is the Old Basement, am I right?"

"Right," said Ippolito.

"Where the two children were found."

"Bingo," said D'Agosta.

"This Secure Area sounds interesting, Mr. Ippolito. Shall we take a stroll?"

Beyond the rusty metal door, a row of light bulbs stretched down a long basement corridor. The floor was covered in shabby linoleum, and the walls were hung with murals of Southwestern Pueblo Indians grind-ing corn, weaving, and stalking deer.

"Lovely," said Pendergast. "A shame they're down here. They look like early Fremont Ellis."

"They used to hang in the Hall of the Southwest," said Ippolito. "It closed in the twenties, I think."

"Ah!" said Pendergast, scrutinizing one of the murals. "It *is* Ellis. My heavens, these are lovely. Look at the light on that adobe facade."

"So," said Ippolito. "How do you know?"

"Why," said Pendergast, "anyone who knows Ellis would recognize these."

"I mean, how do you know the killer came through here?"

"I suppose I was guessing," said Pendergast, examining the next painting. "You see, when someone says 'it's impossible,' I have this very bad habit, I can't help myself, I immediately contradict that person in the most positive terms possible. A very bad habit, but one that I find hard to break. But of course, now we *do* know the killer came through here."

"How?" Ippolito seemed confused.

"Look at this marvelous rendition of old Santa Fe. Have you ever been to Santa Fe?"

There was a momentary silence. "Er, no," said Ippolito.

"There is a mountain range behind the town, called the Sierra de Sangre de Cristo. It means the 'Blood of Christ Mountains' in Spanish."

"So?"

"Well the mountains *do* look quite red in the setting sun, but not, I dare say, *that* red. That's real blood, and it's fresh. A shame, really, it's ruined the painting."

"Holy shit," said D'Agosta. "Look at that."

A broad streak of blood was smeared waist-high across the painting.

"You know, murder is a messy thing. We should find traces of blood all along this corridor. Lieutenant, we'll need the crime lab people in here. I think we have your egress, at any rate." He paused. "Let's finish our little tour, and then call them in. I'd like to go ahead and look for evidence, if you don't mind."

"Be my guest," said D'Agosta.

"Careful where you walk, Mr. Ippolito, we'll be asking them to check the floors as well as the walls."

They came to a locked door marked RESTRICTED. "This is the Secure Area," said Ippolito.

"I see," said Pendergast. "And what exactly is the point of this Secure Area, Mr. Ippolito? Is the rest of the Museum insecure?"

"Not at all," the Security Director replied quickly. "The Secure Area is for storing especially rare and valuable objects. This is the best-protected museum in the country. We've recently installed a system of sliding metal doors throughout the Museum. They're all linked to our computer system, and in the event of a burglary we can seal off the Museum in sections, just like the watertight compartments on a—"

"I get the picture, Mr. Ippolito, thank you very much," Pendergast said. "Interesting. An old copper-sheathed door," he said, examining it closely.

D'Agosta saw that the copper covering was riddled with shallow dents.

"Fresh dents, by the look of them," Pendergast said. "Now, what do you make of this?" He pointed downward.

"Jesus H. Christ," breathed D'Agosta, looking at the lower section of the door. The wooden doorframe was scored and gouged into a welter of fresh splinters, as if something with claws had been scrabbling at it.

Pendergast stepped back. "I want the entire door analyzed, if you please, Lieutenant. And now to see what's inside. Mr. Ippolito, if you would be so kind as to open the door without getting your hands all over it?"

"I'm not supposed to let anyone in there without clearance."

D'Agosta looked at him in disbelief. "You mean you want us to get a damn warrant?"

"Oh, no, no, it's just that—"

"He forgot the key," said Pendergast. "We'll wait."

"I'll be right back," said Ippolito, and his hurried footsteps echoed down the corridor. When he was out of hearing D'Agosta turned to Pendergast. "I hate to say it, Pendergast, but I like the way you work. That was pretty slick, the painting, and the way you handled Ippolito. Good luck with the New York boys."

Pendergast looked amused. "Thank you. The feeling is mutual. I'm glad I am working with you, Lieutenant, and not one of these hard-boiled fellows. Judging from what happened back there, you still have a heart. You're still a normal human being."

D'Agosta laughed. "Naw, it wasn't that. It was the fucking scrambled eggs with ham and cheese and ketchup I had for breakfast. And that crew cut. I hate crew cuts."

= **15** =

The herbarium door was shut, as usual, despite the sign that read DO
NOT CLOSE THIS DOOR. Margo knocked. *Come on, Smith, I know you're
in there.* She knocked again, louder, and heard a querulous voice: "All
right, hold your horses! I'm coming!"

The door opened and Bailey Smith, the old Curatorial Assistant of
the herbarium, sat back down at his desk with an enormous sigh of
irritation and began shuffling through his mail.

Margo stepped forward resolutely. Bailey Smith seemed to consider
his job a gross imposition. And when at last he got around to things,
it was hard to shut him up. Normally Margo would have merely sent
down a requisition slip and avoided the ordeal. But she needed to
examine the Kiribitu plant specimens as soon as possible for her next
dissertation chapter. Moriarty's write-up was still unfinished, and she'd
been hearing rumors of another horrible killing that might shut the
Museum down for the rest of the day.

Bailey Smith hummed, ignoring her. Though he was nearly eighty,
Margo suspected he only feigned deafness to annoy people.

"Mr. Smith!" she called out. "I need these specimens, please." She
pushed a list over the counter top. "Right away, if possible."

Smith grunted, rose from his chair, and slowly picked up the list,
scanning it disapprovingly. "May take awhile to locate, you know. How
about tomorrow morning?"

"Please, Mr. Smith. I've heard they might close down the Museum
at any moment. I really need these specimens."

Scenting the chance to gossip, the old man became friendlier. "Terrible business," he said, shaking his head. "in my forty-two years here I've never seen anything like it. But I can't say I'm surprised," he added, with a significant nod.

Margo didn't want to get Smith going. She said nothing.

"But not the first, from what I hear. And not the last, either." He turned with the list, holding it in front of his nose. "What's this? *Muhlenbergia dunbarii?* We don't have any of that."

Then Margo heard a voice behind her.

"Not the first?"

It was Gregory Kawakita, the young Assistant Curator who had accompanied her to the staff lounge the previous morning. Margo had read the Museum's bio of Kawakita: born to wealthy parents, orphaned young, he had left his native Yokohama and grown up with relatives in England. After studying at Magdalene College, Oxford, he moved to M.I.T. for graduate work, then on to the Museum and an assistant curatorship. He was Frock's most brilliant protégé, which made Margo occasionally resentful. To her, Kawakita didn't seem the kind of scientist who'd wish to be allied with Frock. Kawakita had an instinctual sense for Museum politics, and Frock was controversial, an iconoclast. But despite his self-absorption, Kawakita was undeniably brilliant, and he was working with Frock on a model of genetic mutation that no one but the two of them seemed to fully understand. With Frock's guidance, Kawakita was developing the Extrapolator, a program that could compare and combine genetic codes of different species. When they ran their data through the Museum's powerful computer, the system's throughput was reduced to such a degree that people joked it was in "hand calculator mode."

"Not the first what?" asked Smith, giving Kawakita an unwelcoming stare.

Margo flashed a warning glance at Kawakita, but he continued. "You said something about this murder not being the first."

"Greg, did you *have* to?" Margo groaned sotto voce. "I'll never get my plant specimens now."

"I'm not surprised by any of this," Smith continued. "Now, I'm not a superstitious man," he said, leaning on the counter, "but this isn't the first time some creature has prowled the halls of the Museum. At least that's what people say. Not that I believe a word of it, mind you."

"Creature?" asked Kawakita.

Margo gave Kawakita a light kick in the shins.

"I'm only repeating what everyone's talking about, Dr. Kawakita. I don't believe in starting false rumors."

"Of course not," said Kawakita, winking at Margo.

Smith fixed Kawakita with a stern glare. "They say it's been around a long time. Living down in the basement, eating rats and mice and cockroaches. Have you noticed there aren't any rats or mice loose in the Museum? There *should* be, God knows they're all over the rest of New York. But not here. Curious, don't you think?"

"I hadn't noticed," said Kawakita. "I'll make a special effort to check that out."

"Then there was a researcher here who was breeding cats for some experiment," Smith continued. "Sloane I think his name was, Doctor Sloane, in the Animal Behavior Department. One day a dozen of his cats escaped. And you know what? They were never seen again. Vanished. Now that's kind of funny. You'd expect one or two at least to show up."

"Maybe they left because there weren't any mice to eat," said Kawakita.

Smith ignored him. "Some say it hatched from one of those crates of dinosaur eggs brought back from Siberia."

"I see," said Kawakita, trying to suppress a grin. "Dinosaurs loose in the Museum."

Smith shrugged. "I only say what I hear. Others think it was something brought back from one of the graves they've robbed over the years. Some artifact with a curse. You know, like the King Tut curse. And if you ask me, those fellows deserve what they get. I don't care what they call it, archaeology, anthropology, or hoodoo-ology, it's just plain old grave robbing to me. You don't see them digging up *their* grandmother's graves, but they sure don't hesitate to dig up somebody else's and take all the goodies. Am I right?"

"Absolutely," said Kawakita. "But what was that you said about these murders not being the first?"

Smith looked at them conspiratorially. "Well, if you tell anybody I told you this I'll deny it, but about five years back, something strange happened." He paused for a minute, as if to gauge the effect his story was having. "There was this curator, Morrissey, or Montana, or something. He was involved with that disastrous Amazon expedition. You know the one I mean, where everyone was killed. Anyway, one day he simply vanished. Nobody ever heard from him again. So people started to whisper about it. Apparently, a guard was overheard saying that his body had been found in the basement, horribly mutilated."

"I see," Kawakita said. "And you think the Museum Beast did it?"

"I don't think anything," Smith responded quickly. "I'm just telling you what I've heard, that's all. I've heard a lot of things from a lot of people, I can tell you."

"So has anyone seen this, ah, creature?" Kawakita asked, unsuccessfully stifling a smile.

"Why, yessir. Couple of people, in fact. You know old Carl Conover in the metal shop? Three years ago now he says he saw it, came in early to get some work done and saw it slouching around a corner in the basement. Saw it right there, plain as day."

"Really?" said Kawakita. "What'd it look like?"

"Well—" Smith began, then stopped. Even he finally noticed Kawakita's amusement. The old man's expression changed. "I expect, Dr. Kawakita, that it looked a bit like Mr. Jim Beam," he said.

Kawakita was puzzled. "Beam? I don't believe I know him—"

Bailey Smith suddenly roared with laughter, and Margo couldn't help grinning herself. "George," she said, "I think he meant that Conover was drunk."

"I see," said Kawakita stiffly. "Of course."

All his good humor had vanished. *Doesn't like having the joke turned on him,* Margo thought. *He can dish it out, but he can't take it.*

"Well, anyway," said Kawakita briskly, "I need some specimens."

"Now, wait just a minute!" Margo protested as Kawakita pushed his own list onto the counter. The old man eyed it and peered at the scientist.

"Week after next okay?" he asked.

= 16 =

Several floors above, Lieutenant D'Agosta sat in a huge leather sofa in the curator's study. He smacked his lips contentedly, propped one chubby leg upon the knee of the other, and looked around. Pendergast, absorbed in a book of lithographs, was reclining in an armchair behind a desk. Above his head, in a gold rococo frame, hung a massive Audubon painting depicting the mating ritual of the snowy egret. Oak paneling with a century's patina ran along the walls above a beadboard wainscot. Delicate gilded lights of hand-blown glass hung just below the pressed tin ceiling. A large fireplace of elaborately carved Dolomite limestone dominated one corner of the room. *Nice place*, D'Agosta thought. *Old money. Old New York. It has class. Not the place to smoke a two-bit cigar.* He lit up.

"It's come and gone two-thirty, Pendergast," he said, exhaling blue smoke. "Where the hell do you think Wright is?"

Pendergast shrugged. "Trying to intimidate us," he said, turning another page.

D'Agosta looked at the FBI agent for a minute.

"You know these Museum big shots, they think they can keep anybody waiting," he said finally, watching for a reaction. "Wright and his cronies have been treating us like second-class citizens since yesterday morning."

Pendergast turned another page. "I had no idea the Museum had a complete collection of Piranesi's Forum sketches," he murmured.

D'Agosta snorted to himself. *This should be interesting*, he thought.

Over lunch, he'd made a few surreptitious calls to some friends in the Bureau. Turned out they'd not only heard of Pendergast, but they'd heard several rumors about him. Graduated with honors from some English university—probably true. A special forces officer who'd been captured in Vietnam and had later walked out of the jungle, the only survivor of a Cambodian death camp—D'Agosta wasn't sure about *that* one. But he was revising his opinion nevertheless.

Now the massive door opened silently and Wright came in, the Security Director at his heels. Abruptly, Wright sat down opposite the FBI agent. "You're Pendergast, I suppose," the Director sighed. "Let's get this over with."

D'Agosta sat back to watch the fun.

There was a long silence while Pendergast turned pages. Wright shifted. "If you're busy," he said irritably, "We can come back another time."

Pendergast's face was invisible behind the large book. "No," he said finally. "Now is a good time." Another page was leisurely turned. Then another.

D'Agosta watched with amusement as the Director reddened.

"The Security Director isn't needed for this meeting," came the voice from behind the book.

"Mr. Ippolito is part of the investigation—"

The agent's eyes suddenly appeared over the spine of the book. "I'm in charge of the investigation, Dr. Wright," Pendergast said quietly. "Now, if Mr. Ippolito would be so kind—?"

Ippolito glanced nervously at Wright, who flicked his hand in dismissal.

"Look, Mr. Pendergast," Wright began as the door closed. "I've got a Museum that needs running, and I don't have much time. I hope this can be brief."

Pendergast laid the open book carefully on the desk in front of him.

"I've often thought," he said slowly, "that this early classicist stuff of Piranesi's was his best. Do you agree?"

Wright looked utterly astonished. "I fail to see," he stammered, "what that has to do with—"

"His later work was interesting, of course, but too fantastical for my taste," Pendergast replied.

"Actually," said the Director in his best lecture voice, "I've always thought—"

The book slammed shut like a shot. "*Actually*, Dr. Wright," Pendergast said tightly, his courtly manner gone, "it's time to forget what you've *always* thought. We're going to play a little game here. I'm going to talk, and y'all are going to listen. Understood?"

Wright sat speechless. Then his face mottled in anger. "Mr. Pendergast, I will not be spoken to in that manner—"

Pendergast cut him off. "In case you haven't read the headlines, Dr. Wright, there have been three grisly murders in this Museum in the last forty-eight hours. *Three.* The press is speculating that some kind of ferocious beast is responsible. Museum attendance is down fifty percent since the weekend. Your staff is *very* upset, to put it mildly. Have you bothered taking a stroll through your Museum today, Dr. Wright? You might find it edifying. The feeling of dread is almost palpable. Most people, if they leave their offices at all, travel in twos and threes. The maintenance staff is finding any reasons it can to avoid the Old Basement. Yet you prefer to act as if nothing is wrong. Believe me, Dr. Wright, something is extremely wrong."

Pendergast leaned forward, and slowly folded his arms on top of the book. There was something so menacing in his deliberateness, so cold in his pale eyes, that the Director sat back involuntarily. D'Agosta unconsciously held his breath. Then Pendergast continued.

"Now we can handle this one of three ways," he said. "Your way, my way, or the Bureau's way. So far, your way has been far too much in evidence. I understand that the police investigation has been subtly obstructed. Phone calls are returned late, if at all. Staff are busy or not to be found. Those who *are* available—such as Mr. Ippolito—have not proven particularly useful. People are late to appointments. Why, it's enough to make one suspicious. As of now, your way is no longer acceptable."

Pendergast waited for a response. There was none, and he went on.

"Ordinarily, the Bureau's way would be to close the Museum, suspend operations, cancel exhibitions. Very bad publicity, I assure you. Very expensive, to the taxpayers and to you. But *my* way is a bit more hospitable. All other things being equal, the Museum can remain open. Still, there will be certain conditions. Number one," he said, "I want you to assure complete cooperation of Museum personnel. We will need to speak to you and other senior staff members from time to time, and I want total compliance. I will also need a list of the entire staff. We want to interview everyone who works in, or has had any reason to be in, the vicinity of the murders. There will be no exceptions. I would appreciate your making sure of this personally. We'll be setting up a schedule, and *everyone* is to show up on time."

"But there are twenty five hundred employees—" began Wright.

"Number two," Pendergast continued. "Starting tomorrow, we're going to be limiting employee access to the Museum, until such time as this investigation is concluded. The curfew is to be for the safety of the staff. At least, that is what you will tell them."

"But there's vital research going on here that—"

"Number three—" Pendergast casually pointed three fingers, derringer-like, at Wright "—from time to time we may need to close the Museum, either fully or in part. In some instances, only visitors will be denied entry; in others, the Museum will be closed to staff as well. Notice may be short. Your cooperation will be expected."

Wright's fury mounted. "This Museum is closed only three days a year: Christmas, New Year's, and Thanksgiving," he said. "This is unprecedented. It will look terrible." He gave Pendergast a long, appraising look. "Besides, I'm not convinced you have the authority to do that. I think we should—" He stopped. Pendergast had picked up the telephone.

"What's that for?" Wright demanded.

"Dr. Wright, this is growing tiresome. Perhaps we should discuss this with the Attorney General."

Pendergast started to dial.

"Just a moment," said Wright. "Surely we can discuss this without involving other people."

"That's up to you," said Pendergast as he finished dialing.

"For Heaven's sake, put down that phone," Wright said angrily. "Of course, we'll cooperate fully—within reason."

"Very good," Pendergast said. "And if in the future you start to feel that anything is unreasonable, we can always do this again." He replaced the receiver gently.

"If I'm going to cooperate," Wright continued, "I think I've a right to be informed about just what's been done since this latest atrocity. As far as I can see, you've made precious little progress."

"Certainly, Doctor," Pendergast said. He looked at papers on the desk. "According to your time clocks, the most recent victim, Jolley, met his demise shortly after ten-thirty last night," he said. "The autopsy should confirm this. He was, as you know, lacerated in a fashion similar to the previous victims. He was killed while making his rounds, although the stairwell where he was found wasn't part of his normal route. He may have been investigating a suspicious noise or something of that nature. He may have just stopped for some reefer. A recently smoked marijuana cigarette was found near the archway directly outside the stairwell exit. We will, naturally, be testing the body for drug use."

"God, that's all we need," said Wright. "But haven't you found any *useful* clues? What about this wild animal business? You—"

Pendergast held his palm up and waited for silence. "I would prefer not to speculate until we discuss the available evidence with experts. Some of these experts may be from among your own staff. For the record, we've found no signs as yet that any kind of animal had been in the vicinity.

"The body was found lying at the bottom of the stairwell, although it was clear that the attack occurred near the top, as blood and viscera were found along the length of the stairs. He either rolled or was dragged to the bottom. But don't take my word for it, Dr. Wright," Pendergast said, picking up a manila envelope from the desk, "see for yourself." He pulled out a glossy photograph and laid it carefully on the tabletop.

"Oh, my God," Wright said, staring at the photograph. "Heaven help us."

"The right-hand wall of the stairwell was covered with splattered blood," Pendergrast said. "Here's a photograph."

He handed it to Wright, who slid it quickly on top of the first.

"It's a simple matter to do a ballistics analysis on splattered blood," Pendergast went on. "In this case, the evidence is consistent with a massive blow directed downward, instantaneously disemboweling the victim."

Pendergast replaced the photographs and checked his watch. "Lieutenant D'Agosta will be checking in with you to make sure that everything is proceeding along the lines we've discussed," he said. "One last question, Doctor. Which of your curators knows the most about the anthropology collections here?"

Dr. Wright seemed not to have heard. Finally he said, "Dr. Frock," in a barely audible voice.

"Very good," said Pendergast. "Oh, and Doctor—I told you earlier that the Museum can remain open, *all other things being equal.* But if anybody else dies inside these walls, the Museum will have to be shut down immediately. The matter will be out of my hands. Understood?"

After a long moment, Wright nodded.

"Excellent," Pendergast replied. "I'm very aware, Doctor, that your *Superstition* exhibition is scheduled to open this coming weekend, and that you have a large preview planned for Friday evening. I'd like to see your opening proceed unvexed, but everything will depend on what we discover in the next twenty-four hours. Prudence may require us to delay the opening party."

Wright's left eyelid began to twitch. "That's quite impossible. Our entire marketing campaign would be derailed. The publicity would be devastating."

"We shall see," Pendergast replied. "Now, unless there's anything else, I don't think we need keep you any longer."

Wright, his face drained of color, stood up and, without a word, walked stiffly out of the room.

D'Agosta grinned as the door closed. "Softened up that bastard nicely," he said.

"What's that again, Lieutenant?" Pendergast asked, leaning back in the leather chair and picking up the book with renewed enthusiasm.

"Come on, Pendergast," D'Agosta said, looking cagily at the FBI agent. "I guess you can drop the genteel act when it suits you."

Pendergast blinked innocently at D'Agosta. "I'm sorry, Lieutenant. I apologize for any unseemly behavior. It's simply that I can't stand pompous, bureaucratic individuals. I'm afraid I can become quite short with them." He raised the book. "It's a bad habit, but very hard to break."

= 17 =

The laboratory looked out over the East River and across to the warehouses and decaying industrial buildings of Long Island City. Lewis Turow stood in the window and watched an enormous barge, piled with garbage and surrounded by countless seagulls, being pushed out to sea. *Probably one minute's worth of New York City garbage*, he thought.

Turow turned away from the window and sighed. He hated New York, but one had to make choices. The choice for him was enduring the city and working in one of the best genetic labs in the country, or working in some half-assed facility in a nice rural spot somewhere. So far he'd chosen the city, but his patience was running out.

He heard a low beeping, then the soft hiss of a miniprinter. The results were coming through. Another soft beep indicated the print job was finished. The three-million-dollar Omega-9 Parallel Processing Computer, which took up a series of large gray boxes along one wall, was now completely silent. Only a few lights indicated that anything was happening. It was a special, hardwired model designed for sequencing DNA and mapping genes. Turow had come to the lab six months before specifically because of this machine.

He fetched the paper out of the bin and scanned it. The first page was a summary of the results, followed by a sequence of nucleic acids found in the sample. Next to those were columns of letters that identified primer sequences and mapped genes from the target group.

The target group, in this case, was unusual: big cats. They had asked for gene matches with Asiatic tiger, jaguar, leopard, bobcat. Turow had thrown in the cheetah, since its genetics were so well known. The outgroup chosen was, as usual, Homo sapiens, a control to check that the genetic matching process had been accurate and the sample sound.

He scanned the summary.

Run 3349A5 990
SAMPLE: NYC Crime Lab LA-33
SUMMARY

TARGET GROUP

	% matches	degree of confidence
Panthera leo	5.5	4%
Panthera onca	7.1	5%
Felis lynx	4.0	3%
Felis rufa	5.2	4%
Acinonyx jubatus	6.6	4%

OUTGROUP CONTROL

Homo sapiens	45.2	33%

Well, this is complete bullshit, thought Turow. The sample matched the outgroup a lot more than it matched the target group—the opposite of what should have happened. Only a 4 percent chance that the genetic material was from a big cat, but a 33 percent chance it was from a human being.

Thirty-three percent. Still low, but within the realm of probability.

So that meant trying GenLab for a match. GenLab was an enormous international DNA database—two hundred gigs and growing—that contained DNA sequences, primers, and mapped genes for thousands of organisms, from the Escherichia coli bacterium to *Homo sapiens*. He would run the data against the GenLab database, and see just what this DNA was from. Something close to *Homo sapiens*, it looked like. Not high enough to be an ape, but maybe something like a lemur.

Turow's curiosity was piqued. Till now, he didn't even know that his laboratory did work for the police department. *What the hell made them think this sample came from a big cat?* he wondered.

The results ran to a hefty eighty pages. The DNA sequencer printed out the identified nucleotides in columnar format, indicating species, identified genes, and unidentified sequences. Turow knew that most of the sequences would be unidentified, since the only organism with a complete genetic map was *E. coli.*

C-G	*		G-T	Unidentified
G-G			G-T	*
G-G	*Homo sapiens*		T-T	*
C-G			T-T	*
A-T	A-1 allele		T-T	*
T-G	marker		G	*
G-G			C	*
T-T	A1		C-C	*
A-A	Polymorphism		C-T	*
A-A	begin		G-T	*
A-A	*		T-A	*
G-T	*		G-G	*
T-T	*		T	*
G-T	*		T	*
T-A	'		T	
A-T	'			
T-T	'			
G-T	'			
C-C	'			
C-G	A1 Poly end			

Turow glanced over the figures, then carried the paper over to his desk. With a few keystrokes on his SPARCstation 10, Turow could access information from thousands of databases. If the Omega-9 did not have the information he sought, it would automatically dial into the Internet and find a computer that did.

Scanning the printout more closely, Turow frowned. *It must be a degraded sample,* he thought. *Too much unidentified DNA.*

A-A	Unidentified		A-T	*Hemidactylus*
A-T	'		T	*turcicus*
A-T	'		C	cont'd
A-T	'		T-C	*
A-T	'		C-C	*
A-T	'		T-G	*
T-T	'		G-G	*

G-G	-	G-G	*
G-G	-	G-G	*
A-A	*Hemidactylus	G-G	*
T-T	turcicus	G-G	*
T-G	*	G-G	*
G-C	*	G-G	*
G-T	*	G-G	*
T-G	*	G-G	*
C-A	*	G-G	*
A-C	*	G-G	*

He stopped flipping the pages. Here was something truly odd: the program had identified a large chunk of DNA as belonging to an animal named Hemidactylus turcicus.

Now what the hell is that? thought Turow.

The Biological Nomenclature Database told him:

COMMON NAME: TURKISH GECKO

What? thought Turow. He typed, EXPAND.

HEMIDACTYLUS TURCICUS: TURKISH GECKO. ORIGINAL RANGE: NORTHERN AFRICA PRESENT BIOLOGICAL RANGE: FLORIDA, BRAZIL, ASIA MINOR, NORTHERN AFRICA. MEDIUM-SIZE LIZARD OF THE GECKO FAMILY, GEKKONIDAE, ARBOREAL, NOCTURAL, LACKING MOVEABLE EYELIDS

Turow flicked out of the database while the information was still scrolling by. It was pure nonsense, obviously. Lizard DNA and human DNA in the same sample? But this wasn't the first time something like this had happened. You couldn't blame the computer, really. It was an inexact procedure, and only the smallest fractions of the DNA sequences of any given organism were known.

He scanned down the printed list. Less than 50 percent of the matches were human—a very low proportion, assuming the subject was human, but not out of the question in a degraded sample. And there was always the possibility of contamination. A stray cell or two could ruin an entire run. This last possibility was looking more and more likely to Turow. *Well, what can you expect from the NYPD?* They couldn't even get rid of the guy who sold crack openly on the corner across from his apartment building.

He continued his scan. *Wait,* he thought, *here's another long sequence:* Tarentola mauritanica. He punched up the database, entered the name. The screen read:

TARENTOLA MAURITANICA: WALL GECKO

Give me a break, Turow thought. *This is some kind of joke.* He glanced at the calendar: April first was Saturday.

He started to laugh. It was a very good joke. A very, very good joke. He didn't think old Buchholtz had it in him. Well, he had a sense of humor, too. He started his report.

Sample LA-33
**Summary: Sample conclusively identified as *Homo Gekkopiens,*
common name Gecko-man . . .**

When he finished the report he sent it upstairs immediately. Then he went out for coffee, still chuckling. He was proud of how he'd handled it. He wondered where in the world Buchholtz got his gecko samples from. *Probably sold them in pet stores.* He could see Buchholtz blending up sample cells from two or three geckos in the ultrablender with a few drops of his own blood. *Let's see what our new man Turow makes of this, he'd probably been thinking.* Turow, returning with the coffee, had to laugh out loud. He found Buchholtz waiting for him in the lab, only Buchholtz wasn't laughing.

= 18 =

Wednesday

Frock sat in his wheelchair, dabbing his forehead with a Gucci handkerchief. "Sit down, please," he said to Margo. "Thank you for coming so promptly. It's dreadful, just dreadful."

"The poor guard," she replied. Nobody in the Museum was talking about anything else.

"Guard?" Frock looked up. "Oh yes, quite a tragedy. No, I mean this." He held up a memorandum.

"All sorts of new rules," said Frock. "Very inconvenient. Effective today, staff are only allowed in the building between ten and five. No working late or on Sundays. There will be guards stationed in each department. You'll be expected to sign in and out of Anthropology each day. They are asking everybody to carry IDs at all times. Nobody will be allowed to enter or leave the Museum without one."

He continued reading. "Let's see, what else . . . ah, yes. Try as much as possible to keep to your assigned section. And I'm supposed to tell you not to go into isolated areas of the Museum alone. If you need to go somewhere, go with someone. The police will be interviewing everyone who works in the Old Basement. Yours is scheduled for early next week. And various sections of the Museum are being posted as off-limits." He pushed the memo across the desk.

Margo saw a floor plan attached, the off-limits areas shaded in red. "Don't worry," Frock continued. "I note your office is just outside the area."

Lovely, thought Margo. *Just outside where the murderer is probably lurking.* "This seems like a complicated arrangement, Professor Frock. Why didn't they just close the whole Museum?"

"No doubt they tried, my dear. I'm sure Winston talked them out of it. If *Superstition* doesn't open on schedule, the Museum will be in deep trouble." Frock held out his hand for the memo. "Shall we consider this discussed? There are other things I wish to talk to you about."

Margo nodded. *The Museum will be in deep trouble.* It seemed to her that it already was. Her office mate, along with half of the Museum staff, had called in sick that morning. Those who did show up were spending most of their time at the coffee machines or photocopiers, trading rumors and staying in groups. If that wasn't bad enough, the Museum's exhibit halls were nearly empty. The vacationing families, school groups, shouting children—the normal visitors—were few and far between. Now the Museum attracted mostly ghoulish rubber-neckers.

"I was curious whether you'd obtained any of the plants for your chapter on the Kiribitu yet," Frock continued. "I thought it might be a useful exercise for both of us to run them through the Extrapolator."

The telephone rang. "Blast," Frock said, picking up the receiver. "Yes?" he demanded.

There was a long silence. "Is this necessary?" Frock asked. Then he paused. "If you insist," he concluded, dropping the phone into its cradle and heaving a great sigh.

"The authorities want me down in the basement, Heaven knows why. Somebody named Pendergast. Would you mind wheeling me down? We can chat along the way."

In the elevator, Margo continued. "I was able to get a few specimens from the herbarium, though not as many as I'd wanted. But I don't understand. You're suggesting we run them through the G.S.E.?"

"Correct," Frock replied. "Depending on the condition of the plants, of course. Is there printable material?"

G.S.E. stood for Genetic Sequence Extrapolator, the program being developed by Kawakita and Frock for analyzing genetic "prints."

"The plants are in good condition, for the most part," Margo admitted. "But, Dr. Frock, I don't see what use they could be to the Extrapolator." *Am I just jealous of Kawakita?* She wondered to herself. *Is that why I'm resisting?*

"My dear Margo, your situation is tailor-made!" Frock exclaimed, using her first name in his excitement. "You can't replay evolution. But you can *simulate* it with computers. Perhaps these plants are allied genetically, along the same lines as the Kiribitu shamans have developed for their own classification. Wouldn't that make an interesting sidebar for your dissertation?"

"I hadn't thought of that," Margo said.

"We're beta-testing the program now, and this is exactly the kind of scenario we need," Frock continued eagerly. "Why don't you talk to Kawakita about working together?"

Margo nodded. Privately, she thought that Kawakita didn't seem like the type who wanted to share his spotlight—or even his research—with anybody.

The elevator door opened onto a checkpoint manned by two police officers armed with shotguns. "Are you Dr. Frock?" one asked.

"Yes," Frock replied irritably.

"Come with us, please."

Margo wheeled Frock through several intersections, arriving at last at a second checkpoint. Behind the barricade stood two more policemen and a tall, thin man in a somber black suit, blond white hair combed severely back from his forehead. As the policemen moved the barricade, he stepped forward.

"You must be Dr. Frock," he said, extending his hand. "Thank you for coming down. As I told you, I'm expecting another visitor, so I wasn't able to come by your office myself. Had I known you were—" he indicated the wheelchair with a nod,"—I would never have asked. Special Agent Pendergast." He held out his hand. *Interesting accent*, thought Margo. *Alabama? This guy doesn't look anything like an FBI agent.*

"Quite all right," said Frock, mollified by Pendergast's courtesy. "This is my assistant, Miss Green." Pendergast's hand felt cool in Margo's grasp.

"It's an honor to meet such a distinguished scientist as yourself," Pendergast continued. "I hope time will permit me to read your latest book."

"Thank you." Frock nodded.

"In it, do you apply the 'Gambler's Ruin' scenario to your theory of evolution? I always thought that backed up your hypothesis rather well, especially if you assume most genera start out close to the absorbing boundary."

Frock sat up in his wheelchair. "Well, ah, I was planning to make certain references to that in my next book." He seemed at a loss for words.

Pendergast nodded to the officers, who readjusted the barrier. "I need your help, Dr. Frock," he said in a lower tone.

"Certainly," Frock said amiably. Margo was amazed at how quickly Pendergast had won Frock's cooperation.

"I must ask, first of all, that this discussion be kept among ourselves for the time being," said Pendergast. "May I have your assurance? And that of Ms. Green?"

"Of course," said Frock. Margo nodded.

Pendergast motioned to one of the officers, who brought forward a large plastic bag marked EVIDENCE. From it he removed a small, dark object, which he handed to Frock.

"What you're holding," he said, "is the latex cast of a claw found embedded in one of the children that were murdered last weekend."

Margo leaned forward for a closer look. It was about an inch long, perhaps a little less, curved and jagged.

"A claw?" Frock said, bringing the object close to his face and examining it. "Very unusual. But I'd guess it's a fake."

Pendergast smiled. "We haven't been able to identify its source, Doctor. But I'm not sure it's a fake. In the root canal of the claw we found some matter, which is now being sequenced for DNA. The results are still ambiguous, and our tests are continuing."

Frock raised his eyebrows. "Interesting."

"Now this," said Pendergast, reaching into the bag and withdrawing a much larger object, "is a reconstruction of the instrument that raked the same child." He handed it to Frock.

Margo looked at the cast with disgust. At one end, the latex was mottled and uneven, but at the other, details were clear and well-defined. It ended in three hooked claws: a large central claw, and two shorter talons on either side.

"Good heavens!" said Frock. "This looks saurian."

"Saurian?" asked Pendergast dubiously.

"*Dino*-saurian," said Frock. "Typical ornithischian forelimb, I should say, with one difference. Look here. The central digital process is thickened enormously, while the talons themselves are undersized."

Pendergast raised his eyebrows in mild surprise. "Well, sir," he said slowly, "we'd been leaning toward the big cats, or some other mammalian carnivore."

"But *surely* you know, Mr. Pendergast, that all mammalian predators have five digits."

"Of course, Doctor," said Pendergast. "If you would indulge me for a moment, I'd like to describe a scenario to you."

"Certainly," said Frock.

"There is a theory that the murderer is using this—" he hefted the forelimb—"as a weapon to rake his victims. We feel that what I'm holding might be the impression of an *artifact* of some kind, something made by a primitive tribe out of, say, a jaguar or lion forelimb. The DNA appears to be degraded. It may be an old artifact, collected by the Museum a long time ago, then stolen."

Frock's head lowered until his chin was on his chest. The silence stretched out, broken only by the shuffling of the policemen by the barricade. Then Frock spoke.

"The guard who was killed? Did his wounds show evidence of a broken or missing claw?"

"Good question," Pendergast said. "See for yourself." He slid his hand into the plastic bag and removed a heavy plaque of latex, a long rectangle with three jagged ridges down its middle.

"This is a cast of one of the guard's abdominal wounds," Pendergast explained. Margo shuddered. It was a vile-looking thing.

Frock peered at the deep ridges intently. "The penetration must have been remarkable. But the wound shows no indication of a broken claw. Therefore, you are suggesting that *two* such artifacts are in use by the murderer."

Pendergast looked a little uncomfortable, but nodded.

Frock's head sank once more. The silence went on for minutes. "Another thing," he suddenly said, quite loudly. "Do you see how the claw marks *draw together* slightly? How they are farther apart at the top than at the bottom?"

"Yes?" said Pendergast.

"Like a hand clenching into a fist. That would indicate flexibility in the instrument."

"Granted," said Pendergast. "Human flesh, however, is rather soft and easily distorted. We cannot read too much into these casts." He paused. "Dr. Frock, is any artifact capable of doing this missing from the collection?"

"There is no such artifact *in* the collection," said Frock with a faint smile. "You see, this comes from no living animal I've studied. Do you see how this claw has a conical shape, a deep fully enclosed root? See how it tapers to an almost perfect tripyramidal cross section near the top? This appears in only two classes of animal: dinosaur and bird. That is one of the reasons some evolutionary biologists think birds evolved from dinosaurs. I would say it *is* from a bird, except that it is far too large. Thus, dinosaurian."

He placed the latex claw in his lap and looked up again. "Certainly, a clever person familiar with dinosaur morphology could have shaped a claw like this, and used it as a tool for murder. I assume you have tested the original fragment to see if it indeed is composed of a genuine biological material, such as keratin, rather than being cast or carved from some inorganic material?"

"Yes, Doctor. It is real."

"And you are sure that the DNA was real, and not simply blood or flesh from the victim?"

"Yes," Pendergast replied. "As I said, it came from the root canal, not under the cuticle."

"And what, pray tell, *was* the DNA from?"

"The final report isn't in yet."

Frock held up his hand. "Understood. But tell me, why aren't you making use of our own DNA laboratory, here in the Museum? We have facilities equal to that of anybody in the state."

"Equal to anybody in the country, Doctor. But you must understand that our procedures forbid it. Could we be sure of the results if the tests were conducted at the crime scene? With perhaps the murderer himself operating the equipment?" Pendergast smiled. "I hope you'll forgive my persistence, Doctor, but would you be willing to *consider* the possibility that this weapon is constructed from relics belonging to the Anthropology collection, and to think about what artifact or artifacts this cast most closely resembles?"

"If you'd like," Frock replied.

"Thank you. We can discuss it again in a day or so. Meanwhile, would it be possible to obtain a printed inventory of the Anthropology collection?"

Frock smiled. "Six million items? You can use the computer catalog, however. Would you like a terminal set up?"

"Perhaps later," said Pendergast, replacing the latex plaque in the plastic bag. "It's kind of you to offer. Our command post is currently in the unused gallery behind reprographics."

Footsteps sounded behind them. Margo turned to see the tall form of Dr. Ian Cuthbert, Deputy Director of the Museum, followed by the two officers from the elevator.

"Look here, how long is this going to take?" Cuthbert was complaining. He stopped at the barricade. "Oh, Frock, so they've got you, too. What a damned nuisance this is."

Frock nodded imperceptibly.

"Dr. Frock," said Pendergast, "I'm sorry. This is the gentleman I'd been waiting for when we first spoke. You're welcome to remain, if you'd care to." Frock nodded again.

"Now, Dr. Cuthbert," said Pendergast briskly, turning to the Scotsman. "I asked you to come down because I'd like some information about this area behind me." He indicated a large doorway.

"The Secure Area? What about it? Surely somebody else could—" Cuthbert began.

"Ah, but my questions are for you," Pendergast interrupted, politely but firmly. "Shall we step inside?"

"If it won't take much time," Cuthbert said. "I've got an exhibition to mount."

"Yes, indeed," said Frock, his tone faintly sardonic. "An *exhibition*." He motioned Margo to wheel him forward.

"Dr. Frock?" Pendergast said politely.

"Yes?"

"I wonder if I might have that cast back."

The copper-sheathed door to the Museum's Secure Area had been removed and a new steel one installed in its place. Across the hall was a small door labelled PACHYDERMAE. Margo wondered how the staff had been able to fit huge elephant bones through it.

Turning away, she wheeled Frock into the narrow walkway beyond the open door to the Secure Area. The Museum kept its most valuable artifacts in small vaults on either side: sapphires and diamonds; ivory and rhinoceros horns heaped on racks like cordwood; bones and skins of extinct animals; Zuni war gods. Two men in dark suits stood at the far end, talking in low tones. They straightened up when Pendergast entered.

Pendergast stopped at one open vault door, much like the others, sporting a large black combination knob, brass lever, and ornate decorative scrollwork. Inside, a bulb threw a harsh light across the metal walls. The vault was empty except for several crates, all of which were quite large except one. The smaller crate's lid was removed, while one of the larger crates was badly damaged, with excelsior stuffing protruding.

Pendergast waited until everybody was inside the vault. "Allow me to provide some background," Pendergast said. "The murder of the guard took place not far from this spot. It appears that afterward, the murderer came down the hallway just outside. The murderer attempted to break down the door that leads to the Secure Area. He may have tried before. The attempts were unsuccessful.

"At first we weren't sure what the killer was after. As you know, there is a lot of valuable material in here." Pendergast motioned to one of the policemen, who came over and handed him a piece of paper. "So we asked around, and found that nothing has come in or out of the Secure Area for six months. Except these crates. They were moved into this vault last week. On your orders, Dr. Cuthbert."

"Mr. Pendergast, allow me to explain—" said Cuthbert.

"One moment, if you please," said Pendergast. "When we inspected the crates, we found something very interesting." He pointed to the damaged crate. "Notice the slats. The two by sixes here are deeply scored by claw marks. Our forensic people tell me the marks on the victims were probably made by the same object or instrument."

Pendergast stopped and looked intently at Cuthbert.

"I had no idea—" said Cuthbert. "Nothing had been taken. I merely thought that . . ." His voice trailed away.

"I wonder, Doctor, if you could enlighten us as to the history of these crates?"

"That's easily explained," said Cuthbert. "There's no mystery about it. The crates are from an old expedition."

"I gathered that," Pendergast said. "Which expedition?"

"The Whittlesey expedition," Cuthbert replied.

Pendergast waited.

Finally Cuthbert sighed. "It was a South American expedition that took place over five years ago. It was . . . not entirely successful."

"It was a disaster," Frock said derisively. Oblivious to Cuthbert's angry glance, he continued. "It caused a scandal in the Museum at the time. The expedition broke up early, due to personality conflicts. Some of the expedition members were killed by hostile tribesmen; the rest were killed in a plane crash on the way back to New York. There were the inevitable rumors of a curse, that kind of thing."

"That's an exaggeration," Cuthbert snapped. "There was no scandal of any sort."

Pendergast looked at them. "And the crates?" he said mildly.

"They were shipped back separately," Cuthbert said. "But this is all beside the point. There was a very unusual object in one of these crates, a figurine created by an extinct South American tribe. It's to be an important element in the *Superstition* exhibition."

Pendergast nodded. "Go on."

"Last week, when we went to retrieve the figurine, I found that one of the crates had been broken into." He pointed. "So I ordered all of the crates moved temporarily to the Secure Area."

"What was taken?"

"Well, now, that was a little odd," said Cuthbert. "None of the artifacts were missing from the crate. The figurine itself is worth a fortune. It's unique, the only one of its kind in the world. The Kothoga tribe that made it vanished years ago."

"You mean *nothing* was missing?" Pendergast asked.

"Well, nothing important. The only thing that seemed to be missing were the seed pods, or whatever they were. Maxwell, the scientist who packed them, died in the plane crash near Asunción."

"Seed pods?" asked Pendergast.

"I honestly don't know what they were. None of the documentation survived except for the anthropological material. We had Whittlesey's journal, you see, but that was all. There was a little reconstructive work done when the crates first came back, but since then . . ." he stopped.

"You'd better tell me about this expedition," said Pendergast.

"There's not much to tell. They had originally assembled to search for traces of the Kothoga tribe, and to do a survey and general collection in a very remote area of the rain forest. I think the preliminary work estimated that ninety-five percent of the plant species in the area were unknown to science. Whittlesey, an anthropologist, was the leader. I believe there was also a paleontologist, a mammalogist, a physical anthropologist, perhaps an entomologist, a few assistants. Whittlesey and an assistant named Crocker disappeared and were probably killed by tribesmen. The rest died in the plane crash. The only thing we had any documentation on was the figurine, from Whittlesey's journal. The rest of the stuff is just a mystery, no locality data, nothing."

"Why did the material sit in these crates for so long? Why wasn't it unpacked and cataloged and put in the collections?"

Cuthbert stirred uncomfortably. "Well," he said defensively, "ask Frock. He's the chairman of the department."

"Our collections are enormous," said Frock. "We have dinosaur bones still crated up from the 1930s that have never been touched. It costs a tremendous amount of money and time to curate these things." He sighed. "But in this particular case, it's not a question of mere oversight. As I recall, the Anthropology Department was forbidden to curate these crates upon their return." He looked pointedly at Cuthbert.

"That was years ago!" Cuthbert replied acidly.

"How do you know there are no rare artifacts in the unopened boxes?" Pendergast asked.

"Whittlesey's journal implied that the figurine in the small crate was the only item of importance."

"May I see this journal?"

Cuthbert shook his head. "It's gone missing."

"Were the crates moved on your own authority?"

"I suggested it to Dr. Wright after I learned the crates had been tampered with," Cuthbert said. "We kept the material together in its original crates until it could be curated. That's one of the Museum's rules."

"So the crates were moved late last week," Pendergast murmured, almost to himself. "Just prior to the killing of the two boys. What could the killer have been after?" Then he looked back at Cuthbert. "What did you say had been taken from the crates? Seed pods, was it?"

Cuthbert shrugged. "As I said, I'm not sure what they were. They looked like seed pods to me, but I'm no botanist."

"Can you describe them?"

"It's been years, I don't really remember. Big, round, heavy. Rugose on the outside. Light brown color. I've only seen the inside of the crate twice, you understand; once when it first came back, and then last week, looking for Mbwun. That's the figurine."

"Where is the figurine now?" Pendergast asked.

"It's being curated for the show. It should be on display already, we're sealing the exhibition today."

"Did you remove anything else from the box?"

"No. The figurine is the unique piece of the lot."

"I would like to arrange to see it," said Pendergast.

Cuthbert shifted irritably on his feet. "You can see it when the show opens. Frankly, I don't know what you're up to. Why waste time on a broken crate when there's a serial killer loose in the Museum and you chaps can't even find him?"

Frock cleared his throat. "Margo, bring me closer, if you will," he asked.

Margo wheeled him over to the crates. With a grunt he bent forward to scrutinize the broken boards.

Everyone watched.

"Thank you," he said, straightening up. He eyed the group, one at a time.

"Please note that these boards are scored on the *inside* as well as the outside," he said finally. "Mr. Pendergast, are we not making an assumption here?" he finally said.

"I never make assumptions," replied Pendergast, with a smile.

"But you are," Frock persisted. "All of you are making an assumption—that some one, or some thing, broke *into* the crate."

There was a sudden silence in the vault. Margo could smell the dust in the air, and the faint odor of excelsior.

And then Cuthbert began to laugh raucously, the sound swelling harshly through the chamber.

As they approached Frock's office once again, the curator was unusually animated.

"Did you see that cast?" he said to Margo. "Avian attributes, dinosaurian morphology. This could be the very thing!" He could scarcely contain himself.

"But, Professor Frock, Mr. Pendergast believes it was constructed as a weapon of some sort," Margo said quickly. As she said it, she realized that *she* wanted to believe it, too.

"Stuff!" Frock snorted. "Didn't you get the sense, looking at that cast, of something tantalizingly familiar, yet utterly foreign? We're looking at an evolutionary aberration, the vindication of my theory." Inside the office, Frock immediately produced a notebook from his jacket pocket and started scribbling.

"But, Professor, how could such a creature—?" Margo stopped as she felt Frock's hand close over hers. His grip was extraordinarily strong.

"My dear girl," he said, "there are more things in heaven and earth, as Hamlet pointed out. It isn't always for us to speculate. Sometimes we must simply observe." His voice was low, but he trembled with excitement. "We can't miss this opportunity, do you hear? Damn this steel prison of mine! You must be my eyes and ears, Margo. You must go everywhere, search up and down, be an extension of my fingers. We must *not* let this chance pass us by. Are you willing, Margo?"

He gripped her hand tighter.

= 19 =

The old freight elevator in Section 28 of the Museum always smelled like something had died in it, Smithback thought. He tried breathing through his mouth.

The elevator was huge, the size of a Manhattan studio, and the operator had decorated it with a table, chair, and pictures cut from the Museum's nature magazine. The pictures focused on a single subject. There were giraffes rubbing necks, insects mating, a baboon displaying its rump, native women with pendulous breasts.

"You like my little art gallery?" the elevator man asked, with a leer. He was about sixty years old and wore an orange toupee.

"It's nice to see someone so interested in natural history," Smithback said sarcastically.

As he stepped out, the smell of rotting flesh hit him with redoubled force; it seemed to fill the air like a Maine fog. "How do you stand it?" he managed to gasp to the elevator man.

"Stand what?" the man said, pausing as he rolled the hoistway doors shut.

A cheerful voice came ringing down the corridor. "Welcome!" An elderly man shouted over the sound of the forced-air ducts as he grasped Smithback's hand. "Nothing but zebra cooking today. You miss the rhinoceros. But come in anyway, come in, please!" Smithback knew his thick accent was Austrian.

Jost Von Oster ran the osteological preparation area, the Museum Laboratory in which animal carcasses were reduced to bones. He was over eighty, but looked so pink, cheerful, and plump that most people thought he was much younger.

Von Oster had started at the Museum in the late twenties, preparing and mounting skeletons for display. His crowning achievement in those days had been a series of horse skeletons, mounted walking, trotting, and galloping. It was said that these skeletons had revolutionized the way animals were exhibited. Von Oster had then turned to creating the lifelike habitat groups popular in the forties, making sure every detail—down to the saliva on an animal's mouth—looked perfectly real.

But the era of the habitat group had passed, and Von Oster had eventually been relegated to the Bug Room. Disdaining all offers of retirement, he cheerfully presided over the osteological lab, where animals—now mostly collected from zoos—were turned into clean white bones for study or mounting. However, his old skills as a master habitat sculptor were still intact, and he had been called in to work on a special shaman life-group for the *Superstition* exhibition. It was the painstaking preparation of this display group that Smithback wanted to include as one chapter in his book.

Following Von Oster's gesture, Smithback stepped into the preparation area. He'd never seen this famous room before. "So glad you could come see my workshop," Von Oster said. "Not many people down here now, what with these dreadful killings. Very glad indeed!"

The workshop looked more like a bizarre industrial kitchen than anything else. Deep stainless-steel tanks lined one wall. On the ceiling near the tanks hung massive pulleys, chains, and grappling hooks for handling the larger carcasses. A drain was drilled into the center of the floor, a small broken bone caught in its grill. In a far corner of the workshop a stainless-steel gurney stood, bearing a large animal. If it hadn't been for the large, hand-lettered sign taped to one leg of the gurney, Smithback wouldn't have guessed that the creature had once been a Sargasso Sea Dugong; it was now almost fully decomposed. Around the corpse lay picks, pliers, tiny knives.

"Thanks for taking time to see me," Smithback managed.

"Not at all!" Von Oster exploded. "I wish we could give tours, but you know this area is off limits to the tourists, the more is the pity. You should have been here for the rhinoceros. *Gott,* she was something!"

Walking briskly across the room, he showed Smithback the maceration tank containing the zebra carcass. Despite a hood drawing the vapors away, the smell was still strong. Von Oster lifted the lid and stood back like a proud cook.

"What you think of *zat!*"

Smithback looked at the soupy brown liquid filling the vat. Under the muddy surface lay the macerating zebra carcass, its flesh and soft tissues slowly liquefying.

"It's a little ripe," Smithback said weakly.

"What you mean, ripe? It just perfect! Under here we got the burner. It keep the water at an even ninety-five degrees. See, first we gut the carcass and drop it in the vat here. Then it rot and in two weeks we pull the plug and drain everything down the sink. What we got left is this big pile of greasy bones. So then we refill the vat and add a little alum and boil those bones. You don't want to boil them too long, they get soft."

Von Oster paused again for air. "You know, just like when they cook the chicken too long. Phhhhtui! Bad! But those bones still greasy, so we wash them *mit* the benzene. That make them pure white."

"Mr. Von Oster—" Smithback began. If he didn't redirect this interview quickly, he would never get out. And he couldn't stand the smell much longer. "I was wondering if you could tell me a little about the shaman group you worked on. I'm writing a book about *Superstition*. You remember our conversation?"

"*Ja, ja!* Of course!" He charged over to a desk and pulled out some drawings. Smithback switched on his microcassette recorder.

"First, you paint the background on a double-curved surface, so you get no corners, see? You want the illusion of depth."

Von Oster began describing the process, his voice pitched with excitement. *This is going to be good,* Smithback thought. *The guy's a writer's dream.*

Von Oster went on for a long time, stabbing the air, making sweeping gestures, taking deep breaths between his heavily accented sentences. When he was finished, he beamed at Smithback. "Now, you want to see the bugs?" he asked.

Smithback couldn't resist. The bugs were famous. It was a process Von Oster himself had invented, but was now in use by all the large natural history museums in the country: the beetles would strip a small carcass of its flesh, leaving behind a cleaned, perfectly articulated skeleton.

The "safe" room that housed the beetles was hot and humid, and little larger than a closet. The beetles, called dermestids, came from Africa and lived in white porcelain tubs with slick sides, roofed with screens. The beetles slowly crawled over rows of dead, skinned animals.

"What are those things?" Smithback asked, peering at the bug-covered carcasses inside the tubs.

"Bats!" said Von Oster. "Bats for Dr. Huysmans. It will take about ten days to clean up those bats." He pronounced it "zose bets."

Between the odors and the bugs, Smithback had had enough. He stood up and extended his hand toward the old scientist. "I gotta go. Thanks for the interview. And those bugs are really something."

"You're most welcome!" Von Oster responded. "Now, wait. Interview, you say. Who you writing this book for?" The idea had suddenly occurred to him that he'd been interviewed.

"For the Museum," said Smithback. "Rickman's in charge of it."

"Rickman?" Von Oster's eyes suddenly narrowed.

"Yes. Why?" Smithback asked.

"You working for Rickman?" Von Oster said.

"Not really. She's just, well, interfering mostly," Smithback said.

Von Oster broke into a pink grin. "*Ach,* she poison, that one! Why you working for her?"

"That's just the way it happened," Smithback said, gratified at having found an ally. "You wouldn't believe the kind of crap she's put me through. Oh, God."

Von Oster clapped his hands. "I believe it! I believe it! She making trouble everywhere! This exhibit, she making all kind of trouble!"

Suddenly Smithback was interested. "How so?" he asked.

"She in there every day, saying *zis* not good, *zat* not good. *Gott,* that woman!"

"That sounds like her," Smithback said with a grim smile. "So what wasn't good?"

"That, what you call it, that Kothoga tribe stuff. I was in there just yesterday afternoon and she was carrying on. 'Everybody leave the exhibition! We bring in Kothoga figurine!' Everybody had to drop work and leave."

"The figurine? What figurine? What's so sensitive about it?" It suddenly occurred to Smithback that something so upsetting to Rickman might someday be useful to him.

"That Mbwun figurine, big deal in the exhibition. I not know much about. But she was very upset, I tell you!"

"Why?"

"Like I tell you, that figurine. You not heard? Lots of talk about it, very very bad. I try not to hear."

"What kind of talk would that be, for instance?"

Smithback listened to the old man for quite a while longer. Finally, he backed himself out of the workshop, Von Oster pursuing as far as the elevator.

As the doors rolled shut, the man was still talking. "You unlucky, working for her!" he called after Smithback just before the elevator lurched upward. But Smithback didn't hear him. He was busy thinking.

= 20 =

As the afternoon drew to a close, Margo looked up wearily from her terminal. Stretching, she punched a command to the printer down the hall, then sat back, rubbing her eyes. Moriarty's case write-up was finally done. A little rough around the edges, perhaps; not as comprehensive as she would have liked; but she couldn't afford to spend any more time on it. Secretly, she was rather pleased, and found herself eager to take a printout up to Moriarty's office on the fourth floor of the Butterfield Observatory, where the project team for the *Superstition* exhibition was housed.

She thumbed through her staff directory, looking for Moriarty's extension. Then she reached for her phone and dialed the four-digit number.

"Exhibition central," drawled a voice. There were loud good-byes in the background.

"Is George Moriarty there?" Margo asked.

"I think he's down at the exhibition," the voice responded. "We're locking up here. Any message?"

"No, thanks," Margo replied, hanging up. She looked at her watch: almost five. Curfew time. But the exhibition was being unveiled Friday evening, and she'd promised Moriarty the material.

As she was about to get up, she remembered Frock's suggestion that she call Greg Kawakita. She sighed, picking up the phone again. *Better give him a try.* Chances are he'd be out of the building now, and she could just leave a message on phone-mail.

"Greg Kawakita speaking," came the familiar baritone voice.

"Greg? This is Margo Green." *Stop sounding so apologetic. It's not like he's a department head or anything.*

"Hi, Margo. What's up?" She could hear the clacking of keys coming over the line.

"I have a favor to ask. It's a suggestion of Dr. Frock's, actually. I'm doing an analysis of some plant specimens used by the Kiribitu tribe, and he suggested I run them through your Extrapolator. Perhaps it will find some genetic correspondences in the samples."

There was silence. "Dr. Frock thought it might be a useful test of your program, as well as a help to me," she urged.

Kawakita paused. "Well, you know, Margo, I'd like to help you out, I really would. But the Extrapolator really isn't in shape yet to be used by just anybody. I'm still chasing down bugs, and I couldn't vouch for the results."

Margo's face burned. "Just anybody?"

"Sorry, that was a poor choice of words. You know what I mean. Besides, it's a really busy time for me, and this curfew won't help matters any. Tell you what, why don't you check with me again in a week or two? Okay? Talk to you then."

The line went dead.

Margo stood up, grabbed her jacket and purse, and went down the hall to retrieve her printout. She knew he was planning to postpone her indefinitely. Well, to hell with Kawakita. She'd hunt Moriarty down and give him the copy before she left. If nothing else, it might get her that guided tour of the exhibition, maybe find out what all the fuss was about.

A few minutes later, Margo walked slowly across the deserted Selous Memorial Hall. Two guards were stationed at the entrance, and a single docent stood inside the information center, locking away ledgers and arranging sale items in preparation for the next day's visitors. *Assuming there are any,* thought Margo. Three policemen stood just under the huge bronze statue of Selous, talking among themselves. They didn't notice Margo.

Margo found her thoughts returning to the morning's talk with Frock. If the killer wasn't found, the security measures could get stricter. Maybe her dissertation defense would be delayed. Or the entire Museum could be closed. Margo shook her head. If that happened, she was Massachusetts-bound for sure.

She headed for the Walker Gallery and the rear entrance to *Superstition*. To her dismay, the large iron doors were closed, and a velvet

rope was suspended between two brass posts in front of them. A policeman stood beside the sign, motionless.

"Can I help you, Miss?" he said. His nameplate read F. BEAUREGARD.

"I'm going to see George Moriarty," Margo replied. "I think he's in
the exhibition galleries. I have to give him something." She brandished
the printout in front of the policeman, who looked unimpressed.

"Sorry, Miss," he said. "It's past five. You shouldn't be here. Besides,"
he said more gently, "the exhibition's been sealed until the opening."

"But—" Margo began to protest, then turned and walked back toward the rotunda with a sigh.

After rounding a corner, she stopped. At the end of the empty hallway she could see the dim vastness of the Hall. Behind her, Officer F.
Beauregard was out of sight around the corner. On impulse, she veered
sharply left through a small, low passage that opened into another,
parallel walkway. Maybe it wasn't too late to find Moriarty, after all.

She moved up a wide flight of stairs, and, looking carefully around
before proceeding, walked slowly into a vaulted hall devoted to insects.
Then she turned right and entered a gallery that ran around the second
level of the Marine Hall. Like everyplace else in the Museum, it felt
eerie and deserted.

Margo descended one of the twin sweeping staircases to the granite
floor of the main hall. Moving more slowly now, she passed by a life-
size walrus habitat group and a meticulously constructed model of an
underwater reef. Dioramas such as these, originally fashioned in the
thirties and forties, could no longer be made, she knew—they had
become much too expensive to produce.

At the far end of the Hall was the entrance to the Weisman Gallery,
where the larger temporary exhibitions were held. This was one of the
suite of galleries in which the *Superstition* exhibition was being
mounted. Black paper covered the inside of the double glass doors,
fronted by a large sign that read: GALLERY CLOSED. NEW EXHIBITION
IN PROGRESS. THANK YOU FOR YOUR UNDERSTANDING.

The left-hand door was locked. The right one, however, pushed
open easily.

As casually as possible, she looked over her shoulder: nobody.

The door hissed shut behind her, and she found herself in a narrow
crawl space between the outer walls of the gallery and the back of the
exhibition proper. Plywood boards and large nails were strewn around
in disarray, and electrical cables snaked across the floor. On her left a
huge structure of sheetrock and boards, hammered clumsily together

and supported by wooden buttresses, looked very much like the back side of a Hollywood set. It was the side of the *Superstition* exhibition that no Museum visitor would ever see.

She moved carefully down the crawl space, scouting for some way to get into the exhibition. The light was poor—metal-shielded light bulbs, spaced about twenty feet apart—and she didn't want to stumble and fall. Soon she came across a small gap between the wooden panels—just big enough, she decided, to squeeze through.

She found herself in a large, six-sided anteroom. Gothic arches in three of the walls framed passages that receded into the gloom. Most of the light came from several backlit photographs of shamans high up on the walls. She looked speculatively at the three exits. She had no idea where she was in the exhibition—where it began, where it ended, or which way she should go to find Moriarty. "George?" she called softly, somehow unable to raise her voice in the silence and gloom.

She took the central passage to another dark hall, longer than the last and crowded with exhibits. At intervals, a brilliant spot illuminated some artifact: a mask, a bone knife, a strange carving covered with nails. The artifacts appeared to float in the velvet darkness. Crazy, dim patterns of light and shadow played across the ceiling.

At the far end of the gallery, the walls narrowed. Margo had the odd feeling that she was walking back into a deep cave. *Pretty manipulative,* she thought. She could see why Frock was upset.

She went deeper into the gloom, hearing nothing but her own footsteps padding on the thick carpet. She couldn't see the exhibits until she was almost on top of them, and she wondered how she'd retrace her steps to the room of the shamans. Perhaps there would be an unlocked exit—a well-lit unlocked exit—someplace else in the exhibit.

Ahead of her, the narrow hall forked. After a moment's hesitation, Margo chose the right-hand passage. As she continued, she noticed small alcoves to either side, each containing a single grotesque artifact. The silence was so intense that she found herself holding her breath.

The hall widened into a chamber, and she stopped in front of a set of Maori tattooed heads. They weren't shrunken—the skulls were clearly still inside, preserved, the label said, by smoking. The eye sockets were stuffed with fibers, and the mahogany-colored skins glistened. The black, shriveled lips were drawn back from the teeth. There were six of them, a crowd grinning hysterically, bobbing in the night. The blue tattoos were breathtakingly complex: intricate spirals that intersected and reintersected, curving in endless patterns around the cheeks and nose and chin. The tattooing had been done in life, the label said, and the heads preserved as a sign of respect.

Just beyond, Margo could see the gallery narrowing to a point. A massive, squat totem pole stood before it, lit from beneath by a pale, orange light. The shadows of giant wolf heads and birds with cruel, hooked beaks thrust upward from the pole and splashed across the ceiling, gray against black. Certain she had reached a dead end, Margo approached the totem pole unwillingly. Then she noticed a small opening, ahead and on the left, leading into an alcove. She continued slowly, walking as quietly as possible. Any thought of calling out again for Moriarty had long since vanished. *Thank God I'm nowhere near the Old Basement*, she thought.

The alcove held a display of fetishes. Some were simple stones carved in the shapes of animals, but the majority were monsters depicting the darker side of human superstition. Another opening brought Margo into a long, narrow room. Thick black felt covered all of the room's surfaces, and a dim blue light filtered from hidden recesses. The ceiling was low above Margo's head. *Smithback would have to go through here on his hands and knees*, she thought.

The room broadened into an octagonal space beneath a high groined vault. A dappled light filtered down from stained-glass depictions of medieval underworlds set into the vaulted ceiling. Large windows dominated each wall.

She approached the closest window and found herself looking down into a Mayan tomb. A skeleton lay in the center, covered with a thick layer of dust. Artifacts were scattered around the site. A gold breastplate sat on the ribcage, and gold rings encircled bony fingers. Painted pots were arranged in a semicircle around the skull. One of these contained an offering of tiny, dried corncobs.

The next window displayed an Eskimo rock burial, including an Eskimo mummy-bundle wrapped in skins. The next was even more startling: a lidless, rotting European-style coffin, complete with corpse. The corpse was dressed in a much-decayed frock coat, tie, and tails, and was well on its way toward decomposition. Its head was bent stiffly toward Margo as if prepared to tell her a secret, sightless eye sockets bulging, mouth ossified into a rictus of pain. She took a step backward. *Good God*, she thought, *that's somebody's great-grandfather*. The matter-of-fact tone of the label, which tastefully described the rituals associated with a typical nineteenth-century American burial, belied the visual hideousness of the scene. *It's true*, she thought; *the Museum is definitely taking a chance with stuff as strong as this*.

She decided to forego the other windows and proceeded through a low archway in the far side of the octagonal room. Beyond, the passage forked. To her left was a small cul-de-sac; to her right, a long, slender passage led into darkness. She didn't want to go that way; not just yet. She wandered into the dead-end room, and stopped suddenly. Then she moved forward to examine one of the cases more closely.

The gallery dealt with the concept of ultimate evil in its many mythic forms. There were various images of a medieval devil; there was the Eskimo evil spirit, Tornarsuk. But what arrested her was a crude stone altar, placed in the center of the gallery. Sitting on the altar, lit by a yellow spot, was a small figurine, carved in such detail it took Margo's breath away. Covered in scales, it crouched on all fours. Yet there was something—the long forearms, the angle of its head—that was disturbingly human. She shuddered. *What kind of imagination gave rise to a being with both scales and hair?* Her eyes dropped to the label.

MBWUN. This carving is a representation of the mad god Mbwun, possibly carved by the Kothoga tribe of the Upper Amazon basin. This savage god, also known as He Who Walks On All Fours, was much feared by the other indigenous tribes of the area. In local myth, the Kothoga tribe was said to be able to conjure Mbwun at will, and send him on errands of destruction against neighboring tribes. Very few Kothoga artifacts have ever been found, and this is the sole image of Mbwun known to exist. Except for trace references in Amazonian legends, nothing else is known about the Kothoga, or about their mysterious "devil."

Margo felt a chill creep over her. She looked closer, repulsed by the reptilian features, the small, wicked eyes . . . the talons. Three on each forelimb.

Oh, dear God. It couldn't be.

Suddenly, she realized that every instinct she had was telling her to keep absolutely still. A minute passed, then two.

Then it came again—the sound that had galvanized her. An odd rustling, slow, deliberate, maddeningly soft. On the thick carpet, the footsteps had to be close . . . very close. A horrible goatish stench threatened to choke her.

She looked around wildly, fighting down panic, searching for the safest exit. The darkness was complete. As quietly as possible, she moved out of the cul-de-sac and across the fork. Another rustling noise and she was running, running, headlong through the darkness, past the ghoulish displays and leering statues that seemed to leap out of the blackness, down twisting forks and passages, trying always to take the most hidden path.

At last, thoroughly lost and out of breath, she ducked into an alcove containing a display on primitive medicine. Gasping, she crouched behind a case holding a trepanned human skull upon an iron pole. She hid in its shadow, listening.

There was nothing; no noise, no movement. She waited as her breath slowed and reason returned. There was nothing out there. There had never been anything out there, in fact—it was her overzealous imagination, fueled by this nightmarish tour. *I was foolish to sneak in,* she thought. *Now, I don't know if I'll ever want to come back—even on the busiest Saturday.*

Anyway, she had to find a way out. It was late now, and she hoped people were still around to hear her knocking, should she come up against a locked exit. It would be embarrassing, having to explain herself to a guard or policeman. But at least she'd be out.

She peeked over the case lid. Even if it *had* all been her imagination, she didn't care to go back in the same direction. Holding her breath, she stepped quietly out, then listened. Nothing.

She turned left and moved slowly down the corridor, searching for a likely looking route out of the exhibit. At a large fork she stopped, eyes straining in the darkness, debating which of the branching pathways to take. *Shouldn't there be exit signs? Guess they haven't been installed yet. Typical.* But the hall to her left looked promising: the passage seemed to open up into a large foyer, ahead in the blackness where sight failed.

Movement registered in her peripheral vision. Limbs frozen, she glanced hesitatingly to the right. A shadow—black against black—was gliding stealthily toward her, moving with an inky sinuousness over the display cases and grinning artifacts.

With a speed born of horror, she shot down the passage. She felt, more than saw, the walls of the passage roll back and widen about her. Then she saw twin slits of vertical light ahead, outlining a large double doorway. Without slackening her pace, she threw herself against it. The doors flew back, and something on the far side clattered. Dim light rushed in—the subdued red light of a museum at night. Cool air moved across her cheek.

Weeping now, she slammed the doors closed and leaned against them, eyes shut, forehead pressed against the cold metal, sobbing, fighting to catch her breath.

From the crimson gloom behind her came the unmistakable sound of something clearing its throat.

**SUPERSTITION
EXHIBITION**

PART TWO

= 21 =

"What's going on here?" came the stern voice.

Margo whirled around and almost collapsed with relief. "Officer Beauregard, there's—" she began, stopping in mid-sentence.

F. Beauregard, who was righting the brass posts that the swinging door had knocked over, looked up at the sound of his name. "Hey, you're the girl who tried to get in earlier!" The policeman's eyes narrowed. "What's wrong, Miss, can't take no for an answer?"

"Officer, there's a—" Margo tried to start again, then faltered.

The officer stepped back and folded his arms across his chest, waiting. Then a look of surprise crossed his face. "What the hell? Hey, you okay, lady?"

Margo was slumped over, laughing—or crying, she wasn't sure which—and wiping tears from her face.

The policeman freed one folded hand and took her arm. "I think you should come with me."

The implications of that last sentence—sitting in a room full of policemen, telling her story again and again, maybe having Dr. Frock or even Dr. Wright called in, having to go back into that exhibition— forced Margo to straighten up. *They'll just think I'm crazy.* "Oh no, that's not necessary," she said, snuffling. "I just had a bit of a scare."

Officer Beauregard looked unconvinced. "I still think we should go talk to Lieutenant D'Agosta." With his other hand, he pulled a large, leather-bound notebook out of his back pocket. "What's your name?" he asked. "I'll have to make a report."

It was clear he wouldn't let her go until she gave him the information. "My name's Margo Green," she said finally. "I'm a graduate student working under Dr. Frock. I was doing an assignment for George Moriarty—he's curating this exhibition. But you were right. Nobody was in there." She gently freed her arm from the policeman's grip as she spoke. Then she started backing away, toward Selous Memorial Hall, still talking. Officer Beauregard watched her and finally, with a shrug, he flipped open the notebook and started writing.

Back in the Hall, Margo paused. She couldn't go back to her office; it was almost six, and the curfew was sure to be enforced by now. She didn't want to go home—she *couldn't* go home, not just yet.

Then she remembered Moriarty's copy. She pressed one elbow against her side—sure enough, her carryall was still there, hanging unnoticed through the ordeal. She stood still another moment, then walked over to the deserted information kiosk. She picked up the receiver of an internal phone and dialed.

One ring, then: "Moriarty here."

"George?" she said. "It's Margo Green."

"Hi, Margo," Moriarty answered. "What's up?"

"I'm in the Selous Hall," she replied. "I just came from the exhibition."

"My exhibition?" Moriarty said, surprised. "What were you doing there? Who let you in?"

"I was looking for you," she answered. "I wanted to give you the Cameroon copy. *Were you in there?*" She felt panic rising once again to the surface.

"No. The exhibition's supposed to be sealed, in preparation for Friday night's opening," Moriarty said. "Why?"

Margo was breathing deeply, trying to control herself. Her hands were trembling, and the receiver knocked against her ear.

"What did you think of it?" Moriarty asked curiously.

A hysterical giggle escaped Margo. "Scary."

"We brought in some experts to work out the lighting and the placement of the visuals. Dr. Cuthbert even hired the man who designed Fantasyworld's Haunted Mausoleum. That's considered the best in the world, you know."

Margo finally trusted herself to speak again. "George, something was in that exhibition with me." A security guard on the far side of the Hall had spotted her, and was walking in her direction.

"What do you mean, *something?*"

"Exactly that!" Suddenly, she was back in the exhibit, in the dark, beside that horrible figurine. She remembered the bitter taste of terror in her mouth.

"Hey, stop shouting!" Moriarty said. "Look, let's go to The Bones and talk this over. We're both supposed to be out of the Museum, anyway. I hear what you're saying, but I don't understand it."

The Bones, as it was called by everyone in the Museum, was known to other local residents as the Blarney Stone Tavern. Its unimposing facade was nestled between two huge, ornate co-op buildings, directly across Seventy-second Street from the Museum's southern entrance. Unlike typical Upper West Side fern bars, the Blarney Stone did not serve hare pâté or five flavors of mineral water; but you could get home-made meatloaf and a pitcher of Harp for ten dollars.

Museum staffers called it The Bones because Boylan, the owner, had hammered and wired an amazing number of bones into every available flat surface. The walls were lined with countless femurs and tibias, arranged in neat ivory ranks like bamboo matting. Metatarsals, scapulas, and patellas traced bizarre mosaics across the ceiling. Craniums from strange mammals were lodged in every conceivable niche. Where he got the bones was a mystery, but some claimed he raided the Museum at night.

"People bring 'em in," is all Boylan would ever say, shrugging his shoulders. Naturally, the place was a favorite hangout among the Museum staff.

The Bones was doing brisk business, and Moriarty and Margo had to push their way back through the crowd to an empty booth. Looking around, Margo spotted several Museum staffers, including Bill Smithback. The writer was seated at the bar, talking animatedly to a slender blonde woman.

"Okay," Moriarty said, raising his voice over the babble. "Now what were you saying over the phone? I'm not quite sure I caught it."

Margo took a deep breath. "I went down to the exhibition to give you the copy. It was dark. Something was in there. Following me. *Chasing* me."

"There's that word again, *something*. Why do you say that?"

Margo shook her head impatiently. "Don't ask me to explain. There were these sounds, like padded steps. They were so stealthy, so deliberate, I—" she shrugged, at a loss. "And there was this strange smell, too. It was horrible."

"Look, Margo—" Moriarty began, then paused while the waitress took their drink orders. "That exhibition was designed to be creepy. You told me yourself that Frock and others consider it too sensational. I can imagine what it must have been like: being locked in there, alone in the dark . . ."

"In other words, I just imagined it." Margo laughed mirthlessly. "You don't know how much I'd like to believe that."

The drinks arrived: a light beer for Margo, and a pint of Guinness for Moriarty, topped with the requisite half-inch of creamy foam. Moriarty sipped it critically. "These killings, all the rumors that have been going around," he said. "I probably would have reacted the same way."

Margo, calmer now, spoke hesitantly. "George, that Kothoga figurine in the exhibition . . . ?"

"Mbwun? What about it?"

"Its front legs have three claws."

Moriarty was enjoying the Guinness. "I know. It's a marvelous piece of sculpture, one of the highlights of the show. Of course, though I hate to admit it, I suppose its biggest attraction is the curse."

Margo took an exploratory sip from her beer. "George. I want you to tell me, in as much detail as you can, what you know about the Mbwun curse."

A shout came bellowing over the din of conversation. Looking up, Margo saw Smithback appear out of the smoky gloom, carrying an armful of notebooks, his hair backlit and sticking out from his head at a variety of angles. The woman he'd been talking to at the bar was nowhere to be seen.

"A meeting of the shut-outs," he said. "This curfew is a real pain. God save me from policemen and PR directors." Uninvited, he dropped his notebooks on the table and slid in next to Margo.

"I've heard that the police are going to start interviewing those working in the vicinity of the murders," he said. "Guess that means you, Margo."

"Mine's set for next week," Margo replied.

"I haven't heard anything about it," said Moriarty. He didn't look pleased at Smithback's appearance.

"Well, you don't have much to worry about, perched up in that garret of yours," Smithback told Moriarty. "The Museum Beast probably can't climb stairs, anyway."

"You're in a foul mood this evening," Margo said to Smithback. "Did Rickman perform another amputation on your manuscript?"

Smithback was still talking to Moriarty. "Actually, you're just the man I wanted to see. I've got a question for you." The waitress came by again, and Smithback waved his hand. "Macallan, straight up."

"Okay," Smithback went on. "What I wanted to know is, what's the story behind this Mbwun figurine?"

There was a stunned silence.

Smithback looked from Moriarty to Margo. "What'd I say?"

"We were just talking about Mbwun," Margo said uncertainly.

"Yeah?" Smithback said. "Small world. Anyway, that old Austrian in the Bug Room, Von Oster, told me he heard Rickman kicking up a fuss about Mbwun being put on display. Something about sensitive issues. So I did a little digging."

The scotch arrived and Smithback held the glass high in a silent toast, then tossed it off.

"I've obtained a little background so far," he continued. "It seems there was this tribe along the Upper Xingú river in the Amazon, the Kothoga. They'd apparently been a bad lot—supernatural-dabbling, human sacrifice, the whole bit. Since the old boys hadn't left many traces around, anthropologists assumed they died out centuries ago. All that remained was a bunch of myths, circulated by local tribes."

"I know something of this," Moriarty began. "Margo and I were just discussing it. Except not everybody felt—"

"I know, I know. Hold your water."

Moriarty settled back, looking annoyed. He was more used to giving lectures than listening to them.

"Anyway, several years ago, there was this guy named Whittlesey at the Museum. He mounted an expedition to the Upper Xingú, purportedly to search for traces of the Kothoga—artifacts, ancient dwelling sites, whatever." Smithback leaned forward conspiratorially. "But what Whittlesey didn't tell anybody was that he wasn't just going in search of this old tribe's traces. He was going in search of the tribe *itself*. He'd got it into his noggin that the Kothoga still existed, and he was pretty certain he could locate them. He'd developed something he called 'myth triangulation.'"

This time, Moriarty wouldn't be stopped. "That's where you locate all the spots on a map where legends about a certain people or place are heard, identify the areas where the legends are most detailed and consistent, and locate the exact center of this myth region. That's where the source of the myth cycles is most likely to be found."

Smithback looked at Moriarty for a moment. "No kidding," he said.

"Anyway, this Whittlesey goes off in 1987 and disappears into the Amazon rain forest, never to be seen again."

"Von Oster told you all this?" Moriarty rolled his eyes. "Tiresome old guy."

"He may be tiresome, but he knows a hell of a lot about this Museum." Smithback examined his empty glass forlornly. "Apparently, there was a big confrontation in the jungle, and most of the expedition team started back early. They'd found something so important they wanted to leave right away, and Whittlesey disagreed. He stayed, along with a fellow named Crocker. Apparently, they both died in the jungle. But when I asked Von Oster for more details about this Mbwun figurine, he suddenly clammed up." Smithback stretched languorously and began looking for the waitress. "Guess I'll have to hunt down somebody who was part of that expedition."

"Lots of luck," Margo said. "They were all killed in a plane crash coming back."

Smithback peered at her intently. "No shit. And how do you know that?"

Margo hesitated, remembering Pendergast's request for confidentiality. Then she thought of Frock, and how he'd gripped her hand so fiercely that morning. *We can't miss this opportunity. We must not let this chance slip us by.* "I'll tell you what I know," she said slowly. "But you must keep this to yourselves. And you must agree to help me in any way you can."

"Be careful, Margo," Moriarty cautioned.

"Help you? Sure, no problem," said Smithback. "With what, by the way?"

Hesitantly, Margo told them about the meeting with Pendergast in the Secure Room: the casts of the claw and wound, the crates, Cuthbert's story. Then she described the sculpture of Mbwun she'd seen in the exhibition—omitting her panic and flight. She knew Smithback wouldn't believe her any more than Moriarty had.

"So what I was asking George when you came up," she concluded, "is exactly what he knows about this curse of the Kothoga."

Moriarty shrugged. "Not all that much, really. In local legend, the Kothoga tribe was a shadowy group, a witch-doctor cult. They were supposed to be able to control demons. There was a creature—a familiar if you will—they used for vengeance killings. That was Mbwun, He Who Walks On All Fours. Then, Whittlesey came across this figurine, and some other objects, packed them up, and sent them back to the Museum. Of course, such disturbance of sacred objects has been done countless times before. But then when he gets lost in the jungle and never comes out, and the rest of the expedition dies on the return trip . . ." He shrugged his shoulders. "The curse."

"And now, people are dying in the Museum," Margo said.

"What are you saying—that the Mbwun curse, the stories of a Museum Beast, and these killings are all linked?" asked Moriarty. "Come on, Margo, don't read too much into it."

She looked at him intently. "Didn't you tell me that Cuthbert kept the figurine out of the exhibition until the last minute?"

"That's right," Moriarty said. "He handled all work on that relic himself. Not unusual, considering it's such a valuable piece. As for delaying its placement in the exhibition, that was Rickman's idea, I believe. Probably thought it would generate more interest."

"I doubt it," Smithback replied. "That's not the way her mind works. If anything, she was trying to *avoid* interest. Blow scandal at her, and she shrivels up like a moth in a flame." He chuckled.

"Just what's *your* interest in all this, anyway?" Moriarty demanded.

"You don't think a dusty old artifact would interest me?" Smithback finally caught the eye of the waitress and ordered another round for the table.

"Well, it's obvious Rickman wouldn't let you write about it," Margo said.

Smithback made a face. "Too true. It might offend all the ethnic Kothoga tribesmen in New York. Actually, it's because Von Oster said that Rickman was bent out of shape about this. So I thought maybe I could dig around, get some dirt. Something that will put me in a better bargaining position when our next *tête-à-tête* comes along. You know, 'This chapter stays, or I'm taking the Whittlesey story to *Smithsonian* magazine,' that sort of thing."

"Now, wait a minute," Margo said. "I didn't take you into my confidence just so you could make some money off it. Don't you understand? We have to learn more about these crates. Whatever is killing people wants something that's in them. We *have* to find out what it is."

"What we really need to do is find that journal," Smithback said.

"But Cuthbert says it's been lost," Margo said.

"Have you checked the accession database?" Smithback said. "Maybe there's some information there. I'd do it myself, but my security rating is rock-bottom."

"So is mine," Margo replied. "And it hasn't been my day for computers." She told them about her talk with Kawakita.

"How about Moriarty, here?" Smithback said. "You're a computer
whiz, right? Besides, as an Assistant Curator, you have high security
access."

"I think you should let the authorities handle this." Moriarty drew
back, dignified. "This isn't for us to mess around with."

"Don't you understand?" Margo pleaded. "*Nobody* knows what we're
dealing with here. People's lives—perhaps the Museum's future—are
at stake."

"I know your motives are good, Margo," Moriarty said. "But I don't
trust Bill's."

"My motives are pure as the Pierian spring," Smithback retorted.
"Rickman is storming the citadel of journalistic truth. I'm just looking
to defend the ramparts."

"Wouldn't it be easier to just do what Rickman wants?" Moriarty
asked. "I think your vendetta is a little childish. And you know what?
You won't win."

The drinks came, and Smithback tossed his off and exhaled with
gusto.

"Someday I'll get that bitch," he said.

= 22 =

Beauregard finished the entry, then stuffed his notebook in a back pocket. He knew he really ought to call the incident in. *Hell with it.* That girl had looked so scared, it was obvious she wasn't up to anything. He'd make his report when he got the chance, and no sooner.

Beauregard was in a bad mood. He didn't like doorshaker duty. Still, it beat directing traffic at a broken light. And it made a good impression down at O'Ryans. *Yeah,* he would say, *I'm assigned to the Museum case. Sorry, can't talk about it.*

For a museum, this place is damn quiet, Beauregard thought. He supposed on a normal day the Museum would be bustling with activity. But the Museum hadn't been normal since Sunday. At least during the day, staff members had come in and out of the new exhibition halls. But then, they'd closed it off for the opening. Except with written permission from Dr. Cuthbert, you couldn't get in unless you were police or security on official business. Thank God his shift ended at six and he could look forward to two days away from this place. A solo fishing trip to the Catskills. He'd been looking forward to it for weeks.

Beauregard ran his hand reassuringly along the holster of his S&W .38 special. Ready for action, as always. And on his other hip, a shotshell pistol loaded with enough capstun to bring an elephant to its knees.

Behind him, Beauregard heard a muffled pattering sound.

He spun around, heart suddenly racing, to face the closed doors of the exhibition. He located a key, unlocked the doors, and peered in.

"Who's there?"

Only a cool breeze fanned his cheek.

He let the doors close and tested the lock. You could come out, but you couldn't go in. That girl must have gone in through the front entrance. But wasn't that kept locked, too? They never told him anything.

The sound came again.

Well, hell, he thought, *it ain't my job to check inside. Can't let anyone into the exhibition. Never said anything about anyone coming out.*

Beauregard started humming a tune, tapping the beat on his thigh with two fingers. Ten more minutes and he'd be out of this frigging spookhouse.

The sound came again.

Beauregard unlocked the doors a second time, and stuck his head deep inside. He could see some dim shapes: exhibition cases, a gloomy-looking entranceway. "This is a police officer. You in there, please respond."

The cases were dark, the walls vague shadows. No answer.

Withdrawing, Beauregard pulled out his radio. "Beauregard to Ops, do you copy?"

"This is TDN. What's up?"

"Reporting noises at the exhibition's rear exit."

"What kind of noises?"

"Uncertain. Sounds like someone's in there."

There was some talk and a stifled laugh.

"Uh . . . Fred?"

"What?" Beauregard was growing more irritated by the minute. The dispatcher in the situation room was a first-class asshole.

"Better not go in there."

"Why not?"

"It might be the monster, Fred. Might get you."

"Go to hell," Fred muttered under his breath. He wasn't supposed to investigate anything without backup, and the dispatcher knew it.

A scratching noise came from behind the doors, as if something with nails was scrabbling against it. Beauregard felt his breath come hard and fast.

His radio squawked. "Seen the monster yet?" came the voice.

Trying to keep his voice as neutral as possible, Beauregard said: "Repeat, reporting unidentified sounds in the exhibition. Request backup to investigate."

"He wants backup." There was the sound of muffled laughter. "Fred, we don't have any backup. Everyone's busy."

"Listen," said Beauregard, losing his temper. "Who's that with you? Why don't you send him down?"

"McNitt. He's on a coffee break. Right, McNitt?"

Beauregard heard some more laughter.

Beauregard switched off the radio. *Fuck those guys*, he thought. *Some professionalism.* He just hoped the Lieutenant was listening in on that frequency.

He waited in the dark hallway. *Five more minutes and I'm history.*

"TDN calling Beauregard. You read?"

"Ten-four," said Beauregard.

"McNitt there yet?"

"No," said Beauregard. "He finally finish his coffee break?"

"Hey, I was just kidding around," TDN said a little nervously. "I sent him right up."

"Well, he's lost, then," said Beauregard. "And my duty ends in five minutes. I'm off the next forty-eight, and nothing's going to interfere with that. You better radio him."

"He isn't reading," said TDN.

An idea suddenly occurred to Beauregard. "How did McNitt go? Did he take the Section 17 elevator, the one behind the sit room?"

"Yep, that's what I told him. Section 17 elevator. I got this map, same one you have."

"So in order to get here he has to go through the exhibition. That was real smart. You should have sent him up through food services."

"Hey, don't talk to me about smart, Freddy boy. He's the one who's lost. Call me when he arrives."

"One way or another, I'm outta here in five minutes," said Beauregard. "It'll be Effinger's headache then. Over and out."

That was when Beauregard heard a sudden commotion from the exhibition. There was a sound like a muffled thud. *Jesus*, he thought, *McNitt.* He unlocked the doors and went in, unsnapping the holster of his .38.

TDN placed another doughnut in his mouth and chewed, swallowing it with a mouthful of coffee. The radio hissed.

"McNitt to Ops. Come in, TDN."

"Ten-four. Where the hell are you?"

"I'm at the rear entrance. Beauregard ain't here. I can't raise him or anything."

"Lemme try." He punched the transmitter. "TDN calling Beauregard. Fred, come in. TDN calling Beauregard . . . Hey, McNitt, I think he got pissed off and went home. His shift just ended. How did you get up there, anyway?"

"I went the way you said, but when I got to the front end of the exhibition it was locked, so I had to go around. Didn't have my keys. Got a little lost."

"Stay tight, all right? His relief should arrive any minute. Effinger, it says here. Radio me when he arrives and then come on back."

"Here comes Effinger now. You gonna report Beauregard?" McNitt asked.

"You kidding? I'm no damn baby-sitter."

= 23 =

D'Agosta looked over at Pendergast, reclining in the shabby backseat of the Buick. *Jesus*, he thought, *a guy like Pendergast ought to pull at least a late model Town Car.* Instead, they gave him a four-year-old Buick and a driver who could barely speak English.

Pendergast's eyes were half closed.

"Turn on Eighty-sixth and take the Central Park transverse," shouted D'Agosta.

The driver swerved across two lanes of Central Park West and roared into the transverse.

"Take Fifth to Sixty-fifth and go across," said D'Agosta. "Then go one block north on Third and take a right at Sixty-sixth."

"Fifty-nine faster," said the driver, in a thick Middle Eastern accent.

"Not in the evening rush hour," called D'Agosta. Christ, they couldn't even find a driver who knew his way around the city.

As the car swerved and rattled down the avenue, the driver flew on past Sixty-fifth Street.

"What the hell are you doing?" said D'Agosta. "You just missed Sixty-fifth."

"Apology," said the driver, turning down Sixty-first into a massive traffic jam.

"I can't believe this," D'Agosta said Pendergast. "You ought to have this joker fired."

Pendergast smiled, his eyes still half closed. "He was, shall we say, a gift of the New York office. But the delay will give us a chance to talk." He settled back into the torn seat.

Pendergast had spent the last half of the afternoon at Jolley's autopsy. D'Agosta had declined the invitation.

"This lab found several kinds of DNA in our sample," Pendergast continued. "One was human, the other, from a gecko."

D'Agosta looked at him. "Gecko? What's a gecko?" he asked.

"A kind of lizard. Harmless enough. They like to sit on walls and bask in the sun. When I was a child, we rented a villa overlooking the Mediterranean one summer, and the walls were covered with them. At any rate, the results were so surprising to the lab technician that he thought it was a joke."

He opened his briefcase. "Here's the autopsy report on Jolley. There's nothing much new, I'm afraid. Same MO, body horrifically mauled, thalamoid region of the brain removed. The coroner's office has estimated that to create such deep lacerations in a single stroke, the required force would exceed—" he consulted a typewritten sheet "—twice what a strong human male can achieve. Needless to say, it's an estimation."

Pendergast turned some pages. "Also, they've now run salivase enzyme tests on brain sections from the older boy and from Jolley."

"And—?"

"Both brains tested positive for the presence of saliva."

"Jesus. You mean the killer's *eating* the fucking brain?"

"Not only eating, Lieutenant, but slobbering over the food as well. Clearly, he, she, or it has no manners. You have the SOC report? May I see it?"

D'Agosta handed it over. "You won't find any surprises there. The blood on the painting was Jolley's. They found traces of blood leading past the Secure Area and down into a stairwell to the subbasement. But last night's rain flushed all traces out of there, of course."

Pendergast scanned the document. "And here's the report on the door to the vault. Someone did quite a lot of pounding and banging, possibly with a blunt instrument. There were also three-pronged scratches consistent with those found on the victims. Once again, the force used was considerable."

Pendergast handed over the files. "It sounds as if we'll need to devote more attention to the subbasement. Basically, Vincent, this DNA business is our best chance for now. If we can trace the origin of that claw fragment, we'll have our first solid lead. That's why I've asked for this meeting."

The car pulled up in front of a warren of ivy-covered redbrick buildings overlooking the East River. A guard ushered them into a side entrance.

Once inside the lab, Pendergast took up a position against a table in the center of the room and chatted with the scientists, Buchholtz and Turow. D'Agosta admired how easily the Southerner could take charge of a scene.

"My colleague and I would like to understand the DNA sequencing process," Pendergast was saying. "We need to know how you arrived at these results, and whether any further analysis might be called for. I'm sure you understand."

"Certainly," said Buchholtz. He was busy and small and as bald as Mount Monadnock. "My assistant, Dr. Turow here, did the analysis."

Turow stepped forward nervously. "When we were given the sample," he said, "we were asked to identify whether it had come from a large carnivorous mammal. Specifically, a big cat. What we do in such a case is compare the DNA in the sample to the DNA of, say, five or six species that are likely matches. But we would also select an animal that was definitely *not* of the sample, and we call this the outgroup. It's a kind of control. Am I making sense?"

"So far," said Pendergast. "But go easy on me. I'm a child in these matters."

"We usually use human DNA as the outgroup, since we've mapped so much of it. Anyway, we do a PCR—that is, a Polymerase Chain Reaction—on the sample. This causes thousands and thousands of copies of the genes to be made. It gives us a lot to work with, you see."

He pointed to a large machine with long clear strips of Plexiglas attached to its flanks. Behind the strips were dark vertical bands arrayed in complicated patterns. "This is a pulsed-field gel electrophoresis machine. We place the sample in here, and portions of the sample migrate out along these strips through the gel, according to their molecular weights. They show up as these dark bands. By the pattern of bands, and with the aid of our computer, we can figure out what genes are present."

He took a deep breath. "Anyway, we got a negative reading on the big cat genes. A *very* negative reading. It wasn't anywhere close. And to our surprise, we got a *positive* reading on the outgroup, that is, *Homo sapiens*. And, as you know, we identified DNA strands from several species of gecko—or so it appears." He looked a little sheepish. "But even so, most of the genes in the sample were unidentified."

"So that's why you presumed it was contaminated."

"Yes. Contaminated or degraded. A lot of repeated base pairs in the sample suggested a high level of genetic damage."

"Genetic damage?" asked Pendergast.

"When DNA is damaged or defective, it often uncontrollably replicates long repeating sequences of the same base pair. Viruses can damage DNA. So can radiation, certain chemicals, even cancer."

Pendergast had begun to roam around the laboratory, examining his surroundings with an almost catlike curiosity. "These gecko genes interest me a great deal. Just what do they mean exactly?"

"That's the big mystery," said Turow. "These are rare genes. Some genes are very common, like the Cytochrome B gene, which can be found in everything from a periwinkle to man. But these gecko genes—well, we don't know anything about them."

"What you're really saying is the DNA *didn't* come from an animal, right?" D'Agosta asked.

"Not from any large carnivorous mammal we know of," Buchholtz answered. "We tested all the relevant taxa. There are not nearly enough matches to say it came from a gecko. So, by a process of elimination, I would say it probably came from a human. But it was degraded or contaminated. The results are ambiguous."

"The sample," said D'Agosta, "was found in the body of a murdered boy."

"Ah!" said Turow. "That could easily explain how it was contaminated with human genetic material. Really, it would be much easier for us if we knew things like this before hand."

Pendergast frowned. "The sample was removed from the root canal of a claw by the forensic pathologist, as I understand it, and every effort was made to prevent contamination."

"All it can take is one cell," said Turow. "A claw, you say?" He thought a moment. "Let me advance an idea. The claw might be from a lizard that was heavily contaminated by blood from its human victim. Any lizard—not necessarily a gecko." He looked at Buchholtz. "The only reason we identified some of the DNA as gecko is because a fellow in Baton Rouge did some research a few years ago on gecko genetics, and logged his results in GenLab. Otherwise it would have turned up unknown, like most of that sample."

Pendergast looked at Turow. "I'd like further tests done to tell us just what those gecko genes do, if you don't mind."

Turow frowned. "Mr. Pendergast, the chance of a successful analysis is not all that high, and it could take weeks. It seems to me the mystery's already been solved—"

Buchholtz clapped his hand on Turow's back. "Let's not second-guess Agent Pendergast. After all, the police are paying for it, and it is a *very* expensive procedure."

Pendergast smiled more broadly. "I'm glad you mentioned that, Dr. Buchholtz. Just send the bill to Director of Special Operations, FBI." He wrote down the address on his business card. "And please don't worry. Cost is no consideration whatsoever."

D'Agosta had to grin. He knew what Pendergast was doing: getting even for the lousy car. He shook his head. *What a devil.*

= 24 =

Thursday

At eleven-fifteen Thursday morning, a man claiming to be the living incarnation of the Egyptian pharaoh Toth ran amok in the Antiquities wing, knocking over two displays in the Temple of Azar-Nar, breaking a case and pulling a mummy out of its tomb. Three policemen were necessary to restrain him, and several curators worked the rest of the day replacing bandages and collecting ancient dust.

Less than an hour later, a woman ran screaming from the Hall of Great Apes, babbling about something she'd seen crouched in a dark bathroom corner. A television team, waiting on the south steps for a glimpse of Wright, got her entire hysterical exit on film.

Around lunchtime, a group calling itself the Alliance Against Racism had begun picketing outside the Museum, calling for a boycott of the *Superstition* exhibition.

Early that afternoon, Anthony McFarlane, a world-renowned philanthropist and big-game hunter, offered a reward of $500,000 for the capture and safe delivery of the Museum Beast. The Museum immediately disclaimed any connection with McFarlane.

All of these events were duly reported in the press. The following incidents, however, went undisclosed to the world outside the Museum:

By noon, four employees had quit without notice. Thirty-five others had taken unscheduled vacations, nearly three hundred had called in sick.

Shortly after lunch, a junior preparator in the vertebrate paleontology department collapsed at her laboratory table. She was taken to Medical, where she demanded extended leave and worker's compensation, citing severe emotional and physical stress.

By three P.M., security had responded to seven requests for investigations of suspicious noises in various remote sections of the museum. By curfew, police from the Museum command post had responded to four suspected sightings, all of which remained unverified.

Later, the Museum switchboard would tabulate the number of creature-related calls it received that day: 107, including crank messages, bomb threats, and offers of assistance from exterminators to spiritualists.

= 25 =

Smithback eased open the grimy door and peered inside. This, he thought, had to be one of the more macabre places in the Museum: the storage area of the Physical Anthropology Laboratory, or, in Museum parlance, the Skeleton Room. The Museum had one of the largest collections of skeletons in the country, second only to the Smithsonian—twelve thousand in this room alone. Most were North and South American Indian or African, collected in the nineteenth century, during the heyday of physical anthropology. Tiers of large metal drawers rose in ordered ranks to the ceiling; each drawer contained at least a portion of a human skeleton. Yellowed labels were slotted into the front of each drawer; on these labels were numbers, names of tribes, sometimes a short history. Other, briefer labels carried the chill of anonymity.

Smithback had once spent an afternoon wandering among the boxes, opening them and reading the notes, almost all of which were written in faded, elegant scripts. He had jotted several down in his notebook:

Spec. No. 1880-1770
Walks in Cloud. Yankton Sioux. Killed in Battle of Medi-
    cine Bow Creek, 1880.

Spec. No. 1899-1206
Maggie Lost Horse. Northern Cheyenne.

Spec. No. 1933-43469
Anasazi. Canyon del Muerto. Thorpe-Carlson expedition,
1900.

Spec. No. 1912-695
Luo. Lake Victoria. Gift of Maj. Gen. Henry Throckmor-
ton, Bart.

Spec. No. 1872-10
Aleut, provenance unknown.

It was a strange graveyard indeed.

Beyond the storage area lay the warren of rooms housing the Physical
Anthropology Lab. In earlier days, physical anthropologists had spent
most of their time in this laboratory measuring bones and trying to
determine the relationship between the races, where humanity had
originated, and similar studies. Now, much more complex biochemical
and epidemiological research was being done in the Physical Anthro
Lab.

Several years earlier, the Museum—at Frock's insistence—had decided to merge its genetics research and DNA laboratories with the
lab. Beyond the dusty bone-storage area lay a spotless assortment of
huge centrifuges, hissing autoclaves, electrophoresis apparatus, glowing
monitors, elaborate blown-glass distillation columns, and titration
setups—one of the most advanced technical facilities of its kind. It
was in the no-man's-land between the old and the new that Greg
Kawakita had set up shop.

Smithback looked through the tall racks of the storage room toward
the lab doors. It was just after ten, and Kawakita was the only one
around. Through the open shelves, Smithback could see Kawakita
standing one or two rows over, making sharp, jerky overhead movements with his left hand, waving something about. Then, Smithback
heard the zing of a line and the whirring of a fly reel. *Well, raise my
rent*, Smithback thought. The man was fishing.

"Catch anything?" he called out loudly.

He heard a sharp exclamation and a clatter of a dropped rod.

"Damn you, Smithback," Kawakita said. "You're always sneaking
about. This isn't a good time to go around scaring people, you know.
I might have been packing a .45, or something."

He walked down his aisle and came around the corner, reeling in his fly rod and scowling good-humoredly at Smithback.

Smithback laughed. "I told you not to work down here with all these skeletons. Now look what's happened: you've gone off the deep end at last."

"Just practicing," Kawakita laughed. "Watch. Third shelf. Buffalo Hump."

He flicked the rod. The line whirred out, and the fly struck, then rebounded off a drawer on the third tier of a shelf at the end of the aisle. Smithback walked over. Sure enough: it contained the bones of someone who had once been Buffalo Hump.

Smithback whistled.

Kawakita drew in some line, loosely holding the loops in his left hand while he gripped the cork butt of the rod in his right. "Fifth shelf, second row. John Mboya," he said.

Again the line arced through the air between the narrow shelves and the tiny fly ticked the correct label.

"Izaak Walton, move over," said Smithback, shaking his head.

Kawakita reeled in the line and started dismantling the bamboo rod. "It's not quite like fishing on a river," he said as he worked, "but it's great practice, especially in this confined space. Helps me relax during breaks. When I don't tangle my line in one of the cases, that is."

When Kawakita was first hired by the Museum, he had declined the sunny fifth-floor office offered him, and instead claimed a much smaller one in the lab, saying he wanted to be closer to the action. Since then, he had already published more papers than some full curators had in their entire careers. His cross-disciplinary studies under Frock had quickly led him to an Assistant Curatorship in evolutionary biology, where he had initially devoted his time to the study of plant evolution. Kawakita skillfully used his mentor's notoriety to advance himself. Lately, he had put aside plant evolution temporarily for the Genetic Sequence Extrapolator program. His only other passion in life, aside from his work, seemed to be fly-fishing; in particular, as he would ex-plain to anyone who listened, his search for the noble and elusive Atlantic salmon.

Kawakita slid the rod into a battered Orvis case and leaned it care-fully in a corner. Motioning Smithback to follow, he led the way down long rows of coffined aisles to a large desk and three heavy wooden chairs. The desk, Smithback noticed, was covered with papers, stacks of well-thumbed monographs, and low trays of plastic-covered sand holding various human bones.

"Look at this," Kawakita said, sliding something in Smithback's direction. It was an engraved illustration of a family tree, etched in brown ink on hand-marbled paper. The branches of the tree were labeled with various Latin words.

"Nice," said Smithback, taking a seat.

"That's one word for it, I guess," Kawakita replied. "A mid-nineteenth century view of human evolution. An artistic masterpiece, but a scientific travesty. I'm working on a little piece for the *Human Evolution Quarterly* about early evolutionary views."

"When will it be published?" Smithback asked with professional interest.

"Oh, early next year. These journals are so slow."

Smithback put the chart down on the desk. "So what does all this have to do with your current work—the GRE, or the SAT, or whatever it is?"

"G.S.E., actually." Kawakita laughed. "Nothing whatsoever. This is just a little idea I had, some after-hours fun. I still enjoy getting my hands dirty from time to time." He replaced the chart carefully in a binder, then turned toward the writer. "So, how's the masterwork coming along?" he asked. "Is Madame Rickman still giving you a hard time?"

Smithback laughed. "Guess my struggles under the tyrant are common knowledge by now. But that's a book in itself. Actually, I came by to talk to you about Margo."

Kawakita took a seat across from Smithback. "Margo Green? What about her?

Smithback started paging aimlessly through one of the monographs scattered about the worktable. "I understand she needs your help on something."

Kawakita's eyes narrowed. "She called last night, asking if she could run some data through the Extrapolation program. I told her it wasn't ready yet." He shrugged. "Technically, that's true. I can't vouch one hundred percent for the accuracy of its correlations. But I'm terribly busy these days, Bill. I just don't have the time to shepherd somebody through the program."

"She's not exactly some scientific illiterate you need to lead around by the nose," Smithback replied. "She's doing some heavy-duty genetics research of her own. You must see her around this lab all the time." He pushed the monographs aside and leaned forward. "It might not hurt to cut the kid a break," he said. "It isn't exactly an easy time for her. Her father died about two weeks ago, you know."

Kawakita looked surprised. "Really? Is that what you were talking about in the staff lounge?"

Smithback nodded. "She hasn't said much, but it's been a struggle. She's considering leaving the Museum."

"That would be a mistake," Kawakita frowned. He started to say something, then stopped abruptly. He leaned back in his chair and gave Smithback a long, appraising look. "This is a mighty altruistic gesture on your part, Bill." He pursed his lips, nodding slowly. "Bill Smithback, the good samaritan. New image for you, eh?"

"That's William Smithback Jr. to you."

"Bill Smithback, the Eagle Scout," Kawakita continued. Then he shook his head. "Nope, it just doesn't ring true. You didn't really come down here to talk about Margo, did you?"

Smithback hesitated. "Well, that was one of my reasons," he admitted.

"I knew it!" Kawakita crowed. "Come on, out with it."

"Oh, all right," Smithback sighed. "Listen: I'm trying to get some information on the Whittlesey expedition."

"The *what?*"

"The South American expedition that brought back the Mbwun figurine. You know, the showpiece for the new exhibition."

Recognition flooded Kawakita's face. "Oh, yes. That's the one old man Smith must have been talking about in the herbarium the other day. What about it?"

"Well, we think there's some kind of link between that expedition and these murders."

"What?" Kawakita said incredulously. "Don't tell me *you're* starting up with this Museum Beast stuff. And what do you mean, 'we'?"

"I'm not saying I believe anything, okay?" Smithback replied evasively. "But I've been hearing a lot of strange stuff recently. And Rickman's all tense about having the Mbwun figurine in the exhibition. Other things came back from that expedition besides this one relic—several crates, in fact. I want to find out more about them."

"And what, exactly, do I have to do with all of this?" Kawakita asked.

"Nothing. But you're an Assistant Curator. You have high-security access to the Museum computer. You can query the accession database, find out about those crates."

"I doubt they've even been logged," Kawakita said. "But either way, it wouldn't matter."

"Why not?" Smithback asked.

Kawakita laughed. "Wait here a minute." He stood up and headed for the lab. In a few minutes he returned, a piece of paper in one hand.

"You must be psychic," he said, handing over the paper. "Look what I found in my mail this morning."

NEW YORK MUSEUM OF NATURAL HISTORY
INTERNAL MEMORANDUM

To: Curators and Senior Staff
From: Lavinia Rickman
CC: Wright, Lewallen, Cuthbert, Lafore

As a result of recent unfortunate events, the Museum is under intense scrutiny by the media and by the public in general. This being the case, I wanted to take the opportunity to review the Museum's policy on external communications.

Any dealings with the press are to be handled through the Museum's public relations office. No comments on Museum matters are to be made, either on or off the record, to journalists or other members of the media. Any statements made or assistance given to individuals who are engaged in preparing interviews, documentaries, books, articles, etc. dealing with the Museum are to be cleared through this office. Failure to follow these guidelines will result in disciplinary action from the Director's Office.

Thank you for your cooperation in this difficult time.

"Christ," muttered Smithback. "Look at this. 'Individuals engaged in preparing books.' "

"She means you, Bill," Kawakita laughed. "So you see? My hands are tied." He extracted a handkerchief from his back pocket and blew his nose. "Allergic to bone dust," he explained.

"I just can't believe this," Smithback said, rereading the memo.

Kawakita clapped an arm around Smithback's shoulder. "Bill, my friend, I know this story would make great copy. And I'd like to help you write the most controversial, outrageous, and salacious book possible. Only I can't. I'll be honest. I've got a career here, and—" he tightened his grip "—I'm coming up for tenure. I can't afford to make those kinds of waves right now. You'll have to go some other route. Okay?"

Smithback nodded with resignation. "Okay."

"You look unconvinced," Kawakita laughed. "But I'm glad you understand, anyway." He gently propelled the writer to his feet. "I'll tell you what. How about a little fishing on Sunday? They're predicting an early hatch on the Connetquot."

Smithback finally grinned. "Tie me some of your devilish little nymphs," he said. "You're on."

= 26 =

D'Agosta was all the way on the other side of the Museum when yet another call came in. Emergency sighting, Section 18, Computer Room.

He sighed, shoving his radio back into its holster, thinking of his tired feet. Everyone in the damn place was seeing bogeymen.

A dozen people were crowding the hall outside the Computer Room, joking nervously. Two uniformed officers were standing by the closed door. "Okay," said D'Agosta, unwrapping a cigar. "Who saw it?"

A young man edged forward. White lab coat, slope-shouldered, Coke bottle glasses, calculator and pager dangling off the belt. *Cripes,* thought D'Agosta, *where did they get these guys?* He was perfect.

"I didn't actually *see* anything," he said, "but there was this loud thumping noise in the Electrical Systems Room. It sounded like banging, someone trying to get through the door—"

D'Agosta turned to the two cops. "Let's check it out."

He fumbled at the door knob and someone produced a key, explaining, "We locked it. We didn't want anything coming out—"

D'Agosta waved his hand. This was getting ridiculous. Everyone was spooked. How the hell could they be planning a big opening party for the following night? They should have shut the damn place down after the first murders.

The room was large, circular, and spotless. In the center, standing on a large pedestal and bathed in bright neon lights, was a five-foot-tall white cylinder that D'Agosta supposed was the Museum's mainframe. It hummed softly, surrounded by terminals, workstations, tables, and bookcases. Two closed doors were visible on the far walls.

"You guys poke around," he told his men, popping the unlit cigar in his mouth. "I wanna talk to this guy, do the paperwork."

He went back outside. "Name?" he asked.

"Roger Thrumcap. I'm the Shift Supervisor."

"Okay," D'Agosta said wearily, making notations. "You're reporting noises in Data Processing."

"No, sir, Data Processing's upstairs. This is the Computer Room. We monitor the hardware, do systems work."

"The Computer Room, then." He scribbled some more. "You first noticed these noises when?"

"A few minutes after ten. We were just finishing up our journals."

"You were reading the paper when you heard the noises?"

"No, sir. The journal tapes. We were just finishing our daily backup."

"I see. You were just *finishing* at ten o'clock?"

"The backups can't be done during peak hours, sir. We have special permission to come in at six in the morning."

"Lucky you. And you heard these noises where?"

"They were coming from the Electrical Room."

"And that is—?"

"The door to the left of the MP-3. That's the computer, sir."

"I saw two doors in there." D'Agosta said. "What's behind the other one?"

"Oh, that's just the lights-out room. It's on a carded-entry system, nobody can get in there."

D'Agosta gave the man a strange look.

"It contains the diskpacks, things like that. You know, the storage devices. It's called a lights-out room because everything's automated, nobody goes in there except for maintenance." He nodded proudly. "We're in a zero-operator environment. Compared to us, DP's still in the Stone Age. They still have operators manually mounting tapes, no silos or anything."

D'Agosta went back inside. "They heard the noises on the other side of that door to the left, there in the back. Let's take a look." He turned around. "Keep them out here," he said to Thrumcap.

The door to the electrical room swung open, releasing a smell of hot wiring and ozone. D'Agosta fumbled along the wall, found the light and snapped it on.

He did a visual first, by the book. Transformers. Grillwork covering ventilation ducts. Cables. Several large air-conditioning units. A lot of hot air. But nothing else.

"Take a look behind that equipment," D'Agosta said.

The officers nosed around thoroughly. One looked back and shrugged.

"All right," said D'Agosta, walking out into the computer room. "Looks clean to me. Mr. Thrumcap?"

"Yes?" He poked his head in.

"You can tell your people to come back in. Looks okay, but we're gonna post a man for the next thirty-six hours." He turned to one of the policemen emerging from the electrical room. "Waters, I want you here till the end of your shift. Pro forma, all right? I'll send your relief." *A few more sightings and I'll be fresh out of officers.*

"Right," said Waters.

"That's a good idea," said Thrumcap. "This room is the heart of the Museum, you know. Or rather, the brain. We run the telephones, physical plant, network, miniprinting, electronic mail, security system—"

"Sure," said D'Agosta. He wondered if this was the same security that didn't have an accurate blueprint of the subbasement.

The staff began filing back into the room and taking up their places at the terminals. D'Agosta mopped his brow. *Hot as balls in here.* He turned to leave.

"Rog," he heard a voice behind him. "We got a problem."

D'Agosta hesitated a moment.

"Oh, my God," said Thrumcap, staring at a monitor. "The system's doing a hex dump. What the hell—?"

"Was the master terminal still in backup mode when you left it, Rog?" a short guy with buck teeth was asking. "If it finished and got no response, it might have gone into a low-level dump."

"Maybe you're right," said Roger. "Abort the dump and make sure the regions are all up."

"It's not responding."

"Is the OS down?" Thrumcap asked, bending over bucktooth's CRT. "Lemme see this."

An alarm went off in the room, not loud, but high-pitched and insistent. D'Agosta saw a red light in a ceiling panel above the sleek mainframe. Maybe he'd better stick around.

"Now what?" said Thrumcap.

Jesus, it's hot, D'Agosta thought. *How can these people stand it?*

"What's this code we're getting?"

"I don't know. Look it up."

"Where?"

"In the manual, fool! It's right behind your terminal. Here, I've got it."

Thrumcap started flipping pages. "2291, 2291 . . . here it is. It's a heat alarm. Oh, Lord, the machine's overheating! Get maintenance up here right away."

D'Agosta shrugged. The thumping noise they'd heard was probably air-conditioner compressors failing. *It doesn't take a rocket scientist to figure that out. It must be ninety degrees in here.* As he began moving down the hall, he passed two maintenance men hurrying in the opposite direction.

Like most modern supercomputers, the Museum's MP-3 was better able to withstand heat than the "big iron" mainframes of ten or twenty years before. Its silicon brain, unlike the older vacuum tubes and transistors, could function above recommended temperatures for longer periods of time without damage or loss of data. However, the hardwired interface to the Museum's security system had been installed by a third party, outside the operating specifications of the computer manufacturer. When the temperature in the computer room reached ninety-four degrees, the tolerances of the. ROM chips governing the Automatic Disaster Control System were exceeded. Failure occurred ninety seconds later.

Waters stood in a corner and glanced around the room. The maintenance men had left over an hour before, and the room was pleasantly chilly. Everything was back to normal, and the only sounds were the hum of the computer and the zombies clicking thousands of keys. He idly glanced at an unoccupied terminal screen and saw a blinking message.

EXTERNAL ARRAY FAILURE AT ROM
ADDRESS 33 B1 4A 0E

It was like Chinese. Whatever it was, why couldn't they just say it in English? He hated computers. He couldn't think of one damn thing computers had done for him except leave the *s* off his last name on bills. He hated those smart-ass computer nerds, too. If there was anything wrong here, let *them* take care of it.

= 27 =

Smithback dumped his notebooks beside one of his favorite library carrels. Sighing heavily, he squeezed himself into the cramped space, placed his laptop on the desk, and turned on the small overhead light. He was only a stone's throw from the oak-panelled reading room, with its red leather chairs and marble fireplace that hadn't seen use in a century. But Smithback preferred the narrow, scuffed carrels. He especially liked the ones that were hidden deep in the stacks, where he could examine documents and manuscripts he'd temporarily liberated —or catch forty winks—in privacy and relative comfort.

The Museum's collection of new, old, and rare books on all aspects of natural history was unrivalled. It had received so many bequests and privately donated collections over the years that its card catalogue was always hopelessly behind. Yet Smithback knew the library better even than most of the librarians. He could find a buried factoid in record time.

Now he pursed his lips, thinking. Moriarty was a stubborn bureaucrat, and Smithback himself had come up empty with Kawakita. He didn't know anyone else who could get him into the accession database. But there was more than one way to approach this puzzle.

At the microfilm card file, he started flipping through the *New York Times* index. He backtracked as far as 1975. Nothing there—or, as he soon discovered, in the relevant natural history and anthropological journals.

He checked the back issues of the Museum's internal periodicals for information on the expedition. Nothing. In the 1985 *Who's Who At*

NYMNH, a two-line bio of Whittlesey told him nothing he didn't already know.

He cursed under his breath. *This guy's hidden deeper than the Oak Island treasure.*

Smithback slowly put the volumes back on their racks, looking around. Then, taking some sheets from a notebook, he strolled nonchalantly up to the desk of a reference librarian, first making sure he hadn't seen her before.

"Gotta put these back in the archives," he told the librarian.

She blinked up at him severely. "Are you new around here?"

"I'm from the science library, just got transferred up last week. On rotation, you know." He gave her a smile, hoped it looked bright and genuine.

She frowned at him, uncertain, as the phone on her desk began to ring. She hesitated, then answered it, distractedly handing him a clipboard and a key on a long, blue cord. "Sign in," she said, covering the mouthpiece with her hand.

The library archives lay behind an unmarked gray door in a remote corner of the library stacks. It was a gamble in more ways than one. Smithback had been inside once before, on legitimate business. He knew that the bulk of the Museum's archives were stored elsewhere, and that the library's files were very specific. But something was nagging him. He closed the door and moved forward, scanning the shelves and the stacks of labeled boxes.

He had progressed down one side of the room and was starting up the other when he stopped. Carefully, he reached up and brought down a box labeled CENTRAL RECVG/SHPG: AIR CARGO RECEIPTS. Squatting down, he rustled quickly through the papers.

Once again, he went back as far as 1975. Disappointed, he rustled through them again. Nothing.

As he returned the box to its high perch, his eye caught another label: BILLS OF LADING, 1970–1990. He couldn't risk more than another five minutes, tops.

His finger stopped near the end of the pile. "Gotcha," he whispered, pulling a smudged sheet free of the box. From his pocket, he extracted his microcassette recorder and quietly spoke the pertinent words, dates, and places: Belém; Port of New Orleans; Brooklyn. The *Strella de Venezuela*—Star of Venezuela. *Odd,* he thought. *Awfully long layover in New Orleans.*

* * *

"You seem pretty pleased with yourself," the librarian said as she stowed the key back in the desk.

"Have a nice day," Smithback said. He finished the entry on the archives clipboard: Sebastian Melmoth, in 11:10, out 11:25.

Back at the microfilm catalog, Smithback paused. He knew the New Orleans newspaper had a strange name, very antebellum-sounding—*Times-Picayune*, that was it.

He scanned the catalog quickly. There it was: *Times-Picayune*, 1840–present.

He snapped the 1988 reel into the machine. As he neared October, he slowed, then stopped completely. A large, 72-point banner headline stared at him out of the microfilm viewer.

"Oh, God," he breathed.

He now knew, without a shred of doubt, why the Whittlesey crates had spent so long in New Orleans.

= 28 =

"I'm sorry, Miss Green, but his door is still closed. I'll give him your message as soon as possible."

"Thanks," Margo said, hanging up her phone with frustration. How could she be Frock's eyes and ears if she couldn't even talk to him?

When Frock was deeply involved in a project, he often locked himself in his office. His secretary knew better than to disturb him. Margo had tried to reach him twice already that morning, and there was no telling when he'd re-emerge.

Margo glanced at her watch. 11:20 A.M.—the morning was almost gone. She turned to her terminal and tried logging on to the Museum's computer.

HELLO MARGO GREEN@BIOTECH@STF
WELCOME BACK TO MUSENET
DISTRIBUTED NETWORKING SYSTEM,
RELEASE 15-5
COPYRIGHT © 1989–1995 NYMNH AND CEREBRAL
SYSTEMS INC.
CONNECTING AT 11:20:45 03-30-95
PRINT SERVICE ROUTED TO LJ56

ALL USERS—IMPORTANT NOTICE
DUE TO THIS MORNING'S SYSTEM OUTAGE, A RESTORE WILL
BE PERFORMED AT NOON.
EXPECT DEGRADED PERFORMANCE. REPORT

ANY MISSING OR CORRUPTED FILES TO SYSTEMS
ADMINISTRATOR ASAP.
ROGER THRUMCAP@ADMIN@SYSTEMS

YOU HAVE 1 MESSAGE(S) WAITING

She brought up the electronic mail menu and read the waiting message.

MAIL FROM GEORGE MORIARTY@EXHIB@STF
SENT 10:14:07 03-30-95

THANKS FOR THE LABEL COPY—LOOKS PERFECT, NO
CHANGES NECESSARY. WE'LL PUT IT IN WITH OTHER
FINISHING TOUCHES BEFORE OPENING TO THE
GENERAL PUBLIC.
CARE TO HAVE LUNCH TODAY?
—GEORGE

REPLY, DELETE, FILE (R/D/F)?

Her telephone rang, shattering the silence. "Hello?" she said.

"Margo? Hi. It's George," came Moriarty's voice.

"Hi," she replied. "Sorry, just got your message now."

"I figured as much," he responded cheerfully. "Thanks again for helping out."

"Glad to," replied Margo.

Moriarty paused. "So . . ." he began hesitantly. "How about that lunch?"

"Sorry," Margo said. "I'd like to, but I'm waiting for a call back from Dr. Frock. Could be five minutes, could be next week."

She could tell by the silence that Moriarty was disappointed.

"Tell you what, though," she said. "You could swing by for me on your way to the cafeteria. If Frock's called by then, maybe I'll be free. If he hasn't . . . well, perhaps you could hang out for a couple of minutes while I wait, help me with the *Times* crossword or something."

"Sure!" Moriarty replied. "I know every three-letter Australian mammal there is."

Margo hesitated. "And perhaps while you're down here, we can take a peek into the accession database, see about the Whittlesey crates . . . ?"

There was a silence. Finally, Moriarty sighed. "Well, if it's that important to you, I guess it couldn't hurt anything. I'll stop by around twelve."

Half an hour later, a knock sounded. "Come in," she called out.

"The damn thing's locked." The voice was not Moriarty's.

She opened the door. "I didn't expect to see *you* here."

"Do you suppose it's luck or fate?" Smithback said, coming in quickly and shutting the door behind him. "Listen, Lotus Blossom, I've been a busy man since last night."

"So have I," she said. "Moriarty will be here any minute to get us into the accession database."

"How did you—"

"Never mind," Margo replied smugly.

The door opened, and Moriarty peered in. "Margo?" he asked. Then he caught sight of Smithback.

"Don't fret, professor, it's safe," the writer said. "I'm not in a biting mood today."

"Don't mind him," Margo said. "He has this annoying habit of popping up unannounced. Come on in."

"Yes, and make yourself comfortable," Smithback said, pointedly gesturing to the chair in front of Margo's terminal.

Moriarty sat down slowly, looking at Smithback, then at Margo, then at Smithback again. "I guess you want me to check the accession records," he said.

"If you wouldn't mind," Margo said quietly. Smithback's presence made the whole thing seem like a setup.

"Okay, Margo." Moriarty put his fingers on the keyboard. "Smithback, turn around. The password, you know."

The Museum's accession database contained information on all the millions of catalogued items in the Museum's collections. Initially, the database had been accessible to all employees. However, someone on the fifth floor had gotten nervous at having the artifacts' detailed descriptions and storage locations available to anyone. Now, access was limited to senior staff—Assistant Curators, such as Moriarty, and above.

Moriarty was sullenly tapping keys. "I could be given a reprimand for this, you know," he said. "Dr. Cuthbert's very strict. Why didn't you just get Frock to do it for you?"

"Like I said, I can't get in to see him," Margo replied.

Moriarty gave the ENTER key a final jab. "Here it is," he said. "Take a quick look, I'm not going to bring it up again."

Margo and Smithback crowded around the terminal as the green letters crawled slowly up the screen:

ACCESSION FILE NUMBER 1989-2006
DATE: APRIL 4, 1989
COLLECTOR: JULIAN WHITTLESEY, EDWARD MAXWELL ET AL
CATALOGUER: HUGO C. MONTAGUE
SOURCE: WHITTLESEY/MAXWELL AMAZON BASIN
EXPEDITION
LOCATION: BUILDING 2, LEVEL 3, SECTION 6, VAULT 144
NOTE: THE FOLLOWING CATALOGUED ITEMS WERE
RECEIVED ON FEBRUARY 1, 1989 IN SEVEN CRATES SENT
BACK BY THE WHITTLESEY/MAXWELL EXPEDITION FROM
THE UPPER XINGU RIVER SYSTEM. SIX OF THE CRATES WERE
PACKAGED BY MAXWELL, ONE BY WHITTLESEY. WHITTLESEY
AND THOMAS R. CROCKER JR. DID NOT RETURN FROM THE
EXPEDITION AND ARE PRESUMED DEAD. MAXWELL AND THE
REST OF THE PARTY PERISHED IN A PLANE CRASH EN ROUTE
TO THE UNITED STATES. ONLY WHITTLESEY'S CRATE HAS
BEEN PARTIALLY CATALOGUED HERE; THIS NOTE WILL BE
SUPERCEDED AS THIS CRATE AND THE MAXWELL CRATES
ARE FULLY CATALOGUED. DESCRIPTIONS ARE TAKEN FROM
JOURNAL WHEREVER POSSIBLE. HCM 4/89

"Did you see that?" Smithback said. "I wonder why the cataloguing was never finished."

"Shh!" Margo hissed. "I'm trying to get all this."

NO. 1989-2006.1
BLOW GUN AND DART, NO DATA
STATUS: C.

NO. 1989-2006.2
PERSONAL JOURNAL OF J. WHITTLESEY, JULY 22 [1987] TO
SEPTEMBER 17 [1987]
STATUS: T.R.

NO. 1989-2006.3
2 GRASS BUNDLES, TIED WITH PARROT FEATHERS, USED AS
SHAMAN'S FETISH, FROM DESERTED HUT
STATUS: C.

NO. 1989-2006.4
FINELY CARVED FIGURINE OF BEAST. SUPPOSED
REPRESENTATION OF "MBWUN" CF. WHITTLESEY JOURNAL,
P. 56–59
STATUS: O.E.

NO. 1989-2006.5
WOODEN PLANT PRESS, ORIGIN UNKNOWN, FROM
VICINITY OF DESERTED HUT.
STATUS: C.

NO. 1989-2006.6
DISK INCISED WITH DESIGNS.
STATUS: C.

NO. 1989-2006.7
SPEAR POINTS, ASSORTED SIZES AND CONDITION.
STATUS: C.

NOTE: ALL CRATES TEMPORARILY MOVED TO SECURE
VAULT, LEVEL 2B, PER IAN CUTHBERT 3/20/95. D.
ALVAREZ, SEC'Y

"What do all those codes mean?" Smithback asked.
"They tell the current status of the artifact," Moriarty said. "C means it's still crated up, hasn't been curated yet. O.E. means 'on exhibit.' T.R. means 'temporarily removed.' There are others—"
"Temporarily removed?" Margo asked. "That's all you need to put down? No wonder the journal got lost."
"Of course that's not all," Moriarty said. "Whoever removes an object has to sign it out. The database is hierarchical. We can see more detail on any entry just by stepping down a level. Here, I'll show you." He tapped a few keys.
His expression changed. "That's odd." The message on the screen read:

INVALID RECORD OR RELATION
PROCESS HALTED

Moriarty frowned. "There's nothing attached to this record for the Whittlesey journal." He cleared the screen and started typing again. "Nothing wrong with the others. See? Here's the detail record for the figurine."

Margo examined the screen.

DETAIL LISTING
Item: 1989–2006.4
####################################
Removed By:	Cuthbert, I.	40123
Approval:	Cuthbert, I.	40123
Removal Date:	3/17/95	
Removal To:	Superstition Exhibition	
	Case 415, Item 1004	
Reason:	Display	
Return Date:		

####################################
Removed By:	Depardieu, B.	72412
Approval:	Cuthbert, I.	40123
Removal Date:	10/1/90	
Removal To:	Anthropology Lab 2	
Reason:	Initial curating	
Return Date:	10/5/90	

####################################
END LISTING
=:?

"So what does that mean? We know the journal's lost," Margo said.

"Even if it's lost, there should still be a detail record for it," Moriarty said.

"Is there a restricted flag on the record?"

Moriarty shook his head and hit a few more keys.

"Here's why," he said at length, pointing at the screen. "The detail record's been erased."

"You mean the information about the journal's location has been deleted?" Smithback asked. "Can they do that?"

Moriarty shrugged. "It takes a high-security ID."

"More importantly, why should somebody do that?" Margo asked. "Did the mainframe problem this morning have anything to do with it?"

"No," Moriarty said. "This file compare dump I've just done implies the file was deleted sometime before last night's backup. I can't be more specific than that."

"Deleted, eh?" Smithback said. "Gone forever. How clean, how neat. How coincidental. I'm beginning to see a pattern here—a nasty one."

Moriarty switched off the terminal and pushed himself back from the desk. "I'm not interested in your conspiracy theories," he said.

"Could it have been an accident? Or a malfunction?" Margo asked.

"Doubtful. The database has all sorts of referential integrity checks built-in. I'd see an error message."

"So what, then?" Smithback pressed.

"I haven't a clue." Moriarty shrugged. "But it's a trivial issue, at best."

"Is that the best you can do?" Smithback snorted. "Some computer genius."

Moriarty, offended, pushed his glasses up his nose and stood up. "I really don't need this," he said. "I think I'll get some lunch." He headed for the door. "Margo, I'll take a rain check on that crossword puzzle."

"Nice going," Margo said as the door closed. "You've got a really subtle touch, you know that, Smithback? George was good enough to get us into the database."

"Yeah, and what did we learn from it?" Smithback asked. "Diddly-squat. Only one of the crates was ever accessioned. Whittlesey's journal is still missing." He looked at her smugly. "I, on the other hand, have struck oil."

"Put it in your book," Margo yawned. "I'll read it then. Assuming I can find a copy in the library."

"*Et tu, Brute?*" Smithback grinned and handed her a folded sheet of paper. "Well, take a look at this."

The sheet was a photocopy reproduction of an article from the New Orleans *Times-Picayune* dated October 17, 1988.

GHOST FREIGHTER FOUND BEACHED NEAR NEW ORLEANS

By Antony Anastasia

Special to the *Times-Picayune*

BAYOU GROVE, October 16 (AP)—A small freighter bound for New Orleans ran aground last night near this small coastal town. Details remain sketchy, but preliminary reports indicate that all crew members had been brutally slain while at sea. The Coast Guard first reported the grounding at 11:45 Monday night.

The ship, the *Strella de Venezuela*, was an 18,000-ton freighter, currently of Haitian registry, that plied the waters of the Caribbean and the main trade routes between South America and the United States. Damage was limited, and the vessel's cargo appeared to be intact.

It is not presently known how the crew members met their deaths, or whether any of the crew were able to escape the ship. Henry La Plage, a private helicopter pilot who observed the beached vessel, reported that "corpses were strewn across the foredeck like some wild animal had gotten at them. I seen one guy hanging out a bridge porthole, his head all smashed up. It was like a slaughterhouse, ain't never seen nothing like it."

Local and federal authorities are cooperating in an attempt to understand the slayings, easily one of the most brutal massacres in recent maritime history. "We are currently looking into several theories, but we've come to no conclusions as of yet," said Nick Lea, a police spokesman. Although there was no official comment, federal sources said that mutiny, vengeance killings by rival Caribbean shippers, and sea piracy were all being considered as possible motives.

"Jesus," Margo breathed. "The wounds described here—"

"—sound just like those on the three bodies found here this week," Smithback nodded grimly.

Margo frowned. "This happened more than seven years ago. It has to be coincidental."

"Does it?" Smithback asked. "I might be forced to agree with you—if it wasn't for the fact that *the Whittlesey crates were on board that ship.*"

"*What?*"

"It's true. I tracked down the bills of lading. The crates were shipped from Brazil in August of 1988—almost a year after the expedition broke up, as I understand it. After this business in New Orleans, the crates sat in customs while the investigation was being conducted. It took them almost a year and a half to reach the Museum."

"The ritualized murders have followed the crates all the way from the Amazon!" Margo said. "But that means—"

"It means," Smithback said grimly, "that I'm going to stop laughing now when I hear talk about a curse on that expedition. And it means you should keep locking this door."

The phone rang, startling them both.

"Margo, my dear." Frock's voice rumbled to her. "What news?"

"Dr. Frock! I wonder if I could come by your office for a few minutes. At your earliest convenience."

"Splendid!" Frock said. "Give me a little time to shuffle some of this paper off my desk and into the wastebasket. Shall we say one o'clock?"

"Thank you," Margo said. "Smithback," she said, turning around, "we've got to—"

But the writer was gone.

At ten minutes to one, another knock sounded.

"Who's there?" Margo said through the locked door.

"It's me, Moriarty. Can I come in, Margo?"

"I just wanted to apologize for walking out earlier," Moriarty said, declining a chair. "It's just that Bill wears on me sometimes. He never seems to let up."

"George, I'm the one who should apologize," Margo said. "I didn't know he was going to appear like that." She thought of telling him about the newspaper article, but decided against it and began to pack up her carryall.

"There's something else I wanted to tell you," Moriarty went on. "While I was eating lunch, I realized there may be some way we can find out more about that deleted database record, after all. The one for Whittlesey's journal."

Margo abruptly put down the carryall and looked at Moriarty, who took a seat in front of her terminal. "Did you see that sign-on message when you logged into the network earlier?" he asked.

"The one about the computer going down? Big surprise. I got locked out twice this morning."

Moriarty nodded. "The message also said they were going to restore from the backup tapes at noon. A full restore takes about thirty minutes. That means they should be done by now."

"So?"

"Well, a backup tape holds about two to three months' worth of archives. If the detail record for the Whittlesey journal was deleted in the last two months—*and* if the backup tape is still on the hub down in data processing—I should be able to resurrect it."

"Really?"

Moriarty nodded.

"Then do it!" Margo urged.

"There's a certain element of risk," Moriarty replied. "If a system operator notices that the tape is being accessed . . . well, he could trace it to your terminal ID."

"I'll risk it," Margo said. "George," she added, "I know you feel this is all a wild goose chase, and I can't really blame you for that. But I'm convinced those crates from the Whittlesey expedition are connected to these killings. I don't know what the connection is, but maybe the journal could have told us something. And I don't know what we're dealing with—a serial killer, some animal, some creature. And not knowing scares me." She gently took Moriarty's hand and gave it a squeeze. "But maybe we're in a position here to be of some help. We have to try."

When she noticed Moriarty blushing, she withdrew her hand.

Smiling shyly, Moriarty moved to the keyboard.

"Here goes," he said.

Margo paced the room as Moriarty worked. "Any luck?" she asked finally, moving closer to the terminal.

"Don't know yet," said Moriarty, squinting at the screen and typing commands. "I've got the tape, but the protocol's messed up or something, the CRC checks are failing. We may get garbled data, if we get anything. I'm going in the back door, so to speak, hoping to avoid attention. The seek rate is really slow this way."

Then the keytaps stopped. "Margo," Moriarty said quietly. "I've got it."

The screen filled.

DETAIL LISTING
Item: 1989–2006.2
################################
Removed By: Rickman, L.   53210
Approval: Cuthbert, I.   40123
Removal Date: 3/15/95
Removal To: Personal supervision

Reason:
Return Date:
###################################
Removed By: Depardieu, B.   72412
Approval: Cuthbert, I.   40123
RemLW/@;oval Date: 10/1/90
Remov~DS*-~@2e34 5WIFU
   = + +ET2 34 h34!~

DB ERROR

=:?

"Hell!" Moriarty exclaimed. "I was afraid of that. It's been partially overwritten, corrupted. See that? It just trails off into garbage."

"Yes, but look!" Margo said excitedly.

Moriarty examined the screen. "The journal was removed by Mrs. Rickman two weeks ago, with Dr. Cuthbert's permission. No return date."

Margo snorted. "Cuthbert said the journal had been lost."

"So why was this record deleted? And by whom?" Suddenly his eyes widened. "Oh, Lord, I have to release my lock on the tape before somebody notices us." His fingers danced over the keys.

"George," Margo said. "Do you know what this means? They took the journal out of the crates before the killings started. Around the time Cuthbert had the crates put in the Secure Area. Now they're concealing evidence from the police. Why?"

Moriarty frowned. "You're starting to sound like Smithback," he said. "There could be a thousand explanations."

"Name one," Margo challenged.

"The most obvious would be that somebody else deleted the detail record before Rickman could add a Lost Artifact notation."

Margo shook her head. "I don't believe it. There are just too many coincidences."

"Margo—" Moriarty began. Then he sighed. "Listen," he went on patiently, "this is a trying time for all of us, you especially. I know you're trying to make a tough decision, and then with a crisis like this . . . well . . ."

"These murders weren't committed by some garden-variety maniac," Margo interrupted impatiently. "I'm *not* crazy."

"I'm not saying that," Moriarty continued. "I just think you ought to let the police handle this. It's a very, very dangerous business. And you should be concentrating on your own life right now. Digging into this won't help you make up your mind about your own future." He swallowed. "And it won't bring your father back."

"Is that what you think?" Margo blazed. "You don't—"

She broke off abruptly as her eye fell on the wall clock. "Jesus. I'm late for my meeting with Dr. Frock." She grabbed her carryall and headed for the door. Halfway into the hall, she turned around. "I'll speak to *you* later," she said.

The door slammed.

God, Moriarty thought, sitting at the darkened terminal and resting his chin in his hands. *If a graduate student in plant genetics actually thinks Mbwun might be loose—if even Margo Green starts seeing conspiracies behind every door—what about the rest of the Museum?*

= 29 =

Margo watched Frock spill his sherry down his shirtfront.

"Blast," he said, dabbing with plump hands. He set the glass down on the desk with exaggerated care and looked up at Margo.

"Thank you for coming to me, my dear. It's an extraordinary discovery. I'd say we should go down there this moment and take another look at the figurine, but that Pendergast fellow will be here shortly to make a further nuisance of himself."

Bless you, Agent Pendergast, Margo thought. The last thing she felt like doing was going back down into the exhibition.

Frock sighed. "No matter, we'll know soon enough. Once Pendergast leaves, we'll learn the truth. This Mbwun figurine could be the additional proof I've been searching for. *If,* that is, you are correct about the claws matching the lacerations in the victim."

"But how could such a creature be loose in the Museum?" Margo asked.

"Ah!" Frock exclaimed, eyes shining. "That's the question, is it not? And let me answer a question with a question. What thing, my dear Margo, is *rugose?*"

"I don't know," Margo said. "Rugose as in bumpy?"

"Yes. It's a regular pattern of ridges, wrinkles, or creases. I'll tell you what's rugose. Reptilian eggs are rugose. As are dinosaur eggs."

A sudden current passed through Margo as she remembered. "That's the word—"

"—that Cuthbert used to describe the seed pods missing from the crate," Frock finished her sentence. "I ask you: were they *really* seed pods? What kind of seed pod would look wrinkled and scaly? But an egg . . ."

Frock drew himself up in his wheelchair. "Next question. *Where have they gone?* Were they stolen? Or did something else happen to them?"

Abruptly, the scientist stopped, sinking back in his wheelchair, shaking his head.

"But if something . . . if something hatched, something broke out of the crates," Margo said, "how does that explain the killings on board the freighter that carried the crates from South America?"

"Margo," Frock said, laughing quietly, "what we have here is a riddle wrapped in a mystery inside an enigma. It is *essential* that we gather more facts without wasting additional time."

There was a soft rapping at the door.

"That must be Pendergast," Frock said, drawing back. Then, louder: "Come in, please!"

The agent walked in, carrying a briefcase, his black suit as ever impeccable, his blond white hair brushed back from his face. To Margo, he looked as collected and placid as before. When Frock gestured to one of the Victorian chairs, Pendergast seated himself.

"A pleasure to see you again, sir," Frock said. "You've met Miss Green. We were once again in the middle of something just now, so I hope you won't mind if she remains."

Pendergast waved his hand. "Of course. I know you'll both continue to respect my request for confidentiality."

"Of course," said Frock.

"Dr. Frock, I know you're busy and I'll keep this short," Pendergast began. "I was hoping you'd had some success in locating the artifact we spoke about. An artifact that might have been used as a weapon in these murders."

Frock shifted in the wheelchair. "As you requested, I considered the matter further. I ran a search of our accession database, both for single items and for items that could potentially have been broken apart and recombined." He shook his head. "Unfortunately, I found nothing that even remotely resembled the imprint you showed us. There has never been anything like it in the collections."

Pendergast's expression betrayed nothing. Then he smiled. "Officially, we'd never admit this, but the case is—shall we say—a trying one." He indicated his briefcase. "I am awash in false sightings, lab reports, interviews. But we're slow in finding a fit."

Frock smiled. "I believe, Mr. Pendergast, that what you do and what

I do are not all that different. I've been in the same predicament myself. And no doubt His Eminence is acting as if nothing out of the ordinary is happening."

Pendergast nodded.

"Wright is very eager that the exhibition go on as scheduled tomorrow night. Why? Because the Museum spent millions it didn't really have to put it together. It's vital that admissions be increased to keep the museum from slipping into the red. This exhibition is seen as the best way to do that."

"I see," Pendergast said. He picked up a fossil lying on a table next to his chair, turning it over idly in his hand. "Ammonite?" he asked.

"Correct," replied Frock.

"Dr. Frock—" Pendergast began. "Pressure is now being brought to bear from a variety of quarters. As a result, I must be doubly careful to conduct this investigation by the book. I can't share our results with outside entities such as yourself—even when the conventional avenues of investigation are proving fruitless." He put down the fossil carefully and crossed his arms. "That said, do I understand correctly that you are an expert on DNA?"

Frock nodded. "That's partly true. I have devoted some study to how genes affect morphology—the shape of an organism. And I oversee the projects of various graduate students—such as Gregory Kawakita, and Margo here—whose studies involve DNA research."

Pendergast retrieved his briefcase, snapped it open, and withdrew a fat computer printout. "I have a report on DNA from the claw found in one of the first victims. Of course, I can't show it to you. It would be highly irregular. The New York office wouldn't like it."

"I see," said Frock. "And you continue to believe that the claw is your best clue."

"It's our only clue of importance, Dr. Frock. Let me explain my conclusions. I believe we have a madman loose in the Museum. He kills his victims in a ritualistic fashion, removes the back of the skull, and extracts the hypothalamus from the brain."

"For what purpose?" asked Frock.

Pendergast hesitated. "We believe he eats it."

Margo gasped.

"The killer may be hiding in the Museum's subbasement," Pendergast continued. "There are many indications that he has returned there after killing, but so far we've been unable to isolate a specific location or retrieve any evidence. Two dogs were killed during searches.

As you probably know, it's a perfect warren of tunnels, galleries, and passages spread over several subterranean levels, the oldest dating back almost 150 years. The Museum has been able to furnish me with maps covering only a small percentage of its total area. I call the killer 'he' because the force used in the killings indicates a male, and a strong one at that. Almost preternaturally strong. As you know, he uses some kind of three-clawed weapon to disembowel his victims, who are apparently chosen at random. We have no motive. Our interviews with selected Museum staff have turned up no leads as yet." He looked at Frock. "You see, Doctor, our best clue remains our only clue—the weapon, the claw. That is why I continue to search for its origin."

Frock nodded slowly. "You mentioned DNA?"

Pendergast waved the computer printout. "The lab results have been inconclusive, to say the least." He paused. "I can see no reason not to tell you that the test on the claw turned up DNA from various species of gecko, in addition to human chromosomes. Hence our assumption that the sample might be degraded."

"Gecko, you say?" Frock murmured in mild surprise. "And it eats the hypothalamus . . . how extraordinary. Tell me, how do you know?"

"We found traces of saliva and teeth marks."

"Human teeth marks?"

"No one knows."

"And the saliva?"

"Indeterminate."

Frock's head sank down on his chest. After a few minutes, he looked up.

"You continue to call the claw a weapon," he said. "I assume, then, that you continue to believe the killer is human?"

Pendergast closed his briefcase. "I simply don't see any other possibility. Do you think, Dr. Frock, an animal could decapitate a body with surgical precision, punch a hole in the skull and locate an internal organ the size of a walnut that only someone trained in human anatomy could recognize? And the killer's ability to elude our searches of the subbasement has been impressive."

"Frock's head had sunk on his chest again. As the seconds ticked off into minutes, Pendergast remained motionless, watching.

Frock suddenly raised his head. "Mr. Pendergast," he said, his voice booming. Margo jumped. "I've heard your theory. Would you care to hear mine?"

Pendergast nodded. "Of course."

"Very well," Frock replied. "Are you familiar with the Transvaal Shales?"

"I don't believe so," said Pendergast.

"The Transvaal Shales were discovered in 1945 by Alistair Van Vrouwenhoek, a paleontologist with South Africa's Witwatersrand University. They were Cambrian, about six hundred million years old. And they were full of bizarre life forms the likes of which had never been seen before or since. Asymmetrical life forms, not showing even the bilateral symmetry of virtually all animal life on earth today. They occurred, coincidentally, at the time of the Cambrian mass extinction. Now most people, Mr. Pendergast, believe the Transvaal Shales represent a dead end of evolution: life experimenting with every conceivable form before settling down to the bilaterally symmetric form you see today."

"But you do not hold such a view," Pendergast said.

Frock cleared his throat. "Correct. A certain type of organism predominates in these shales. It had powerful fins and long suction pads and oversized crushing and tearing mouth parts. Those mouth parts could saw through rock, and the fins allowed it to move at twenty miles per hour through the water. No doubt it was a highly successful and quite savage predator. It was, I believe, *too* successful: it hunted its prey into extinction and then quickly became extinct itself. It thus caused the minor mass extinction at the end of the Cambrian era. *It,* not natural selection, killed off all the other forms of life in the Transvaal Shales."

Pendergast blinked. "And?"

"I've run computer simulations of evolution according to the new mathematical theory of fractal turbulence. The result? Every sixty to seventy million years or so, life starts getting very well adapted to its environment. Too well adapted, perhaps. There is a population explosion of the successful life forms. Then, suddenly, a new species appears out of the blue. It is almost always a predatory creature, a killing machine. It tears through the host population, killing, feeding, multiplying. Slowly at first, then ever faster."

Frock gestured toward the sandstone fossil plaque on his desk. "Mr. Pendergast, let me show you something." The agent stood up and moved forward.

"This is a set of tracks made by a creature that lived during the Upper Cretaceous," Frock continued. "Right on the K-T boundary, to be exact. This is the only such fossil of its kind we've found; there is no other."

"K-T?" asked Pendergast.

"Cretaceous-Tertiary. It's the boundary that marks the mass extinction of the dinosaurs."

Pendergast nodded, but still looked puzzled.

"There is a connection here that has so far gone unnoticed," Frock continued. "The figurine of Mbwun, the claw impressions made by the killer, and these fossil tracks."

Pendergast looked down. "Mbwun? The figurine that Dr. Cuthbert removed from the crates and put on display?"

Frock nodded.

"Hmm. How old are these prints?"

"Approximately sixty-five million years old. They came from a formation where the very last of the dinosaurs were found. Before the mass extinction, that is."

There was another long silence.

"Ah. And the connection? . . ." asked Pendergast after a moment.

"I said that nothing in the anthropology collections matches the claw marks. But I did not say there were no *representations,* no *sculptures* of such a claw. We've learned that the forelimbs on the figurine of Mbwun have three claws, with a thickened central digit. Now look at these tracks," Frock said, pointing to the fossil. "Think back to the reconstruction of the claw and the claw marks in the victim."

"So you think," Pendergast said, "that the killer might be the same animal that made these tracks? A dinosaur?" Margo thought she detected amusement in Pendergast's voice.

Frock looked at the agent, shaking his head vigorously. "No, Mr. Pendergast, not a dinosaur. Nothing as common as a dinosaur. We're talking about the proof of my theory of aberrant evolution. You know my work. This is the creature I believe *killed off* the dinosaurs."

Pendergast remained silent.

Frock leaned closer to the FBI agent. "I believe," he said, "this creature, this freak of nature, is the cause of the dinosaur's extinction. Not a meteorite, not a change in climate, but some terrible predator—the creature that made the tracks preserved in this fossil. The embodiment of the Callisto Effect. It was not large, but it was extremely powerful and fast. It probably hunted in cooperative packs and was intelligent. But because superpredators are so short lived, they aren't well represented in the fossil record. Except in the Transvaal Shales. And in these tracks here, from the Tzun-je-jin Badlands. Are you following me?"

"Yes."

"We are *in* a population explosion today."

Pendergast remained silent.

"*Human beings*, Mr. Pendergast!" Frock continued, his voice rising. "Five thousand years ago there were only ten million of us on the globe. Today there are six billion! We're the most successful form of life the earth has ever seen!" He tapped the copies of *Fractal Evolution* that lay on his desk. "Yesterday, you asked about my next book. It will constitute an extension of my theory on the Callisto Effect, applying it to *modern* life. My theory predicts that at any moment, some grotesque mutation will come about; some creature that will prey on the *human* population. I'm not saying the killer is the same creature that killed off the dinosaurs. But a *similar* creature . . . well, look at these tracks again. They look like Mbwun! We call it convergent evolution, where two creatures look alike not because they're necessarily related, but because they evolve to do the same thing. A creature that's evolved to kill. There are too many similarities, Mr. Pendergast."

Pendergast brought his briefcase onto his lap. "I'm afraid you've lost me, Dr. Frock."

"Don't you see? *Something came back in that crate from South America.* Unleashed in the Museum. A highly successful predator. That figurine of Mbwun is the proof. The indigenous tribes were aware of this creature, and built a religion around it. Whittlesey inadvertently sent it into civilization."

"You've seen this figurine yourself?" Pendergast asked. "Dr. Cuthbert seemed reluctant to show it to me."

"No," Frock admitted. "But I have it on the best authority. I plan to make my own observations at the earliest opportunity."

"Dr. Frock, we looked into the matter of the crates yesterday," Pendergast said. "Dr. Cuthbert assured us there was nothing of value in them, and we have no reason to disbelieve him." He stood up, impassive. "I thank you for your time and help. Your theory is most interesting, and I truly wish I could subscribe to it." He shrugged. "However, my own opinion remains unchanged for the time being. Forgive me for being blunt, but I hope you will be able to separate your conjectures from the cold facts of our investigation, and help us in any way you can." He walked toward the door. "Now, I hope you'll excuse me. If anything comes to mind, please contact me."

And he left.

Frock sat in his wheelchair, shaking his head. "What a shame," he murmured. "I had high hopes for his cooperation, but it seems he's like all the rest."

Margo glanced at the table next to the chair Pendergast had just vacated. "Look," she said. "He left the DNA printout."

Frock's eyes followed Margo's. Then he chuckled.

"I assume that's what he meant by anything else coming to mind." He paused. "Perhaps he isn't like all the rest, after all. Well, we won't tell on him, Margo, will we?" he said, picking up the phone.

"Dr. Frock to speak with Dr. Cuthbert." A pause. "Hello, Ian? Yes, I'm fine, thank you. No, it's just that I'd like to get into the *Superstition* exhibition right away. What's that? Yes, I know it's been sealed, but . . . No, I'm quite reconciled to the idea of the exhibition, it's just that . . . I see."

Margo noticed Frock's face redden.

"In that case, Ian," Frock continued, "I should like to reexamine the crates from the Whittlesey expedition. Yes, the ones in the Secure Area. I know we saw them yesterday, Ian."

There was a long silence. Margo could hear a faint squawking.

"Now look here, Ian," Frock said. "I'm chairman of this department, and I have a right to . . . Don't you speak to me that way, Ian. Don't you *dare*."

Frock was shaking with rage in a way Margo had never seen before. His voice had dropped almost to a whisper.

"Sir, you have no business in this institution. I shall be making a formal grievance to the Director."

Frock slowly returned the phone to its cradle, his hand trembling. He turned toward Margo, fumbling for his handkerchief. "Please forgive me."

"I'm surprised," said Margo. "I thought that as a Chairman . . ." She couldn't quite complete the sentence.

"I had complete control over the collections?" Frock smiled, his composure returning. "So did I. But this new exhibition, and these killings, have aroused sentiments in people that I hadn't suspected. Technically, Cuthbert outranks me. I'm not sure why he's doing this. It would have to be something profoundly embarrassing, something that would delay or prevent his precious exhibition from opening." He thought for a minute. "Perhaps he's aware of this creature's existence. After all, he was the one who moved the crates. Perhaps he found the hatched eggs, made the connection, hid them. And now he wants to deny me my right to study it!" He sat forward in the wheelchair and balled his fists.

"Dr. Frock, I don't think that's a real possibility," Margo warned. Any thoughts she'd had of telling Frock about Rickman's removal of the Whittlesey journal evaporated.

Frock relaxed. "You're right, of course. This isn't the end of it, though, you can be sure. Still, we don't have time for that now, and I trust your observations of Mbwun. But, Margo, we *must* get in to see those crates."

"How?" said Margo.

Frock slid open a drawer of his desk and fished around for a moment. Then he withdrew a form which Margo immediately recognized: a '10-14,' Request for Access.

"My mistake," he went on, "was in asking." He started to fill out the form longhand.

"But doesn't that need to be signed by Central Processing?" Margo asked.

"Of course," said Frock. "I will send the form to Central Processing via the usual procedure. And I'll take the unsigned copy down to the Secure Area and bully my way in. No doubt the request form will be denied. But by the time that happens, I will have had time to examine the crates. And find the answers."

"But Dr. Frock, you can't do that!" Margo replied in a shocked tone.

"Why not?" Frock smiled wryly. "Frock, a pillar of the Museum establishment, acting in an unorthodox manner? This is too important for such considerations."

"I didn't mean that," Margo continued. She let her gaze drop to the scientist's wheelchair.

Frock looked down. His face fell. "Ah, yes," he said slowly. "I see what you mean." Crestfallen, he started to return the paper to his desk.

"Dr. Frock," Margo said. "Give me the form. I'll take it down to the Secure Area."

Frock's hand froze. He looked at Margo appraisingly. "I asked you to be my eyes and ears, but I didn't ask you to walk over coals for me," he said. "I'm a tenured curator, a relatively important figure. They wouldn't dare sack me. But you—" he drew a deep breath, raised his eyebrows. "They could make an example of you, expel you from the Ph.D. program. And I'd be powerless to prevent it."

Margo thought for a moment. "I have a friend who's very clever at this kind of thing. I think he could talk his way into or out of any situation."

Frock remained motionless for a moment. Then he tore off the copy and gave it to her. "I'll have the original delivered upstairs. I have to, if we're going to maintain the facade. The guard may call Central Processing to verify receipt. You won't have much time. As soon as it comes in they'll be on the alert. You will have to be gone by then."

From a desk drawer, he withdrew a yellow paper and a key. He showed them to Margo.

"This paper holds the combination to the Secure Area vaults," he said. "And here's the key to the vault itself. All directors have them. With luck, Cuthbert won't have thought to change the combinations." He handed them to Margo. "These will get you through the doors. It's the guards you'll have to deal with." He was talking fast now, his eyes locked on Margo's. "You know what to look for in the crates. Any evidence of eggs, living organisms, even cult objects associated with the creature. Anything that can prove my theory. Check the smaller crate first, Whittlesey's crate. That's the one that contained the Mbwun figurine. Check the others if you have time, but, for Heaven's sake, expose yourself to as little risk as possible. Go now, my dear, and Godspeed."

The last thing Margo saw as she left the office was Frock beneath the bow windows, his broad back turned away from her, drumming his fists repeatedly against the arms of his wheelchair. "Damn this thing!" he was saying. "Damn it to hell!"

= 30 =

Five minutes later, in her office several floors below, Margo picked up the phone and dialed. Smithback was in a rare mood. As Margo explained Moriarty's discovery of the deleted accession record and—in somewhat less detail—the events in Frock's office, his mood grew even more cheerful.

She heard him chuckling. "Was I right about Rickman, or what? Concealing evidence. Now I'll make her see the book my way, or—"

"Smithback, don't you *dare*," Margo warned. "This isn't for your personal gratification. We don't know the story behind that journal, and we can't worry about it right now. We *have* to get into those crates, and we only have a few minutes to do it."

"All right, all right," came the answer. "Meet me at the landing outside Entomology. I'm leaving now."

"I never thought Frock could be such a radical," Smithback said. "My respect for the old feller has just gone up two notches." He was making his way down a long flight of iron stairs. They'd taken a back way in hopes of avoiding the police checkpoints set up at all elevator banks.

"You've got the key and the combination, right?" he asked from the bottom of the stairs. Margo checked her carryall, then followed him.

She glanced quickly up and down the corridor. "You know how the hall outside the Secure Area has lighted alcoves along it? You go ahead, I'll follow a minute later. Talk to the guard, try to draw him into an alcove where the light is better, on the pretext of showing him this form. Get him to turn his back for a couple of minutes, and then I'll unlock the door and go in. Just keep him occupied. You're a good talker."

"That's your plan?" Smithback scoffed. "All right." He spun on his heels, continued down the corridor, and vanished around the corner.

Margo waited, counting to sixty. Then she moved forward, pulling on a pair of latex gloves.

Soon she could hear Smithback's voice, already raised in righteous protest. "This paper is signed by the Chairman of the department himself! Are you trying to tell me that . . ."

She poked her head around the corner. About fifty feet down the hall was an intersection with another hallway that led to the police barricades. Further down was the door to the Secure Area itself, and, beyond that, Margo could see the guard. He had his back to her, and was holding her form in one hand.

"I'm sorry, sir," she could hear him say, "but this hasn't gone through Processing . . ."

"You're not looking in the right place," Smithback responded. "Take it over here where you can read it, here in the light."

They moved down the hall away from Margo, into an illuminated alcove. As they disappeared from view, Margo came around the corner and walked briskly down the hall. At the Secure Area door, she inserted the key and pushed gingerly. The door swung open on oiled hinges. She peered around the edge to make sure she was alone; the darkened room seemed empty, and she eased the door shut behind her.

Her heart was already racing, the blood pounding in her ears. She caught her breath, fumbled for the light switch. The vaults stretched ahead of her in rows to the left and right. When she noticed the third door on the right had a yellow EVIDENCE sheet taped to it, she grasped its dial with one hand and took out Frock's scrap of paper with the other. 56-77-23. She took a deep breath and began, remembering the locker she'd once used to store her oboe in high school music class. *Right, left, right* . . .

There was a loud click. Immediately, she grabbed the lever and pulled downward. The door opened.

Inside, the crates were dim shapes against the far wall. She turned on the light and glanced at her watch. Three minutes had passed.

She had to work very quickly now. She could see the ragged marks where one of the larger crates had been torn and splintered apart. The marks sent shivers down her spine. Kneeling in front of the smaller crate, she removed its top and plunged her hands into the packing material, parting the stiff fibers to expose the artifacts.

Her hand closed around something hard. Pulling it out, Margo saw a small stone, carved with odd designs. *Not very promising.* She exposed a collection of what looked like jade lip plugs, then flint arrowheads, some points, a blow gun tube with a set of darts, long and sharp, the tips blackened with some hardened substance. *Don't want to be pricked by those,* she thought. Still nothing worth taking. She delved deeper. The next layer held a small plant press, screwed shut; a damaged shaman's rattle covered in grotesque designs; and a beautiful manta made of woven cloth and feathers.

On an impulse she stuffed the plant press, covered with packing fibers, into her bag. The stone disc and rattle followed.

On the bottom layer, she found several jars containing small reptiles. Colorful, but nothing out of the ordinary.

Six minutes had passed. She sat up, listening, expecting any moment to hear the footsteps of the returning guard. But there was nothing.

She hastily stuffed the rest of the artifacts back into the crate and surrounded them with packing material. She picked up the lid, noting its loose inner lining. As she pried the lining away curiously, a brittle, water-damaged envelope slipped out into her lap; hastily, she crammed it into her bag.

Eight minutes. There was no time left.

Back in the central room, she listened, trying to make out the muffled sounds outside. She eased the door open a crack.

"What's your badge number?" Smithback was saying loudly.

Margo couldn't make out the guard's reply. She slipped out and shut the door behind her, quickly peeling off her gloves and stuffing them into her carryall. She straightened up, looked herself up and down, then started walking past the alcove where Smithback and the guard were standing.

"Hey!"

She turned. The guard, flushed, was looking at her.

"Oh, there you are, Bill!" she said, thinking fast, hoping the guard hadn't seen her come out the door. "Am I too late? Have you already been inside?"

"This guy won't let me in!" Smithback complained.

"Listen, you," the guard said, turning back to Smithback. "I've told you a thousand times, and I won't tell you again. That form has to be properly processed before I can give you access. Understand?"

They'd pulled it off.

Margo looked back down the hall. In the distance, she saw a tall, lean figure approaching: Ian Cuthbert.

She grabbed Smithback's arm. "We've got to go. Remember our appointment? We'll have to look at the collections some other time."

"That's right. Of course." Smithback babbled heartily. "I'll get this taken care of later," he said to the guard.

Near the far end of the hall, she pushed Smithback into an alcove.

"Get behind those cabinets," Margo whispered.

They heard Cuthbert's footsteps behind them as they concealed themselves. Then the footsteps stopped, and Cuthbert's voice echoed loudly down the corridor.

"Has anyone tried to gain access to the vaults?" he asked.

"Yes, sir. There was a man trying to get in. They were just here."

"Who?" demanded Cuthbert. "Those people you were just speaking with?"

"Yes, sir. He had a form but it hadn't been properly processed, so I didn't let him in."

"You did *not* let him in?"

"That's right, sir."

"Who issued the form? Frock?"

"Yes, sir. Dr. Frock."

"And you didn't get the name of this person?"

"I think his name was Bill. I don't know about the woman, but—"

"Bill? *Bill?* Oh, that's bloody brilliant. The *first* thing you should do is ask for identification."

"I'm sorry, sir. It was just that he insisted it was—"

But Cuthbert was already striding back angrily. The footfalls faded down the corridor.

At a nod from Smithback, Margo rose gingerly and dusted herself off. They stepped out into the hall.

"Hey, you there!" shouted the guard. "Come here, I need to see your ID! Wait!"

Smithback and Margo took off at a sprint. They raced around a bend, then ducked into a stairwell and dashed up the wide concrete steps.

"Where are we going?" Margo panted.

"Damned if I know."

They reached the next landing, and Smithback stepped out gingerly into the hallway. He looked up and down the corridor, then wrenched open a door marked MAMMALOGY, PONGIDAE STORAGE.

Inside, they stopped to catch their breath. The room was quiet and cool. As Margo's eyes grew accustomed to the dim light, she noticed stuffed gorillas and chimpanzees standing in ranks like sentinels, and heaping piles of hairy skins on wooden racks. Against one wall were dozens of shelves lined with primate skulls.

Smithback listened intently at the door for a moment. Then he turned to Margo. "Lets see what you found," he said.

"There wasn't much," Margo said, breathing heavily. "I took a couple of unimportant artifacts, that's it. I did find this, though," she said, reaching into her carryall. "It was wedged in the lid of the crate."

The unsealed envelope was addressed simply "R. H. Montague, NYMNH."

The yellowed writing paper was embossed with a curious double-arrow motif. As Smithback peered over her shoulder, Margo held the sheet carefully up to the light and began to read.

Upper Xingú
Sept. 17, 1987

Montague,

I've decided to send Carlos back with the last crate and go on alone in search of Crocker. Carlos is trustworthy, and I can't risk losing the crate should anything happen to me. Take note of the shaman's rattle and other ritual objects. They seem unique. But the figurine I've enclosed, which we found in a deserted hut at this site, is the proof I've been looking for. Note the exaggerated claws, the reptilian attributes, the hints at *bipedalia*. The Kothoga exist, and the Mbwun legend is not mere fabrication.

All my field notes are in this notebook. . . .

= 31 =

Mrs. Lavinia Rickman sat in a wine-colored leather armchair in the Director's office. The room was deathly silent. Not even traffic noises from the street three floors below penetrated the thick turret windows. Wright himself sat behind the desk, practically swallowed by the vast length of mahogany. A Reynolds portrait of Ridley A. Davis, the Museum's founder, glared down from behind Wright.

Dr. Ian Cuthbert occupied a sofa along a far wall of the room. He leaned forward, elbows on his knees, his tweed suit loose on his spare frame. He was frowning. Normally humorless and irritable, he looked particularly austere on this afternoon.

Finally, Wright broke the silence.

"He's called twice already this afternoon," the Director snapped at Cuthbert. "I can't avoid him forever. Sooner or later he's going to raise a stink about being denied access to the crates. He may well drag this Mbwun business into it. There's going to be controversy."

Cuthbert nodded. "As long as it's later rather than sooner. When the exhibition is open and running, with forty thousand visitors a day and favorable notices in all the periodicals, let him bloody well raise hell about whatever he likes."

There was another long silence.

"I hate to play devil's advocate," Cuthbert continued at last, "but when the dust settles from all this, you, Winston, are going to have the necessary increase in attendance. These rumors of a curse may be annoying now, but when things are safe again, everyone's going to want a vicarious shudder and some scandal. Everyone's going to want to go inside the Museum and see for themselves. It's good for business. I'm telling you, Winston, we couldn't have arranged it better ourselves."

Wright frowned at the Assistant Director. "Rumors of a curse. Maybe it's true. Look at all the disasters that have followed that ugly little figurine halfway around the world." He laughed mirthlessly.

"You're not serious," said Cuthbert.

"I'll tell you what I'm serious about," Wright snapped. "I don't want to hear you talking like that again. Frock has important friends. If he starts complaining to them . . . well, you know how stories grow and spread. They'll think you're withholding information. They'll think you're banking on these killings bringing people in to see the exhibition. How's *that* for publicity, eh?"

"Agreed," Cuthbert said with a wintry smile. "But I don't need to remind you that, if this exhibition doesn't open on time, everything becomes academic. Frock must be kept on a short leash. Now, he's sending hired help to do his dirty work. One of them tried to get into the Secure Vault less than an hour ago."

"Who?" Wright demanded.

"The security guard made a right hash of it," Cuthbert replied. "But he got the fellow's first name—Bill."

"Bill?" Rickman sat up.

"Yes, I think that was it," Cuthbert said, turning to the public relations director. "Isn't that the name of the journalist who's doing the book on my exhibition? He's your man, isn't he? Is he under control? I hear he's been asking a lot of questions."

"Absolutely," said Rickman, a bright smile on her face. "We've had our ups and downs with him, but he's toeing the line now. Control the sources, and you've controlled the journalist, as I always say."

"Toeing the line, is he?" Wright said. "Then why did you feel it necessary to send that mail message round to half the western world this morning, reminding them not to talk to strangers?"

Mrs. Rickman quickly held up a lacquered hand. "He's been taken care of."

"You'd damned well better make sure of that," Cuthbert said. "You've been in on this little party from the beginning, Lavinia. I'm sure you don't want this journalist of yours digging up any dirty knickers."

There came a hiss of static over the intercom, and a voice said: "Mr. Pendergast to see you."

"Send him in," said Wright. He looked sourly at the others. "This is it."

Pendergast appeared in the doorway, a newspaper tucked under one arm. He paused for a moment.

"My, this *is* a charming tableau," he said. "Dr. Wright, thank you for seeing me again. Dr. Cuthbert, always a pleasure. And you are Lavinia Rickman, ma'am, are you not?"

"Yes," Rickman replied, smiling primly.

"Mr. Pendergast," said Wright, with a small, formal smile. "Please take any seat you wish."

"Thank you, Doctor, but I prefer to stand." Pendergast moved over to the massive fireplace and leaned against the mantle, arms folded.

"Have you come to make a report? No doubt you've asked for this meeting to inform us of an arrest."

"No," said Pendergast. "I'm sorry, no arrests. Frankly, Dr. Wright, we've made very little progress. Despite what Ms. Rickman has been telling the newspapers."

He showed them the newspaper's headline: ARREST NEAR IN "MUSEUM BEAST" MURDERS.

There was a short silence. Pendergast folded the paper and carefully placed it on the mantelpiece.

"What's the problem?" asked Wright. "I don't understand what's taking so long."

"There are many problems, as you are no doubt aware," said Pendergast. "But I'm not really here to brief you on the case. It's enough if I remind you simply that a dangerous serial killer remains loose in the Museum. We have no reason to believe he has stopped killing. As far as we know, all his killings have been nocturnal. In other words, after 5 P.M. As the special agent in charge of this investigation, I'm regretfully informing you that the curfew we've set up must remain in force until such time as the killer is found. There will be no exceptions."

"The opening. . . ." Rickman bleated.

"The opening will have to be postponed. It may be for a week, it may be for a month. I can't make any promises, I'm afraid. I'm very sorry."

Wright stood up, his face livid. "You said the opening could go on as scheduled provided there were no more killings. That was our *agreement*."

"I made no agreement with you, Doctor," Pendergast said mildly. "I'm afraid we are no closer to catching the murderer than we were at the beginning of the week." He gestured toward the newspaper on the mantle. "Headlines like these make people complacent, incautious.

The opening would probably be very well attended. Thousands of people, in the Museum after dark . . ." He shook his head. "I have no other choice."

Wright stared at the agent in disbelief. "Because of your incompetence, you expect us to delay the opening, and do the Museum irreparable harm in the process? The answer is no."

Pendergast, unruffled, walked forward into the center of the room. "Forgive me, Dr. Wright, if I didn't make myself clear. I'm not here to ask your permission; I'm merely notifying you of my decision."

"Right," the Director answered, his voice shaking. "I see. You can't do your own job, but you still want to tell me how to do mine. Do you have any idea what delaying the opening would do to our exhibition? Do you know what kind of message it would send to the public? Well, Pendergast, I'm not going to allow it."

Pendergast stared steadily at Wright. "Any unauthorized personnel found on the premises after five o'clock will be arrested and charged with trespassing at a scene of crime. This is a misdemeanor. Second violations will be charged with obstruction of justice. Which is a felony, Dr. Wright. I trust I make myself sufficiently clear?"

"The only thing that's clear right now is your path to the door," Wright said, his voice rising. "It's unobstructed. Please take it."

Pendergast nodded. "Gentlemen. Ma'am." Then he turned around and moved silently out of the room.

Closing the door quietly, Pendergast stopped for a moment in the Director's outer office. Then, staring at the door, he quoted,

> So I return rebuk'd to my content,
> And gain by ills thrice more than I have spent.

Wright's executive secretary stopped her gum chewing in mid-snap. "Howzat?" she inquired.

"No, Shakespeare," Pendergast replied, heading for the elevator.

Inside, Wright fumbled at the telephone with shaking hands.

"What the hell happens now?" exploded Cuthbert. "I'll be damned if a bloody policeman's going to boot us out of our own Museum."

"Cuthbert, be quiet," said Wright. Then he spoke into the handset. "Get me Albany, right away."

There was a silence while he was put on hold. Wright looked over the receiver at Cuthbert and Rickman, controlling his heavy breathing with an effort. "Time to call in some favors," he said. "We'll see who has the final word here: some inbred albino from the Delta, or the Director of the largest natural history museum in the world."

= 32 =

The vegetation here is very unusual. The cycads and ferns look almost primordial. Too bad there isn't time for more careful study. We've used a particularly resilient variety as packing material for the crates; feel free to let Jörgensen take a look, if he's interested.

I fully expect to be with you at the Explorer's Club a month from now, celebrating our success with a brace of dry martinis and a good Macanudo. Until then, I know I can entrust this material and my reputation to you.

Your colleague,

> Whittlesey

Smithback looked up from the letter. "We can't stay here. Let's go to my office."

His cubbyhole lay deep in a maze of overflow offices on the Museum's ground level. The honeycomb passages, full of noise and bustle, seemed a refreshing change to Margo after the damp, echoing basement corridors outside the Secure Area. They walked past a large green dumpster overflowing with back issues of the Museum's magazine. Outside Smithback's office, a large bulletin board was plastered with a variety of irate letters from subscribers, for the amusement of the magazine staff.

Once before, hot on the trail of an issue of *Science* long overdue from the periodical library, Margo had penetrated Smithback's messy lair. It was as she remembered it: his desk a riot of photocopied articles, half-finished letters, Chinese take-out menus, and numerous books and journals the Museum's libraries were no doubt very eager to find.

"Have a seat," Smithback said, pushing a two-foot stack of paper brusquely off a chair. He closed the door, then walked around his desk to an ancient bentwood rocker. Paper crackled beneath his feet.

"Okay," he said in a low tone. "Now, you're sure the journal wasn't there?"

"I told you, the only crate I had a chance to look at was the one Whittlesey packed himself. But it wouldn't have been in the others."

Smithback examined the letter again. "Who's this Montague the thing's addressed to?" he asked.

"Don't know," Margo replied.

"How about Jörgensen?"

"Haven't heard of him, either."

Smithback pulled down the Museum's telephone listing from a shelf. "No Montague here," he murmured, flipping pages. "Of course, that might be a first name for all we know. Aha! Here's Jörgensen. Botany. Says he's retired. How come he still has an office?"

"Not unusual in this place," Margo replied. "Independently wealthy people with little else to fill up their time. Where's his office?"

"Section forty-one, fourth floor," Smithback said, closing the book and dropping it on his desk. "Near the herbarium." He stood up. "Let's go."

"Wait a minute, Smithback. It's almost four o'clock. I should call Frock and let him know what . . ."

"Later," Smithback said, making for the door. "Come on, Lotus Blossom. My journalist's nose hasn't picked up a decent scent all afternoon."

Jörgensen's office was a small, windowless laboratory with a high ceiling. It held none of the plants or floral specimens Margo expected to see in a botanist's lab. In fact, the room was empty except for a large workbench, a chair, and a coat rack. A drawer of the workbench was open, exposing a variety of worn tools. Jörgensen was bending over the workbench, fiddling with a small motor.

"Dr. Jörgensen?" Smithback asked.

The old man turned and gazed at Smithback. He was almost completely bald, with bushy white eyebrows overhanging intense eyes the color of bleached denim. He was bony and stooped but Margo thought he must be at least six feet four.

"Yes?" he said in a quiet voice.

Before Margo could stop him, Smithback handed Jörgensen the letter.

The man began reading, then started visibly. Without taking his eyes from the letter, he reached around for the battered chair and carefully eased himself into it.

"Where did you get this?" he demanded when he had finished.

Margo and Smithback looked at each other.

"It's genuine," Smithback said.

Jörgensen stared at them. Then he handed the letter back to Smithback. "I don't know anything about this," he said.

There was a silence. "It came from the crate Julian Whittlesey sent back from the Amazon expedition seven years ago," Smithback prompted hopefully.

Jörgensen continued to stare at them. After a few moments, he returned to his motor.

The two watched him tinker for a moment. "I'm sorry we interrupted your work," Margo said at last. "Perhaps this isn't a good time."

"What work?" asked Jörgensen, without turning around.

"Whatever that is you're doing," Margo replied.

Jörgensen suddenly barked out a laugh. "This?" he said, turning to face them again. "This isn't work. This is just a broken vacuum cleaner. Since my wife died, I've had to do the housework myself. Darn thing blew up on me the other day. I only brought it in here because this is where all my tools are. I don't have much work to do anymore."

"About that letter, sir—" Margo pressed.

Jörgensen shifted in the creaky chair and leaned back, looking at the ceiling. "I hadn't known it existed. The double-arrow motif served as the Whittlesey family crest. And that's Whittlesey's handwriting, all right. It brings back memories."

"What kind?" asked Smithback eagerly.

Jörgensen looked over at him, his brows contracting with irritation. "Nothing that's any of your business," he said tartly. "Or at least, I haven't heard just why it might be your business."

Margo shot Smithback a shut-up look. "Dr. Jörgensen," she began, "I'm a graduate student working with Dr. Frock. My colleague here is a journalist. Dr. Frock believes that the Whittlesey expedition, and the crates that were sent back, have a link to the Museum murders."

"A *curse?*" said Jörgensen, raising his eyebrows theatrically.

"No, not a curse," said Margo.

"I'm glad you haven't bought into that one. There's no curse. Unless you define a curse as a mixture of greed, human folly, and scientific jealousy. You don't need Mbwun to explain . . ."

He stopped. "Why are you so interested?" he asked suspiciously.

"To explain what?" Smithback interjected.

Jörgensen looked at him with distaste. "Young man, if you open your mouth one more time I'm going to ask you to leave."

Smithback narrowed his eyes but remained silent.

Margo wondered if she should go into detail about Frock's theories, the claw marks, the damaged crate, but decided not to. "We're interested because we feel that there's a connection here that no one is paying attention to. Not the police, and not the Museum. You were mentioned in this letter. We hoped you might be able to tell us more about this expedition."

Jörgensen held out a gnarled hand. "May I see that again?"

Reluctantly, Smithback complied.

Jörgensen's eyes passed over the letter again, hungrily, as if sucking in memories. "There was a time," he murmured, "I would have been reluctant to talk about this. Maybe afraid would be a better word. Certain parties might have sought to fire me." He shrugged. "But when you get as old as I am, you don't have much to be afraid of. Except maybe being alone."

He nodded slowly to Margo, clutching the letter. "I would have been on that expedition, if it hadn't been for Maxwell."

"He's mentioned in the letter, too! Who's he?" asked Smithback.

Jörgensen shot him a look. "I've knocked down bigger journalists than you," he snapped. "Now I said, be quiet. I'm talking to the lady."

He turned to Margo again.

"Maxwell was one of the leaders of the expedition. Maxwell and Whittlesey. That was the first mistake, letting Maxwell muscle his way in, making the two of them coleaders. They were at odds right from the beginning. Neither one had full control. Maxwell's gain was my loss—he decided they didn't have room for a botanist on the expedition, and that was it for me. But Whittlesey was even less happy about it than I. Having Maxwell along put his hidden agenda at risk."

"What was that?" Margo asked.

"To find the Kothoga tribe. There were rumors of an undiscovered tribe living on a *tepui*, a vast tableland above the rain forest. Although the area had not been scientifically explored, the consensus was that the tribe was extinct, that only relics remained. Whittlesey didn't believe this. He wanted to be their discoverer. The only problem was, the local government denied him a permit to study on the *tepui*. Said it was reserved for their own scientists. Yankee go home."

Jörgensen snorted, shook his head.

"Well, what it was really being reserved for was depredation, land rape. Of course, the local government had heard the same rumors Whittlesey had. If there *were* Indians up there, the government didn't want them in the way of timbering and mining. So anyway, the expedition had to approach from the north. A much less convenient route, but away from the restricted area. And they were forbidden to ascend the *tepui* itself."

"Did the Kothoga still exist?" Margo asked.

Jörgensen slowly shook his head. "We'll never know. The government found something on top that *tepui*. Maybe gold, platinum, placer deposits. You can detect lots of things with satellites these days. Anyway, the *tepui* was fired from the air in the spring of '88."

"Fired?" Margo asked.

"Burned clear with napalm," Jörgensen said. "Unusual and expensive to do it that way. Apparently, the fire got out of hand, spread, burned uncontrollably for months. Then they built a big road in there, coming up the easy way from the south. They hauled in Japanese hydraulic mining equipment and literally washed away huge sections of the mountain. No doubt they leeched the gold and platinum or whatever with cyanic compounds, then just let the poison run into the rivers. There's nothing, I mean *nothing*, left. That's why the Museum never sent a second expedition down to search for the remains of the first." He cleared his throat.

"That's terrible," breathed Margo.

Jörgensen gazed up with his unsettling cerulean eyes. "Yes. It *is* terrible. Of course, you won't read about it in the *Superstition* exhibition."

Smithback held up one hand while slipping out his microcassette recorder with the other. "Excuse me, may I—?"

"No, you may *not* record this. This is not for attribution. Not for quotation. Not for anything. I've received a memo to that effect just this morning, as you probably know. This is for me: I haven't been able to talk about this for years, and I'm going to do it now, just this once. So keep quiet and listen."

There was a silence.

"Where was I?" Jörgensen resumed. "Oh, yes. So Whittlesey had no permit to ascend the *tepui*. And Maxwell was the consummate bureaucrat. He was determined to make Whittlesey play by the rules.

Well, when you get out there in the jungle two hundred miles from any kind of government. . . . What rules?" He cackled.

"I doubt if anybody knows exactly what *did* happen out there. I got the story from Montague, and he pieced it together from Maxwell's telegrams. Not exactly an unbiased source."

"Montague?" Smithback interrupted.

"In any case," Jörgensen continued, ignoring Smithback, "it appears Maxwell stumbled upon some unbelievable botany. Around the base of the *tepui*, ninety-nine percent of the plant species were absolutely new to science. They found strange, primitive ferns and monocotyledons that looked like throwbacks to the Mesozoic Era. Even though Maxwell was a physical anthropologist, he went crazy over the strange vegetation. They filled up crate after crate with odd specimens. That was when Maxwell found those seed pods."

"How important were *they?*"

"They were from a living fossil. Not unlike the discovery of the coelacanth in the 1930s: a species from an entire phylum they thought had become extinct in the Carboniferous. An entire *phylum.*"

"Did these seed pods look like eggs?" asked Margo.

"I couldn't say. But Montague got a look at them, and he told me they were hard as hell. They'd need to be buried deep in the highly acidic soil of a rain forest in order to germinate. I imagine they're still in those crates."

"Dr. Frock thought they *were* eggs."

"Frock should stick to paleontology. He's a brilliant man, but erratic. At any rate, Maxwell and Whittlesey had a falling out. Not unexpected. Maxwell couldn't care less about botany, but he knew a rarity when he saw one. He wanted to get back to the Museum with his seed pods. He learned that Whittlesey intended to scale the *tepui* and look for the Kothoga, and it alarmed him. He was afraid the crates would be seized at dockside and he wouldn't get his precious pods out. They split up. Whittlesey went on deeper into the jungle, up the *tepui*, and was never seen again.

"When Maxwell reached the coast with the rest of the expedition, he sent back a stream of telegrams to the Museum, lambasting Whittlesey and telling his side of the story. Then he and the rest were killed in that plane crash. Luckily, arrangements had been made to ship the crates separately, or maybe it *wasn't* so lucky. Took the Museum a year to untangle the red tape, get the crates back to New York. Nobody seemed in a big hurry to do it." He rolled his eyes in disgust.

"You mentioned somebody named Montague?" Margo asked quietly.

"Montague," Jörgensen said, his eyes looking past Margo. "He was a young Ph.D. candidate at the Museum. Anthropology. Whittlesey's protégé. Needless to say, that didn't exactly put him in the Museum's good graces after Maxwell's telegrams arrived. None of us who'd been friendly with Whittlesey were ever really trusted after that."

"What happened to Montague?"

Jörgensen hesitated. "I don't know," he replied finally. "He just disappeared one day. Never came back."

"And the crates?" Margo pressed.

"Montague had been terribly anxious to see those crates, especially Whittlesey's. But, as I said, he was out of favor, and had been taken off the project. In point of fact, there *was* no project anymore. The whole expedition had been such a disaster that the top brass just wanted to forget anything had happened. When the crates finally arrived, they sat, unopened. Most of the documentation and provenance had burned up in the crash. Supposedly, there was a journal of Whittlesey's, but I never saw it. In any case, Montague complained and pleaded, and in the end they gave him the job of doing the initial curating. And then he just up and left."

"What do you mean, left?" Smithback asked.

Jörgensen looked at him, as if deciding whether or not to answer the question. "He simply walked out of the Museum and never came back. I understand his apartment and all his clothes were abandoned. His family instituted a search and found nothing. But he was a rather strange character. Most people assumed he'd gone off to Nepal or Thailand to find himself."

"But there were rumors," Smithback said. It was a statement, not a question.

Jörgensen laughed. "Of course there were rumors! Aren't there always? Rumors that he embezzled money, rumors that he ran off with a gangster's wife, rumors that he'd been murdered and dumped in the East River. But he was such a nonentity in the Museum that most people forgot about him in a few weeks."

"Rumors that the Museum Beast got him?" Smithback asked.

Jörgensen's smile faded. "Not exactly. But it caused all the rumors of the curse to resurface. Now everyone, they said, who had come in contact with the crates had died. Some of the guards and cafeteria employees—you know those types—said Whittlesey had robbed a temple, that there was something in the crate, a relic with a terrible curse on it. They said the curse followed the relic all the way back to the Museum."

"Didn't you want to study the plants that Maxwell sent back?" Smithback asked. "I mean, you're a botanist, aren't you?"

"Young man, you know nothing of science. There is no such thing as a *botanist* per se. I have no interest in the paleobotany of angiosperms. That whole thing was way out of my field. My specialty is the coevolution of plants and viruses. Or *was*," he said with a certain irony.

"But Whittlesey wanted you to take a look at the plants he sent back as packing material," Smithback continued.

"I have no idea why," Jörgensen said. "This is the first I've heard of it. I never saw this letter before." With a certain reluctance, he handed it back to Margo. "I'd say it's a fake, except for the handwriting and the motif."

There was a silence. "You haven't said what *you* thought about Montague's disappearance," Margo said at last.

Jörgensen rubbed the bridge of his nose and looked at the floor. "It frightened me."

"Why?"

There was a long silence. "I'm not sure," he finally said. "Montague once had a financial emergency and had to borrow money from me. He was very conscientious and went through great difficulties paying it back. It didn't seem in character for him to just disappear like that. The last time I saw him, he was about to do an inventory of the crates. He was very excited about it." He looked up at Margo. "I'm not a superstitious man. I'm a scientist. Like I said, I don't believe in curses and that sort of thing . . ." his voice trailed off.

"But—?" Smithback prodded.

The old man shot a glance at Smithback. "Very well," he glowered. Then he leaned back in his chair and looked at the ceiling. "I told you that Julian Whittlesey was my friend," he said. "Before he left, Whittlesey had collected all the stories he could find about the Kothoga tribe. Mostly from lowland tribes living downstream, Yanomamo and the like. I remember him telling me one story the day before he left. The Kothoga, according to a Yanomamo informant, had made a deal with a being called Zilashkee. This was a creature like our Mephistopheles, but even more extreme: all the evil and death in the world emanated from this thing, which slithered around on the peak of the *tepui*.

Or so the legend went. Anyway, according to their arrangement, the Kothoga would get the Zilashkee's child for a servant in return for killing and eating all of their own children, and vowing forevermore to worship him and only him. When the Kothoga had finished their grisly task, the Zilashkee sent his child to them. But the beast proceeded to run rampant through the tribe, murdering and eating people. When the Kothoga complained, the Zilashkee laughed and said: *What did you expect? I am evil.* Finally, using magic or herbal spells or some such thing, the tribe managed to control the beast. It couldn't be killed, you see. So the Zilashkee child remained under the control of the Kothoga, and they used it to do their own malignant bidding. But using it was always a dangerous proposition. The legend says that the Kothoga have been looking for a way to get rid of it ever since."

Jörgensen looked down at the disassembled motor. "That was the story Whittlesey told me. When I heard about the plane crash, the death of Whittlesey, the disappearance of Montague . . . well, I couldn't help but think the Kothoga had finally managed to get rid of Zilashkee's child."

Picking up a piece of the machine, the old botanist turned it over in his hands with a distant expression. "Whittlesey told me the name of the Zilashkee's child was Mbwun. He Who Walks On All Fours." And he dropped the piece with a clank and grinned.

= 33 =

As closing drew near, the visitors began to trickle out toward the Museum exits. The Museum shop—located directly inside the south entrance—did a brisk business.

In the marble hallways leading away from the south entrance, the sounds of conversation and the drumming of feet could be clearly heard. In the Hall of the Heavens near the West entrance, where the opening party for the new exhibition was to be held, the noise was fainter, echoing inside the huge dome like a vaguely remembered dream. And deeper within the Museum, as more laboratories, antique lecture halls, storage vaults, and book-lined offices interposed themselves, the sounds of visitors did not penetrate. The long corridors were dark and silent.

Within the Butterfield Observatory, the noise and bustle could just as well have been on another planet. The staffers, making the most of the curfew, had gone home early. George Moriarty's office, like all six floors of the observatory, was deathly quiet.

Moriarty stood behind his desk, a balled fist pressed tightly against his mouth. "Damn," he mumbled.

Suddenly, one foot lashed out in frustration, the heel slamming against a file cabinet behind him and knocking a pile of papers onto the floor. "Damn!" he howled, this time in pain, as he sank into his chair and began rubbing his ankle.

Slowly, the pain lifted, and with it, his funk. Sighing heavily, he looked around the room. "Jeez, George, you always manage to screw things up, don't you?" he murmured.

He was hopeless socially, he might as well admit it to himself. Everything he did to catch Margo's attention, everything he did to gain her favor, seemed to backfire. What he'd said about her father was about as tactful as a machine gun.

Suddenly, he swiveled toward his terminal and typed in a command. He'd send her an e-mail message, maybe repair some of his damage. He paused a moment, composing, then began to type.

HI, MARGO! JUST CURIOUS TO KNOW IF YOU

Abruptly, Moriarty hit a key, purging the message. He'd probably just mess things up even worse.

He sat for a moment, staring at the blank screen. He knew of only one surefire method to ease his hurt: a treasure hunt.

Many of the *Superstition* exhibition's most prized artifacts were the direct result of his treasure hunts. Moriarty had a deep love for the Museum's vast collections, and he was more familiar with its obscure and secret corners than many longtime staffers. Shy, Moriarty had few friends and often passed his time researching and locating long-forgotten relics from the Museum's storerooms. It gave him a sense of worth and fulfillment that he had been unable to obtain from others.

He turned once again to the keyboard, opening the Museum's accession database and moving casually yet deliberately through its records. He knew his way around the database, knew its shortcuts and back doors, like an experienced riverboat captain knew the contours of a riverbed.

In a few minutes, his fingers slowed. Here was a region of the database he hadn't explored before: a trove of Sumerian artifacts, discovered in the early twenties but never fully researched. Carefully, he targeted first a collection, then a subcollection, then individual artifacts. This looked interesting: a series of clay tablets, early examples of Sumerian writing. The original collector believed they dealt with religious rituals. Moriarty read over the annotated entries, nodding to himself. Maybe they could use these in the exhibition. There was still room for a few more artifacts in one of the smaller miscellaneous galleries.

He checked his sundial watch: almost five. Still, he knew where the tablets were stored. If they looked promising, he could show them to Cuthbert tomorrow morning and get his approval. He could work up

the display between the Friday night celebration and the public opening. He quickly jotted a few notes, then flicked off his computer.

The sound of the terminal being snapped into darkness sounded like
a pistol shot in the lonely office. Finger still on the power switch,
Moriarty paused. Then he stood up, tucked his shirt inside his trousers,
and—favoring his bruised heel slightly—left the office, closing the
door quietly behind him.

= 34 =

Down in the temporary command post, D'Agosta froze in the act of rapping on Pendergast's window. He peered in to get a better look.

Some tall guy in an ugly suit was moving around Pendergast's office. His face looked sweaty and sunburnt and he swaggered like he owned the place, picking up papers on the desk, laying them down somewhere else, jingling his pocket change.

"Hey, pal," D'Agosta said, opening the door and walking in, "that's FBI property. If you're waiting for Mr. Pendergast, how about doing it outside?"

The man turned. His eyes were small and narrow, and pissed off.

"From now on, ah, *Lieutenant*," he said, staring at the badge hanging from D'Agosta's belt as if trying to read the number, "you'll speak respectfully to the FBI personnel around here. Of which I am now in charge. Special Agent Coffey."

"Well, Special Agent Coffey, as far as I know, and until someone tells me different, Mr. Pendergast is in charge here, and you're messing with his desk."

Coffey gave him a thin smile, reached into his jacket, and pulled out an envelope.

D'Agosta examined the letter inside. It was from Washington, putting the New York Field Office of the FBI, and one Special Agent Spencer Coffey, in charge of the case. Stapled to the directive were two memos. One, from the Governor's office, formally demanded the change and accepted full responsibility for the transfer of power.

The second, with a United States Senate letterhead, D'Agosta folded up without bothering to read.

He handed the envelope back. "So you guys finally snuck in the back door."

"When will Pendergast be back, Lieutenant?" said Coffey, sliding the envelope back into his pocket.

"How would I know?" said D'Agosta. "While you're poking through his desk there, maybe you'd like to check his appointment book."

Before Coffey could respond, Pendergast's voice sounded from outside the office. "Ah, Agent Coffey! How delightful to see you."

Coffey once again reached for the envelope.

"No need," Pendergast said. "I know why you're here." He sat down behind his desk. "Lieutenant D'Agosta, please make yourself comfortable."

D'Agosta, noting only one other chair in the office, sat down with a grin. Watching Pendergast in action was something he'd grown to enjoy.

"A madman is apparently loose in the Museum, Mr. Coffey," Pendergast said. "Therefore, Lieutenant D'Agosta and I have both come to the conclusion that tomorrow night's opening party must not be allowed to proceed. This murderer works at night. He's well overdue for another attack. We cannot be responsible for more people being killed because the Museum is kept open for, shall we say, pecuniary reasons."

"Yeah," said Coffey, "well, you're not responsible anymore. My orders are that the opening proceeds as planned, and on schedule. We're bolstering the police presence with additional field agents. This place is going to be more secure than the Pentagon lavatory. And I'll tell you something else, Pendergast: once this little party is over and done with and the big shots have gone home, we're gonna wrap this sucker. You're supposed to be hot shit, but you know something? I'm not impressed. You've had four days and all you've caught is your own dick. We're through wasting time."

Pendergast smiled. "Yes, I expected as much. If that's your decision, so be it. You should know, however, that I will be sending a formal memorandum to the Director, stating my own views on the matter."

"Do what you want," Coffey said, "but do it on your own time. Meanwhile, my people will be setting up shop down the hall. I'll expect a briefing from you at curfew."

"My closing report is already prepared," Pendergast said mildly. "Now, Mr. Coffey, is there anything else?"

"Yes," Coffey said. "I expect full cooperation from you, Pendergast." He left the door open behind him.

D'Agosta watched him walk down the hall. "He looks a lot more pissed off now than before you came in," he said. Then he turned toward Pendergast. "You're not just going to give in to that jerk-off, are you?"

Pendergast smiled. "Vincent, I'm afraid this had grown inevitable. In a sense, I'm surprised it didn't happen sooner. This isn't the first time I've trod on Wright's toes this week. Why should I fight it? This way, at least, no one can accuse us of lack of cooperation."

"But I thought you had pull." D'Agosta tried to keep the disappointment out of his voice.

Pendergast spread his hands. "I have quite a bit of pull, as you put it. But remember, I'm off my turf. Because the killings were similar to those I investigated in New Orleans several years ago, I had good cause to be here—as long as there was no controversy, no call for local involvement. But I knew that Dr. Wright and the Governor had been at Brown together. With the Governor making a formal request for FBI intervention, there's only one possible outcome."

"But what about the case?" D'Agosta asked. "Coffey's gonna build on all the work you've done, and take the credit himself."

"You assume there's going to be credit here at all," Pendergast said. "I have a bad feeling about this opening, Lieutenant. A very bad feeling. I've known Coffey for a long time, and he can be relied upon to make a bad situation worse. But you notice, Vincent, that he did *not* send me packing. That he can't do."

"Don't tell me you're happy to lose the responsibility," said D'Agosta. "My main goal in life may be to keep the mower off my ass, but I always figured you different."

"Vincent, I'm surprised at you," Pendergast said. "It has nothing to do with shirking responsibility. However, this arrangement does allow me a certain degree of freedom. It's true that Coffey has the final say, but his ability to direct *my* actions is limited. The only way I could come up here initially was if I took charge of the case. That tends to make one more circumspect. Now, I'll be able to follow my own instincts." He sat back in his chair, fixing D'Agosta with his pale stare. "I would continue to welcome your help. I may need someone inside the department to help expedite a few things."

D'Agosta looked thoughtful for a few moments. "There's one thing I could tell about this Coffey right from the get-go," he said.

"What is that?"

"The guy's dipped in green shit."

"Ah, Vincent," said Pendergast, "you have such a colorful way with words."

= 35 =

Friday

The office, Smithback noted glumly, looked exactly the same: not a knickknack out of place. He slumped in his chair, feeling a strong sense of déjà vu.

Rickman returned from her secretary's office carrying a slim file, the ubiquitous prim smile frozen on her face. "Tonight's the night!" she said cheerfully. "Planning to attend?"

"Yeah, sure," said Smithback.

She passed him the file. "Read this, Bill," she said, her voice a little less pleasant.

NEW YORK MUSEUM OF NATURAL HISTORY
INTERNAL MEMORANDUM

To: William Smithback Jr.
From: Lavinia Rickman
Re: Untitled work on Superstition Exhibition

Effective immediately, and until further notice, your work at the Museum will be governed by the following provisions:

1. All interviews conducted for the Work in Progress are to be done in my presence.
2. Recording of interviews by you, or the taking of notes during interviews by you, is forbidden. In the interests of timeliness and consistency, I will take on the responsi-

bility of note-taking myself, and pass the edited scripts
on to you for inclusion in the Work in Progress.

3. Discussion of Museum matters with employees, or any
persons encountered upon the Museum grounds, is pro-
hibited without first obtaining my written approval.
Please sign in the space provided below to acknowledge
your understanding of and agreement to these provisions.

Smithback read it twice, then looked up.

"Well?" she asked, tilting her head. "What do you think?"

"Let me get this straight," said Smithback. "I'm not even allowed
to talk to someone at, say, lunch without your permission?"

"About Museum matters. That is correct," Rickman said, patting
the paisley scarf around her neck.

"Why? Wasn't that memo you sent around yesterday a big enough
ball and chain?"

"Bill, you know why. You've proven yourself unreliable."

"How so?" Smithback said in a strangled voice.

"I understand you've been running wild all over the Museum, talking
to people you have no business with, asking absurd questions about
matters that do not pertain to the new exhibition. If you think you
can gather information about the . . . ah . . . recent circumstances that
have occurred, then I must remind you of paragraph seventeen of your
contract, which forbids the use of any information not authorized by
myself. Nothing, I repeat, *nothing* related to the unfortunate situation
will be authorized."

Smithback sat up. "Unfortunate situation!" he exploded. "Why
don't you call it what it is: murder!"

"Please don't raise your voice in my office," Rickman said.

"You hired me to write a book, not crank out a three-hundred-page
press release. There's been a string of brutal murders in the week before
the Museum's biggest opening ever. You mean to tell me that's not
part of the story?"

"I and I alone define what will be in this book and what will not.
Understood?"

"No."

Rickman stood up. "This is growing tiresome. You will either sign
this document now, or you will be terminated."

"Terminated? What, do you mean shot or fired?"

"I will not stand for that kind of levity in my office. Either sign this agreement, or I will accept your resignation immediately."

"Fine," Smithback said. "I'll simply take my manuscript to a commercial publisher. You need this book as much as I do. And you and I both know I could get a huge advance for the inside story on the Museum murders. And, believe me, I know the inside story. All of it."

Rickman's face was ghastly, yet still she held her smile. Her knuckles whitened against her desk.

"That would be a violation of your contract," she said slowly. "The Museum has the Wall Street law firm of Daniels, Soller and McCabe on retainer. Undoubtedly you've heard of them. Should you take such action, you would instantly be party to a breach of contract lawsuit, as would your agent and any publisher foolish enough to sign a contract with you. We'd bring everything we have to bear on this case, and I wouldn't be surprised if, after you lose, you never find work in your chosen field again."

"This is a gross violation of my First Amendment rights," Smithback managed to croak out.

"Not at all. We would merely be seeking remedy for breach of contract. Nothing heroic in it for you, and it wouldn't even make the *Times*. If you are really thinking of taking this course of action, Bill, I'd consult a good lawyer first and show him the contract you signed with us. I'm sure he'll tell you it's as airtight as they come. Or if you'd prefer, I'll accept your resignation right now." She opened a desk drawer and extracted a second piece of paper, leaving the drawer open as she did so.

Her intercom buzzed noisily. "Mrs. Rickman? Dr. Wright on line one."

Rickman picked up the telephone. "Yes, Winston. What? The *Post* again? Yes, I'll talk to them. You sent for Ippolito? Good."

She hung up and went to the office door. "Make sure Ippolito's on his way to the Director's office," she said to her secretary. "As for you, Bill, I don't have any more time to bandy civilities. If you won't sign the agreement, then pack your things and get out."

Smithback had grown very quiet. All of a sudden, he smiled. "Mrs. Rickman, I see your point."

She leaned toward him, simpering, eyes bright. "And—?" she prompted.

"I'll agree to the restrictions," he said.

Rickman moved back behind her desk, triumphant. "Bill, I'm very glad I won't need to use this." She put the second sheet of paper back in her drawer and closed it. "I suppose you're intelligent enough to know you have no choice."

Meeting her eyes, Smithback reached for the folder. "You don't mind if I read this over again before I sign, do you?"

Rickman hesitated. "No, I suppose not. Although you'll find it says exactly what it did the first time you read it. There's no room for misinterpretation, so please don't look for gray areas." She looked around the office, swept up her pocketbook, and headed for the door. "Bill, I'm warning you. Don't forget to sign it. Please follow me out, and give the signed document to my secretary. You'll be sent a copy."

Smithback's lips pursed in distaste as he watched her fanny sway under the pleated skirt. He gave a final, furtive glance toward the outer office. Then he quickly slid open the drawer Rickman had just closed and extracted a small object, which he slipped into his jacket pocket. Closing the drawer, he looked around once again and started for the exit.

Then, moving back to the desk, he grabbed the memo and scrawled an illegible signature across the bottom. He handed it to the secretary on the way out. "Save that signature, it'll be valuable someday," he said over his shoulder, letting the door close with a bang.

Margo was hanging up her phone as Smithback walked in. Once again, she had the lab to herself: her office mate, the preparator, had apparently taken a sudden extended vacation.

"I just talked to Frock," she said. "He was pretty disappointed that we didn't find anything more in the crate, and that I didn't get a chance to look for any remaining seed pods. I think he was hoping for evidence of a creature. I wanted to tell him about the letter and Jörgensen, but he said he couldn't talk. I think Cuthbert was in there with him."

"Probably asking about that Request for Access form he sent up," Smithback said. "Doing his Torquemada imitation." He gestured toward the door. "How come this was unlocked?"

Margo looked surprised. "Oh. Guess I forgot again."

"Mind if I lock it, just in case?" He fumbled with the door, then, grinning, he reached into his jacket and slowly withdrew a small, battered book, its leather cover stamped with two overlapping arrowheads. He held it up like a trophy fish for her inspection.

Margo's look of curiosity turned to astonishment. "My God! Is that the journal?"

Smithback nodded proudly.

"How did you get it? *Where* did you get it?"

"Rickman's office," he said. "I had to make a terrible sacrifice for it. I signed a piece of paper forbidding me ever to speak to you again."

"You're joking."

"Only partly. Anyway, at one point in the torture she opened her desk drawer, and I saw this little beat-up book. Looked like a diary. Seemed like a strange thing for Rickman to keep in her desk. Then I remembered your story about how she'd supposedly borrowed the journal." He nodded smugly. "As I always suspected. So I nicked it as I was leaving her office."

He opened the journal. "Now be quiet, Lotus Blossom. Daddy's going to read you a bedtime story."

Margo listened as Smithback began to read; slowly at first, but faster as he got the hang of the sloppy handwriting and frequent abbreviations. Most of the early entries were very short; cursory sentences giving a few details about the day's weather and the expedition's position.

> Aug. 31. Rain all night—Canned bacon for breakfast—Something wrong with helicopter this morning, had to waste day doing nothing. Maxwell insufferable. Carlos having more trouble with Hosta Gilbao—demanding additional wages for . . .

"This is boring," said Smithback, interrupting his reading. "Who cares that they ate canned bacon for breakfast?"

"Keep going," urged Margo.

"There really isn't that much here," Smithback said, paging ahead. "Guess Whittlesey was a man of few words. Oh, God. I hope I didn't sign my life away for nothing."

The journal described the expedition's progress deeper and deeper into the rain forest. The first part of the journey was made by jeep. Then the party was helicoptered two hundred miles to the upper reaches of the Xingú. From there, hired guides rowed the party up the sluggish flow of the river toward the *tepui* of Cerro Gordo. Smithback read on.

> Sept. 6. Left dugouts at dropoff site. On foot all the way now. First glimpse of Cerro Gordo this afternoon—rain forest rising into clouds. Cries of tutitl birds, captured several specimens. Guards murmuring among themselves.

Sept. 12. Last of corned beef hash for breakfast. Less humid than yesterday. Continued toward *tepui*—clouds broke free at noon—altitude of plateau possibly eight thousand feet—temperate rain forest—saw five rare candelaria ibex—recovered blow darts and tube, excellent condition—mosquitoes bad—Xingú dried peccary for dinner—not bad, tastes like smoked pork. Maxwell filling crates with useless rubbish.

"Why did Rickman snag this?" Smithback wailed. "There's no dirt in here. What's the big deal?"

Sept. 15. Wind from the S.W. Oatmeal for breakfast. Three portages today owing to brush jams in river—water up to chest—leeches lovely. Around dinner, Maxwell stumbled upon some specimens of flora he is extremely excited about. Indigenous plants indeed quite unique—odd symbiosis, morphology seems very ancient. But more important discoveries lie ahead, I am sure.

Sept. 16. Stayed late in camp this morning, repacking gear. Maxwell now insists on returning with his "find." Idiotic fellow, nuisance is that almost everyone else is returning also. They turned back with all but two of our guides just after lunch. Crocker, Carlos, and I press on. Almost immediately, stopped to repack crate. Specimen jar had broken inside. While I repacked, Crocker wandered off trail, came upon ruined hut . . .

"Now we're getting somewhere," Smithback said.

. . . brought gear down to investigate, reopened crate, retrieved toolbag—before we could investigate hut, old native woman wanders out from brush, staggering—sick or drunk impossible to tell—points to crate, wailing loudly. Breasts down to her waist—no teeth, nearly bald—great sore on her back, like a boil. Carlos reluctant to translate, but I insist:

Carlos: She says, devil, devil.
Myself: Ask her, what devil?

Carlos translates. Woman goes into hysterics, wailing, clutching chest.

Myself: Carlos, ask her about the Kothoga.

Carlos: She say you come to take devil away.

Myself: What about the Kothoga?

Carlos: She say, Kothoga gone up mountain.

Myself: Up mountain! Where?

More caterwauling from woman. Points at our open crate.

Carlos: She say you take devil.

Myself: What devil?

Carlos: Mbwun. She say you take devil Mbwun in box.

Myself: Ask her more about Mbwun. What is it?

Carlos talks to woman, who calms down a little, and speaks for an extended period of time.

Carlos: She says that Mbwun is son of devil. The foolish Kothoga sorcerer who asked devil Zilashkee for his son to help them defeat their enemies. Devil made them kill and eat all their children—then sent Mbwun as gift. Mbwun helps defeat Kothoga enemies, then turns on Kothoga, starts killing everyone. Kothoga flee to *tepui*, Mbwun follow. Mbwun not ever die. Have to rid Kothoga of Mbwun. Now white man come and take Mbwun away. Beware, Mbwun curse will destroy you! You bring death to your people!

I am flabbergasted, and elated—this tale fits into myth cycles we had only heard secondhand. I tell Carlos to get more details about Mbwun—woman breaks away—great strength for one so old—melts into brush. Carlos follows her, comes back empty-handed—he looks frightened, I don't push matters. Investigate hut. When we return to trail, guides gone.

"She knew they were going to take the figurine back!" Smithback said. "That must have been the curse she was talking about!"

He read on.

Sept. 17. Crocker missing since last night. I fear the worst. Carlos very apprehensive. I will send him back after Maxwell, who must be halfway to the river by now—can't afford to lose this relic, which I believe priceless. I will continue on in search of Crocker. There are trails throughout these

woods that must be Kothogan—how civilization can harness this kind of landscape is beyond me—perhaps the
Kothoga will be saved after all.

That was the end of the journal.

Smithback closed the book with a curse. "I can't believe it! Nothing
we didn't already know. And I sold my soul to Rickman . . . for *this!*"

= 36 =

Behind his desk in the command post, Pendergast was fiddling with an ancient Mandarin puzzle made of brass and knotted silken cord. He seemed totally absorbed. Behind him, the learned sounds of a string quartet emerged from the speakers of a small cassette player. Pendergast did not look up as D'Agosta walked in.

"Beethoven's String Quartet in F Major, Opus 135," he said. "But no doubt you knew that, Lieutenant. It's the fourth movement Allegro, known as *Der schwer gefaβte Entschuluβ*—the 'Difficult Resolution.' A title that could be bestowed on this case, as well as the movement, perhaps? Amazing, isn't it, how art imitates life."

"It's eleven o'clock," D'Agosta said.

"Ah, of course," Pendergast said, rolling his chair back and standing up. "The Security Director owes us a guided tour. Shall we go?"

The door of Security Command was opened by Ippolito himself. To D'Agosta, the place looked like the control room of a nuclear power plant, all dials and buttons and levers. Across one wall was a vast miniature city of lighted grids, arranged in intricate geometries. Two guards monitored a battery of closed-circuit screens. In the center, D'Agosta recognized the relay box for the repeater stations used to ensure strong signals for the radios the police and Museum guards carried.

"This," said Ippolito, spreading his hands and smiling, "is one of the most sophisticated security systems in any museum in the world. It was designed especially for us. It cost us a pretty penny, I can tell you."

Pendergast looked around. "Impressive," he said.

"It's state of the art," said Ippolito.

"No doubt," Pendergast said. "But what concerns me right now, Mr. Ippolito, is the safety of the five thousand guests who are expected here tonight. Tell me how the system works."

"It was primarily designed to prevent theft," the security director went on. "A large number of the Museum's most valuable objects have small chips attached in inconspicuous places. Each chip transmits a tiny signal to a series of receivers located around the Museum. If the object is moved even one inch, an alarm goes off, pinpointing the location of the object."

"And then what happens?" asked D'Agosta.

Ippolito grinned. At a console, he pressed some buttons. A large screen illuminated floor plans of the Museum.

"The interior of the Museum," Ippolito continued, "is divided into five cells. Each cell includes a number of exhibit halls and storage areas. Most of these run from basement to roof, but, because of the Museum's structural framework, the perimeters in cells two and three are a little more complicated. When I flick a switch on this panel here, thick steel doors drop down from the ceilings to seal off the interior passages between cells. The Museum windows are all barred. Once we've sealed off a certain cell, the burglar is trapped. He can move around within one section of the Museum, but he can't get out. The grid was laid out in such a way that the exits are external to it, making monitoring easy." He moved over to the layouts. "Let's say someone manages to steal an object, and by the time the guards arrive, he's left the room. It won't make any difference. Within a few seconds, the chip will have sent a signal to the computer, instructing it to seal off that entire cell. The whole process is automatic. The burglar is trapped inside."

"What happens if he takes the chip off before he runs?" D'Agosta asked.

"The chips are motion sensitive," Ippolito continued. "That would set off the alarm, too, and the security doors would instantly descend. A burglar couldn't move fast enough to get out."

Pendergast nodded. "How do you reopen the doors once the burglar has been caught?"

"We can open any set of doors from this control room, and each security door has a manual override on it. It's a keypad, actually. Punch in the right code, and the door comes up."

"Very nice," Pendergast murmured. "But the entire system is geared toward preventing someone from getting out. What we're dealing with here is a killer who wants to stay *in*. How will all this help keep tonight's guests safe?"

Ippolito shrugged. "No big deal. We'll just use the system to create a secure perimeter around the reception hall and the exhibition. All the festivities are taking place inside Cell Two." He pointed to the schematic. "The reception is taking place in the Hall of the Heavens, here. That's just outside the entrance to the *Superstition* exhibition, which is itself within Cell Two. All the steel doors for this cell will be closed. We'll be leaving only four doors open: the East Door of the Great Rotunda—which is the gateway to the Hall of the Heavens— and three emergency exits. All will be heavily guarded."

"And what parts of the Museum exactly does Cell Two consist of?" asked Pendergast.

Ippolito pushed some buttons on the console. A large central section of the Museum glowed green on the panels.

"This is Cell Two," Ippolito said. "As you can see, it reaches from the basement to the ceiling, as do all the cells. The Hall of the Heavens is here. The computer lab and the room we're in now, Security Command, are both inside this cell. So is the Secure Area, the central archives, and a variety of other high-security areas. There will be no exit from the Museum except through the four steel doors, which we'll keep open on override. We'll seal the perimeter an hour before the party, drop all the other doors, and set up guards at the access points. I'm telling you, it'll be more secure than a bank vault."

"And the rest of the Museum?"

"We thought about sealing all five cells, but decided against it."

"Good," said Pendergast, eyeing another panel. "In the event of a crisis, we wouldn't want any emergency personnel to be hampered." He pointed at the illuminated panel. "But what about the subbasement? The basement areas of this cell may well connect with it. And that subbasement could lead almost anywhere."

"Nobody would dare try to use that," Ippolito snorted. "It's a maze."

"But we're not talking about an ordinary burglar. We're talking about a killer that's eluded every search you, I, or D'Agosta here have mounted. A killer that seems to call the subbasement home."

"There is only one stairwell connecting the Hall of the Heavens to other floors," Ippolito explained patiently, "and it'll be guarded by my men, just like the emergency exits. I'm telling you, we've got this figured out. The entire perimeter is going to be secure."

Pendergast examined the glowing map for some time in silence. "How do you know this schematic is accurate?" he asked finally.

Ippolito looked a little flustered. "Of course it's accurate."

"I asked: how do you *know?*"

"The system was designed straight off the architectural drawings from the 1912 reconstruction."

"No changes since then? No doors knocked open here, sealed off there?"

"All changes were taken into account."

"Did those architectural drawings cover the Old Basement and sub-basement areas?"

"No, those are older areas. But, like I told you, they'll either be sealed or guarded."

There was a long silence while Pendergast continued to look at the panels. Finally, he sighed and turned to face the Security Director.

"Mr. Ippolito, I don't like it."

A throat was cleared behind them. "What doesn't he like now?"

D'Agosta didn't have to turn around. That abrasive Long Island accent could belong only to Special Agent Coffey.

"I'm just reviewing the security procedures with Mr. Pendergast," said Ippolito.

"Well, Ippolito, you're gonna have to review them all over again with me." He turned his narrow eyes on Pendergast. "Remember in the future to invite me to your private parties," he said irritably.

"Mr. Pendergast—" Ippolito began.

"Mr. Pendergast is up here from the Deep South to give us a little help here and there when we need it. I'm running the show now. Got it?"

"Yes, sir," said Ippolito. He reviewed the procedures again while Coffey sat in an operator's chair, twirling a set of earphones around his finger. D'Agosta wandered around the room, looking at the control panels. Pendergast listened carefully to Ippolito, looking for all the world as if he hadn't heard the speech before. When the Security Director finished, Coffey leaned back in his chair.

"Ippolito, you got four holes in this perimeter." He paused for effect. "I want three of them plugged. I want only one way in and one way out."

"Mr. Coffey, fire regulations require—"

Coffey waved his hand. "Let me worry about the fire regulations. You worry about the holes in your security net. The more holes we have, the more trouble we have waiting to happen."

"That, I'm afraid, is precisely the *wrong* way to go," Pendergast said. "If you close these three exits, the guests are going to be locked in. Should something happen, there would be only one way out."

Coffey spread his hands in a gesture of frustration. "Hey, Pendergast, that's just the point. You can't have it both ways. Either you have a secure perimeter or you don't. Anyway, according to Ippolito here, each security door has an emergency override. So what's your problem?"

"That's right," said Ippolito, "the doors can be opened using the keypad in an emergency. All you need is the code."

"May I ask what controls the keypad?" asked Pendergast.

"The central computer. The computer room is right next door."

"And if the computer goes down?"

"We've got backup systems, with redundancies. Those panels on the far wall control the backup system. Each panel has its own alarm."

"That's another problem," said Pendergast quietly.

Coffey exhaled loudly and spoke to the ceiling. "He still doesn't like it."

"I counted eighty-one alarm lights on that bank of controls alone," Pendergast continued, oblivious to Coffey. "In a true emergency, with multiple system failure, most of those alarms would be blinking. No team of operators could deal with that."

"Pendergast, you're slowing me down," Coffey snapped. "Ippolito and I are going to work out these details, okay? We've got less than eight hours to showtime."

"Has the system been tested?" Pendergast asked.

"We test it every week," said Ippolito.

"What I mean is, has it ever been put to the test in a real situation? An attempted theft, perhaps?"

"No, and I hope it never is."

"I regret to say it," said Pendergast, "but this strikes me as a system designed for failure. I'm a great advocate of progress, Mr. Ippolito, but I'd strongly recommend an old-fashioned approach here. In fact, during the party, I would disable the whole system. Just turn it off. It's too complex, and I wouldn't trust it in an emergency. What we need is a proven approach, something we are all familiar with. Foot patrols, armed guards at every ingress and egress point. I'm sure Lieutenant D'Agosta will provide us with extra men."

"Just say the word," said D'Agosta.

"The word is no." Coffey began to laugh. "Jesus, he wants to *disable* the system right at the moment when it's most needed!"

"I must register my strongest objections to this plan," said Pendergast.

"Well, you can write up your objections, then," said Coffey, "and send them by slow boat to your New Orleans office. Sounds to me like Ippolito here's got things pretty well under control."

"Thank you," Ippolito said, swelling visibly.

"This is a very unusual and dangerous situation," Pendergast continued. "It's not the time to rely on a complex and unproven system."

"Pendergast," said Coffey, "I've heard enough. Why don't you just head down to your office and eat that catfish sandwich your wife put in your lunchbox?"

D'Agosta was startled at the change that came over Pendergast's face. Instinctively, Coffey took a step back. But Pendergast simply turned on his heel and walked out the door. D'Agosta moved to follow him.

"Where're you going?" asked Coffey. "You better stick around while we work out the details."

"I agree with Pendergast," D'Agosta said. "This isn't the time to start messing with video games. You're talking about people's lives here."

"Listen up, D'Agosta. We're the big boys, we're the FBI. We're not interested in the opinions of a traffic cop from Queens."

D'Agosta looked at Coffey's sweaty red face. "You're a disgrace to law enforcement," he said.

Coffey blinked. "Thank you, and I will note that gratuitous insult in my report to my good friend, Chief of Police Horlocker, who will no doubt take appropriate action."

"You can add this one, then: you're a sack of shit."

Coffey threw back his head and laughed. "I love people who slit their own throats and save you the trouble. It's already occurred to me that this case is much too important to have a lieutenant acting as NYPD liaison. You're gonna be pulled off this case in twenty-four hours, D'Agosta. Did you know that? I wasn't going to tell you until after the party—didn't want to spoil your fun—but I guess now's a good time after all. So put your last afternoon on this case to good use. And we'll see you at the four o'clock briefing. Be on time."

D'Agosta said nothing. Somehow, he wasn't surprised.

= 37 =

An explosive sneeze rattled beakers and dislodged dried plant specimens in the Museum's auxiliary botanical lab.

"Sorry," Kawakita apologized, sniffling. "Allergies."

"Here's a tissue," Margo said, reaching into her carryall. She'd been listening to Kawakita's description of his genetic Extrapolator program. *It's brilliant,* she thought. *But I'll bet Frock supplied most of the theory behind it.*

"Anyway," Kawakita said, "you start with gene sequences from two animals or plants. That's the input. What you get is an extrapolation— a guess from the computer of what the evolutionary link is between the two species. The program automatically matches up pieces of DNA, compares like sequences, then figures out what the extrapolated form might be. As an example, I'll do a test run with chimp and human DNA. What we should get is a description of some intermediate form."

"The Missing Link," Margo nodded. "Don't tell me it draws a picture of the animal, too?"

"No!" Kawakita laughed. "I'd get a Nobel Prize if it could do that. What it does instead is give you a list of morphological and behavioral features the animal or plant might possess. Not definite, but probable. And not a complete list, of course. You'll see when we finish this run."

He typed a series of instructions, and data began flowing across the computer screen: a rapid, undulating progression of zeros and ones. "You can turn this off," said Kawakita. "But I like to watch the data download from the gene sequencer. It's as beautiful as watching a river. A trout stream, preferably."

In about five minutes the data stopped and the screen went blank, glowing a soft blue. Then the face of Moe, from the Three Stooges, appeared, saying through the computer's speaker: "I'm thinking, I'm thinking, but nothing's happening!"

"That means the program's running," Kawakita said, chuckling at his joke. "It can take up to an hour, depending on how far apart the two species are."

A message popped on the screen:

ESTIMATED TIME TO COMPLETION: 3.03.40 min.

"Chimps and humans are so close—they share ninety-eight percent of the same genes—that this one should be fairly quick."

A light bulb suddenly popped on the screen over Moe's head.

"Done!" said Kawakita. "Now for the results."

He pressed a key. The computer screen read:

FIRST SPECIES:
Species: *Pan troglodytes*
Genus: *Pan*
Family: *Pongidae*
Order: *Primata*
Class: *Mammalia*
Phylum: *Chordata*
Kingdom: *Animalia*

SECOND SPECIES:
Species: *Homo sapiens*
Genus: *Homo*
Family: *Hominidae*
Order: *Primata*
Class: *Mammalia*
Phylum: *Chordata*
Kingdom: *Animalia*

Overall Genetic Match: 98.4%

"Believe it or not," said Kawakita, "the identification of these two species was made solely on the genes. I didn't tell the computer what these two organisms were. That's a good way to show unbelievers that the Extrapolator isn't just a gimmick or a kludge. Anyway, now we get a description of the intermediate species. In this case, as you said, the Missing Link."

Intermediate form morphological characteristics:
Gracile
Brain capacity: 750cc
Bipedal, erect posture
Opposable thumb
Loss of opposability in toes
Below average sexual dimorphism
Weight, male, full grown: 55 kg
Weight, female, full grown: 45 kg
Gestation period: eight months
Aggressiveness: low to moderate
Estrus cycle in female: suppressed

The list went on and on, growing more and more obscure. Under "osteology," Margo could make out almost nothing.

Atavistic parietal foramina process
Greatly reduced iliac crest
10–12 thoracic vertebrae
Partially rotated greater trochanter
Prominent rim of orbit
Atavistic frontal process with prominent zygomatic process

That must mean beetle browed, thought Margo to herself.

Diurnal
Partially or serially monogamous
Lives in cooperative social groups

"Come on. How can your program tell something like this?" Margo asked, pointing to *monogamous*.

"Hormones," said Kawakita. "There's a gene that codes for a hormone seen in monogamous mammal species, but not in promiscuous species. In humans, this hormone has something to do with pair bonding. It isn't present in chimps, who are notoriously promiscuous animals. And the fact that the female's estrus cycle is suppressed—you also see that only in relatively monogamous species. The program uses a whole arsenal of tools—subtle AI algorithms, fuzzy logic—to interpret the effect of whole suites of genes on the behavior and look of a proposed organism."

"AI algorithms? Fuzzy logic? You're losing me," Margo said.

"Well, it really doesn't matter. You don't need to know all the secrets, anyway. What it boils down to is making the program think more like a person than a normal computer would. It makes educated guesses, uses intuition. That one trait, 'cooperative,' for example, is extrapolated from the presence or absence of some eighty different genes."

"That's all?" Margo said jokingly.

"No," Kawakita replied. "You can also use the program to guess at a *single* organism's size, shape, and behavior by entering the DNA for one creature instead of two, and disabling the extrapolation logic. And assuming the funding holds up, I plan to add two other modules for this program. The first will extrapolate back in time from a single species, and the second will extrapolate forward. In other words, we'll be able to learn more about extinct creatures of the past, and guess at beings of the future." He grinned. "Not bad, huh?"

"It's amazing," said Margo. She feared her own research project seemed puny by comparison. "How did you develop it?"

Kawakita hesitated, staring at her a little suspiciously. "When I first started working with Frock, he told me he was frustrated by the spottiness of the fossil record. He said he wanted to fill in the gaps, learn what the intermediate forms were. So I wrote this program. He gave me most of the rule tables. We started testing it with various species. Chimps and humans, as well as various bacteria for which we had a lot of genetic data. Then an incredible thing happened. Frock, the old devil, was expecting it, but I wasn't. We compared the domesticated dog with the hyena, and what we got was not a smoothly intermediate species, but a bizarre life form, totally different from either dog or hyena. This happened with a couple of other species pairs, too. You know what Frock said to that?"

Margo shook her head.

"He just smiled and said, 'Now you see the true value of this program.' " Kawakita shrugged. "You see, my program vindicated Frock's theory of the Callisto Effect by showing that small changes in DNA can sometimes produce extreme changes in an organism. I was a little miffed, but that's the way Frock works."

"No wonder Frock was so anxious that I use this program," Margo said. "This can revolutionize the study of evolution."

"Yeah, except nobody is paying any attention to it," said Kawakita bitterly. "Anything connected with Frock these days is like the kiss of death. It's really frustrating to pour your heart and soul into something, and then just get ignored by the scientific community. You know, Margo, between you and me, I'm thinking of dumping Frock as an adviser and joining Cuthbert's group. I think I'd be able to carry much of my work over with me. You might want to consider it yourself."

"Thanks, but I'll stick with Frock," Margo said, offended. "I wouldn't have even gone into genetics if it weren't for him. I owe him a lot."

"Suit yourself," said Kawakita. "But then, you might not even stay at the Museum, right? At least, that's what Bill Smithback tells me. But I've invested everything in this place. My philosophy is, you don't owe anyone but yourself. Look around the Museum: look at Wright, Cuthbert, the whole lot. Are they out for anyone but themselves? We're scientists, you and I. We *know* about survival of the fittest and 'nature red in tooth and claw.' And survival applies to scientists, too."

Margo looked at Kawakita's glittering eyes. He was right in a way. But at the same time, Margo felt that human beings, having figured out the brutal laws of nature, could perhaps transcend some of them.

She changed the subject. "So the G.S.E. works the same way with plant DNA as with animal DNA?"

"Exactly the same," Kawakita replied, returning to his businesslike manner. "You run the DNA sequencer on two plant species, and then download the data into the Extrapolator. It'll tell you how closely the plants are related, and then describe the intermediate form. Don't be surprised if the program asks questions or makes comments. I added a lot of little bells and whistles here and there while I was developing my artificial intelligence chops."

"I think I've got the idea," said Margo. "Thanks. You've done some amazing work."

Kawakita winked and leaned over. "You owe me one now, kid."

"Anytime," said Margo. *Kid. Owing him one.* She disliked people who talked like that. And when Kawakita said it, he meant it.

Kawakita stretched, sneezed again. "I'm off. Gotta grab some lunch, then go home and pick up my tux for the party tonight. I wonder why I even bothered to come in today—everybody else is home preparing for tonight. I mean, look at this lab. It's deserted."

"Tux, eh?" said Margo. "I brought my dress with me this morning. It's nice, but it's not a Nipon original or anything."

Kawakita leaned toward her. "Dress for success, Margo. The powers that be take a look at some guy wearing a T-shirt, and even though he's a genius they can't *visualize* him as Director of the Museum."

"And you want to be Director?"

"Of course," said Kawakita, surprised. "Don't you?"

"What about just doing good science?"

"Anybody can do good science. But someday I'd like a larger role. As Director, you can do a lot more for science than some researcher fiddling in a dingy lab like this. Today it's just not enough to do outstanding research." He patted her on the back. "Have fun. And don't break anything."

He left, and the lab settled into silence.

Margo sat for a moment, motionless. Then she opened up the folder with the Kiribitu plant specimens. But she couldn't help thinking there were more important things to be done. When she'd finally reached Frock on the phone, and told him about what little she'd found in the crate, he had grown very quiet. It was as if, suddenly, all the fight had gone out of him. He'd sounded so depressed, she hadn't bothered to tell him about the journal and its lack of new information.

She looked at her watch: after one o'clock. The DNA sequencing of each Kiribitu plant specimen was going to be time-consuming, and she had to complete the sequencing before she could use Kawakita's Extrapolator. But as Frock had reminded her, this was the first attempt to do a systematic study of a primitive plant classification system. With this program, she could confirm that the Kiribitu, with their extraordinary knowledge of plants, had actually classified them biologically. The program would allow her to come up with intermediate plants, hypothetical species whose real counterparts might still be found in the Kiribitu rain forest. At least, that was Frock's intention.

To sequence DNA from a plant, Margo had to remove part of each specimen. After a lengthy exchange of electronic mail that morning, she had finally been given permission to take 0.1 gram from each specimen. It was just barely enough.

She stared at the delicate specimens, smelling faintly of spice and grass. Some of them were powerful hallucinogens, used by the Kiribitu for sacred ceremonies; others were medicinal and quite possibly of great value to modern science.

She picked up the first plant with tweezers, slicing off the top portion of the leaf with an X-Acto knife. In a mortar and pestle, she ground it up with a mild enzyme that would dissolve the cellulose and lyse the cells' nuclei, releasing the DNA. She worked swiftly but meticulously, adding the appropriate enzymes, centrifuging the result and performing a titration, then repeating the process with other plants.

The final centrifuging took ten minutes, and while the centrifuge vibrated in its gray metal case, Margo sat back, her mind wandering. She wondered what Smithback was doing in his new role as Museum pariah. She wondered, with a small thrill of fear, whether Mrs. Rickman had discovered the missing journal. She thought about what Jörgensen had said, and about Whittlesey's own description of his last days on earth. She imagined the old woman pointing a withered finger at the figurine in the box, warning Whittlesey about the curse. She imagined the setting: the ruined hut overgrown by vines, the flies droning in the sunlight. Where had the woman come from? Why had she run off? Then she imagined Whittlesey taking a deep breath, entering that dark hut of mystery for the first time . . .

Wait a minute, she thought. The journal had said they encountered the old woman before entering the deserted hut. And yet, the letter she found wedged in the lid of the crate clearly stated that Whittlesey discovered the figurine *inside* the hut. He didn't enter the hut until after the old woman ran away.

The old woman was *not* looking at the figurine when she cried out that Mbwun was in the crate! *She must have been looking at something else in the crate and calling it Mbwun!* But nobody had realized that, because they hadn't found Whittlesey's letter. They'd only had the journal for evidence, so they'd assumed Mbwun was the figurine.

But they were wrong.

Mbwun, the *real* Mbwun, wasn't the figurine at all. What had the woman said? *Now white man come and take Mbwun away. Beware, Mbwun curse will destroy you! You bring death to your people!*

And that's just what had happened. Death had come to the Museum. But what inside the crate could she have been referring to?

Grabbing the notebook from her carryall, she quickly reconstructed a list of what she had found in Whittlesey's crate the day before:

Plant press with plants
Blow darts with tube
Incised disk (found in the hut)
Lip plugs
Five or six jars with preserved frogs and salamanders (I think?)

Bird skins
Flint arrowheads and spear points
Shaman's rattle
Manta

What else? She rummaged in her handbag. The plant press, disc, and shaman's rattle were still there. She laid them on the table.

The damaged shaman's rattle was interesting, but far from unusual. She'd seen several more exotic specimens in the *Superstition* exhibition.

The disk was obscure. It showed some kind of ceremony, people standing in a shallow lake, bending over, some with plants in their hands, baskets on their backs. Very odd. But it certainly didn't seem to be an object of veneration.

The list wasn't helpful. Nothing inside the crate had looked remotely like a devil, or whatever else could inspire such terror in an old woman.

Margo carefully unscrewed the small, rusty plant press, its screws and plywood holding the blotter paper in place. She eased it open and lifted off the first sheet.

It held a plant stem and several small flowers. Nothing she had ever seen before, but not particularly interesting at first glance.

The next sheets in the press contained flowers and leaves. It was not, Margo thought, a collection made by a professional botanist. Whittlesey was an anthropologist, and he had probably just picked these specimens because they looked showy and unusual. But why would he collect them at all? She went through all the specimens, and in the back found the note she was looking for.

"Selection of plants found in overgrown abandoned garden near hut (Kothoga?) on September 16, 1987. May be cultivated species, some may also be invasive after abandonment." There was a little drawing of the overgrown plot, showing the location of the various plants. *Anthropology,* thought Margo, *not botany.* Still, she respected Whittlesey's interest in the relationship the Kothoga had to their plants.

She continued her inspection. One plant caught her eye: it had a long fibrous stem, with a single round leaf at the top. Margo realized it was some kind of aquatic plant, similar to a lily pad. *Probably lived in an area of floods,* she thought.

Then she realized that the incised disk found in the hut showed the very same plant. She looked at the disk more closely: it depicted people harvesting these very plants from the swamp in a ceremony of sorts.

The faces on the figures were twisted, full of sorrow. Very strange. But she felt satisfied to have made the connection; it might make a nice little paper for the *Journal of Ethnobotany*.

Putting the disk aside, she reassembled the press and screwed it down tight. A loud beeping sounded: the centrifuge was finished, the material prepared.

She opened the centrifuge and slid a glass rod into the thin layer of material at the bottom of the test tube. She carefully applied it to the waiting gel, then eased the gel tray into the electrophoresis machine. Her finger moved to the power switch. *Now for another half-hour wait,* she thought.

She paused, her finger still on the switch. Her thoughts kept returning to the old woman and the mystery of Mbwun. Could she have been referring to the seed pods—the ones that resembled eggs? No, Maxwell had taken those back himself. They weren't in Whittlesey's crate. Was it one of the frogs or salamanders in jars, or one of the bird skins? That seemed an unlikely locus for the son of the devil himself. And it couldn't have been the garden plants, because they were hidden in the plant press.

So what was it? Was the crazy old woman ranting about nothing?

With a sigh, Margo switched on the machine and sat back. She replaced the plant press and the incised disk in her carryall, brushing away a few packing fibers clinging to the press, packing fibers from the crate. There were additional traces inside her handbag. Yet another reason to clean the damn thing out.

The packing fibers.

Curious, she picked one up with the tweezers, laid it on a slide, and placed it under the stereozoom. It was long and irregular, like the fibrous vein of a tough-stemmed plant. Perhaps it had been pounded flat by Kothoga women for household uses. Through the microscope, she could see the individual cells gleaming dully, their nuclei brighter than the surrounding ectoplasm.

She thought back to Whittlesey's journal. Hadn't Whittlesey mentioned specimen jars being broken, and his need to repack the crate? So, in the area of the deserted hut, they must have thrown out the old packing material, which had become soaked in formaldehyde, and repacked the crate with material found lying near the abandoned hut. Fibers prepared by the Kothoga, perhaps; probably for weaving into coarse cloth or for the production of rope.

Could the fibers have been what the woman was referring to? It seemed impossible. And yet, Margo couldn't help a little professional curiosity about it. Had the Kothoga actually cultivated the plant?

She plucked out a few fibers and dropped them in another mortar, added a few drops of enzyme, and ground them up. If she sequenced the DNA, she could use Kawakita's program to at least identify the plant's genus or family.

Soon, the centrifuged DNA from the fibers was ready for the electrophoresis machine. She followed her usual procedure, then switched on the current. Slowly, the dark bands began forming along the electrified gel.

A half hour later, the red light on the electrophoresis machine winked out. Margo removed the gel tray and began recording the position of the dots and bands of migrated nucleotides, typing her results into the computer.

She punched in the last position, instructed Kawakita's program to search for matches with known organisms, directed the output to the printer, and waited. Finally, the pages began scrolling out.

At the top of the first sheet, the computer had printed:

Species: Unknown. 10% randomized genetic matches with known species.
Genus: Unknown
Family: Unknown
Order: Unknown
Class: Unknown
Phylum: Unknown
Kingdom: Unknown
Cripes, Margo! What did you put in here? I don't even know if this is an animal or plant. And you won't believe how much CPU time it took to figure that out!

Margo had to smile. So *this* was how Kawakita's sophisticated experiment in artificial intelligence communicated with the outside world. And the results were ridiculous. Kingdom *unknown?* The damn program couldn't even tell if it were a plant or an animal. Margo suddenly felt she knew why Kawakita had been reluctant to show her the program in the first place, why it took a call from Frock to get things in motion. Once you strayed out of its known provinces, the program grew flaky.

She scanned the printout. The computer had identified very few genes from the specimen. There were the usual ones common to almost all life: a few respiration cycle proteins, cytochrome Z, various other universal genes. And there were also some genes linked to cellulose, chlorophylls, and sugars, which Margo knew were specific plant genes.

At the waiting prompt, she typed:

How come you don't even know if it is an animal or plant? I see lots of plant genes in here.

There was a pause.

Didn't you notice the animal genes in there, too? Run the data through GenLab.

Good point, thought Margo. She dialed up GenLab on the modem and soon the familiar blue logo popped up on the screen. She uploaded the DNA data from the fibers and ran it against their botanical sub-bank. Same results: almost nothing. A few matches with common sugars and chlorophylls.

On an impulse she ran the DNA data through the entire databank.

There was a long pause, and then a flood of information filled the screen. Margo quickly hit a series of keys, instructing the terminal to capture the data. There were numerous matches with a variety of genes she had never heard of.

Logging off GenLab, she fed the data she'd captured into Kawakita's program, instructing it to tell her what proteins the genes coded for.

A complicated list of the specific proteins created by each gene started to scroll down the screen.

Glycotetraglycine collagenoid
Weinstein's thyrotropic hormone, 2,6 adenosine [gram positive]
1,2,3, oxytocin 4-monoxytocin supressin hormone
2,4 diglyceride diethylglobulin ring-alanine
Gammaglobulin A,x-y, left positive
Hypothalamic corticotropic hormone, left negative
1-1-1 sulphagen (2,3 murine) connective keratinoid,
III-IV involution
Hexagonal ambyloid reovirus protein coat
Reverse transcriptase enzyme

The list went on and on. *A lot of these seem to be hormones*, she thought. *But what kind of hormones?*

She located a copy of *Encyclopedia of Biochemistry* that was busily gathering dust on a shelf, dragged it down and looked up *glycotetra-glycine collagenoid*:

> A protein common to most vertebrate life. It is the protein that bonds muscle tissue to cartilage.

She flipped through to *Weinstein's thyrotropic hormone.*

> A thalamoid hormone present in mammals that elevates release of the neurotransmitter epinephrine from the thyroid gland. It plays a role in the well-known "fight or flight" syndrome by speeding up the heart, elevating body temperature, and possibly increasing mental alertness.

A terrible thought began to form inside her head. She looked up the next, *1,2,3 oxytocin 4-monoxytocin supressin hormone*:

> A hormone secreted by the human hypothalamus gland. Its function is not clearly understood. Recent studies have shown that it might regulate levels of testosterone in the bloodstream during periods of high stress. (Bouchard, 1992; Dennison, 1991).

Margo sat back with a start, the book dropping to the floor with a hollow thud. As she picked up the phone, she glanced at the clock. It was three-thirty.

= 38 =

When the Buick's driver had pulled away, Pendergast mounted the steps to a Museum side entrance, juggling two long cardboard tubes beneath one arm as he showed his identification to the waiting security guard.

At the temporary command post, he shut the door to his office and extracted several yellowed blueprints from the tubes, which he spread across his desk.

For the next hour, he remained nearly motionless, head resting on tented hands, studying. Occasionally he jotted a few words in a notebook, or referred to typewritten sheets that lay on one corner of the desk.

Suddenly, he stood up. He took a final look at the curling blueprints, and slowly ran his finger from one point to another, pursing his lips. Then he gathered up most of the sheets, returned them carefully to the cardboard tubes, and stowed them in his coat closet. The rest he folded carefully and placed in a two-handled cloth bag that lay open on his desk. Opening a drawer, he removed a double-action Colt .45 Anaconda, narrow and long and evil-looking. The weapon fit snugly into the holster under his left arm. A handful of ammunition went into his pocket. From the drawer he also removed a large, bulky yellow object, which he placed in the cloth bag. Then, smoothing his black suit and straightening his tie, he slipped his notebook into the breast pocket of his jacket, picked up the cloth bag, and left his office.

New York City had a short memory for violence, and in the vast public spaces of the Museum streams of visitors could be seen once again. Groups of children crowded around exhibits, pressing noses against the glass, pointing and laughing. Parents hovered nearby, maps and cameras in hand. Tour guides walked along, reciting litanies; guards stood warily in doorways. Through it all, Pendergast glided unnoticed.

He walked slowly into the Hall of the Heavens. Potted palms lined two sides of the enormous room, and a small army of workers made last-minute preparations. The speaking platform on the podium was being sound-checked by two technicians, and imitation native fetishes were being placed on a hundred white linen tablecloths. A hum of activity floated up past the Corinthian columns into the vast circular dome.

Pendergast checked his watch: four o'clock precisely. All the agents would be at Coffey's briefing. He walked briskly across the Hall toward the sealed entrance of *Superstition*. A few brief words were exchanged, and a uniformed officer on duty unlocked the door.

Several minutes later, Pendergast emerged from the exhibition. He stood for a moment, thinking. Then he walked back across the Hall and out into the corridors beyond.

Pendergast moved into the quieter backwaters of the Museum, out of the public spaces. Now he was in the storage areas and laboratories where no tourist was permitted. The high ceilings and vast decorative galleries gave way to drab cinder-block corridors lined with cabinets. Steam pipes rumbled and hissed overhead. Pendergast stopped once at the top of a metal staircase, to look around for a moment, consult his notebook, and load his weapon. Then he moved downward into the narrow labyrinths of the Museum's dark heart.

= **39** =

The door to the lab banged open, then eased back slowly. Margo looked up to see Frock backing himself inside, his wheelchair creaking. She quickly stood up and helped wheel him over to the computer terminal. She noticed he was already dressed in his tuxedo. *Probably put it on before he came to work,* she thought. The usual Gucci handkerchief protruded from his breast pocket.

"I can't understand why they put these labs in such out-of-the-way places," he grumbled. "Now what's the great mystery, Margo? And why did I have to come down to hear it? Tonight's foolishness is getting underway shortly, and my presence will be required on the dais. It's a hollow honor, of course—it's only due to my best-selling status. Ian Cuthbert made that abundantly clear in my office this morning." His voice again sounded bitter, resigned.

Quickly, she explained how she had analyzed the fibers from the packing crate. She showed him the incised disk with its harvest scene. She described the discovery and contents of Whittlesey's journal and letter, and the talk with Jörgensen. And she mentioned how the hysterical old woman described in Whittlesey's journal could not have been referring to the figurine when she warned the scientist about Mbwun.

Frock listened, gently turning the stone disk over in his hands. "It's an interesting story," he said. "But why the urgency? Chances are your sample just got contaminated. And for all we know, that old woman was insane, or Whittlesey's recollections just got a bit scrambled."

"That's what I thought originally. But look at this," Margo said, handing Frock the printout.

He scanned it quickly. "Curious," he said. "But I don't think that this . . ."

His voice trailed off as his pudgy fingers ran down the columns of proteins.

"Margo," he said, looking up. "I was far too hasty. It *is* contamination of sorts, but not from a human being."

"What do you mean?" Margo asked.

"See this hexagonal ambyloid reovirus protein? This is the protein from the shell of a virus that infects animals and plants. Look at how much of it there is in here. And you have reverse transcriptase, an enzyme almost always found in association with viruses."

"I'm not sure I understand."

Frock turned to her impatiently. "What you have here is a plant heavily infected with a virus. Your DNA sequencer was mixing them up, coding for both. Many plants carry viruses like this. A bit of DNA or RNA in a protein coat. They infect the plant, take over some of its cells, then they insert their genetic material into the plant's genes. The plant genes start producing more viruses, instead of what they're supposed to produce. The oak-gall virus makes those brown balls you see on oak leaves, but otherwise it's harmless. Burls on maple and pine trees are also caused by viruses. They're just as common in plants as they are in animals."

"I know, Dr. Frock, but—"

"There *is* something in here I don't understand," he said, laying down the printout. "A virus normally codes for other viruses. Why would a virus code for all these human and animal proteins? Look at all these. Most of them are hormones. What good are human hormones in a plant?"

"That's what I wanted to tell you," Margo said. "I looked up some of the hormones. A lot of them seem to be from the human hypothalamus gland."

Frock's head jerked as if he had been slapped. "Hypothalamus?" His eyes were suddenly alive.

"That's right."

"And the creature that's loose in this Museum is *eating* the hypothalamus of its victims! So it must need these hormones—perhaps it's even *addicted* to these hormones," Frock blurted. "Think: there are only two sources: the plants—which, thanks to this unique virus, are probably saturated with the hormones—and the human hypothalamus. When the creature can't get the fibers, it eats the brain!"

"Jesus, how awful," Margo breathed.

"This is stunning. It explains *exactly* what's behind these terrible murders. With this, we can now put the pieces together. We have a creature loose in the Museum, killing people, opening the calvaria, removing the brain, and eating the thalamoid region where the hormones are most concentrated."

He continued to look at her, his hands trembling slightly. "Cuthbert told us that he'd hunted up the crates in order to retrieve the Mbwun figurine, only to find one of the crates broken open and the fibers scattered about. In fact, now that I think of it, one of the larger crates was nearly empty of fibers. So this creature must have been *eating* the fibers for some time. Maxwell obviously used the same fibers to pack his crates. The creature may not need to eat much—the hormonal concentration in the plants must be very high—but it obviously needs to eat regularly."

Frock leaned back in the wheelchair. "Ten days ago, the crates were moved into the Secure Area, and then three days later, the two boys are killed. Another day, and a guard is killed. What has happened? Simple: the beast cannot *get* to the fibers anymore, so it kills a human being and eats its hypothalamus, thus satisfying its craving. But the hypothalamus only secretes minute amounts of these hormones, making it a poor substitute for this fiber. Based on the concentrations described in this printout, I'd hazard a guess that it would require fifty human brains to equal the concentration found in half an ounce of these plants."

"Dr. Frock," Margo said, "I think the Kothoga were *growing* this plant. Whittlesey collected some specimens in his plant press, and the picture on this incised disk is of a plant being harvested. I'm sure these fibers are just the pounded stems from the lily pad in Whittlesey's press—the plant depicted on this disk. And now we know: these *fibers* are what the woman was referring to when she screamed 'Mbwun.' *Mbwun*, son of the devil: That's the name of this plant!"

She quickly brought the strange plant out of the press. It was dark brown and shrivelled, with a web of black veins. The leaf was thick and leathery, and the black stem as hard as a dried root. Gingerly, Margo brought her nose close to it. It smelled musky.

Frock looked at it with a mixture of fear and fascination. "Margo, that's brilliant," he said. "The Kothoga must have built a whole ceremonial facade around this plant, its harvest and preparation—no doubt to appease the creature. And no doubt that very beast is depicted in the figurine. But how did it get here? Why did it come?"

"I think I can guess," Margo said, her thoughts racing. "Yesterday, the friend who helped me search the crates told me he read of a similar series of murders in New Orleans several years ago. They'd occurred on a freighter coming in from Belém. My friend located the shipping records of the Museum crates, and he found that the crates were on board that ship."

"So the creature was following the crates," said Frock.

"And that's why the FBI man, Pendergast, came up from Louisiana," Margo replied.

Frock turned, his eyes burning. "Dear God. We've lured some terrible beast into a museum in the heart of New York City. It's the Callisto Effect with a vengeance: a savage predator, bent on *our* destruction this time. Let's pray there's only one."

"But just what kind of creature could it be?" asked Margo.

"I don't know," Frock answered. "Something that lived up on the *tepui*, eating these plants. A bizarre species, perhaps surviving since the time of the dinosaurs in tiny numbers. Or perhaps the product of a freak turn of evolution. The *tepui*, you see, is a highly fragile ecosystem, a biological island of unusual species surrounded by rain forest. In such places, animals and plants can develop strange parallels, strange dependencies on each other. A shared DNA pool—think of it! And then—"

Frock was silent.

"*Then!*" he said loudly, slapping his hand on the arm of the wheelchair. "Then they discover gold and platinum on that *tepui*! Isn't that what Jörgensen told you? Shortly after the expedition fell apart, they fired the *tepui*, built a road, brought in heavy mining equipment. They destroyed the entire ecosystem of that *tepui*, and the Kothoga tribe with it. They polluted the rivers and swamps with mercury and cyanide."

Margo nodded vigorously. "The fires burned for weeks, out of control. And the plant that sustained this creature became extinct."

"So the creature started on a journey, to follow these crates and the food it so desperately craved."

Frock fell into silence, his head settling on his chest.

"Dr. Frock," Margo finally said quietly. "How did the creature know the crates had gone to Belém?"

Frock looked at her and blinked. "I don't know," he finally said. "That's strange, isn't it?"

Suddenly Frock was gripping the sides of the wheelchair, rising up in his excitement. "Margo!" he said. "We *can* find out exactly what this creature is. We have the means right here. The Extrapolator! We've got the creature's DNA: we'll feed it into the program and get a description."

Margo blinked. "You mean the claw?"

"Exactly!" He wheeled around to the lab's workstation and his fingers began moving over the keys. "I had the printout Pendergast left us scanned into the computer," he said. "I'll load its data into Gregory's program right now. Help me set things up, will you?"

Margo took Frock's place at the keyboard. In a moment, another message flashed:

ESTIMATED TIME TO COMPLETION: 55.30 minutes.

Hey, Margo, this looks like a big job. Why don't you send out for pizza? The best place in town is Antonio's. I recommend the green chili and pepperoni. Shall I fax them your order now?

The time was quarter past five.

= **40** =

D'Agosta watched with amusement as two burly workmen unrolled a red carpet between two lines of palm trees in the Museum's Great Rotunda, out through the bronze doors and down the front steps.

That's gonna get rained on, he thought. It was dusk, and outside D'Agosta could see big thunderheads piling up to the north and west, rising like mountains above the wind-lashed trees along Riverside Drive. A distant roll of thunder rattled the artifacts in the Rotunda's preview case, and a few stray drops began to pelt the frosted glass of the bronze doors. It was going to be a monster storm—the satellite picture on the morning news left no doubt. That fancy red carpet was going to get soaked. And a lot of fancy people along with it.

The Museum had closed its doors to the public at five o'clock. The beautiful people wouldn't be arriving until seven. The press was there already: television vans with satellite uplinks, photographers talking loudly to each other, equipment everywhere.

D'Agosta spoke into his police radio, giving orders. He had close to two dozen men stationed strategically around the Hall of the Heavens and in other areas inside and outside the Museum. It was lucky, he thought, that he'd finally figured out his way around much of the place. Already, two of his men had become lost and had to be radioed back out.

D'Agosta wasn't happy. At the four o'clock briefing, he had re-quested a final sweep through the exhibition. Coffey had vetoed it, as well as heavy weapons for the plainclothes and uniformed men inside the party. Might scare the guests, Coffey had said. D'Agosta glanced over toward the four walk-through metal detectors, equipped with X-ray conveyor belts. *Thank God for those, at least,* he thought.

D'Agosta turned and, once again, looked around for Pendergast. He hadn't been at the briefing. In fact, D'Agosta hadn't seen him since the meeting with Ippolito that morning.

His radio crackled.

"Hey, Lieutenant? This is Henley. I'm here in front of the stuffed elephants, but I can't seem to find the Marine Hall. I thought you said—"

D'Agosta cut him short, watching a crew testing what had to be the biggest bank of lights since *Gone with the Wind*. "Henley? You see the big doorway with the tusks? Okay, just go through that and take two hard rights. Call me when you're in position. Your partner is Wilson."

"Wilson? You know I don't like partnering with a woman, sir—"

"Henley? There's something else."

"What's that?"

"Wilson's gonna be carrying the twelve-gauge."

"Wait a minute, Lieutenant, you're—"

D'Agosta snapped him off.

There was a loud grinding sound behind him, and a thick steel door began to descend from the ceiling at the north end of the Great Rotunda. They were starting to seal the perimeter. Two FBI men stood in the dimness just beyond the doorway, short-barrel shotguns not quite concealed beneath their loose suit jackets. D'Agosta snorted.

There was a great hollow boom as the steel plate came to rest on the floor. The sound echoed and reechoed through the Hall. Before the echo faded, the boom was duplicated by the descending door at the south end. Only the east door would be left up—where the red carpet ended. *Christ,* thought D'Agosta, *I'd hate to see this place in a fire.*

He heard a loud voice barking at the far end of the Hall and turned to see Coffey, pointing his scurrying men in all directions.

Coffey spotted him. "Hey, D'Agosta!" he shouted, gesturing him over.

D'Agosta ignored him. Now Coffey came swaggering up, his face perspiring. Gizmos and weapons D'Agosta had heard about but had never seen were dangling off Coffey's thick service belt.

"You deaf, D'Agosta? I want you to send two of your men over here for a while and watch this door. Nobody goes in or out."

Jesus, thought D'Agosta. *There are five FBI guys just hanging around in the Great Rotunda, picking their noses.* "My men are tied up, Coffey. Use one of your Rambos over there. I mean, you're deploying most of your men just *outside* the perimeter. I have to station my forces inside to protect the guests, not to mention the traffic duty outside. The rest of the Museum's going to be almost empty, and the party will be underpatrolled. I don't like that."

Coffey hitched up his belt and glared at D'Agosta. "You know what? I don't give a shit what you don't like. Just do your job. And keep a channel open for me." He strode off.

D'Agosta swore. He looked at his watch. Sixty minutes and counting.

= 41 =

The CRT on the computer went blank, and another message came up:

COMPLETED: DO YOU WANT TO PRINT DATA, VIEW DATA, OR BOTH (P/V/B)?

Margo hit the B key. As the data marched across the screen, Frock wheeled his chair to a stop and brought his face close to the screen, his ragged breath misting the terminal glass.

SPECIES: Unidentified
GENUS: Unidentified
FAMILY: 12% match to Pongidae; 16% match to Hominidae
ORDER: Possibly primata; 66% common genetic markers lacking; large standard deviation.
CLASS: 25% match to Mammalia; 5% match to Reptilia
PHYLUM: Chordata
KINGDOM: Animalia
Morphological characteristics: Highly robust
Brain capacity: 900–1250cc
Quadrupedal, extreme posterior-anterior dimorphism
Potentially high sexual dimorphism
Weight, male, full grown: 240–260 kg
Weight, female, full grown: 160 kg
Gestation period: Seven to nine months
Aggressiveness: extreme

Estrus cycle in female: enhanced
Locomotor speed: 60–70 kph
Epidermal covering: Anterior pelt with posterior
bony plates
Nocturnal

Frock scanned the list, running his finger down.

"Reptilia!" he said. "There are those gecko genes appearing again! It appears that the creature combines reptile and primate genes. And it has posterior scales. They must also be from the gecko genes."

Margo read down the list of characteristics as they became more and more obscure.

Gross enlargement and fusion of metacarpal bones in rear limb
Probable atavistic fusion of forelimb No. 3 & 4 digits
Fusion of proximal and middle phalanx on forelimb
Extreme thickening of calvaria
Probable 90% (?) negative rotation of ischium
Extreme thickening and prismatic cross-sectioning in femur
Nasal cavity enlarged
Three (?) highly involute conchae
Enlarged olfactory nerves and olfactory region of cerebellum
Probable external mucoid nasal glands
Reduced optic chiasm, reduced optic nerve

Frock slowly backed himself away from the monitor.

"Margo," he said, "this describes a killing machine of the highest order. But look how many 'probables' and 'possibles' there are. This is a hypothetical description, at best."

"Even so," said Margo, "it sounds an awful lot like the Mbwun figurine in the exhibition."

"No doubt. Margo, I particularly want to direct your attention to the brain size."

"Nine to twelve hundred and fifty cubic centimeters," Margo said, retrieving the printout. "That's high, isn't it?"

"High? It's unbelievable. The upper limit is within human range. This beast, whatever it is, appears to have the strength of a grizzly bear, the speed of a greyhound, and the intelligence of a human being. I say *appears;* so much of this is conjecture on the part of the program. But look at this cluster of traits."

He stabbed his finger at the list.

"Nocturnal—active at night. External mucoid nasal glands—that means it has a 'wet' nose, possessed by animals with a keen scent. Highly involute conchae—also a trait of animals with enhanced olfactory organs. Reduced optic chiasm—that is the part of the brain that processes eyesight. What we have is a creature with a preternatural sense of smell and very poor eyesight that hunts nocturnally."

Frock thought for a moment, his brows contracted.

"Margo, this frightens me."

"If we're right, the whole *idea* of this creature frightens me," Margo replied. She shuddered at the thought that she'd been working with the fibers herself.

"No, I mean this cluster of olfactory traits. If the program's extrapolation is to be believed, the creature lives by smell, hunts by smell, *thinks* by smell. I've often heard it said that a dog sees an entire landscape of smell, as complex and beautiful as any landscape we see with our eyes. But the olfactory sense is more primitive than sight, and as a result, such animals also have a highly instinctual, primitive reaction to smell. *That* is what frightens me."

"I'm not sure I understand."

"In a few minutes, thousands of people will be arriving in the Museum. They will be congregating together in an enclosed space. The creature will be smelling the concentrated hormonal scent of all these people. That may very well irritate or even anger it."

A silence settled in the lab.

"Dr. Frock," Margo said, "you said that a couple of days elapsed from the locking up of the crates and the first killing. Then, another day to the second killing. It's been three days since then."

"Go on," said Frock.

"It just seems to me the creature may be desperate by now. Whatever effect the thalamoid hormones have on the beast must have worn off—after all, those brain hormones are a poor substitute for the plant. If you're right, the creature must be almost like a drug addict unable to get a fix. All the police activity has kept it lying low. But the question is—how long can it wait?"

"My God," said Frock. "It's seven o'clock. We must warn them. Margo, we *must* stop this opening. Otherwise, we might as well be ringing the dinner bell." He moved toward the door, motioning her to follow.

HE WHO WALKS
ON ALL FOURS

PART THREE

= **42** =

As seven o'clock neared, a tangle of cabs and limousines formed outside the Museum's west entrance. Elegantly dressed occupants emerged gingerly, the men in near-identical dinner jackets, the women in furs. Umbrellas jousted as the guests rushed up the red carpet toward the Museum's awning, trying to avoid the pelting rain that was already turning the sidewalks to streams and the gutters to rushing rivers.

Inside, the Great Rotunda, accustomed to silence at this advanced hour, was resounding with the echoes of a thousand expensive shoes crossing its marble expanse between the rows of palm trees leading to the Hall of the Heavens. The Hall itself held towering stands of bamboo in massive tubs festooned with violet lights. Clusters of drooping orchids had been artfully fixed to the bamboo, recalling tropical hanging gardens.

Somewhere deep inside, an invisible band briskly played "New York, New York." An army of waiters in white tie threaded their way expertly through the crowd, carrying large silver platters crowded with champagne glasses and ranks of hors d'oeuvres. Streams of incoming guests joined the ranks of Museum scientists and staff already grazing on the free food. Spotlights, muted blue, caught the glitter of long sequined evening dresses, strings of diamonds, polished gold cufflinks, and tiaras.

Almost overnight, the opening of the *Superstition Exhibition* had become the preferred event among fashionable New York. Coming-out balls and fund-raising dinners took a backseat to the chance to see, firsthand, what all the fuss was about. Three thousand invitations had gone out and five thousand acceptances had come back.

Smithback, wearing an ill-fitting tuxedo with the twin faux pas of wide, spiked lapels and a frilled shirt, peered into the Hall of the Heavens, scanning for familiar faces. At the far end of the hall, a giant platform had been erected. Along one side was the elaborately decorated entrance to the exhibition, currently locked and guarded. A massive dance floor in the center was quickly filling up with couples. Once inside the hall, Smithback immediately found himself surrounded by innumerable conversations, all conducted at a painfully high volume.

". . . that new psychohistorian, Grant? Well, she finally fessed up yesterday, told me what she's been working on all this time. Get this: She's trying to prove that the wanderings of Henry the Fourth after the second crusade were really just a fugue state brought on by acute stress response. It was all I could do to keep from telling her that . . ."

". . . came up with the ridiculous idea that the Stabian Baths were really just a lot of horse stables! I mean, the man's never even been to Pompeii. He wouldn't know the Villa of the Mysteries from a Pizza Hut. But he's got the gall to call himself a papyrologist . . ."

". . . that new research assistant of mine? You know, the one with the enormous hooters? Well, yesterday she was standing by the autoclave, see, and she dropped this test-tube full of . . ."

Smithback took a deep breath and made the plunge, cutting a path toward the hors d'oeuvres tables. *This is going to be great*, he thought.

Outside the main doors of the Great Rotunda, D'Agosta saw more rapid-fire flashing from the group of photographers, and yet another VIP came through the door, a wimpy handsome guy with an emaciated-looking woman clinging to each arm.

He stood where he could keep an eye on the metal detectors, the people coming in, and the throngs moving through the single door into the Hall of the Heavens. The floor of the Rotunda was slick with rainwater, and the coatcheck counter was stowing umbrellas briskly. In a far corner, the FBI had set up its forward security station: Coffey wanted a ringside seat from which to monitor the evening's events. D'Agosta had to laugh. They had tried to make it inconspicuous, but the network of electrical, telephone, fiber-optic and ribbon cables snaking out like an octopus from the station made it as easy to ignore as a bad hangover.

There was a rumble of thunder. The tops of the trees along the Hudson River promenade, new leaves still budding, were sawing about wildly in the wind.

D'Agosta's radio hissed.

"Lieutenant, we got another argument over the metal detector."

D'Agosta could hear a shrill voice in the background. "Surely you know *me*."

"Pull her aside. We gotta keep this crowd moving. If they won't go through, just pull 'em out of the line. They're holding things up."

As D'Agosta holstered his radio, Coffey walked up with the Museum's Security Director in tow. "Report?" Coffey asked brusquely.

"Everyone's in place," D'Agosta said, removing the cigar and examining the soggy end. "I've got four plainclothes circulating in the party. Four uniforms patrolling the perimeter with your men. Five controlling traffic outside, and five supervising the metal detectors and the entrance. I got uniformed men inside the hall. Two of them will follow me into the exhibition when the ribbon's cut. I got one man in the computer room, one man in the Security Control Room . . ."

Coffey squinted. "These uniformed men going into the exhibition with the crowd. That wasn't part of the plan."

"It's nothing formal. I just want us to be at or near the front of the crowd as they go through. You wouldn't let us do a sweep, remember?"

Coffey sighed. "You can do your thing, but I don't want a goddamn escort service. Unobtrusive, not blocking the exhibits. Okay?"

D'Agosta nodded.

He turned toward Ippolito. "And you?"

"Well, sir, all my men are in place, too. Exactly where you wanted them."

"Good. My base of operations will be here in the Rotunda during the ceremony. Afterward, I'll deploy. Meanwhile, Ippolito, I want you up front with D'Agosta. Get up there near the Director and the Mayor. You know the routine. D'Agosta, I want you to stay in the background. No glory-boy shit, don't fuck up your last day. Got it?"

Waters stood in the cool of the computer room, bathed in neon light, his shoulder aching from the heavy shotgun. This had to be the most boring assignment he'd ever caught. He glanced at the geek—he had started thinking of him as that—tapping away at the computer. Tapping, tapping, for hours the guy had been tapping. And drinking Diet Cokes. Waters shook his head. First thing in the morning, maybe he should ask D'Agosta for a rotation. He was going crazy in here.

The geek scratched the back of his neck and stretched.

"Long day," he said to Waters.

"Yeah," said Waters.

"I'm almost done. You won't believe what this program can do."

"You're probably right," said Waters without enthusiasm. He checked his watch. Three more hours until his relief.

"Watch." The geek hit a button. Waters moved a little closer to the screen. He peered at it. Nothing, just a bunch of writing, gibberish that he supposed was the program.

Then, the image of a bug appeared on the screen. At first it was still. Then it stretched its green legs and started walking across the lettering on the screen. Then another animated bug appeared on the screen. The two bugs noticed each other, and moved closer. They started screwing.

Waters looked at the geek. "What *is* this?" he asked.

"Just watch," the geek said.

Soon, four bugs were born, and they started screwing. Pretty soon the screen was full of bugs. Then, the bugs began to eat the letters on the screen. In a couple of minutes, all the words on the screen were gone, and there was nothing left but bugs walking around. Then, the bugs started eating each other. Soon, nothing was left but blackness.

"Pretty cool, huh?" the geek said.

"Yeah," said Waters. He paused. "What does the program do?"

"It's just . . ." the geek looked a little confused. "It's just a cool program, that's all. It's doesn't *do* anything."

"How long did it take you to write that?" asked Waters.

"Two weeks," said the geek proudly, sucking air through his teeth. "On my own time, of course."

The geek turned back to his terminal, and the tapping resumed. Waters relaxed, leaning against the wall nearest the Computer Room door. He could hear the faint sounds of the dance band over his head, the thump of the drums, the low vibration of the basses, the whine of the saxophones. He thought he could even hear the sounds of thousands of footsteps, shuffling and sliding. And here he was, stuck in this psycho ward with nothing but a key-tapping geek for company. The biggest excitement he had was when the geek got up for another Diet Coke.

At that moment, he heard a noise from inside the electrical systems room.

"You hear that?" he asked.

"No," said the geek.

There was another long silence. Then, a definite thump.

"What the hell was that?" said Waters.

"I dunno," said the geek. He stopped typing and looked around. "Maybe you ought to go take a look."

Waters ran his hand over the smooth buttstock of his shotgun and eyed the door leading to the electrical room. *Probably nothing. Last time, with D'Agosta, it had been nothing.* He should just go in there and check things out. Of course, he could always call for backup from Security Command. It was just down the hall. His buddy Garcia was supposed to be in there . . . right?

Perspiration broke across his brow. Instinctively, Waters raised an arm to wipe it off. But he made no move toward the electrical room door.

= 43 =

As Margo rounded the corner into the Great Rotunda, she saw a scene of pandemonium: people shaking off drenched umbrellas, chattering in small and large groups, the racket of their conversations adding to the din from the reception beyond. She pushed Frock up to a velvet rope strung beside the metal detectors, a uniformed policeman standing watchfully next to it. Beyond, the Hall of the Heavens was flooded with yellow light. An enormous chandelier hung from the ceiling, sending flashing rainbows everywhere.

They displayed their Museum IDs to the policeman, who obediently opened the rope and let them through, checking Margo's carryall as he did so. As Margo passed by, the cop gave her a funny glance. Then she looked down, and understood: She was still dressed in jeans and a sweater.

"Hurry," said Frock. "Up front, to the lectern."

The lectern and podium were on the far end of the hall, near the entrance to the exhibition. The hand-carved doors were chained, and the word SUPERSTITION was formed by an arc of crude bone-like letters across the top. On either side were wooden stelae, resembling huge totem poles or the pillars of a pagan temple. Margo could see Wright, Cuthbert, and the Mayor gathered on the platform, talking and joking, while a sound man fiddled with the nearby mikes. Behind them stood Ippolito amid a gaggle of administrators and aides, talking into his radio and gesturing furiously at someone out of sight. The noise was deafening.

"Excuse us!" bellowed Frock. Reluctantly, people moved aside.

"Look at all these people," he yelled back at Margo. "The phero-monal level in this room must be astronomical. It will be irresistible to the beast! We've got to stop this right now." He pointed to one side. "Look—there's Gregory!" He gestured to Kawakita, standing by the edge of the dance floor, drink in hand.

The Assistant Curator worked his way toward them. "There you are, Dr. Frock. They've been looking for you. The ceremony's about to start."

Frock reached out and gripped Kawakita's forearm. "Gregory!" he shouted. "You've got to help us! This event has got to be cancelled, and the Museum cleared at once!"

"What?" said Kawakita. "Is this some kind of joke?" He looked quiz-zically at Margo, then back at Frock.

"Greg," said Margo over the commotion, "we've discovered what's been killing people. It's not a human being. It's a creature, a beast. It's nothing we've ever come across before. Your Extrapolation program helped us to identify it. It feeds on the packing fibers in the Whittlesey crates. When it can't get those, it needs the human hypothalamus hormones as a substitute. We believe it must have a regular—"

"Whoa! Hold on. Margo, what are you talking about?"

"Dammit, Gregory!" Frock thundered. "We don't have any more time to explain. We've got to get this place cleared *now*."

Kawakita backed up a step. "Dr. Frock, with all due respect . . ."

Frock clutched his arm harder and spoke slowly and deliberately. "Gregory, listen to me. There is a terrible creature loose in this Mu-seum. It needs to kill, and it *will* kill. Tonight. We must get everyone out."

Kawakita backed up another step, looking toward the podium. "I'm sorry," he said over the noise. "I don't know what this is all about, but if you're using my extrapolation program for some kind of joke . . ." He prized his arm free of Frock's gasp. "I really think you should go up to the platform, Dr. Frock. They're waiting for you."

"Greg—" Margo tried to say, but Kawakita had moved away, looking at them speculatively.

"To the podium!" said Frock. "Wright can do it. He can order this place evacuated."

Suddenly they heard a drumroll and a fanfare.

"Winston!" shouted Frock, rolling into the open space in front of the platform. "Winston, listen! We've got to evacuate!"

Frock's final words hung in the air as the fanfare faded away.

"There is a deadly beast loose in the Museum!" Frock shouted into the silence.

A sudden murmur arose in the crowd. Those closest to Frock backed away, looking at each other and muttering in low tones.

Wright glared at Frock while Cuthbert quickly separated himself from the group. "Frock," he hissed. "What in bloody hell are you doing?" He bounded off the platform and came over.

"What is the matter with you, Frock? Have you gone mad?" he said in a vicious whisper.

Frock reached out. "Ian, there is a terrible beast loose in the Museum. I know we've had our differences, but trust me, *please*. Tell Wright we've got to get these people out. Now."

Cuthbert looked at Frock intently. "I don't know what you're thinking," the Scotsman said, "or what your game is. Perhaps it's some desperate eleventh-hour attempt to derail the exhibition, to turn me into a laughingstock. But I will tell you this, Frock: If you make one more outburst, I will have Mr. Ippolito forcibly remove you from these premises and I will see to it that you never set foot in here again."

"Ian, I beg of you—"

Cuthbert turned and walked back to the podium.

Margo laid a hand on Frock's shoulder. "Don't bother," she said quietly. "They're not going to believe us. I wish George Moriarty were here to help. This is his show, he must be around somewhere. But I haven't seen him."

"What can we do?" Frock asked, trembling with frustration. The conversations around them resumed as the guests near the podium assumed some kind of joke had taken place.

"I guess we should find Pendergast," Margo said. "He's the only one with enough clout to do something about this."

"He won't believe us, either," Frock said, dispiritedly.

"Maybe not right away," Margo said, wheeling him around. "But he'll hear us out. We've got to hurry."

Behind them, Cuthbert signalled for another drumroll and fanfare. Then he walked over to the podium and held up his hands.

"*Ladies and gentlemen!*" he cried out. "*I have the honor to introduce to you the Director of the New York Museum of Natural History, Winston Wright!*"

Margo looked around as Wright took the podium, smiling and waving to the crowd.

"*Welcome!*" he cried out. "*Welcome my friends, fellow New Yorkers, citizens of the world! Welcome to the unveiling of the greatest museum show ever mounted!''* Wright's amplified words echoed through the Hall. A tremendous burst of applause rose to the domed ceiling.

"We'll call security," said Margo. "They'll know where Pendergast is. There's a bank of phones out in the Rotunda."

She began to push Frock toward the entrance. Behind her, she could hear Wright's voice booming through the PA system: *"This is a show about our deepest beliefs, our deepest fears, the brightest and the darkest sides of human nature . . .''*

= 44 =

D'Agosta stood behind the podium, watching Wright's back as he addressed the listening crowd. Then he grabbed his radio. "Bailey?" he said in a low tone. "When they cut that ribbon, I want you and McNitt to get in ahead of the crowd. Just behind Wright and the Mayor, but ahead of everyone else. You got that? Blend in as much as possible, but don't let them push you out of the way."

"Roger, Loo."

"*When the human mind evolved to understand the workings of the universe, the first question it asked was: What is life? Next, it asked: What is death? We've learned a lot about life. But, despite all our technology, we've learned very little about death and what lies beyond . . .*"

The crowd was rapt, listening.

"*We have sealed the exhibition so that you, our honored guests, will be the first inside. You will see many rare and exquisite artifacts, most on display for the first time ever. You will see images of beauty and ugliness, great good and ultimate evil, symbols of man's struggle to cope with and comprehend the ultimate mystery . . .*"

D'Agosta wondered what that business with the old curator in the wheelchair had been. Frock, the name was. He'd shouted something, but then Cuthbert, the honcho of the event, had sent him off. Museum politics, worse even than down at One Police Plaza.

"*. . . most fervent hope that this exhibition will launch a new era at our Museum: an era in which technological innovation and a renaissance in the scientific method will combine to reinvigorate the interest of the museum-going public in today's . . .*"

D'Agosta scanned the room, mentally spot-checking his men. Everyone seemed to be in place. He nodded to the guard at the exhibition entrance, instructing him to remove the chain from the heavy wooden doors.

As the speech ended, a roar of applause filled the vast space once again. Then Cuthbert returned to the podium.

"I want to thank a number of people . . ."

D'Agosta glanced at his watch, wondering where Pendergast was. If he was in the room, D'Agosta would have known it. Pendergast was a guy that stuck out in a crowd.

Cuthbert was holding up an enormous pair of scissors, which he handed to the Mayor. The Mayor grasped one handle and offered the other to Wright, and the two of them walked down the platform steps to a huge ribbon in front of the exhibition entrance. "What are we waiting for?" said the Mayor facetiously, drawing a laugh. They snipped the ribbon in half to an explosion of flashbulbs, and two of the Museum guards slowly pulled open the doors. The band swung into "The Joint Is Jumpin'."

"Now," said D'Agosta, speaking fast into his radio. "Get into position."

As the applause and cheers echoed thunderously, D'Agosta walked briskly forward along the wall, then ducked past the doors into the empty exhibition. He did a quick scan inside, then spoke into his radio. "Clear." Ippolito came up next, scowling at D'Agosta. Arm in arm, the Mayor and the Director stood in the doorway, posing for the cameras. Then, beaming, they walked forward into the exhibition.

As D'Agosta moved deeper into the exhibition ahead of the group, the cheering and applause grew fainter. Inside, it was cool and smelled of new carpeting and dust, with a faint unpleasant odor of decay.

Wright and Cuthbert were giving the Mayor a tour. Behind them, D'Agosta could see his two men, and behind them a vast sea of people, crowding in, craning their necks, gesturing, talking. From D'Agosta's perspective within the exhibition, it looked like a tidal wave. *One exit. Shit.*

He spoke into his radio. "Walden, I want you to tell those Museum guards to slow down the flow. Too many goddamn people are crowding in here."

"Ten-four, Lieutenant."

"This," said Wright, still holding the Mayor's arm, "is a very rare sacrificial gurney from Mesoamerica. That's the Sun God depicted on the front, guarded by jaguars. The priests would sacrifice the victim on this table, cut out the beating heart, and hold it up to the sun. The blood flowed down these channels and collected here at the bottom."

"Impressive," said the Mayor. "I could use one of those up in Albany."

Wright and Cuthbert laughed, the sound reverberating off the still artifacts and display cases.

Coffey stood in the forward security station, legs apart, hands on hips, his face expressionless. Most of the guests had arrived, and those who hadn't were probably not going to venture out. It was raining in earnest now, sheets of water cascading onto the pavement. Across the expanse of the Rotunda, through the east door, Coffey could clearly see the festivities in the Hall of the Heavens. It was a beautiful room, with coruscating stars covering the velvety black dome that floated sixty feet overhead. Swirling galaxies and nebulae glowed softly along the walls. Wright was speaking at the podium, and the cutting ceremony would be starting soon.

"How's it look?" Coffey asked one of his agents.

"Nothing exciting," the agent said, scanning the security board. "No breaches, no alarms. Perimeter's quiet as a tomb."

"The way I like it," Coffey replied.

He glanced back into the Hall of the Heavens in time to see two guards pulling open the huge doors to the *Superstition Exhibition.* He'd missed the ribbon cutting. The crowd was moving forward now, all five thousand at once, it seemed.

"What the hell do you think Pendergast is up to?" Coffey said to another of his agents. He was glad Pendergast was out of his hair for the time being, but he was nervous at the thought of the Southerner wandering around, beholden to no one.

"Haven't seen him," came the response. "Want me to check with Security Command?"

"Naw," Coffey said. "It's nice without him. Nice and peaceful."

D'Agosta's radio hissed. "Walden here. Listen, we need some help. The guards are having a hard time controlling the flow. There's just too many people."

"Where's Spenser? He should be floating around there somewhere. Have him bar the entrance, let people out but not in, while you and the Museum guards set up an orderly line. This crowd has to be con-trolled."

"Yes, sir."

The exhibition was filling up quickly now. Twenty minutes had gone by and Wright and the Mayor were deep inside the exhibition, near the locked rear exit. They'd moved quickly at first, keeping to the central halls and avoiding the secondary passages. But now, Wright had stopped at a particular exhibit to explain something to the Mayor, and people were streaming past them into the exhibition's farthest recesses.

"Keep near the front," D'Agosta said to Bailey and McNitt, the two men on advance duty.

He skipped ahead and did a quick visual through two side alcoves. *Spooky exhibition*, he thought. A very sophisticated haunted house, with all the trimmings. The dim lighting, for instance. Not so dim, though, that you couldn't make out nasty little details. Like the Congo power figure, with its bulging eye sockets and torso riddled with sharp nails. Or the nearby mummy, vertical in a freestanding case, that was streaked with dripped blood. *Now that*, thought D'Agosta, *is a little overdone*.

The crowd continued to spread out, and he ducked into the next set of alcoves. All clear.

"Walden, how'd you make out?" D'Agosta radioed.

"Lieutenant, I can't find Spenser. He doesn't seem to be around, and I can't leave the entrance to find him with the crowd the way it is."

"Shit. Okay, I'm calling Drogan and Frazier over to help you."

D'Agosta radioed one of the two plainclothes units patrolling the party. "Drogan, you copy?"

A pause. "Yes, Lieutenant."

"I want you and Frazier to back up Walden at the *Exhibition* en-trance, on the double."

"Ten-four."

He looked around. More mummies, but none with blood all over them.

D'Agosta stopped, frozen. *Mummies don't bleed*.

Slowly, he turned around and started pushing past the eager phalanx of gawkers. It was just some curator's sick little idea. Part of the exhibit.

But he had to be sure.

The case was surrounded by people, as were all the others. D'Agosta made his way through the crowd and glanced at the label: "Anasazi burial from Mummy Cave, Canyon del Muerto, Arizona."

The streaks of dried blood on the head and chest of the mummy looked like they had come from above. Trying to remain inconspicuous, he leaned as close to the case as possible and peered up.

Above the mummy's head, the top of the case was open, exposing a ceiling crawling with steam pipes and ductwork. A hand, a watch, and the cuff of a blue shirt protruded over the edge of the case. A small icicle of dried blood hung from the middle finger.

D'Agosta backed into a corner, looked around, and spoke urgently into his radio.

"D'Agosta calling Security Command."

"This is Garcia, Lieutenant."

"Garcia, I've got a dead body in here. We've got to get everybody out. If they see it and panic, we're fucked."

"Jesus," said Garcia.

"Get in touch with the guards and Walden. *Nobody* else is to be allowed into the exhibition. You got that? And I want the Hall of the Heavens cleared in case there's a stampede. Get everyone out, but don't cause any alarm. Now get Coffey for me."

"Roger."

D'Agosta looked around, trying to spot Ippolito. His radio squawked.

"Coffey here. What the hell is it, D'Agosta?"

"We got a dead body in here. It's lying on top of a case. I'm the only one who's spotted it, but that could change at any moment. We've got to get everyone out while there's still time."

As he opened his mouth to speak again, D'Agosta heard, over the noise of the crowd, "That blood looks so *real.*"

"There's a hand up there," D'Agosta heard someone else say.

Two woman were backing away from the case, looking up.

"It's a body!" one said loudly.

"It's not real," the other replied. "It's a gimmick for the opening, it has to be."

D'Agosta held up his hands, moving up to the case. "Please, everyone!"

There was a brief, terrible, listening silence. *"A body!"* someone else screamed.

There was a brief movement of the crowd, followed by a sudden stillness. Then, another scream: *"He's been murdered!"*

The crowd peeled back in two directions, and several people stumbled and fell. A large woman in a cocktail dress toppled backward onto D'Agosta, slamming him up against the case. The air was slowly forced out of his chest as the weight of more bodies pressed against him. Then he felt the case behind him start to give.

"Wait!" he gasped.

From the darkness above, something big slid off the top of the case and flopped onto the tight mass of people, knocking several more down. From his awkward angle, D'Agosta could only tell that it was bloody, and that it had been human. He didn't think it had a head.

Utter pandemonium broke out. The close space filled with screaming and shouting, and people started to run, clawing at each other, stumbling. D'Agosta felt the case topple. Suddenly, the mummy fell to the floor, with D'Agosta on top. As he grabbed the side of the case he felt glass slice into his palm. He tried to stand, but was knocked back into the case by the surging crowd.

He heard the hiss from his radio, found it was still in his right hand, and raised it to his face.

"This is Coffey. What the hell is going on, D'Agosta?"

"We've got a panic on our hands, Coffey. You're going to have to evacuate the Hall immediately, or—

"*Shit!*" he roared as the radio was knocked from his hand by the surging crowd.

= 45 =

Margo watched dispiritedly as Frock shouted into an internal phone set in the granite walls of the Great Rotunda. Wright's amplified speech poured out of the Hall of the Heavens, preventing Margo from hearing a word Frock said. Finally, Frock reached up, slamming the phone onto its cradle. He wheeled himself around to face her. "This is absurd. Apparently, Pendergast is in the basement somewhere. Or at least, he was. He radioed in about an hour ago. They refuse to contact him without authorization."

"In the basement? Where?" Margo asked.

"Section 29, they said. Why he's down there, or *was* down there, they refuse to say. My guess is they don't know. Section 29 covers a lot of ground." He turned to Margo. "Shall we?"

"Shall we what?"

"Go down to the basement, of course," Frock replied.

"I don't know," Margo said dubiously. "Perhaps we should get the authorization they need to summon him up."

Frock moved impatiently in his wheelchair. "We don't even know who could give such authorization." He stared at her, becoming aware of her uncertainty. "I don't think you need worry about the creature confronting *us*, my dear," he said. "If I'm right, it will be drawn to the concentration of people here at the exhibition. It's our obligation to do whatever we can to prevent a catastrophe; we took that on when we made these discoveries."

Still Margo hesitated. It was one thing for Frock to speak in grandiose terms. He hadn't been inside that exhibition. He hadn't heard the stealthy padding of feet. He hadn't run blindly in the screaming dark . . .

She took a deep breath. "You're right, of course," she said. "Let's go."

Since Section 29 was inside the Cell Two security perimeter, Margo and Frock had to show their IDs twice on their way to the proper elevator. Apparently, the curfew being suspended for the evening, guards and police officers were more concerned about detaining suspicious or unauthorized characters than restricting the movement of Museum employees.

"Pendergast!" Frock shouted as Margo wheeled him out of the elevator into the dim basement corridor. "This is Doctor Frock. Can you hear me?"

His voice echoed and died.

Margo knew a little of the history behind Section 29. When the Museum's powerplant had been located nearby, the area housed steam pipes, supply tunnels, and the subterranean cubbyholes used by troglodyte workers. After the Museum switched to a more modern power plant in the 1920s, the old works had been removed, leaving a series of ghostly warrens now used for storage.

Margo wheeled Frock down the low-ceilinged hallways. Every so often, Frock would bang on a door or call Pendergast's name. Each time, his shouts were greeted by silence.

"We're getting nowhere," Frock said as Margo stopped for a breather. Frock's white hair was in disarray, and his tuxedo jacket was rumpled.

Margo looked nervously around. She knew approximately where they were: somewhere, at the far end of the confusion of passages, lay the vast, silent space of the old powerhouse: a lightless, subterranean pantheon now used to hold the Museum's collection of whale bones. Despite Frock's predictions of the creature's behavior, the shouting made her nervous.

"This could take hours," Frock said. "He may not be here anymore. Perhaps he never was." He sighed deeply. "Pendergast was our last hope."

"Maybe the noise and confusion will frighten the creature, keep it in hiding, away from the party," Margo said with a hope she didn't feel.

Frock rested his head in his hands. "Not likely. The beast must be driven by smell. It may be intelligent, it may be cunning, but like a human serial killer, when its blood lust is up it cannot control itself."

Frock sat up, his eyes filled with renewed vigor. "Pendergast!" he shouted again. *"Where are you?"*

Waters stood listening, his body tensed. He could feel his heart pounding, and he couldn't seem to gulp enough air into his lungs.

He'd been in plenty of dangerous situations before, been shot at, knifed, even had acid thrown at him once. Every time he'd been cool, almost detached, when he'd had to be. *Now, one little thump and I'm panicking.* He clawed at his collar. *The air's stuffy in this damn room.* He willed himself to breathe slowly and deeply. *I'll just call Garcia. We'll investigate together. And find nothing.*

Then he noticed that the rustling of feet overhead had changed its rhythm. Instead of the scraping and sliding he'd heard before, now he heard a constant drumming, like the sound of running feet. As he listened, he thought he heard a faint screaming. Dread flooded through him.

There was another thump in the electrical room.

Sweet Jesus, something big's happening.

He grabbed his radio. "Garcia? You copy? Requesting backup to investigate suspicious noises in the electrical systems room."

Waters swallowed. Garcia wasn't responding on the regular frequency. As Waters holstered his radio, he noticed that the geek had stood up and was heading for the electrical room.

"What are you doing?" Waters asked.

"I want to see what that noise is," the geek said, opening the door. "I think the air conditioner might have failed again." He put his hand around the doorframe, feeling for a light switch.

"Wait a minute, you," Waters said. "Don't—"

Waters's radio burst into static. "We got a stampede in here!" There was more static. ". . . All units, mobilize for emergency evacuation!" More static. "Can't hold this crowd, we need backup now, now . . ."

Jesus. Waters grabbed his radio, punched buttons. In an instant, all bands had been taken. He could hear something terrible happening right over his head. *Shit.*

Waters looked up. The geek was gone, and the door to the electrical room was open, but the light inside was still off. *Why was the light still off?* Without taking his eyes from the open door, he carefully unshouldered his shotgun, pumped a slug into the chamber, and started forward.

Carefully, he moved up to the edge of the door, looked around. Blackness.

"Hey, you," he said. "You in there?" As he moved inside the darkened room, he felt his mouth go dry.

There was a sudden loud thump to his left, and Waters instinctively dropped to his knee and pumped three rounds, each one a flash of light and a deafening blast.

There was a shower of sparks and a gout of flame licked upward, briefly illuminating the room with lambent orange light. The geek was on his knees, looking up at Waters.

"Don't shoot!" the geek said, his voice breaking. "Please, don't shoot anymore!"

Waters raised himself on trembling legs, ears ringing. "I heard a sound," he cried. "Why didn't you answer me, you stupid shit?"

"It was the air conditioner," the geek said, tears streaming down his face. "It was the air-conditioner pump failing, like before."

Waters backed up, feeling behind him for the wall switch. Gunpowder hung in the air like a blue fog. On the far wall, a large mounted box of metal was smoking from three large, ragged holes in its front casing.

Waters hung his head, sank back against the wall.

With a sudden pop, an electrical arc sliced across the ruined box, followed by a crackling and another shower of sparks. The acrid air grew foul. The lights in the Computer Room flickered, dimmed, brightened. Waters heard one alarm go off, and then another.

"What's happening?" he shouted. The lights dimmed again.

"You destroyed the central switching box," the geek cried, rising to his feet and running past him into the Computer Room.

"Oh, shit," Waters breathed.

The lights went out.

= 46 =

Coffey shouted again into the radio. "D'Agosta, come in!" He waited. *"Shit!"*

He switched to the Security Command channel. "Garcia, what the hell is going on?"

"I don't know, sir," Garcia said nervously. "I think Lieutenant D'Agosta said there was a body in . . ." There was a pause. "Sir, I'm getting reports of panic in the exhibition. The guards are—"

Coffey cut him off and switched the bands, listening. "We got a stampede in here!" the radio squawked.

The agent switched back to Security Command. "Garcia, get the word out. All units, prepare for emergency evacuation procedures." He turned to look across the Great Rotunda, through the east door into the Hall of the Heavens.

A visible ripple passed through the crowd, and the background chatter began to die away. Over the sounds of the band, Coffey could hear clearly now the sound of muffled screams and the low thunder of running feet. The movement toward the exhibition entrance faltered. Then the crowd surged backward, rebounding like a pressure wave. There were some angry yells and confused shouts, and Coffey thought he heard crying. Again the crowd was still.

Coffey unbuttoned his jacket, and turned toward the agents in the forward station. "Emergency crowd control procedures. Move out."

Suddenly the crowd surged backward, and a frenzy of shouting and screaming broke from the open door of the Hall. The band faltered, then fell silent. In an instant, everyone was running toward the exit to the Great Rotunda.

"Go, you son of a bitch!" said Coffey, shoving one of his men in the back, holding his radio in his right hand. "D'Agosta, you copy?"

As the crowd began to pour out of the Hall, the agents collided with the surging mass and were forced back. Thrusting himself from the roiling mass of bodies, Coffey backed away slightly, panting and cursing.

"It's like a tidal wave!" one of his men yelled. "We'll never make it in!"

Suddenly the lights dimmed. Coffey's radio crackled again.

"Garcia here. Listen, sir, all the security lights have gone red, the board's lit up like a Christmas tree. The perimeter alarms are all coming on."

Coffey moved forward again, fighting to stand his ground against the crowd streaming past him. He could no longer see the other agents. The lights flickered a second time, and then he felt a low rumble from the direction of the Hall. Coffey looked up and saw the thick edge of the metal security door descending from a slot in the ceiling.

"Garcia!" Coffey shouted into the radio. "The east door is coming down! Shut it off! Get it back up, for Chrissake!"

"Sir, their controls indicate it's still up. But something's happening down here. All the systems are—"

"I don't give a fuck what their controls say. It's coming down!" He was suddenly spun around by the fleeing crowd. The screaming was continuous now, a strange, banshee-like keening noise that raised the hair on a person's neck. Coffey had never seen anything like it, never: smoke, emergency lights blinking, people running over other people, glassy panic in their eyes. The metal detectors had been knocked over and the X-ray machines shattered as people in tuxedos and gowns went running out into the pouring rain, clawing past each other, stumbling and falling across the red carpet and onto the soaked pavement. Coffey saw little flashes on the steps outside the Museum, first a few, and then several.

He yelled into his radio. "Garcia, alert the cops outside. Have them restore order, get the press the hell out of there. And have them get that door up, now!"

"They're trying, sir, but all the systems are failing. We're losing power. The emergency doors drop independent of the power grid, and they can't activate the fail-safe controls. Alarms are going off all over the place—"

A man coming through nearly bowled Coffey over as he heard Garcia shout, "Sir! Total system failure!"

"Garcia, where the fuck is the backup system?" He forced a path sideways and found himself pinned against the wall. It was no use, he wasn't going to get inside through the stampede. The door was now halfway down. "Give me the technician! I need the manual override code!"

The lights flickered a third time and went out, plunging the Rotunda into darkness. Over the screams, the rumble of the descending door continued relentlessly.

Pendergast ran his hand over the rough stone wall of the cul-de-sac, rapping a few places lightly with his knuckles. The plaster was cracking and flaking off in pieces, and the light bulb in the ceiling was broken.

Opening the bag, he withdrew the yellow object—a miner's hat—adjusted it carefully on his head and flicked its switch. Tilting his head, he ran the powerful beam of light over the wall in front of him. Then he pulled out the creased blueprints, directing the light onto them. He walked backward, counting his steps. Then, taking a penknife from his pocket, he placed its point into the plaster and gently twisted the blade. A piece of plaster the size of a dinner plate fell away, revealing the faint tracings of an ancient doorway.

Pendergast jotted in his notebook, stepped out of the cul-de-sac, and paced along the hall, counting under his breath. He stopped opposite a stack of crumbling sheetrock. Then, he pulled it sharply away from the wall. The material fell with a crash and a great billowing of white dust. Pendergast's light exposed an old panel set low in the wall.

He pressed the panel appraisingly. It held fast. When he kicked it savagely, it flew open with a screech. A narrow service tunnel slanted steeply downward, opening onto the ceiling of the subbasement beneath. One floor below him, a thread of water trickled along like an inky ribbon.

Pendergast pulled the panel back into place, made another marking on the blueprint, and continued on.

"Pendergast!" came the faint cry. "This is Doctor Frock. Can you hear me?"

Pendergast stopped, his brows knitted in surprise. He opened his mouth to answer. Suddenly, he froze. There was a peculiar smell in the air. Leaving his bag open on the floor, he ducked into a storage room, locked the door behind him, and reached up, snapping off his light.

The door had a small wired-glass window set into its middle, grimy and cracked. Fishing in a pocket, he drew out a tissue, spat on it, rubbed the window and peered out.

Something big and dark had just entered the lower edge of his field of view. Pendergast could hear a snuffling sound, like a winded horse breathing heavy and fast. The smell grew stronger. In the dim light, Pendergast could see a muscled withers, covered with coarse black hair.

Moving slowly, taking short, choppy breaths through his nose, Pendergast reached inside his suit jacket and drew out the .45. In the darkness, he passed his finger across the cylinder, checking the loaded chambers. Then, steadying the revolver with both hands and levelling it at the door, he began to back up. As he moved away from the window, the shape dropped from view. But he knew beyond any doubt that it was still out there.

There was a faint bump on the door, followed by a low scratching. Pendergast tightened his grip on the revolver as he saw, or thought he saw, the doorknob begin to turn. Locked or not, the rickety door wouldn't stop whatever was outside. There was another muffled thump, then silence.

Pendergast quickly peered out the window. He could see nothing. He held the revolver at twelve-o'clock with one hand and placed his other hand on the door. In the listening silence, he counted to five. Then, quickly, he unlocked the door and swung it open, moving into the center of the passageway and around a corner. At the far end of the hall a dark shape paused at another door. Even in the dim light he could make out the strong, sloping movements of a quadruped. Pendergast was the most rational of men, but he barked a brief laugh of disbelief as he saw the creature claw for the doorknob. The lights in the hallway dimmed, then brightened. Pendergast slowly dropped to one knee, held the gun in combat position, and took aim. The lights dimmed a second time. He saw the creature sit back on its haunches and then rise up, turning toward him. Pendergast centered on the side of the head, let his breath flow out. Then he slowly squeezed the trigger.

There was a roar and a flash as Pendergast relaxed to absorb the kickback. For a split second he saw a white streak move straight up the beast's cranium. Then the creature was gone, around a far corner, and the hallway was empty.

Pendergast knew exactly what had happened. He had seen that streak of white once before, hunting bear: the bullet had ricocheted off the skull, taking a strip of hair and skin while exposing the bone. The perfectly placed shot with a metal-jacketed, chromium-alloy-tipped .45 caliber bullet had bounced off the creature's skull like a spitball. Pendergast slumped forward and let his gun hand sink toward the floor as the lights flickered again and went out.

= 47 =

From where he'd stood next to the hors d'oeuvres tables, Smithback had a great view of Wright standing at the microphone, gesturing, voice booming out from a nearby loudspeaker. Smithback hadn't bothered to listen; he knew, with gloomy certainty, that Rickman would provide him with a hard copy of the speech later. Now, the speech was over, and the crowd had been eagerly piling into the new exhibition for the past half hour. But Smithback remained where he stood, oblivious. He gazed once again down at the table, debating whether to eat a fat gulf prawn or a tiny blini *au caviare*. He took the blini, actually five, and began grazing. The caviar, he noted, was gray and not salty—real sturgeon, not the fake whitefish they tried to pass off at publishing parties and the like.

He snagged a prawn anyway, made it two, followed by a spoonful of *ceviche* and three crackers covered with Scottish smoked cod roe with capers and lemon, a few paper-thin slices of cold red Kobe beef, no steak tartare, thank you very much, but definitely two pieces of that *uni sushi* . . . His gaze followed the array of delicacies that went on for fifty feet worth of table. He had never seen anything like it and he wasn't about to let any of it get away.

The band suddenly faltered, and almost simultaneously somebody elbowed him, hard, in the ribs.

"Hey!" Smithback started to say, when, looking up, he almost instantly found himself engulfed in a shoving, grunting, screaming mass of people. He was thrown against the banquet table; he struggled to regain his footing, slipped and fell, then rolled under the table. He crouched, watching the thundering feet go by. There were screams and the horrifying noises of bodies crashing full tilt into one another. He heard a few snatches of shouted phrases: "... dead body!" "... murder!" Had the killer struck again, in the middle of thousands of people? It wasn't possible.

A woman's shoe, black felt with a painfully high spiked heel, bounced under the table and came to rest near his nose. He shoved it away with disgust, noticed he was still clutching a morsel of shrimp in his hand, and bolted it down. Whatever was happening, it was happening fast. It was shocking how quickly panic could sweep a crowd.

The table shuddered and slid, and Smithback saw an enormous platter land just beyond the fringe of the tablecloth. Crackers and Camembert went flying. He grabbed crackers and cheese off his frilled shirt and started eating. Twelve inches from his face, he could see scores of feet stamping and churning a loaf of pâté into mud. Another platter landed with a splat, spraying caviar across the floor in a gray mist.

The lights dimmed. Smithback quickly shoved a wedge of Camembert into his mouth, holding it between his teeth, realizing suddenly that he was eating while the biggest event he'd ever seen was being handed him on a silver platter. He checked his pockets for the microcassette recorder as the lights dimmed and brightened.

Smithback talked as fast as he could, mouth close to the microphone, hoping his voice would come through over the deafening roar of humanity. This was an incredible opportunity. The hell with Rickman. Everyone was going to want this story. He hoped that if any other journalists were at the party, they were running like hell to get out.

The lights flickered again.

A hundred thousand for the advance, he wasn't going to take a dime less. He was here, he'd covered the story from the beginning. Nobody could touch his access.

The lights flickered for a third time, then went out.

"Son of a bitch!" yelled Smithback. "Somebody turn on the lights!"

Margo pushed Frock around another corner, then waited while he called again for Pendergast. The sound echoed forlornly.

"This is growing pointless," said Frock in exasperation. "There are several larger storage rooms in this section. Maybe he's inside one and can't hear us. Let's try a few. It's all we have left." He grunted as he fished in a jacket pocket. "Don't leave home without it," he smiled, holding up a curator's master key.

Margo unlocked the first door and peered into the gloom. "Mr. Pendergast?" she called out. Metal shelves stacked with enormous bones rose out of the gloom. A big dinosaur skull, the size of a Volkswagen Beetle, sat near the door on a wooden skid, still partially encased in matrix, black teeth gleaming dully.

"Next!" said Frock.

The lights dimmed.

No answer in the next storage room, either.

"One more try," Frock said. "Over there, across the hall."

Margo stopped at the indicated door, marked PLEISTOCENE—12B, noting as she did so a stairwell door at the far end of the hall. She was pushing open the storage room door as the lights flickered a second time.

"This is—" she began.

Suddenly, a sharp explosion resounded down the narrow hall. Margo looked up, heart pounding, trying to locate the source of the noise. It seemed to have come from around a corner they had not yet explored.

Then the lights went out.

"If we wait a moment," Frock said finally, "the emergency backup system will come on."

Only the faint creaking of the building pierced the silence. The seconds stretched into a minute, two minutes.

Then Margo noticed a strange smell, goatish, fetid, almost rank. With a sob of despair, she remembered where she had smelled it once before: in the darkened exhibition.

"Do you—?" she whispered.

"Yes," hissed Frock. "Get inside and lock the door."

Breathing fast, Margo groped at the doorframe. She called out quietly as the smell grew stronger. "Dr. Frock? Can you follow the sound of my voice?"

"There's no time for that," came his whisper. "Please, forget about me and get inside."

"No," said Margo. "Just come toward me slowly."

She heard his chair rattle. The smell was growing overpowering, the earthy, rotting odor of a swamp, mixed with the sweet smell of warm raw hamburger. Margo heard a wet snuffling.

"I'm right here," she whispered to Frock. "Oh, hurry, please."

The darkness seemed oppressive, a suffocating weight. She cringed against the doorframe, flattening herself to the wall, fighting down an urge to flee.

In the pitch black, wheels rattled and the chair bumped gently against her leg. She grabbed its handles and pulled Frock inside. Turning, she slammed the door closed, locked it, and then sank to the floor, her body rocked by noiseless sobs. Silence filled the room.

There was a scraping on the door, soft at first, then louder and more insistent. Margo shrank away, banging her shoulder against the frame of the wheelchair. In the dark, she felt Frock gently take her hand.

= **48** =

D'Agosta sat up amid the broken glass, grabbed for his radio, and watched the retreating backs of the last guests, their screams and shouts fading.

"Lieutenant?" One of his officers, Bailey, was getting up from underneath another broken case. The Hall was a shambles: artifacts broken and scattered across the floor; broken glass everywhere; shoes, purses, pieces of clothing. Everybody had left the gallery except D'Agosta, Bailey, and the dead man. D'Agosta looked briefly at the headless body, registering the gaping wounds in the chest, the clothing stiffened by dried blood, the man's insides generously exposed like so much stuffing. Dead for some time, apparently. He looked away, then looked back quickly. The man was wearing a policeman's uniform.

"Bailey!" he shouted. "Officer down! Who is this man?"

Bailey came over, his face pale in the dim light. "Hard to say. But I think Fred Beauregard had a big old Academy ring like that."

"No *shit*," D'Agosta whistled under his breath. He bent closer, got the badge number.

Bailey nodded. "That's Beauregard, Loo."

"Christ!" D'Agosta said, straightening up. "Wasn't he on his forty-eight?"

"That's correct. Last tour was Wednesday afternoon."

"Then he's been in here since—" D'Agosta started. His face hardened into a scowl. "That fucking Coffey, refusing to sweep the exhibition. I'm gonna tear him a new asshole."

Bailey helped him up. "You're hurt."

"I'll bind it up later," D'Agosta said tersely. "Where's McNitt?"

"I don't know. Last I looked, he was caught in the crowd."

Ippolito stepped from around the far corner, talking into his radio. D'Agosta's respect for the Security Director went up a notch. *He may not be the brightest guy, but he's got balls when it comes to the pinch.*

The lights dimmed.

"There's panic in the Hall of the Heavens," said Ippolito, ear at his radio. "They say the security wall is coming down."

"Those idiots! That's the only exit!" He raised his own radio. "Walden! You copy? What's going on?"

"Sir, it's chaos here! McNitt just came out of the exhibition. He got pretty roughed up in there. We're at the exhibition entrance, trying to slow the crowd, but it's no use. There's a lot of people getting trampled, Lieutenant."

The lights dimmed a second time.

"Walden, is the emergency door coming down over the exit to the Rotunda?"

"Just a second." For a moment, the radio buzzed. "Shit, yes! It's halfway down and still dropping! People are jammed into that door like cattle, it's gonna crush a dozen or two—"

Suddenly, the exhibition went black. A dull crash of something heavy toppling to the ground momentarily overpowered the cries and screams.

D'Agosta pulled out his flashlight. "Ippolito, you can raise the door with the manual override, right?"

"Right. Anyway, the backup power should come on in a second—"

"We can't wait around for that, let's get the hell over there. And, for Chrissake, be careful."

Gingerly, they picked their way back toward the exhibition entrance, Ippolito leading the way through the welter of glass, broken wood, and debris. Broken pieces of once-priceless artifacts lay strewn about. The shouting and screaming grew louder as they neared the Hall of the Heavens.

Standing behind Ippolito, D'Agosta could see nothing in the vast blackness of the Hall. Even the votive candles had guttered. Ippolito was playing his flashlight around the entrance. *Why isn't he moving?* D'Agosta wondered irritably. Suddenly, Ippolito jerked backward, retching. His flashlight dropped to the ground and rolled away in the darkness.

"What the hell?" D'Agosta shouted, running forward with Bailey. Then he stopped short.

The huge Hall was a shambles. Shining his flashlight into the gloom, D'Agosta was reminded of earthquake footage he'd seen on the evening news. The platform was broken into several pieces, the lectern splintered and shattered. The bandstand was deserted, chairs toppled over, crushed instruments lying in heaps. The floor was a maelstrom of food, clothing, printed programs, toppled bamboo trees, and trampled orchids, twisted and smashed into a strange landscape by the thousands of panicked feet.

D'Agosta brought the flashlight in toward the exhibition entrance itself. The huge wooden stelae surrounding the entrance had collapsed in giant pieces. D'Agosta could see limp arms and legs protruding from beneath the intricately carved columns.

Bailey rushed over. "There're at least eight people crushed here, Lieutenant. I don't think any of them are still alive."

"Any of them ours?" D'Agosta asked.

"I'm afraid so. Looks like McNitt and Walden, and one of the plainclothesmen. There are a couple of guard's uniforms here, too, and three civilians, I think."

"All dead? Every one of them?"

"Far as I can tell. I can't budge these columns."

"Shit." D'Agosta looked away, rubbing his forehead. A loud thud resonated from across the Hall.

"That's the security door closing," said Ippolito, wiping his mouth. He knelt at Bailey's side. "Oh, no. Martine . . . Christ, I can't believe it." He turned to D'Agosta. "Martine here was guarding the back stairwell. He must have come over to help control the crowd. He was one of my best men . . ."

D'Agosta threaded his way between the broken columns and moved out into the Hall, dodging the upturned tables and broken chairs. His hand was still bleeding freely. There were several other still forms scattered about, whether dead or alive D'Agosta couldn't tell. When he heard screaming from the far end of the Hall, he shined his light toward the noise. The metal emergency door was fully shut, and a crowd of people were pressed against it, pounding on the metal and shouting. Some of them turned around as D'Agosta's light illuminated them.

D'Agosta ran over to the group, ignoring his squawking radio. "Everybody calm down, and move away! This is Lieutenant D'Agosta of the New York City police."

The crowd quieted a little, and D'Agosta called Ippolito over. Scanning the group, D'Agosta recognized Wright, the Director; Ian Cuthbert, head of this whole farce; some woman named Rickman who seemed pretty important—basically, the first forty or so people who'd entered the exhibition. First in, last out.

"Listen up!" he shouted. "The Security Director's going to raise the emergency door. Everybody, please step back."

The crowd moved aside, and D'Agosta involuntarily groaned. There were several limbs pinned under the heavy metal door. The floor was slick with blood. One of the limbs was moving feebly, and he could hear faint screaming from the far side of the door.

"Dear Jesus," he whispered. "Ippolito, open the son of a bitch."

"Shine your light over here." Ippolito pointed to a small keypad next to the door, then crouched and punched in a series of numbers.

They waited.

Ippolito looked nonplussed. "I can't understand—" He punched in the numbers again, more slowly this time.

"There's no power," said D'Agosta.

"Shouldn't matter," said Ippolito, frantically punching a third time. "The system's got redundant backups."

The crowd started to murmur.

"We're trapped!" one man yelled.

D'Agosta whirled his light onto the crowd. "All of you, just calm down. That body in the exhibition has been dead at least two days. You understand? *Two days.* The murderer's long gone."

"How do you know?" shouted the same man.

"Shut up and listen," said D'Agosta. "We're going to get you out of here. If we can't open the door, they'll do it from the outside. It may take a few minutes. In the meantime, I want you all to get away from the door, stick together, find yourself some chairs that aren't broken, and sit down. Okay? There's nothing you can do here."

Wright stepped forward into the light. "Listen, officer," he said, "We've got to get out of here. Ippolito, for the love of God, open the door!"

"Just a moment!" said D'Agosta sharply. "Dr. Wright, please return to the group." He looked around at the wide-eyed faces. "Are there any physicians here?"

There was a silence.

"Nurses? First aid?"

"I know some first aid," someone volunteered.

"Great. Mister, ah—"

"Arthur Pound."

"Pound. Get one or two volunteers to help you. There are several people who look like they got trampled. I need to know number and their condition. I've got a guy back at the exhibition entrance, Bailey, who can help you. He's got a flashlight. We also need a volunteer to help collect some candles."

A young, lanky fellow in a wrinkled tuxedo came out of the gloom. He finished chewing, swallowed. "I'll help with that," he said.

"Name?"

"Smithback."

"Okay, Smithback. You got matches?"

"Sure do."

The Mayor stepped forward. His face was smeared with blood and a large purple welt was emerging beneath one eye. "Let me help," he said.

D'Agosta looked at him with amazement. "Mayor Harper! Maybe you can take charge of everyone. Keep them calm."

"Certainly, Lieutenant."

D'Agosta's radio squawked again, and he grabbed it. "D'Agosta, this is Coffey. D'Agosta, do you read? What the hell's going on in there? Give me a sit-ref!"

D'Agosta talked fast. "Listen up, I'm not going to say this twice. We've got at least eight dead, probably more, and an undetermined number of wounded. I guess you know about the people caught under the door. Ippolito can't get the fucking door open. There's about thirty, maybe forty of us here. Including Wright and the Mayor."

"The Mayor! Shit. Look, D'Agosta, the system's failed totally. The manual override doesn't work on this side, either. I'll get a crew with acetylene to cut you guys out. It may take awhile, this door's built like a bank vault. Is the Mayor okay?"

"He's fine. Where's Pendergast?"

"I don't have a clue."

"Who else is trapped inside the perimeter?"

"Don't know yet," said Coffey. "We're taking reports now. There should be some men in the Computer Room and Security Command, Garcia and a few others. Might be a few on the other floors. We got several plainclothes officers and guards out here. They were pushed out with the crowd, some of them got messed up pretty bad. What the hell happened in the exhibition, D'Agosta?"

"They found the body of one of my men stuffed on top of an exhibit. Gutted, just like the rest." He paused, then spoke bitterly. "If you'd let me do the sweep I requested, none of this would have happened."

The radio squawked again and went silent.

"Pound!" D'Agosta called. "What's the extent of the injuries?"

"We've got one man alive, but just barely," Pound said, looking up from an inert form. "The rest are dead. Trampled. Maybe one or two heart attacks, it's hard to say."

"Do what you can for the live one," D'Agosta said.

His radio buzzed. "Lieutenant D'Agosta?" said a scratchy voice. "This is Garcia, in Security Command, sir. We got . . ." The voice trailed out in a burst of static.

"Garcia? Garcia! What is it?" D'Agosta shouted into the radio.

"Sorry, sir, the batteries on this mobile transmitter I'm using are weak. We got Pendergast on the honk. I'm patching him over to you."

"Vincent," came the familiar drawl.

"Pendergast! Where are you?"

"I'm in the basement, Section Twenty-nine. I understand the power is out throughout the Museum, and that we're trapped inside Cell Two. I'm afraid I've got a little more bad news of my own to add. Could you please move to a spot where we can speak privately?"

D'Agosta walked away from the crowd. "What is it?" he asked in a low tone.

"Vincent, listen to me carefully. There is something down here. I don't know what it is, but it's big, and I don't think it's human."

"Pendergast, don't play with me. Not now."

"Vincent, I'm entirely serious. That isn't the bad news. The bad news is, it may be headed your way."

"What do you mean? What kind of animal is it?"

"You'll know when it's near. The smell is unmistakable. What kind of weapons do you have?"

"Let's see. Three twelve gauges, a couple of service revolvers, two shot pistols loaded with capstun. A few odds and ends, maybe."

"Forget the capstun. Now, listen, we have to talk fast. Get everyone out of there. This thing went by me just before the lights went out. I saw it through a window in one of the storage rooms down here, and it looked very big. It walks on all fours. I got off two shots at it, then it went into a stairwell at the end of this hall. I've got a set of old blueprints here with me, and I've checked them. You know where that stairwell comes out?"

"No," said D'Agosta.

"It only has access to alternate floors. It leads down into the sub-basement, too, but we can't assume the thing would go that way. There's an egress on the fourth floor. And there's another one behind the Hall of the Heavens. It's back in the service area behind the platform."

"Pendergast, I'm having a hard time with this. What the hell exactly do you want us to do?"

"I'd get your men—whoever has the shotguns—and line up at that door. If the creature comes through, let the thing have it. It may have already *come* through, I don't know. Vincent, it took a .45 metal-jacketed slug in the skull at close range, and the bullet grazed right off."

If anyone else had been speaking, D'Agosta would have suspected a joke. Or madness. "Right," he said. "How long ago was this?"

"I saw it a few minutes ago, just before the power went out. I shot at it once, then followed it down the hall after the lights went. I got off another shot, but my light wasn't steady and I missed it. I went down to reconnoiter just now. The hall dead-ends, and the thing has vanished. The only way out is the stairwell leading up to you. It may be hiding in the stairwell, or maybe, if you're lucky, it's gone to a different floor. All I know is that it hasn't come back this way."

D'Agosta swallowed.

"If you can get into the basement safely, do it. Meet up with me here. These blueprints seem to show the way out. We'll talk again once you're in a more secure place. Do you understand?"

"Yes," said D'Agosta.

"Vincent? There's something else."

"What now?"

"This creature can open and close doors."

D'Agosta holstered his radio, licked his lips, and looked back toward the group of people. Most were sitting on the floor, stunned, but a few were trying to help light the armload of candles the lanky guy had scrounged.

D'Agosta spoke to the group as softly as he could. "All of you, move over here and get down against the wall. Put those candles out."

"What is it?" somebody cried. D'Agosta recognized the voice as Wright's.

"Quiet. Do as I say. You, what's your name, Smithback, drop that and get over here."

D'Agosta's radio buzzed into speech as he did a quick visual sweep of the Hall with his flashlight. The remote corners of the hall were so black they seemed to eat the beam of his light. In the center of the hall a few candles were lit next to a still form. Pound and somebody else were bending over it.

"Pound!" he called out. "Both of you. Get back over here!"

"But he's still alive—"

"Get back *now!*" He turned to the crowd that was huddling behind him. "None of you move or make a sound. Bailey and Ippolito, bring those shotguns and follow me."

"Did you hear that? Why do they need their guns!" cried Wright.

Recognizing Coffey's voice on the radio, D'Agosta switched if off with a brusque movement. Moving carefully, flashlights probing the darkness ahead of them, the group crept toward the center of the Hall. D'Agosta played his beam along the wall, found the service area, the dark outlines of the stairwell door. It was closed. He thought he smelled something strange in the air; a peculiar, rotten odor he couldn't place. But the room stunk to begin with. Half the damn guests must have lost control of their plumbing when the lights failed.

He led the way into the service area, then stopped. "According to Pendergast, there's a creature, an animal, maybe in this stairwell," he whispered.

"According to Pendergast," said Ippolito sarcastically under his breath.

"Stow that shit, Ippolito. Now listen up. We can't stay here waiting in the dark. We're gonna go in nice and easy. Okay? Do it by the numbers. Safeties off, shells in the chambers. Bailey, you're gonna open the door, then cover us with the light, *fast*. Ippolito, you'll cover the upward staircase and I'll cover the down. If you see a person, demand identification and shoot if you don't get it. If you see anything else, shoot immediately. We move on my signal."

D'Agosta switched off his flashlight, slipped it in a pocket, and tightened his grip on the shotgun. Then he nodded for Bailey to direct his own light onto the stairwell door. D'Agosta closed his eyes and murmured a brief prayer in the close darkness. Then he gave the signal.

Ippolito moved to the side of the door while Bailey yanked it open. D'Agosta and Ippolito rushed in, Bailey behind them, sweeping the light in a quick semicircle.

A horrible stench awaited them inside the stairwell. D'Agosta took a few steps down into the darkness, sensed a sudden movement *above* him, and heard an unearthly, throaty growl that turned his knees to putty, followed by a dull, slapping sound, like the smacking of a damp towel against the floor. Then wet things were hitting the wall around him and gobs of moisture splattered his face. He spun around and fired at something large and dark. The light was gyrating wildly. "Shit!" he heard Bailey wail.

"Bailey! Don't let it go into the Hall!" He fired into the darkness, again and again, up the stairwell and down, until he was pumping an empty chamber. The acrid smell of gunpowder blended with the nauseating reek as screams resounded in the Hall of the Heavens.

D'Agosta stumbled up the stairs to the landing, almost tripped over something, and moved into the Hall. "Bailey, where is it?" he yelled as he jammed shells into his shotgun, temporarily blinded by the muzzle flare.

"I don't know!" Bailey shouted. "I can't see!"

"Did it go down or through?" *Two shells in the shotgun. Three . . .*

"I don't know! I don't know!"

D'Agosta pulled out his flashlight and shone it on Bailey. The officer was soaked in thick clots of blood. Pieces of flesh were in his hair, hanging from his eyebrows. He was wiping his eyes. A hideous smell hung in the air.

"I'm fine," Bailey reassured D'Agosta. "I think. I just got all this shit on my face, I can't see."

D'Agosta swept the light around the room in a fast arc, the shotgun braced against his thigh. The group, huddled together against the wall, blinked in terror. He turned the light back toward the stairwell, and saw Ippolito, or what was left of him, lying partway on the landing, dark blood rapidly spreading from his torn gut.

The thing had been waiting for them just a few steps up from the landing. *But where the fuck was it now?* He shined the light in desperate circles around the Hall. It was gone—the huge space was still.

No. Something *was* moving in the center of the Hall. The light was dim at that distance, but D'Agosta could see a large, dark shape crouched over the injured man on the dance floor, lunging downward with odd, jerking motions. D'Agosta heard the man wail once—then there was a faint crunching noise and silence. D'Agosta propped the flashlight in his armpit, raised his gun, aimed, and squeezed the trigger.

There was a flash and a roar. Screams erupted from the huddled group. Two more shots and the chamber was again empty.

He reached for more shells, came up empty, dropped the shotgun and drew his service revolver. "Bailey!" he yelled. "Get over there fast, get everyone together and prepare to move." He swept the light across the floor of the Hall, but the shape was gone. He moved carefully toward the body. At ten feet, he saw the one thing he'd wanted not to see: the split skull and the brains spread across the floor. A bloody track led into the exhibition. Whatever it was had rushed inside to escape the shotgun blast. It wouldn't stay there long.

D'Agosta leaped up, raced around the columns, and yanked one of the heavy wooden exhibition doors free. With a grunt, he slammed it to, then raced over to the far side. There was a noise inside the exhibition, a swift heavy tread. He slammed the second door 'shut and heard the latch fall. Then the doors shuddered as something heavy hit them.

"Bailey!" he yelled. "Get everyone down the stairwell!"

The pounding grew stronger, and D'Agosta backed up involuntarily. The wood of the door began to splinter.

As he aimed his gun toward the door, he heard screams and shouts behind him. They'd seen Ippolito. He heard Bailey's voice raised in argument with Wright. There was a sudden shudder and a great crack opened at the base of the door.

D'Agosta ran across the room. "Down the stairs, now! Don't look back!"

"No," screamed Wright, who was blocking the stairwell. "Look at Ippolito! I'm not going down there!"

"There's a way out!" shouted D'Agosta.

"No there isn't. But through the exhibition, and—"

"There's something *in* the exhibition!" D'Agosta yelled. "Now get going!"

Bailey moved Wright forcibly aside and started pushing people through the door, even as they cried and stumbled across the body of Ippolito. *At least the Mayor seems calm*, D'Agosta thought. *Probably saw worse than this at his last press conference.*

"I'm not going down there!" Wright cried. "Cuthbert, Lavinia, listen to me. That basement's a death trap. I know. We'll go upstairs, we can hide on the fourth floor, come back when the creature's gone."

The people were through the door and staggering down the stairwell. D'Agosta could hear more wood splintering. He paused a moment. There were thirty-odd people below him, only three hesitating on the landing. "This is your last chance to come with us," he said.

"We're going with Doctor Wright," said the Public Relations Director. In the gleam of the flashlight, Rickman's drawn and fearful face looked like an apparition.

Without a word, D'Agosta turned and followed the group downward. As he ran, he could hear Wright's loud, desperate voice, calling for them to come upstairs.

= **49** =

Coffey stood just inside the tall archway of the Museum's west entrance, watching the rain lash against the elaborate glass-and-bronze doors. He was shouting into his radio but D'Agosta wasn't responding. And what was this shit Pendergast was slinging about a monster? The guy was bent to begin with, he figured, and the blackout sent him over the edge. As usual, everyone had screwed up, and once again it was up to Coffey to clean up the mess. Outside, two large emergency response vehicles were pulling up at the entrance and police in riot gear were pouring out, moving quickly to erect A-frames across Riverside Drive. He could hear the wailing of ambulances frantically trying to nose their way through the steel grid of radio cars, fire engines, and press vans. Crowds of people were scattered around, crying, talking, standing in the rain or lying beneath the Museum's vast awning. Members of the press were trying to slip past the cordon, snaking their microphones and cameras into faces before being pushed back by the police.

Coffey sprinted through the pelting rain to the silver bulk of the Mobile Command Unit. He yanked open the rear door and jumped inside.

Within the MCU, it was cool and dark. Several agents were monitoring terminals, their faces glowing green in the reflected light. Coffey grabbed a headset and sat down. "Regroup!" he shouted on the command channel. "All FBI personnel to the Mobile Command Unit!"

He switched channels. "Security Command. I want an update."

Garcia's voice came on, weary and tense. "We still have total system failure, sir. The backup power hasn't kicked in, they don't know why.

All we have are our flashlights and the batteries in this mobile transmitter."

"So? Start it manually."

"It's all computer-driven, sir. Apparently there is no manual start."

"And the security doors?"

"Sir, when we took those power dips the entire security system mal-
functioned. They think it's a hardware problem. All the security doors
were released."

"Whaddya mean, *all?*"

"The security doors on all five cells closed. It isn't just Cell Two.
The whole Museum's shut down tight."

"Garcia, who there knows the most about this security system?"

"That'd be Allen."

"Put him on."

There was a brief pause. "Tom Allen speaking."

"Allen, what about the manual overrides? Why aren't they working?"

"Same hardware problem. The security system was a third-party in-
stallation, a Japanese vendor. We're trying to get a representative on
the phone now, but it's tough, the phone system is digital and it went
out when the computer shut down. We're routing all calls through
Garcia's transmitter. Even the T1 lines are out. It's been a chain reaction since the switching box was shot to hell."

"Who? I didn't know—"

"Some cop—what's his name? Waters?—on duty in the Computer
Room, thought he saw something, fired a couple of shotgun rounds
into the main electrical switching box."

"Look, Allen, I want to send a team in to evacuate those people
trapped in the Hall of the Heavens. The Mayor's in there, for Chrissake. How can we get in? Should we cut through the east door into
the Hall?"

"Those doors are designed to retard cutting. You could do it, but it
would take forever."

"What about the subbasement? I've heard it's like a frigging cata-
comb down there."

"There might be ingress points from where you are, but on-line
charts are down. And the area isn't fully mapped. It would take time."

"The walls, then. How about going through the walls?"

"The lower load-bearing walls are extremely thick, three feet in most
places, and all the older masonry walls have been heavily reinforced

with rebar. Cell Two only has windows on the third and fourth floor, and they're reinforced with steel bars. Most of them are too small to climb through, anyway."

"Shit. What about the roof?"

"All the cells are closed off, and it would be pretty tough—"

"Goddammit, Allen, I'm *asking* you the *best* way to get some men inside."

There was a silence.

"The best way to get in would be through the roof," came the voice. "The security doors on the upper floors are not as heavy. Cell Three extends above the Hall of the Heavens. That's the fifth floor. You can't enter there, though—the roof is shielded because of the radiography labs. But you could come in through the roof of Cell Four. In some of the narrower halls you might be able to blow a security door to Cell Three with one charge. Once you were in Cell Three you could go right through the ceiling of the Hall of the Heavens. There's an access port for servicing the chandelier in the Hall ceiling. It's sixty feet to the floor, though."

"I'll get back to you. Coffey out."

He punched at the radio and shouted, "Ippolito! Ippolito, you copy?" What the hell was happening inside that Hall? He switched to D'Agosta's frequency. "D'Agosta! This is Coffey. Are you reading me?"

He ran frantically through the bands.

"Waters!"

"Waters here, sir."

"What happened, Waters?"

"There was a loud noise in the electrical room, sir, and I fired as per regulations, and—"

"Regulations? You fucking turkey, there's no regulation for firing at a noise!"

"Sorry, sir. It was a loud noise, and I heard a lot of screaming and running in the exhibition and I thought—"

"For this, Waters, you're dead. I'm gonna have your ass roasted and sliced up like luncheon meat on a platter. Think about it."

"Yes, sir."

Outside there was a cough, sputter, and a roar as a large portable generator started up. The rear door to the Mobile Command Unit opened and several agents ducked in, their suits dripping. "The rest are on their way, sir," one of them said.

"Okay. Tell them we're having a crisis-control meeting here in the MCU in five minutes."

He stepped out into the rain. Emergency services workers were moving bulky equipment and yellow acetylene tanks up the Museum steps.

Coffey ran back through the rain and up the steps into the debris-laden Rotunda. Medics clustered at the metal emergency door blocking the east entrance to the Hall of the Heavens. Coffey could hear the whine of a bone saw.

"Tell me what you've got," Coffey asked the leader of the medical team.

The doctor's eyes looked strained above his blood-flecked mask. "I don't know the full extent of the injuries yet, but we've got several criticals here. We're performing some field amputations. I think a few others might be saved if you can get this door open in the next half hour."

Coffey shook his head. "Doesn't look like that will happen. We're gonna have to cut through it."

An emergency worker spoke up. "We've got some heat-proof blankets we can lay across these people as we work."

Coffey stepped back and raised his radio. "D'Agosta! Ippolito! Come in!"

Silence. Then, he heard a hiss of static.

"D'Agosta here," came the tense voice. "Listen, Coffey—"

"Where have you been? I told you—"

"Shut up and listen, Coffey. You were making too much noise, I had to shut you off. We're down in the subbasement, I'm not sure where. There's a creature loose somewhere in Cell Two. I'm not kidding you, Coffey, it's a fucking *monster*. It killed Ippolito and ran into the Hall. We had to get out."

"A *what*? You're losing it, D'Agosta. Get a grip, you hear me? We're sending men in through the roof."

"Yeah? Well, they'd better have some heavy shit ready if they plan on meeting up with this thing."

"D'Agosta, let me handle it. What's this about Ippolito?"

"He's dead, slashed open, just like all the other stiffs."

"And a monster did this. Okay, sure. Any other police officers with you, D'Agosta?"

"Yeah, there's Bailey."

"I'm relieving you of duty. Put Bailey on."

"Fuck you. Here's Bailey."

"Sergeant," Coffey barked, "You're in charge now. What's the situation?"

"Mr. Coffey, he's right. We had to leave the Hall of the Heavens. We went down the back stairwell near the service area. There's over thirty of us, including the Mayor. No shit, there's really something in here."

"Give me a break, Bailey. Did you see it?"

"I'm not sure what I saw, sir, but D'Agosta saw it, and Jesus, sir, you should see what it did to Ippolito—"

"Listen to me, Bailey. Are you gonna calm down and take over?"

"No sir. As far as I'm concerned, he's in charge."

"I just put *you* in charge!"

Coffey snorted and looked up, enraged. "The son of a bitch just cut me off."

Outside in the rain, Greg Kawakita stood motionless amid a cacophony of yelling, sobbing, and cursing. He remained oblivious to the pelting rain that plastered his black hair to his forehead; the emergency vehicles that passed by, sirens shrieking; the panicky guests that jostled him as they ran past. Again and again he replayed in his mind what Margo and Frock had barked at him. He opened and closed his mouth, moved forward as if to reenter the Museum. Then, slowly, he turned, pulled his sodden tuxedo closer around his narrow shoulders, and walked thoughtfully into the darkness.

= 50 =

Margo jumped as a second gunshot echoed down the hall.

"What's happening?" she cried. In the darkness, she felt Frock's grip tighten.

Outside, they heard running steps. Then the yellow glow of a flashlight streaked by beneath the doorframe.

"That smell is growing fainter," she whispered. "Do you think it's gone?"

"Margo," Frock replied quietly, "you saved my life. You risked your own life to save mine."

There came a soft knocking at the door. "Who is it?" Frock asked in a steady tone.

"Pendergast," a voice said, and Margo rushed to open the door. The FBI agent stood outside, a large revolver in one hand and crumpled blueprints in the other. His crisp well-tailored black suit contrasted with his dirt-streaked face. He shut the door behind him.

"I'm pleased to see you both safe and sound," he said, shining his light first on Margo and then Frock.

"Not half as pleased as we are!" Frock cried. "We came down here searching for you. Were those shots yours?"

"Yes," Pendergast said. "And I assume it was you I heard calling my name?"

"Then you *did* hear me!" Frock said. "That's how you knew to look for us in here."

Pendergast shook his head. "No." He handed Margo a flashlight as he started unfolding his crumpled blueprints. Margo saw they were covered with handwritten notes.

"The New York Historical Society will be very unhappy when they see the liberties I've taken with their property," the agent observed dryly.

"Pendergast," Frock hissed, "Margo and I have discovered exactly what this killer is. You *must* listen. It isn't a human being or any animal we know. Please, let me explain."

Pendergast looked up. "I don't need any convincing, Doctor Frock."

Frock blinked. "You don't? You will? I mean, you will help us stop the opening upstairs, get the people out?"

"It's too late for that," Pendergast said. "I've been talking by police radio to Lieutenant D'Agosta and others. This power failure isn't just affecting the basement, it's affecting the entire Museum. The security system has failed, and all the emergency doors have come down."

"You mean—" Margo began.

"I mean the Museum has been compartmentalized into five isolated cells. We're in Cell Two. Along with the people in the Hall of the Heavens. And the creature."

"What happened?" Frock asked.

"There was a panic even before the power went out and the doors came down. A dead body was discovered inside the exhibition. A police officer. Most of the guests managed to get out, but thirty or forty are trapped inside the Hall of the Heavens." He smiled ruefully. "I was in the exhibition myself, just a few hours before. I wanted to get a look at this Mbwun figurine you mentioned. If I'd gone in by the rear exit instead of the front, perhaps I would have found the body myself, and prevented all this. However, I did get a chance to see the figurine, Doctor Frock. And it's an excellent representation. Take it from somebody who knows."

Frock stared, his mouth open.

"You've seen it?" Frock managed to whisper.

"Yes. That's what I was shooting at. I was down around the corner from this storeroom when I heard you call my name. Then I noticed an awful smell. I ducked into a room and watched it go by. I came out after it and got off a shot, but it grazed off the thing's scalp. Then the lights went out. I followed it around the corner and saw it grasping at this door, snuffling." Pendergast flicked open the revolver's cylinder, and replaced the two spent cartridges. "*That's* how I knew you were in here."

"My God," Margo said.

Pendergast holstered his gun. "I got off a second shot at it, but I was having trouble aiming my weapon, and I missed. I came down this way to look for it, but the thing had vanished. It must have gone into the stairwell at the end of the corridor. There's no other way out from this cul-de-sac."

"Mr. Pendergast," Frock said urgently. "Tell me, please: *what did it look like?*"

"I saw it only briefly," Pendergast said slowly. "It was low, extremely powerful-looking. It walked on all fours, but could rear upright. It was partially covered with hair." He pursed his lips, nodded. "It was dark. But I'd say whoever made that figurine knew what he was doing."

In the glow of Pendergast's light, Margo saw a strange mix of fear, exhilaration, and triumph cross Frock's face.

Then a series of muffled explosions echoed and reechoed above them. There was a brief silence, and then more reports, sharper and louder, boomed nearby.

Pendergast looked upward, listening intently. "D'Agosta!" he said. Drawing his gun and dropping the blueprints, he raced out into the corridor.

Margo ran to the door and shined the flashlight down the hallway. In its thin beam, she could see Pendergast rattling the stairwell door. He knelt to inspect the lock, then, standing, he gave the door a series of savage kicks.

"It's jammed shut," he said when he returned. "Those shotgun blasts we heard sounded like they came from inside the stairwell. Some of the shells must have bent the doorframe and damaged the lock. It won't budge." He holstered the gun and pulled out his radio. "Lieutenant D'Agosta! Vincent, can you hear me?" He waited a moment, then shook his head and replaced the radio in his jacket pocket.

"So we're stuck here?" Margo asked.

Pendergast shook his head. "I don't think so. I've spent the afternoon down in these vaults and tunnels, trying to determine how the beast was able to elude our searches. These blueprints were drafted well before the turn of the century, and they are complicated and contradictory, but they seem to show a route out of the Museum through the subbasement. With everything sealed off, there's no other feasible way out for us. And there are several ways to access the subbasement from this section of the Museum."

"That means we can meet up with the people still upstairs, then escape together!" Margo said.

Pendergast looked grim. "But that also means the beast can find its way back into the subbasement. Personally, I think that while these emergency doors may prevent our own rescue, they won't hamper the beast's movement much. I believe it's been around long enough to find its own secret ways, and that it can move throughout the Museum— or, at least, the lower levels—practically at will."

Margo nodded. "We think it's been living in the Museum for years. And we think we know how and why it came here."

Pendergast looked searchingly at Margo for a long moment. "I need you and Doctor Frock to tell me everything you know about this creature, as quickly as possible," he said.

As they turned to enter the storeroom, Margo heard a distant drumming, like slow thunder. She froze, listening intently. The thunder seemed to have a voice: crying or shouting, she wasn't sure which.

"What was that?" she whispered.

"That," Pendergast said quietly, "is the sound of people in the stairwell, running for their lives."

= 51 =

In the faint light filtering in through the barred laboratory window, Wright could barely make out the old filing cabinet. It was damned lucky, he thought, that the lab was inside the perimeter of Cell Two. Not for the first time, he was glad he'd kept this old laboratory when he'd been promoted to Director. It would provide them with a temporary safe haven, a little breathing room. Cell Two was now completely cut off from the rest of the Museum, and they were effectively prisoners. Everything, all the emergency bars, shutters, and security gates, had come down during the loss of power. At least that's what he'd heard that incompetent police officer, D'Agosta, say.

"Someone is going to pay dearly for this," Wright muttered to himself. Then they all fell quiet. Now that they had stopped running, the enormity of the disaster began to sink in.

Wright moved gingerly forward, pulling out one file-cabinet drawer after another, fishing behind the folders until at last he found what he was looking for.

"Ruger .38 magnum," he said, hefting it in his hands. "Great pistol. Excellent stopping power."

"I'm not sure that's going to stop whatever killed Ippolito," said Cuthbert. He was standing near the laboratory door, a still figure framed in black.

"Don't worry, Ian. One of these speedball bullets would perforate an elephant. I bought this after old Shorter was mugged by a vagrant. Anyway, the creature isn't coming up here. And if he does, this door is solid oak two inches thick."

"What about that one?" Cuthbert pointed toward the rear of the office.

"That goes into the Hall of Cretaceous Dinosaurs. It's just like this one—solid oak." He tucked the Ruger into his belt. "Those fools, going into the basement like so many lemmings. They should have listened to me."

He rummaged in the file drawer again and pulled out a flashlight. "Excellent. Haven't used this in years."

He snapped it on and a feeble beam shot out, wavering as his hand shook a little.

"Not much juice left in that torch, I'd say," Cuthbert murmured.

Wright turned it off. "We'll only use it in an emergency."

"Please!" Rickman spoke suddenly. "Please leave it on. Just for a minute." She was sitting on a stool in the center of the room, clenching and unclenching her hands. "Winston, what are we going to do? We must have a plan."

"First things first," said Wright. "I need a drink, that's Plan A. My nerves are shot." He made his way to the far side of the lab and shone the light in an old cabinet, finally pulling out a bottle. There was a clink of glass.

"Ian?" asked Wright.

"Nothing for me," Cuthbert replied.

"Lavinia?"

"No, no, I couldn't."

Wright came back and sat down at a worktable. He filled the tumbler and drank it off in three gulps. Then he refilled it. Suddenly, the room was full of the warm, peaty scent of single-malt scotch.

"Easy there, Winston," said Cuthbert.

"We can't stay here, in the dark," Rickman said nervously. "There must be an exit somewhere on this floor."

"I'm telling you, everything's sealed off," Wright snapped.

"What about the Dinosaur Hall?" said Rickman, pointing to the rear door.

"Lavinia," said Wright, "the Dinosaur Hall has only one public entrance, and that's been sealed by a security door. We're completely locked in. But you don't need to worry, because whatever killed Ippolito and the others won't be after us. It'll go after the easy kill, the group blundering around in the basement."

There was a swallowing sound, then the loud *snack* of glass hitting the table. "I say we stay here for another half-hour, wait it out. Then, we'll go back down into the exhibition. If they haven't restored power and unsealed the doors by then, I know of another way out. *Through the exhibition.*"

"You seem to know all kinds of hiding places," Cuthbert said.

"This used to be my lab. Once in awhile I still like to come down here, get away from the administrative headaches, be near my dinosaurs again." He chuckled and drank.

"I see," said Cuthbert acidly.

"Part of the *Superstition* exhibition is mounted in what used to be the old Trilobite Alcove. I put in a lot of hours down there many years ago. Anyway, there was a passageway to the Broadway corridor behind one of the old trilobite displays. The door was boarded up years ago to make room for another display case. I'm sure that when they were building *Superstition*, they just nailed a piece of plywood over it and painted it. We could kick it in, shoot off the lock with this if necessary."

"That sounds feasible," said Rickman eagerly.

"I don't recall hearing about any such door in the exhibition," Cuthbert said dubiously. "I'm sure Security would have known about it."

"It was years ago, I tell you," Wright snapped. "It was boarded over and forgotten."

There was a long silence while Wright poured another drink.

"Winston," Cuthbert said, "put that drink down."

The Director took a long swig, then hung his head. His shoulders slumped.

"Ian," he murmured finally. "How could this have happened? We're ruined, you know."

Cuthbert was silent.

"Let's not bury the patient before the diagnosis," said Rickman, in a desperately bright voice. "Good public relations can repair even the worst damage."

"Lavinia, we aren't talking about a few poisoned headache tablets here," Cuthbert said. "There's half a dozen dead people, maybe more, lying two floors below us. The bloody *Mayor* is trapped down there. In a couple of hours, we'll be on every late news show in the country."

"We're ruined," Wright repeated. A small, strangled sob escaped from his throat, and he laid his head down on the table.

"Bloody hell," muttered Cuthbert, reaching over for Wright's bottle and glass and putting them back in the cabinet.

"It's over, isn't it?" Wright moaned without raising his head.

"Yes, Winston, it's over," said Cuthbert. "Frankly, I'll be happy just to get out of here with my life."

"Please, Ian, let's leave here? *Please?*" Rickman pleaded. She stood up and walked over to the door Wright had closed behind them and swung it open slowly.

"This wasn't locked!" she said sharply.

"Good Lord," Cuthbert said, jumping up. Wright, without lifting his head, fished in his pocket and held out a key.

"Fits both doors," he said in a muffled voice.

Rickman's shaking hand rattled the key loudly in the lock.

"What did we do wrong?" Wright asked plaintively.

"That's clear enough," said Cuthbert. "Five years ago, we had a chance to solve this thing."

"What do you mean?" asked Rickman, coming back toward them.

"You know very well what. I'm talking about Montague's disappearance. We should have taken care of the problem then, instead of pretending it never happened. All that blood in the basement near the Whittlesey crates, Montague gone missing. In hindsight, we now know exactly what happened to him. But we should have gotten to the bottom of it *then*. You remember, Winston? We were sitting in your office when Ippolito came in with the news. You ordered the floor cleaned and the incident forgotten. We washed our hands of it, and hoped whoever or *what*ever killed Montague would disappear."

"There was no proof anyone was killed!" Wright wailed, lifting his head. "And certainly no proof it was Montague! It could have been a stray dog, or something. How could we have known?"

"We didn't know. But we might have found out had you allowed Ippolito to report that monstrous great bloodstain to the police. And you, Lavinia—as I recall, you agreed that we should simply wash that blood away."

"Ian, there was no sense in creating a needless scandal. You know very well that blood could have been from anything," Rickman said. "And Ian, it was you who insisted those crates be moved. You who worried the exhibition would raise questions about the Whittlesey expedition, you who took the journal and then asked me to keep it for you until the exhibition was over. The journal didn't fit in with your theories, did it?"

Cuthbert snorted. "How little you know. Julian Whittlesey was my friend. At least, he was once. We had a falling-out over an article he published, and we never patched things up. Anyway, it's rather too late for that now. But I didn't want to see that journal come to light, his theories held up for ridicule."

He turned and stared at the Public Relations Director. "What I did, Lavinia, was simply try to protect a colleague who'd gone a bit barmy. I didn't cover up a killing. And what about the sightings? Winston, you received several reports a year about people seeing or hearing strange things after hours. You never once did anything about it, did you?"

"How could I have known?" came the spluttering response. "Who'd have believed it? They were crank reports, ridiculous . . ."

"Can we change the subject, please?" cried Rickman. "I can't wait here, in the dark. Maybe the windows? Perhaps they'll spread a net for us?"

"No," said Wright, sighing deeply and rubbing his eyes. "Those bars are case-hardened steel, several inches thick." He peered around the darkened room. "Where's my drink?"

"You've had enough," said Cuthbert.

"You and your damned Anglican moralizing." He lurched to his feet and headed for the cabinet with a slightly unsteady gait.

In the stairwell, D'Agosta looked toward the dim figure of Bailey.

"Thanks," he said.

"You're in charge, Loo."

Below them, the large group of guests was waiting, huddled together on the steps, sniffling and sobbing. D'Agosta turned to face them.

"Okay," he said quietly. "We've got to move fast. The next landing down has a door leading into the basement. We're going to go through it and meet up with some others who know a way out of here. Everybody understand?"

"We understand," came a voice that D'Agosta recognized as the Mayor's.

"Good," D'Agosta nodded. "Okay, let's go. I'll get to the front and lead the way with my light. Bailey, you cover our rear. Let me know if you see anything."

Slowly, the group descended. On the landing, D'Agosta waited until Bailey gave him the all-clear sign. Then he grabbed the door handle.

It didn't budge.

D'Agosta gave it another yank, harder this time. No luck.

"What the—?" He brought his flashlight to bear on the handle. "Shit," he muttered. Then, in a louder tone, he said, "Everybody stay where you are for a moment, be as quiet as possible. I'm going up to talk to my officer at the rear." He retraced his steps.

"Listen, Bailey," he told him softly, "we can't get into the basement. Some of our shells ripped into the door and they've bent the jamb all to hell. There's no way we can get the thing open without a crowbar."

Even in the dark he could see Bailey's eyes widen. "So what are we gonna do?" the sergeant asked. "Go back upstairs?"

"Let me think a minute," D'Agosta said. "How much ammo do you have? I've got six rounds in my service piece."

"I don't know. Fifteen, sixteen rounds, maybe."

"Damn," D'Agosta said, "I don't think—"

He stopped, abruptly shutting off his flashlight and listening to the close darkness. A slight movement of air down the stairwell brought a ripe, goatish smell.

Bailey dropped to one knee, aiming the shotgun up the staircase. D'Agosta quickly turned to the group waiting below him. "Everybody," he hissed, "down to the next landing. Quick!"

There was a series of low murmurs. "We can't go down there!" somebody cried. "We'll be trapped underground!"

D'Agosta's response was drowned by the blast of Bailey's shotgun. "The Museum Beast!" somebody screamed, and the group turned, stumbling and falling down the stairs. "Bailey!" D'Agosta shouted, his ears ringing from the blast. "Bailey, follow me!"

Walking backward down the stairs, one hand holding his handgun, the other feeling its way against the wall, D'Agosta noticed the surface of the stairwell turn to damp stone as he moved below the level of the basement. Farther up the stairwell, he could see the dim form of Bailey following, gasping and cursing under his breath. After what seemed an eternity, D'Agosta's foot hit the subbasement landing. All around him, people held their breaths; then Bailey bumped into him gently.

"Bailey, what the fuck was it?" he whispered.

"I don't know," came the response. "There was that horrible smell, then I thought I saw something. Two red eyes in the dark. I fired."

D'Agosta shone his flashlight up the stairwell. The light showed only shadows and rough-hewn yellow rock, crudely carved. The smell lingered.

He shone the flashlight toward the group, and did a quick head count. Thirty-eight, including himself and Bailey. "Okay," he whispered to the group. "We're in the subbasement. I'm gonna go in first, then you follow at my signal."

He turned and shined his light over the door. *Christ,* he thought, *this thing belongs in the Tower of London.* The blackened metal door was reinforced with horizontal strips of iron. When he pushed it open, cool, damp, moldy air rushed into the stairwell. D'Agosta started forward. At the sound of gurgling water, he stepped back, then played the light downward.

"Listen, everybody," he called. "There's running water down here, about three inches deep. Come forward one at a time, quickly but carefully. There are two steps down on the far side of the door. Bailey, take up the rear. And, for God's sake, close the door behind you."

Pendergast counted the remaining bullets, pocketed them, then looked in Frock's direction. "Truly fascinating. And a clever bit of detection on your part. I'm sorry I doubted you, Professor."

Frock gestured magnanimously. "How were you to know?" he asked. "Besides, it was Margo here who discovered the most important link. If she hadn't tested those packing fibers, we never would have known."

Pendergast nodded at Margo, huddled on top of a large wooden crate. "Brilliant work," he said. "We could use you in the Baton Rouge crime lab."

"Assuming I let her go," Frock said. "And assuming we get out of here alive. Dubious assumptions, at best."

"And assuming I'm willing to leave the Museum," Margo said, surprising even herself.

Pendergast turned to Margo. "I know you understand this creature better than I do. Still, do you truly believe this plan you've described will work?"

Margo took a deep breath, nodded. "If the Extrapolator is correct, this beast hunts by smell rather than sight. And if its need for the plant is as strong as we think it is—" She paused, shrugged. "It's the only way."

Pendergast remained motionless a moment. "If it will save those people below us, we have to try." He pulled out his radio.

"D'Agosta?" he said, adjusting the channel. "D'Agosta, this is Pendergast. Do you read?"

The radio squealed static. Then: "D'Agosta here."

"D'Agosta, what's your status?"

"We met up with that creature of yours," came the response. "It got into the Hall, killed Ippolito and an injured guest. We moved into the stairwell, but the basement door was jammed. We had to go to the subbasement."

"Understood," Pendergast said. "How many of your weapons were you able to take?"

"We only had time to grab one twelve-gauge and a service revolver."

"What's your current position?"

"In the subbasement, maybe fifty yards from the stairwell door."

"Listen closely, Vincent. I've been speaking with Professor Frock. The creature we're dealing with is extremely intelligent. Maybe even as smart as you or I."

"Speak for yourself."

"If you see it again, don't aim for the head. The slugs will just bounce off the skull. Aim for the body."

There was silence for a moment, then D'Agosta's voice returned. "Look, Pendergast, you need to tell Coffey some of this. He's sending some men in, and I don't think he has any idea of what's waiting for him."

"I'll do my best. But first let's talk about getting you out of here. That beast may be hunting you."

"No *shit*."

"I can direct you out of the Museum through the subbasement. It won't be easy. These blueprints are very old, and they may not be completely reliable. There may be water."

"We're standing in half a foot of it now. Look, Pendergast, are you sure about this? I mean, there's a mother of a storm outside."

"It's either face the water, or face the beast. There are forty of you; you're the most obvious target. You've got to move, and move quickly—it's the only way out."

"Can you link up with us?"

"No. We've decided to stay here and lure it away from you. There's no time to explain now. If our plan works, we'll join you further on. Thanks to these blueprints, I've discovered more than one way to get into the subbasement from Cell Two."

"Christ, Pendergast, be careful."

"I intend to. Now, listen carefully. Are you in a long, straight passage?"

"Yes."

"Very good. Where the hall forks, go right. The hall should fork a second time in another hundred yards or so. When you get to the second fork, radio me. Got it?"

"Got it."

"Good luck. Pendergast out."

Pendergast quickly switched frequencies.

"Coffey, this is Pendergast. Do you copy?"

"Coffey here. Goddammit, Pendergast, I've been trying to reach you for—"

"No time for that now. Are you sending a rescue team in?"

"Yes. They're preparing to leave now."

"Then make sure they're armed with heavy-caliber automatic weapons, flak helmets, and bulletproof vests. There's a powerful, murderous creature in here, Coffey. I saw it. It has the run of Cell Two."

"For Chrissakes, you *and* D'Agosta! Pendergast, if you're trying to—"

Pendergast spoke rapidly into the radio. "I'll only warn you once more. You're dealing with something monstrous here. Underestimate it at your peril. I'm signing off."

"No, Pendergast, wait! I order you to—"

Pendergast switched off the radio.

= 52 =

They slogged into the water, dim flashlight beams licking the low ceiling in front and behind. The flow of air in the tunnel continued to blow gently into their faces. D'Agosta was alarmed now. The beast could come up behind them unannounced, its stench wafted away from them.

He paused a moment to let Bailey catch up. "Lieutenant," said the Mayor, catching his breath, "are you certain there's a way out through here?"

"I can only go by what Agent Pendergast said, sir. He's got the blueprints. But I sure as hell know we don't want to go back."

D'Agosta and the group started forward again. Dark, oily drops were falling from a ceiling of arched herringbone bricks. The walls were crusted with lime. Everyone was silent except for one woman, who was quietly weeping.

"Excuse me, Lieutenant?" said a voice. The young, lanky guy. Smithback.

"Yes?"

"Would you mind telling me something?"

"Shoot."

"How does it feel to have the lives of forty people, including the Mayor of New York City, in your hands?"

"What?" D'Agosta stopped a moment, glared over his shoulder. "Don't tell me we've got a fucking *journalist* with us!"

"Well, I—" began Smithback.

"Call downtown and make an appointment to see me at headquarters."

D'Agosta played the light ahead and found the fork in the tunnel. He took the right-hand passage, as Pendergast had directed. It had a slight downhill grade, and the water began to move faster, tugging on his pants legs as it rushed past into the blackness beyond. The wound in his hand throbbed. As the group moved around the corner behind him, D'Agosta noted with relief that the breeze was no longer blowing in their faces.

A bloated dead rat came floating past, bumping against people's legs like a lazy, oversized billiard ball. One person groaned and tried to kick it away, but no one complained.

"Bailey!" called D'Agosta behind him.

"Yeah?"

"See anything?"

"You'll be the first to know if I do."

"Gotcha. I'm going to call in upstairs, see if they've made any progress in restoring power."

He grabbed his radio. "Coffey?"

"Reading. Pendergast just shut me off. Where are you?"

"We're in the subbasement. Pendergast has a blueprint. He's leading us out by radio. When are the lights coming on?"

"D'Agosta, don't be an idiot. He'll get you all killed. It doesn't look as if we'll be getting power back any time soon. Go back to the Hall of the Heavens and wait there. We'll be sending the SWAT team in through the roof in a couple of minutes."

"Then you should know that Wright, Cuthbert, and the Public Relations Director are upstairs somewhere, the fourth floor, probably. That's the only other exit point for that stairwell."

"What are you talking about? You didn't take them with you?"

"They refused to come along. Wright cut out on his own and the others followed him."

"Sounds like they had more sense than you did. Is the Mayor all right? Let me talk to the him."

D'Agosta handed the radio over. "Are you all right, sir?" Coffey asked urgently.

"We're in capable hands with the Lieutenant."

"It's my strong opinion, sir, that you should head back to the Hall of the Heavens and wait there for assistance. We're sending in a SWAT team to rescue you."

"I have every confidence in Lieutenant D'Agosta. As should you."

"Yes, of course, sir. Rest assured that I'm going to get you safely out of there, sir."

"Coffey?"

"Sir?"

"There are three dozen people in here besides me. Don't forget that."

"But I just want you to know, sir, we're being extra—"

"Coffey! I don't think you understood me. Every life down here is worth all the effort you've got."

"Yes, sir."

The Mayor handed the radio back to D'Agosta. "Am I wrong, or is that fellow Coffey a horse's ass?" he muttered.

D'Agosta holstered the radio and proceeded down the passage. Then he stopped, playing his flashlight over an object that loomed out of the blackness in front of them. It was a steel door, closed. The oily water rushed through a thickly barred grating in its bottom panel. He waded closer. It was similar to the door at the base of the stairwell: thick, double-plated, studded with rusty rivets. An old copper lock, covered with verdigris, was looped through a thick metal D ring along the door's side. D'Agosta grabbed the lock and pulled, but it held fast.

"Pendergast?" said D'Agosta, removing his radio once again.

"Reading."

"We're past the first fork, but we've hit a steel door, and it's locked."

"A locked door? Between the first and second forks?"

"Yes."

"And you took a right at the first fork?"

"Yes."

"One minute." There was a shuffling sound.

"Vincent, go back to the fork and take the left-hand tunnel. Hurry."

D'Agosta wheeled around. "Bailey! We're heading back to that last fork. All of you, let's go. On the double!"

The group turned wearily, murmuring, and started moving back through the inky water.

"Wait!" came the voice of Bailey, from the head of the group. "Christ, Lieutenant, do you smell it?"

"No," said D'Agosta; then "*shit!*" as the fetid stench enveloped him. "Bailey, we're going to have to make a stand! I'm coming up. Fire at the son of a bitch!"

Cuthbert sat on the worktable, absently tapping its scarred surface with a pencil eraser. At the far end of the table, Wright sat motionless, his head in his hands. Rickman stood on her tiptoes by the small window. She was angling the flashlight through the bars in front of the glass, switching it on and off with a manicured finger.

A brief flash of lightning silhouetted her thin form, then a low rumble of thunder filled the room.

"It's pouring out," she said. "I can't see a thing."

"And nobody can see you," said Cuthbert wearily. "All you're doing is wearing out the battery. We may need it later."

With an audible sigh, Rickman switched off the light, plunging the lab once again into darkness.

"I wonder what it did with Montague's body," came the slurred voice of Wright. "Ate him up?" Laughter spluttered out of the gloom. "Where's my whisky? Ian, you damned Scotsman, where'd you hide my whisky?"

Cuthbert continued tapping the pencil.

"Ate him up! With a little curry and rice, maybe! Montague pilaf!" Wright chuckled.

Cuthbert stood up, reached over toward the Director, and plucked the .38 from Wright's belt. He checked the bullets, then tucked it into his own belt.

"Return that at once!" Wright demanded.

Cuthbert said nothing.

"You're a bully, Ian. You've always been a bully, a small-minded, jealous bully. First thing Monday morning, I'm going to fire you. In fact, you're fired now." Wright stood up unsteadily. "Fired, you hear me?"

Cuthbert was standing at the front door of the laboratory, listening.

"What is it?" Rickman asked in alarm. Cuthbert held his hand up sharply.

Silence.

At length, Cuthbert turned away from the door. "I thought I heard a noise," he said. He looked toward Rickman. "Lavinia? Could you come here a moment?"

"What is it?" she asked, breathless.

Cuthbert drew her aside. "Hand me the torch," he said. "Now, listen. I don't want to alarm you. But should something happen—"

"What do you mean?" she interrupted, her voice breaking.

"Whatever it was that's been killing people is still loose. I'm not sure we're safe in here."

"But the door! Winston said it was two inches thick—"

"I know. Maybe everything will be fine. But those doors to the exhibition were even thicker than that, and I'd like to take a few precautions. Help me move this table up against the door." He turned toward the Director.

Wright looked up vaguely. "Fired! Clean out your desk by five o'clock Monday."

Cuthbert pulled Wright to his feet, and sat him in a nearby chair. With Rickman's help, Cuthbert positioned the table in front of the oak door of the laboratory.

"That will slow it down, anyway," he said, dusting off his jacket. "Enough for me to get in a few good shots, with luck. At the first sign of trouble, I want you to go through that back door into the Dinosaur Hall and hide. With the security gates down, there's no other way into the Hall. At least that will put two doors between you and whatever's out there." Cuthbert looked around again restlessly. "In the meantime, let's try to break this window. At least then maybe someone will be able to hear us yelling."

Wright laughed. "You can't break the window, you can't, you can't. It's high-impact glass."

Cuthbert hunted around the lab, finally locating a short piece of angle iron. When he swung it vertically through the bars, it bounced off the glass and was knocked out of his hands.

"Bloody hell," he muttered, rubbing his palms together. "We could shoot out the window," he speculated. "Do you have any more bullets hidden away?"

"I'm not talking to you anymore," Wright retorted.

Cuthbert opened the filing cabinet and started fumbling in the dark. "Nothing," he said at last. "We can't waste bullets on that window. I've only got five shots in here."

"Nothing, nothing, nothing. Didn't King Lear say that?"

Cuthbert sighed heavily and sat down. Silence filled the room once again, save only the wind and rain, and the distant roll of thunder.

Pendergast lowered the radio and turned toward Margo. "D'Agosta's in trouble. We've got to move fast."

"Leave me behind," said Frock quietly. "I'm just going to slow you down."

"A gallant gesture," Pendergast told him. "But we need your brains."

He moved slowly out into the hall, sweeping his light in both directions. Then he signaled all clear. They moved down the hall, Margo pushing the wheelchair before her as quickly as possible.

As they threaded their way, Frock would occasionally whisper a few words of direction. Pendergast stopped at every intersection, gun drawn. Frequently, he halted to listen and smell the air. After a few minutes, he took the chair's handlebars from an unprotesting Margo. Then they rounded a corner, and the door of the Secure Area stood before them.

For the hundredth time, Margo prayed silently that her plan would work; that she wasn't simply condemning all of them—including the group trapped in the subbasement—to a horrible death.

"Third on the right!" Frock called as they moved inside the Secure Area. "Margo, do you remember the combination?"

She dialed, pulled the lever, and the door swung open. Pendergast strode over and knelt beside the smaller crate.

"Wait," said Margo.

Pendergast stopped, eyebrows raised quizzically.

"Don't let the smell of it get onto you," she said. "Bundle the fibers in your jacket."

Pendergast hesitated.

"Here," Frock said. "Use my handkerchief to remove them."

Pendergast inspected it. "Well," he said ruefully, "if the Professor here can donate a hundred-dollar handkerchief, I suppose I can donate my jacket." He took the radio and notebook, stuffed them into the waistband of his pants, then removed his suit jacket.

"Since when did FBI agents start wearing hand-tailored Armani suits?" Margo asked jokingly.

"Since when did graduate students in ethnopharmacology start appreciating them?" Pendergast replied, spreading the jacket carefully on the floor. Then, gingerly, he scooped out several fistfuls of fiber and laid them carefully across his open jacket. Finally, he stuffed the handkerchief into one of the sleeves, folded the garment, and tied the sleeves together.

"We'll need a rope to drag it with," said Margo.

"I see some packing cord around the far crate," Frock pointed out.

Pendergast tied the jacket and fashioned a harness, then dragged the bundle across the floor.

"Seems to be snug," he said. "Pity, though, that they haven't dusted these floors in a while." He turned to Margo. "Will this leave enough of a scent for the creature to follow?"

Frock nodded vigorously. "The Extrapolator estimates the creature's sense of smell to be exponentially keener than ours. It was able to trace the crates to this vault, remember."

"And you're sure the—er—meals it's already had this evening won't satiate it?"

"Mr. Pendergast, the human hormone is a poor substitute. We believe the beast *lives* for this plant." Frock nodded again. "If it smells an abundance of fibers, it will track them down."

"Let's get started, then," said Pendergast. He lifted the bundle gingerly. "The alternate access to the subbasement is several hundred yards from here. If you're right, we're at our most vulnerable from now on. The creature will home in on *us*."

Pushing the wheelchair, Margo followed the agent into the corridor. He shut the door, then the three moved quickly down the hall, back into the silence of the Old Basement.

= 53 =

D'Agosta moved forward, crouching low in the water, his revolver nosing ahead into the inky darkness. He had turned off his flashlight to avoid betraying his position. The water flowed briskly between his thighs, its smell of algae and lime mixing with the fetid reek of the creature.

"Bailey, you up there?" he whispered into the gloom.

"Yeah," came Bailey's voice. "I'm waiting at the first fork."

"You've got more rounds than I. If we drive off this motherfucker, I want you to stand guard while I go behind and try shooting off the lock."

"Roger."

D'Agosta started toward Bailey, his legs numbing in the frigid water. Suddenly, there was a confusion of sounds in the blackness ahead of him: a soft splash, then another, much closer. Bailey's shotgun went off twice, and several people in the group behind him started whimpering.

"Jesus!" he heard Bailey yell, then there was a low crunching noise and Bailey screamed and D'Agosta felt thrashing in the water ahead of him.

"Bailey!" he cried out, but all he could hear was the gurgle of running water. He pulled out his flashlight and shined it up the tunnel. Nothing.

"Bailey!"

Several people were crying behind him now and somebody was screaming hysterically.

"Shut up!" D'Agosta pleaded. "I have to listen!"

The screams were abruptly muffled. He played the light ahead, off the walls and ceiling, but he could see nothing. Bailey had vanished, and the smell had receded once again. Maybe Bailey had hit the fucker. Or maybe it had just temporarily retreated from the noise of the shotgun. He shone the flashlight downward, and noticed the water flowing red around his legs. A torn shred of NYPD regulation blue cloth floated by.

"I need help up here!" he hissed over his shoulder.

Smithback was suddenly at his side.

"Point this flashlight down the passage," D'Agosta told him.

D'Agosta probed the stone floor with his fingers. The water, he noticed, seemed to be a little higher: as he bent forward, reaching down, it grazed his chest. Something floated by beneath his nose, a piece of Bailey, and he had to turn away for a moment.

There was no shotgun to be found.

"Smithback," he said, "I'm going back to shoot off the lock. We can't backtrack any farther with that thing waiting for us. Feel around in this water for a shotgun. If you see anything, or smell anything, shout."

"You're leaving me here alone?" Smithback asked a little unsteadily.

"You've got the flashlight. It'll just be for a minute. Can you do it?"

"I'll try."

D'Agosta grasped Smithback's shoulder briefly, then started back. For a journalist, the guy had guts.

A hand tugged at him as he waded through the group. "Please tell us what's happening," a feminine voice sobbed.

He gently shook her off. D'Agosta could hear the Mayor talking soothingly to her. Maybe he'd vote for the old bastard next time.

"Everyone get back," he said, and positioned himself in front of the door. He knew he should stand well back from the door to avoid potential ricochets. But it was a thick lock, and he'd have a hard time aiming in the dark.

He moved to within a few feet of the door, placed the barrel of the .38 near the lock, and fired. When the smoke cleared, he found a clean hole in the lock's center. The lock held fast.

"Fuck it," he muttered, placing the muzzle of the revolver directly against the hasp and firing again. Now the lock was gone. He heaved his weight against the door.

"Give me a hand here!" he called out.

Immediately, several people began throwing themselves against it. The rusty hinges gave way with a loud screech, and water gushed through the opening.

"Smithback! Find anything?"

"I got his flashlight!" came the disembodied voice.

"Good boy. Now come on back!"

As D'Agosta moved through the door, he noticed an iron D ring on the other side as well. He stood back and ushered the group through, counting. Thirty-seven. Bailey was gone. Smithback brought up the rear.

"All right, let's shut this thing!" D'Agosta yelled.

Against the heavy flow of the water, the door groaned slowly shut.

"Smithback! Shine one of the lights here. Maybe we can find a way to bar this door."

He looked at it for a second. If they could jam a piece of metal through the D ring, it just might hold. He turned to the group. "I need something, *anything*, made of metal!" he called. "Does anyone have a piece of metal we can use to bar this door?"

The Mayor passed quickly through the group, then came up to D'Agosta, thrusting a small collection of metal items into his hands. As Smithback held the light, D'Agosta inspected the pins, necklaces, combs. "There's nothing here," he muttered.

They heard a sudden splashing on the other side of the door, and a deep grunt. A stench filtered through the low slats in the door. A soft thump and a brief squeal of hinges, and the door was pushed ajar.

"Christ! You there, help me shut this door!"

As before, people flung themselves against the door, forcing it shut. There was a rattle and then a louder boom as the thing met their force, then pushed them back. The door creaked open farther.

At D'Agosta's shout, others joined the effort.

"Keep pushing!"

Another roar; then a tremendous thump heaved everyone back once again. The door groaned under the opposing weights, but continued to open, first six inches, then a foot. The stench became intolerable. Watching the door inch its way from the frame, D'Agosta saw three long talons snake their way around the edge. The shape felt along the door, then swiped forward, the talons alternately sheathing and unsheathing.

"Jesus, Mary, and Joseph," D'Agosta heard the Mayor say, quite matter-of-factly. Somebody else began chanting a prayer in a strange singsong. D'Agosta placed the barrel of the gun near the monstrosity and fired once. There was a terrible roar and the shape vanished into churning water.

"The flashlight!" Smithback cried. "It'll fit perfectly! Shove it into the ring!"

"That'll leave us with just one light," D'Agosta panted.

"Got a better idea?"

"No," D'Agosta said under his breath. Then, louder: "Everybody, *push!*"

With a final heave they slammed the door back into its iron frame, and Smithback shoved the flashlight through the D ring. It slid through easily, its flared end coming to rest against the metal hasp. As D'Agosta caught his breath, they heard another, sudden crash and the door shuddered, but held firm.

"Run, people!" cried D'Agosta. "Run!" They thrashed through the roiling water, falling and sliding. D'Agosta, buffeted from behind, fell face first into the rushing water. He rose and continued forward, trying to ignore the monster's roaring and pounding—he did not think he could hear it and remain sane. He willed himself to think about the flashlight instead. It was a good, heavy police-issue flashlight. It would hold. He hoped to God it would hold. The group stopped at the second fork in the tunnel, crying and shivering. *Time to radio Pendergast and get the fuck out of this maze*, D'Agosta thought. He clapped his hand to his radio holster, and with a shock realized it was empty.

Coffey stood inside the forward security station, staring moodily at a monitor. He was unable to reach either Pendergast or D'Agosta. Inside the perimeter, Garcia in Security Command and Waters in the Computer Room were still responding. Had everybody else been killed? When he thought of the Mayor dead, and the headlines that were sure to follow, a hollow feeling grew in his stomach.

An acetylene torch, flickering near the silver expanse of the metal security door at the east end of the Rotunda, cast ghostly shadows across the tall ceiling. The acrid smell of molten steel filled the air. The Rotunda had grown strangely quiet. Field amputations were still taking place by the security door, but all the other guests had left for home or area hospitals. The journalists had finally been contained behind police barriers. Mobile intensive care units were set up on nearby side streets and medevacs were standing by.

The SWAT team commander came over, buckling an ammo belt over his black fatigues. "We're ready," he said.

Coffey nodded. "Give me a tactical."

The leader pushed a bank of emergency phones aside and unfolded a sheet.

"Our spotter will be leading us by radio. He's got the detailed diagrams from this station. Phase One: We're punching a hole through the roof, here, and dropping to the fifth floor. According to the specs of the security system, this door here will blow with one charge. That gives us access to the next cell. Then we proceed down to this props storage room on the fourth floor. It's right above the Hall of the Heavens. There's a trapdoor in the floor that Maintenance uses for cleaning and servicing the chandelier. We'll lower our men and haul the wounded up in sling chairs. Phase Two: Rescue those in the subbasement, the Mayor and the large group with him. Phase Three: Search for those who may be elsewhere within the perimeter. I understand that people are trapped in the Computer Room and Security Command. The Museum Director, Ian Cuthbert, and a woman as yet unidentified may have gone upstairs. And don't you have agents of your own within the perimeter, sir? The man from the New Orleans field office—"

"Let me worry about him," Coffey snapped. "Who developed these plans?"

"We did, with the assistance of Security Command. That guy Allen has the cell layouts down cold. Anyway, according to the specs of this security system—"

"You did. And who's in charge here?"

"Sir, as you know, in emergency situations the SWAT team commander—"

"I want you to go in there and kill the son of a bitch. Got it?"

"Sir, our first priority is to rescue hostages and save lives. Only then can we deal with—"

"Calling me stupid, Commander? If we kill the thing in there, all our other problems are solved. Right? This is not your typical situation, commander, and it requires creative thinking."

"In a hostage situation, if you take away the killer's hostages, you've removed his base of power—"

"Commander, were you asleep during our crisis-control briefing? We may have an animal in there, not a person."

"But the wounded—"

"Use some of your men to *get* the damn wounded out. But I want the rest of you to go after what's in there and kill it. Then we rescue any stragglers at leisure, in safety and comfort. Those are your direct orders."

"I understand, sir. I would recommend, however—"

"Don't recommend jack shit, Commander. Go in the way you planned, but do the job right. Kill the motherfucker."

The commander looked curiously at Coffey. "You sure about this thing being an animal?"

Coffey hesitated. "Yes," he finally said. "I don't know a hell of a lot about it, but it's already killed several people."

The Commander looked steadily at Coffey for a moment.

"Yeah," he finally said, "well, whatever it is, we've got enough firepower to turn a herd of lions into a fine red mist."

"You're going to need it. Find the thing. Take it out."

Pendergast and Margo looked down the narrow service tunnel into the subbasement. Pendergast's flashlight sent a circle of light onto a sheet of black, oily water roiling past beneath them.

"It's getting deeper," Pendergast said. Then he turned to Margo. "Are you sure the creature can make it up this shaft?" he asked.

"I'm nearly certain," Margo said. "It's highly agile."

Pendergast stepped back and tried once again to raise D'Agosta on the radio. "Something's happened," he said. "The Lieutenant has been out of contact for fifteen minutes. Ever since they hit that locked door." He glanced down again through the shaft that sloped toward the subbasement below. "How are you planning to lay a scent with all this water?" he asked.

"You estimate they passed beneath here some time ago, right?" Margo asked.

Pendergast nodded. "The last time I spoke to him, D'Agosta told me the group was between the first and second forks," he said. "Assuming they haven't backtracked, he's well beyond this spot."

"The way I see it," Margo continued, "if we sprinkle some fibers on the water, the flow should carry them to the creature."

"That's assuming the creature's smart enough to realize the fibers came floating from upstream. Otherwise, he might just chase them further downstream."

"I think it's smart enough," Frock said. "You mustn't think of this creature as an *animal*. It may be nearly as intelligent as a human being."

Using the handkerchief, Pendergast carefully removed some fibers from the bundle and sprinkled them along the base of the shaft. He dropped another handful into the water below.

"Not too much," Frock warned.

Pendergast looked at Margo. "We'll sprinkle a few more fibers to establish a good upwater trail, then drag the bundle back to the Secure Area and wait. Your trap will be set." After scattering a few more fibers, he secured the bundle.

"At the rate this water is moving," he said, "it should take only a few minutes to reach the creature. How fast do you expect the thing to respond?"

"If the extrapolation program is correct," Frock said, "the creature can move at a high rate of speed. Perhaps thirty miles an hour or greater, especially when in need. And its need for the fibers seems overpowering. It won't be able to travel at full speed down these corridors—the residual scent trail we leave will be harder to track—but I doubt the water will slow it much. And the Secure Area is close by."

"I see," Pendergast said. "How unsettling. *'He that has a mind to fight, let him fight, for now is the time.'* "

"Ah," said Frock, nodding. "Alcaeus."

Pendergast shook his head. "Anacreon, Doctor. Shall we go?"

= 54 =

Smithback held the light, but it hardly seemed to penetrate the palpable darkness. D'Agosta, slightly in front, held the gun. The tunnel went on and on, black water rushing past and vanishing into the low-vaulted darkness. Either they were still descending, or the water was getting higher. Smithback could feel it pushing against his thighs.

He glanced at D'Agosta's face, shadowy and grim, his thick features smeared with Bailey's blood.

"I can't go any farther," someone wailed from the rear. Smithback could hear the Mayor's familiar voice—a politician's voice—reassuring, soothing, telling everyone what they wanted to hear. Once again, it seemed to work. Smithback stole a glance backward at the dispirited group. The lean, gowned, bejeweled women; the middle-aged businessmen in their tuxedos; the smattering of yuppies from investment banks and downtown law firms. He knew them all now, had even given them names and occupations in his head. And here they all were, reduced to the lowest common denominator, wallowing around in the dark of a tunnel, covered with slime, pursued by a savage beast.

Smithback was worried, but still rational. Early on, he'd felt a moment of sheer terror when he realized the rumors about a Museum Beast were true. But now, tired and wet, he was more afraid of dying before he wrote his book than he was of dying itself. He wondered if that meant he was brave, or covetous, or just plain stupid. Whatever the case, he knew that what was happening to him down here was going to be worth a fortune. Book party at Le Cirque. *Good Morning America*, the *Today Show*, *Donahue*, and *Oprah*.

No one could do the story like he could, no one else had his first-person perspective. And he'd been a hero. He, William Smithback Jr., had held the light against the monster when D'Agosta went back to shoot off the lock. He, Smithback, had thought of using the flashlight to brace the door. He'd been Lieutenant D'Agosta's right-hand man.

"Shine the light up to the left, there." D'Agosta intruded upon his thoughts, and Smithback dutifully complied. Nothing.

"I thought I saw something moving in the darkness," D'Agosta muttered. "Must've been a shadow, I guess."

God, Smithback thought, *if only he lived to enjoy his success.*

"Is it just my imagination, or is the water getting deeper?" he asked.

"It's getting deeper *and* faster," said D'Agosta. "Pendergast didn't say which way to go from here."

"He didn't?" Smithback felt his guts turn to water.

"I was supposed to radio from the second fork," D'Agosta said. "I lost my radio somewhere back before the door."

Smithback felt another surge against his legs, a strong one. There was a shout and a splash.

"It's all right," the Mayor called out when Smithback aimed the flashlight to the rear. "Someone fell down. The current's getting stronger."

"We can't tell them we're lost," Smithback muttered to D'Agosta.

Margo swung open the door to the Secure Area, looked quickly inside, and nodded to Pendergast. The agent moved past the door, dragging the bundle.

"Shut it in the vault with the Whittlesey crates," Frock said. "We want to keep the beast in here long enough for us to close the door on it."

Margo unlocked the vault as Pendergast threaded a complex pattern across the floor. They put the bundle inside, then closed and locked the ornate vault door.

"Quick," Margo said. "Across the hall."

Leaving the main door to the Secure Area open, they crossed the hall to the elephant bone storage room. The small window in the door had long ago been broken, and a worn piece of cardboard now covered the opening. Margo unlocked the door with Frock's key, then Pendergast pushed Frock inside. Switching Pendergast's flashlight to its low setting, she balanced it on a ledge above the door, pointing the thin beam in the direction of the Secure Area. Finally, with a pen, she reamed a small hole in the cardboard and, with a last look down the corridor, stepped inside.

The storage room was large, stuffy, and full of elephant bones. Most of the skeletons were disassembled, and the great shadowy bones had been stacked on shelves like oversized cordwood. One mounted skeleton stood in a far corner, a dark cage of bones, two curving tusks gleaming in the pale light.

Pendergast shut the door, then switched off his miner's lamp.

Peering through the hole in the cardboard, Margo had a clear view of the hallway and the open door of the Secure Area.

"Take a look," she said to Pendergast, stepping away from the door.

Pendergast moved forward. "Excellent," he said after a moment. "It's a perfect blind, as long as those flashlight batteries hold out." He stepped back from the door. "How did you happen to remember this room?" he asked curiously.

Margo laughed shyly. "When you took us down here on Wednesday, I remember seeing this door marked PACHYDERMAE and wondering how a person could fit an elephant skull through such a small door." She moved forward. "I'll keep watch through the peephole," she said. "Be ready to rush out and trap the creature in the Secure Area."

In the darkness behind them, Frock cleared his throat. "Mr. Pendergast?"

"Yes?"

"Forgive me for asking, but how experienced *are* you with that weapon?"

"As a matter of fact," the agent replied, "before the death of my wife I spent several weeks each winter big-game hunting in East Africa. My wife was an avid hunter."

"Ah," Frock replied. Margo detected relief in his voice. "This will be a difficult creature to kill, but I don't think it will be impossible. I was never much of a hunter, obviously. But working together we may be able to bring it down."

Pendergast nodded. "Unfortunately, this pistol puts me at a disadvantage. It's a powerful handgun, but nothing like a .375 nitro express rifle. If you could tell me where the creature might be most vulnerable, it would help."

"From the printout," Frock said slowly, "we can assume the creature is heavy boned. As you discovered, you won't kill it with a head shot. And an upper shoulder or chest shot toward the heart would almost certainly be deflected by the massive bones and heavy musculature of the creature's upper body. If you could catch the creature sideways, you might get a shot into the heart from behind the foreleg. But again, the ribs are probably built like a steel cage. Now that I think about it, I don't believe any of the vital parts of the beast are particularly vulnerable. A shot to the gut might kill eventually, but not before it took its revenge."

"Cold comfort," Pendergast said.

Frock moved restlessly in the darkness. "That leaves us in a bit of a quandary."

There was silence for a moment. "There may still be a way." Pendergast said at length.

"Yes?" Frock replied eagerly.

"Once, a few years ago, my wife and I were hunting bushbuck in Tanzania. We preferred to hunt alone, without gun bearers, and the only guns we had were 30-30 rifles. We were in light cover near a river when we were charged by a cape buffalo. It had apparently been wounded a few days earlier by a poacher. Cape buffalo are like mules— they never forget an injury, and one man with a gun looks much like any other."

Sitting in the dim light, waiting for the arrival of a nightmarish creature, listening to Pendergast narrate a hunting story in his typical unhurried manner, Margo felt a sense of unreality begin to creep over her.

"Normally, in hunting buffalo," Pendergast was saying, "one tries for a head shot just below the horn bosses, or for a heart shot. In this case, the 30-30 was an insufficient caliber. My wife, who was a better shot than I, used the only tactic a hunter could use in such a situation. She knelt and fired at the animal in such a way as to break it down."

"Break it down?"

"You don't attempt a kill shot. Instead, you work to stop forward locomotion. You aim for the forelegs, pasterns, knees. You basically shatter as many bones as you can until it can't move forward."

"I see," said Frock.

"There is only one problem with this approach," said Pendergast.

"And that is—?"

"You must be a consummate marksman. Placement is everything. You've got to remain serenely calm and steady, unbreathing, firing between heartbeats—in the face of a charging beast. We each had time for four shots. I made the mistake of aiming for the chest and scored two direct hits before I realized the bullets were just burying themselves in muscle. Then I aimed for the legs. One shot missed and the other grazed but didn't break the bone." He shook his head. "A poor performance, I'm afraid."

"So what happened?" Frock asked.

"My wife scored direct hits on three out of her four shots. She shattered both front cannons and broke the upper foreleg as well. The buffalo tumbled head over heels and came to rest a few yards from where we were kneeling. It was still very much alive but it couldn't move. So I 'paid the insurance,' as a professional hunter would put it."

"I wish your wife was here," Frock said.

Pendergast was quiet. "So do I," he said at length.

Silence returned to the room.

"Very well," Frock said at last. "I understand the problem. The beast has some unusual qualities that you should know about, if you are planning to, ah, break it down. First, the hind quarters are most likely covered in bony plates or scales. I doubt if you could penetrate them effectively with your gun. They armor the upper and lower leg, down to the metatarsal bones, I'd estimate."

"I see."

"You will have to shoot low, aim for the phalanx prima or secunda."

"The lowest bones of the leg," said Pendergast.

"Yes. They would be equivalent to the pasterns on a horse. Aim just below the lower joint. In fact, the joint itself might be vulnerable."

"That's a difficult shot," said Pendergast. "Virtually impossible if the creature is facing me."

There was a short silence. Margo continued her vigil through the peephole, but saw nothing.

"I believe the anterior limbs of the creature are more vulnerable," Frock continued. "The Extrapolator described them as being less robust. The metacarpals and the carpals should both be vulnerable to a direct hit."

"The front knee and the lower leg," Pendergast said, nodding. "The shots you've described already are hardly garden variety. To what extent would the creature have to be broken down to immobilize it?"

"Difficult to say. Both front legs and at least one rear leg, I'm afraid. Even then, it could crawl." Frock coughed. "Can you do it?"

"To have a chance, I'd need at least a hundred and fifty feet of shooting space if the creature were charging. Ideally, I'd get the first shot in before the creature knew what was happening. That would slow it down."

Frock thought for a moment. "The Museum contains several straight, long corridors, three or four hundred feet long. Unfortunately, most of them are now cut in half by these damned security doors. I believe that there's at least one unobstructed corridor within Cell Two, however. On the first floor, in Section Eighteen, around the corner from the Computer Room."

Pendergast nodded. "I'll remember that," he said. "In case this plan fails."

"I hear something!" Margo hissed.

They fell silent. Pendergast moved closer to the door.

"A shadow just passed across the light at the end of the hall," she whispered.

There was another long silence. Margo could hear a soft *click* as Pendergast slid back the safety on his gun.

"It's here," Margo breathed, "I can see it." Then, even softer: "Oh, my God."

Pendergast murmured in Margo's ear: "Move away from the door!"

She backed up, hardly daring to breathe. "What's it doing?" she whispered.

"It's stopped at the door to the Secure Area," Pendergast replied quietly. "It went in for a moment, and then backed out very fast. It's looking around, smelling the air."

"What does it look like?" Frock asked, an urgency in his voice.

Pendergast hesitated a moment before answering. "I've got a better view of it this time. It's big, it's massive. Wait, it's turning this way . . . Good Lord, it's a horrible sight, it's . . . Flattened face, small red eyes. Thin fur on the upper body. Just like the figurine. Hold on . . . Hold on a minute . . . it's coming this way."

Margo suddenly realized she had moved back to the far wall. A snuffling sound came through the door. And then the rank, fetid smell. She slid to the floor in the heavy darkness, the peephole in the cardboard wavering like a star. Pendergast's flashlight shone feebly. *Starlight* . . . A small voice in Margo's head was trying to speak.

And then a shadow fell over the peephole and everything went black.

There was a soft muffled thud against the door, and the old wood creaked. The doorknob rattled. There was a long silence, the sound of something heavy moving outside, and a sharp cracking as the creature pressed against the door.

The voice inside Margo's head suddenly became audible.

"Pendergast, turn on your miner's lamp!" she burst out. "Shine it at the beast!"

"What are you talking about!"

"It's nocturnal, remember? It probably hates light."

"That's absolutely correct!" cried Frock.

"Stay back!" Pendergast shouted. Margo heard a small click, then the brilliance of the miner's light blinded her momentarily. As her vision returned, she saw Pendergast on one knee, his gun leveled at the door, the bright circle of light focused directly on its center.

There was another crunching noise, and Margo could see splinters spray into the room from a widening split in the upper panel. The door bowed inward.

Pendergast stayed steady, sighting along the levelled barrel.

There was another tremendous splintering sound and the door broke inward in pieces, swinging crazily on bent hinges. Margo pressed herself against the wall, forcing herself into it until her spine creaked in protest. She heard Frock shout in amazement, wonder, and fear. The creature squatted in the doorway, a monstrous silhouette in the bright light; then, with a sudden throaty roar, it shook its head and backed out.

"Keep back," Pendergast said. He kicked the broken door aside and moved cautiously out into the hall. Margo heard a sudden shot, then another. Then, silence. After what seemed an eternity, Pendergast returned, motioning them forward. A trail of small red droplets led down the hallway and around the corner.

"Blood!" Frock said, bending forward with a grunt. "So you wounded it!"

Pendergast shrugged. "Perhaps. But I wasn't the first. The droplets originate from the direction of the subbasement. See? Lieutenant D'Agosta or one of his men must have wounded it earlier but not disabled it. It moved away with amazing speed."

Margo looked at Frock. "Why didn't it take the bait?"

Frock returned her gaze. "We're dealing with a creature possessed of preternatural intelligence."

"What you're saying is that it detected our trap," Pendergast said, a note of disbelief in his voice.

"Let me ask you, Pendergast. Would *you* have fallen for that trap?"

Pendergast was silent. "I suppose not," he said at length.

"Well, then," said Frock. "We underestimated the creature. We *must* stop thinking of it as a dumb animal. It has the intelligence of a human being. Did I understand correctly that the body they found in the exhibition was *hidden?* The beast knew it was being hunted. Obviously, it had learned to conceal its prey. Besides—" he hesitated. "I think we're dealing with more than simply hunger now. Chances are, it's been temporarily sated by this evening's human diet. But it's also been wounded. If your analogy of the cape buffalo is correct, this creature may not only be hungry, but *angry.*"

"So you think it's gone hunting," Pendergast said quietly.

Frock remained motionless. Then he gave a barely perceptible nod.

"So who's it hunting now?" Margo asked.

No one answered.

= 55 =

Cutbert checked the door again. It was locked and rock solid. He flicked on the flashlight and shined it in the direction of Wright, slumped in his chair and looking morosely at the floor. Cuthbert switched off the flashlight. The room reeked of whisky. There was no noise except for the rain splattering and drumming against the barred window.

"What are we going to do with Wright?" he asked in a low tone.

"Don't worry," Rickman replied, her voice tight and high. "We'll just tell the press he's sick and pack him off to the hospital, then schedule a press conference for tomorrow afternoon—"

"I'm not talking about *after* we get out. I'm talking about *now*. If the beast comes up here."

"Please, Ian, don't talk like that. It scares me. I can't imagine the animal is going to do that. For all we know, it's been in the basement for years. Why would it come up here now?"

"I don't know," said Cuthbert. "That's what worries me." He checked the Ruger once again, spun the cylinder, slid the safety on and off. Five shots.

He went over to Wright and shook the Director's shoulder. "Winston?"

"Are you still here?" Wright asked, looking up hazily.

"Winston, I want you to take Lavinia and go into the Dinosaur Hall. Come along."

Wright slapped Cuthbert's arm away. "I'm fine just where I am. Maybe I'll take a nap."

"The devil with you, then," said Cuthbert. He sat down in a chair opposite the door.

There was a brief noise—a rattle—at the door, as if the doorknob had been turned, then released.

Cuthbert jumped up, gun in hand. He walked close to the door and listened.

"I hear something," he said quietly. "Get into the Dinosaur Hall, Lavinia."

"I'm afraid," she whispered. "Please don't make me go in there alone."

"Do as I say."

Rickman walked over to the far door and opened it. She hesitated.

"Go on."

"Ian—" Rickman pleaded. Behind her, Cuthbert could see the huge dinosaur skeletons looming out of the darkness. The great black ribs and yawning rows of teeth were suddenly illuminated by a streak of livid lightning.

"Damn you, woman, get in there."

Cuthbert turned back, listening. Something soft was rubbing against the door. He leaned forward, pressing his ear against the smooth wood. Maybe it *was* the wind.

Suddenly he was slammed backward into the room by a tremendous force. Cuthbert could hear Rickman screaming within the Dinosaur Hall.

Wright stood unsteadily. "What was that?" he said.

His head ringing, Cuthbert picked the gun off the floor, scrambled to his feet, and ran to the far corner of the room. "Get into the Dinosaur Hall!" he shouted at Wright.

Wright sagged heavily against the chair. "What's that disgusting smell?" he asked.

There was another savage blow to the door, and the crack of splitting wood sounded like a rifle shot. Cuthbert's finger instinctively tightened on the trigger, and the gun fired unexpectedly, bringing down dust from the ceiling. He lowered the weapon momentarily, his hands shaking. *Stupid, one wasted bullet.* Bloody hell, he wished he knew more about handguns. He raised it again and tried to take aim, but his hands were shaking uncontrollably now. *Got to calm down,* he thought. *Take a few deep breaths. Aim for something vital. Four shots.*

The room gradually returned to silence. Wright was slumped against his chair, as if frozen into place.

"Winston, you idiot!" Cuthbert hissed. "Get into the Hall!"

"If you say so," Wright said, and shuffled toward the door. He seemed finally frightened enough to move.

Then Cuthbert heard that soft sound again, and the wood groaned. The thing was pressing against the door. There was another horrible *cra-ack* and the door split wide open, a piece of wood spinning crazily end over end into the room. The table was thrown to one side. Something appeared in the gloom of the hallway, and a three-tined claw reached through the opening and gripped the broken wood. With a tearing noise the remainder of the door was pulled back into the darkness, and Cuthbert saw a dark shape in the doorway.

Wright lurched into the Dinosaur Hall, almost toppling Rickman, who had appeared in the doorway, choking and sobbing.

"Shoot it, Ian, oh please, *please* kill it!" she screamed.

Cuthbert waited, sighting down the barrel. He held his breath. *Four shots.*

The commander of the SWAT team moved along the roof, a catlike shape against the dark indigo of the sky, while the spotter on the street below guided his progress. Coffey stood next to the spotter, under a tarp. They both held rubberized waterproof radios.

"Dugout to Red One, move five more feet to the east," the spotter said into his radio, peering upward through his night-vision passive telescope. "You're almost there." He was studying Museum blueprints spread out on a table under a sheet of Plexiglas. The SWAT team's route had been marked in red.

The dark figure moved carefully across the slate roof, the lights of the Upper West Side twinkling around him; below, the Hudson River, the flashing lights of the emergency vehicles on Museum Drive, the high-rise apartment buildings laid out along Riverside Drive like rows of glowing crystals.

"That's it," the spotter said. "You're there, Red One."

Coffey could see the Commander kneel, working swiftly and silently to set the charges. His team waited a hundred yards back, the medics directly behind them. On the street, a siren wailed.

"Set," said the Commander. He stood up and walked carefully backward, unrolling a wire.

"Blow when ready," murmured Coffey.

Coffey watched as everyone on the roof lay down. There was a brief flash of light, and a second later the sharp slap of sound reached

Coffey. The Commander waited a moment and then eased forward.

"Red One to Dugout, we've got an opening."

"Proceed," said Coffey.

The SWAT team dropped in through the hole in the roof, followed by the medics.

"We're inside," came the voice of the Commander. "We're in the fifth-floor corridor, proceeding as advised."

Coffey waited impatiently. He looked at his watch: nine-fifteen. They'd been stuck in there, without power, for the longest ninety minutes of his life. An unwelcome vision of the Mayor, dead and gutted, kept plaguing him.

"We're at the Cell Three emergency door, fifth floor, Section Fourteen. Ready to set charges."

"Proceed," said Coffey.

"Setting charges."

D'Agosta and his group hadn't reported in for over half an hour. God, if something happened to the Mayor, no one would care whose fault it really was. Coffey would be the one that caught the blame. That's the way things worked in this town. It had taken him so long to get where he was, and he'd been so careful, and now the bastards were just going to take it away from him. It was all Pendergast's fault. If he hadn't started messing around on other people's turf . . .

"Charges set."

"Blow when ready," Coffey said again. Pendergast had fucked up, not him. He himself had only taken over yesterday. Maybe they wouldn't blame him, after all. Especially if Pendergast wasn't around. That son of a bitch could talk the hind legs off a mule.

There was a long silence. No sound of explosion reached Coffey's ears as he waited outside beneath the sodden tarp.

"Red One to Dugout, we're clean," the Commander said.

"Proceed. Get inside and kill the son of a bitch," said Coffey.

"As discussed, sir, our first priority is to evac the wounded," said the Commander in a flat voice.

"I know! But hurry it up, for God's sake!"

He punched savagely at his transmit button.

The Commander stepped out of the stairwell, looking carefully around before motioning the teams to follow him. One by one, the dark figures emerged, gas masks pushed high on their foreheads, fatigue uniforms blending into the shadows, their M-16s and Bullpups equipped with full-tang bayonets. In the rear, a short, stubby officer was carrying a 40mm six-shot grenade launcher, a big-bellied weapon that looked like a pregnant tommy gun. "We've gained the fourth floor," the Commander radioed the spotter. "Laying down an infrared beacon. Hall of Lesser Apes directly ahead."

The spotter spoke into his radio. "Proceed south seventy feet into the Hall, then west twenty feet to a door."

The Commander took a small black box from his belt and pressed a button. A ruby laser shot out, pencil-thin. He moved the beam around until he had the distance reading he needed. Then he moved forward and repeated the procedure, shining the laser toward the west wall.

"Red One to Dugout. Door in sight."

"Good. Proceed."

The Commander moved ahead to the door, motioning his men to follow.

"The door's locked. Setting charges."

The team quickly moulded two small bars of plastique around the doorknob, then stepped back, unrolling more wire.

"Charges set."

There was a low *whump* as the door flew open.

"The trapdoor should be directly in front of you, in the center of the storage room," the spotter directed.

By moving aside several flats of scenery, the Commander and his men exposed the trapdoor. Undoing the latches, the Commander grasped the iron ring and heaved upward. Stale air rushed up to greet them. The Commander leaned forward. In the Hall of the Heavens below, everything was still.

"We've got an opening," he said into the radio. "Looks good."

"Okay," came Coffey's voice. "Secure the Hall. Send down the medics and evac the injured, fast."

"Red One, roger that, Dugout."

The spotter took over. "Tear out the drywall in the center of the north wall. Behind it you'll find an eight-inch I-beam to anchor your ropes to."

"Will do."

"Careful. It's a sixty-foot drop."

The Commander and his team worked swiftly, punching through the drywall, looping two chains around the I-beam, attaching locking carabiners, a block and tackle. A team member hooked a rope ladder to one of the chains and dropped it through the hole.

The Commander leaned over once again, shining his powerful light down into the gloom of the hall.

"This is Red One. We've got some bodies down here," he said.

"Any sign of the creature?" Coffey asked.

"Negative. Looks like ten, twelve bodies, maybe more. Ladder's in place now."

"What are you waiting for?"

The Commander turned to the medic team. "We'll signal when ready. Start lowering the collapsible stretchers. We'll take 'em out one by one."

He grabbed the rope ladder and started down, swinging over the vast empty space. The men followed, one by one. Two fanned out to provide suppressing fire as necessary, while two others set up tripods with clusters of halogen lamps, hooking them to the portable generators being lowered by ropes. Soon the center of the hall was flooded with light.

"Secure all ingress and egress!" shouted the Commander. "Medic team, descend!"

"Report!" Coffey cried over the radio.

"We've secured the Hall," the Commander said. "No sign of any animal. Medic team deploying now."

"Good. You'll need to find the thing, kill it, and locate the Mayor's party. We believe they went down the stairwell back by the service area."

"Roger, Dugout," said the Commander.

As the Commander's radio buzzed into silence, he heard a sudden report, muffled but unmistakable.

"Red One to Dugout, we just heard a pistol shot. Sounded like it was coming from above."

"Dammit, go after it!" cried Coffey. "Take your men and go after it!"

The Commander turned to his men. "All right. Red Two, Red Three, finish up and secure here. Take the grenade launcher. The rest of you come with me."

= 56 =

The viscous water was now lapping at Smithback's waist. Just keeping his balance was exhausting. His legs had long since gone numb, and he was shivering.

"This water is rising awful damn fast." D'Agosta said.

"I don't think we need to worry about that creature anymore," Smithback said hopefully.

"Maybe not. You know," D'Agosta told him slowly, "You were pretty quick back there, jamming the door with the flashlight like that. I guess you saved all our lives."

"Thanks," said Smithback, liking D'Agosta more and more.

"Don't let it go to your head," D'Agosta said over the rush of the water.

"Everyone okay?" D'Agosta turned back to the Mayor.

The Mayor looked haggard. "It's touch and go. There are a few who are slipping into shock or exhaustion, maybe both. Which way from here?" His eyes searched them.

D'Agosta hesitated. "Ah, I really can't say anything conclusively," he said at last. "Smithback and I will to try the right fork first."

The Mayor looked back at the group, then moved closer to D'Agosta. "Look," he said, in a low, pleading tone. "I know you're lost. *You* know you're lost. But if those people back there learn about it, I don't think we'd get them to go any farther. It's very cold standing here, and the water is getting higher. So why don't we all try it together? It's our only chance. Even if we wanted to retrace our steps, half these people would never make it against the current."

D'Agosta looked at the Mayor for a moment. "All right," he said at last. Then he turned to the group. "Listen up now," he shouted. "We're gonna be taking the right tunnel. Everyone join hands, form a line. Hold on tight. Stay against the wall—the current's getting too strong in the center. If anyone slips, give a yell, but don't let go under any circumstances. Everybody got that? Let's go."

The dark shape moved slowly through the broken door, stepping cat-like over the splintered wood. Cuthbert felt pins and needles in his legs. He wanted to shoot, but his hands refused to obey.

"Please go away," he said, so calmly he surprised himself.

It stopped suddenly and looked directly at him. Cuthbert could see nothing in the dim light but the huge, powerful silhouette and the small red eyes. They looked, somehow, intelligent.

"Don't hurt me," Cuthbert pleaded.

The creature remained still.

"I've got a gun," Cuthbert whispered. He aimed carefully. "I won't shoot if you go away," he said quietly.

It moved slowly sideways, keeping its head turned toward Cuthbert. Then there was a sudden movement and it was gone.

Cuthbert backed away in a panic, his flashlight skittering wildly across the floor. He spun around frantically. All was silent. The creature's stench filled the room. Suddenly he found himself stumbling into the Dinosaur Hall, and then he was slamming the door behind him.

"The key!" he cried. "Lavinia, for God's sake!"

He looked wildly around the darkened hall. Before him, a great tyrannosaurus skeleton reared up from the center. In front of it squatted the dark form of a triceratops, its head lowered, the great black horns gleaming in the dull light.

He heard a sobbing, then he felt a key being pressed into his palm. He swiftly locked the door.

"Let's go," he said, guiding her away from the door, past the clawed foot of the tyrannosaur. They moved deeper into darkness. Suddenly, Cuthbert pulled the Public Relations Director to one side, then guided her into a crouch. He peered into the gloom, senses straining. The Hall of Cretaceous Dinosaurs was deathly silent. Not even the sound of the rain penetrated this dark sanctum. The only light came from rows of high clerestory windows.

Surrounding them was a herd of small struthiomimus skeletons, arranged in a defensive ⸪-shaped formation before the monstrous skeleton of a carnivorous dryptosaurus, its head down, jaws open, and huge claws extended. Cuthbert had always relished the scale and drama of this room, but now it frightened him. Now he knew what it was like to be hunted.

Behind them, the entrance to the Hall was blocked by a heavy steel emergency door. "Where's Winston?" Cuthbert whispered, peering through the bones of the dryptosaur.

"I don't know," Rickman moaned, gripping his arm. "Did you kill it?"

"I missed," he whispered. "Please let me go. I need to have a clear shot."

Rickman released him, then crawled backward between two of the struthiomimus skeletons, curling herself into a fetal position with a stifled sob.

"Be silent!" Cuthbert hissed.

The Hall lapsed again into a profound stillness. He looked around, probing the shadows with his eyes. He hoped Wright had found refuge in one of the many dark corners.

"Ian?" came a subdued voice. "Lavinia?"

Cuthbert turned and saw to his horror that Wright was leaning against the tail of a stegosaurus. As he watched, Wright swayed, then recovered.

"Winston!" Cuthbert hissed. "Get under cover!"

But Wright began walking unsteadily toward them. "Is that you, Ian?" Wright said, his voice puzzled. He stopped and leaned for a moment against the corner of a display case. "I feel sick," he said matter-of-factly.

Suddenly an explosive noise rocketed across the hall, echoing crazily in the enormous space. Another crash followed. Dimly, Cuthbert saw that Wright's office door was now a jagged hole. A dark form emerged.

Behind him, Rickman screamed and covered her head.

Through the skeleton of the dryptosaurus, Cuthbert could see the dark shape moving swiftly across the open floor. Straight for him, he thought—but it suddenly veered toward the shadowy figure of Wright. The two shadows merged.

Then Cuthbert heard a wet crunching noise, a scream—and silence.

Cuthbert raised the gun and tried to sight through the ribs of the mounted skeleton.

The silhouette rose up with something in its mouth, shook its head slightly and made a sucking noise. Cuthbert closed his eyes, squeezing the trigger.

The Ruger bucked in his hand, and he heard a blast and a loud clattering. Now Cuthbert saw that the dryptosaurus was missing part of a rib. Behind him, Rickman gasped and moaned.

The dark shape of the creature beyond was gone.

A few moments went by and Cuthbert felt the hinges of his sanity begin to loosen. Then, in a flicker of lightning through the clerestory, Cuthbert clearly saw the beast moving swiftly along the near wall, coming directly toward him, its red eyes fixed on his face.

He swung the barrel and began firing wildly, three quick shots, each white flash illuminating rack upon rack of dark skulls, teeth and claws—the real beast suddenly lost in this wilderness of savage extinct creatures—and then the gun was clicking as the hammer fell harmlessly on the expended chambers.

As if from a half-remembered dream, Cuthbert heard the distant sound of human voices, coming from the direction of Wright's old lab. And suddenly he was running, heedless of obstacles, through the ruined door, through Wright's lab, and into the dark corridor beyond. He heard himself screaming, and then a spotlight was shining in his face and somebody grabbed him and pinned him against a wall.

"Calm down, you're all right! Look, there's blood on him!"

"Get the gun away from him," someone else said.

"Is he the one we're after?"

"No, they said an animal. But don't take any chances."

"Stop struggling!"

Another scream rose in Cuthbert's throat. "It's back there!" he cried. "It'll kill you all! It knows, you can see in its eyes that it knows!"

"Knows what?"

"Don't bother talking to him, he's raving."

Cuthbert suddenly went limp.

The Commander came forward. "Is there anyone else back there?" he asked, shaking Cuthbert's shoulder.

"Yes," Cuthbert finally said. "Wright. Rickman."

The Commander looked up.

"You mean Winston Wright? The Director of the Museum? You must be Dr. Cuthbert, then. Where is Wright?"

"It was eating him," said Cuthbert, "eating the brains. Just eating and eating. It's in the Dinosaur Hall, through the lab there."

"Take him back to the Hall and have the medics evacuate him," said the Commander to two members of his team. "You three, let's go. On the double." He raised his radio. "Red One to Dugout. We've located Cuthbert, and we're sending him out."

"They're in this laboratory, here," said the spotter, pointing at the blueprints. Now that the penetration was complete and the team was deep inside the Museum, the two had moved inside the mobile command unit, away from the hammering rain.

"The lab's clear," the Commander's monotone came over the radio. "Proceeding into the Dinosaur Hall. This other door's been broken down, too."

"Go in and take that thing out!" cried Coffey. "But watch out for Dr. Wright. And keep a clear frequency. I want to be in touch at all times!"

Coffey waited, tensed over the set, hearing the faint hiss and crackle of the static over the open frequency. He heard the clink of a weapon and a few whispers.

"Smell that?" Coffey leaned closer. They were almost there. He gripped the edge of the table.

"Yup," a voice answered.

There was a rattling.

"Kill the light and stay in the shadows. Red Seven, cover the left side of that skeleton. Red Three, go right. Red Four, get your back to the wall, cover the far sector."

There was a long silence. Coffey could hear heavy breathing and faint footfalls.

He heard a sudden explosive whisper. "Red Five, look, there's a body here."

Coffey felt his stomach tighten.

"No head," he heard. "Nice."

"Here's another one," whispered a voice. "See it? Lying in that group of dinosaurs."

More clicking and rattling of weapons, more breathing.

"Red Seven, cover our path of retreat. There's no other way out."

"It may still be here," someone whispered.

"That's far enough, Red Five."

Coffey's knuckles whitened. Why the fuck didn't they get it over with? These guys were a bunch of old women.

More rattling of metal.

"Something's moving! Over there!" The voice was so loud Coffey jumped, and then a burst of automatic weapons fire dissolved immediately into static as the frequency overloaded.

"Shit, shit, shit," Coffey began saying, over and over. Then for an instant he could hear screaming, and then more static; the even cadence of machine-gun fire; then, silence. The tinkling sound of something—what? Shattered dinosaur bones dropping and rolling on the marble floor?

Coffey felt a flood of relief. Whatever it was, it was dead. Nothing could have survived the shitload of firepower just unloaded. The nightmare was finally over. He eased himself down in a chair.

"Red Five! Hoskins! Oh shit!" the voice of the Commander screamed over the frequency. The voice was suddenly buried by the staccato of gunfire, then more static. Or was it a scream?

Coffey surged to his feet and turned to an agent standing behind him. He opened his mouth to speak, but no sound came out. He read his own terror in the agent's eyes.

"Red One!" he yelled into the mike. "Red One! Do you read?"

All he could hear was static.

"Talk to me, Commander! Do you read? Anyone!"

He switched frequencies wildly to the team in the Hall of the Heavens.

"Sir, we're removing the last of the bodies now," came the voice of a medic. "The rear detail of the SWAT team just evacuated Doctor Cuthbert to the roof. We just heard firing from upstairs. Are we going to need more evacuation—?"

"Get the hell out!" Coffey screamed. "Get your asses out! Get the fuck out and pull up the ladder!"

"Sir, what about the rest of the SWAT team? We can't leave those men—"

"They're dead! Understand? That's an order!"

He dropped the radio and leaned back, gazing vaguely out the window. A morgue truck slowly moved up toward the massive bulk of the Museum.

Someone tapped him on the shoulder. "Sir, Agent Pendergast is requesting to speak with you."

Coffey slowly shook his head. "No. I don't want to talk to that fuck, you got that?"

"Sir, he—"

"Don't mention his name to me again."

Another agent opened the rear door and came inside, his suit sodden. "Sir, the dead are coming out now."

"Who? Who are you talking about?"

"The people from the Hall of the Heavens. There were seventeen dead, no survivors."

"Cuthbert? The guy you took out of the lab? Is he out?"

"They've just lowered him to the street."

"I want to talk to him."

Coffey stepped outside and ran down past the ambulance circle, his mind numb. How could a SWAT team buy it, just like that?

Outside, two medics with a stretcher approached. "Are you Cuthbert?" Coffey asked the still form.

The man looked around with unfocused eyes.

The doctor pushed past Coffey, sliced open Cuthbert's shirt, then inspected his face and eyes.

"There's blood here," he said. "Are you hurt?"

"I don't know," said Cuthbert.

"Respiration thirty, pulse one-twenty," said a paramedic.

"You're okay?" the doctor asked. "Is this your blood?"

"I don't know."

The doctor looked swiftly down Cuthbert's legs, felt them, felt his groin, examined his neck.

The doctor turned toward the paramedic. "Take him in for observation." The medics wheeled the stretcher away.

"Cuthbert!" said Coffey, jogging beside him. "Did you see it?"

"See it?" Cuthbert repeated.

"See the fucking creature!"

"It knows," Cuthbert said.

"Knows what?"

"It knows what's going on, it knows exactly what's happening."

"What the hell does that mean?"

"It hates us," said Cuthbert.

As the medics threw open the door of an ambulance, Coffey yelled, "What did it look like?"

"There was sadness in its eyes," said Cuthbert. "Infinite sadness."

"He's a lunatic," said Coffey to no one in particular.

"You won't kill it," Cuthbert added, with calm certainty.

The doors slammed shut.

"The hell I won't!" shouted Coffey at the retreating ambulance. "Fuck you, Cuthbert! *The hell I won't!*"

= 57 =

Pendergast lowered the radio and looked at Margo. "The creature just killed the better part of a SWAT team. Dr. Wright, too, from the sound of it. Coffey withdrew everyone else, and he won't answer my summons. He seems to think everything is my fault."

"He's *got* to listen!" roared Frock. "We know what to do now. All they need to do is come in here with klieg lights!"

"I understand what's happening," said Pendergast. "He's overloaded, looking for scapegoats. We can't rely on his help."

"My God," Margo said. "Dr. Wright . . ." She put a hand to her mouth. "If my plan had worked—if I'd thought everything through—maybe all those people would still be alive."

"And perhaps Lieutenant D'Agosta, and the Mayor, and all those others below us, would be dead," Pendergast said. He looked down the hallway. "I suppose my duty now is to see you two out safely," he said. "Perhaps we should take the route I suggested to D'Agosta. Assuming those blueprints didn't lead him astray, of course."

Then he glanced at Frock. "No, I don't suppose that would work."

"Go ahead!" Frock cried. "Don't stay here on my account!"

Pendergast smiled thinly. "It isn't that, Doctor. It's the inclement weather. You know how the subbasement floods during rainy spells. I heard someone on the police radio saying the rain outside has been approaching monsoon strength for the last hour. When I was sprinkling those fibers into the subbasement, I noticed the water was at least two feet deep and flowing quickly eastward. That would imply drainage from the River. We couldn't get down there now even if we wanted to." Pendergast raised his eyebrows. "If D'Agosta isn't out by now— well, his chances are marginal, at best."

He turned toward Margo. "Perhaps the best thing would be for you two to stay here, inside the Secure Area. We know the creature can't get past this reinforced door. Within a couple of hours, they are sure to restore power. I believe there are several men still trapped in Security Command and the Computer Room. They may be vulnerable. You've taught me a lot about this creature. We know its weaknesses, and we know its strengths. Those areas are near a long, unobstructed hallway. With you two safe in here, I can hunt it for a change."

"No," said Margo. "You can't do it by yourself."

"Perhaps not, Miss Green, but I plan on making a fairly good imitation of it."

"I'm coming with you," she said resolutely.

"Sorry." Pendergast stood by the open door to the Secure Area expectantly.

"That thing is highly intelligent," she said. I don't think you can go up against it alone. If you think that because I'm a woman—"

Pendergast looked astonished. "Ms. Green, I'm shocked you would have such a low opinion of me. The fact is, you've never been in this kind of situation before. Without a gun, you can't do anything."

Margo looked at him combatively. "I saved your ass back there when I told you to switch on your lamp," she challenged.

He raised an eyebrow.

From the darkness, Frock said, "Pendergast, don't be a Southern gentleman fool. Take her."

Pendergast turned to Frock. "Are you sure you'll be all right on your own, Doctor?" he asked. "We'll need to take both the flashlight and the miner's lamp if we're to have any chance of success."

"Of course!" Frock said with a dismissive wave. "I could use a bit of rest after all this excitement."

Pendergast hesitated a moment longer, then looked bemused. "Very well," he said. "Margo, lock the doctor inside the Secure Area, get his keys and what's left of my suit jacket, and let's go."

Smithback gave the flashlight a savage shake. The light flickered, grew brighter for a moment, then dimmed again.

"If that light goes out," D'Agosta said, "we're fucked. Turn it off; we'll switch it on now and then to check our progress."

They moved through the darkness, the sound of rushing water filling the close air. Smithback led; behind him came D'Agosta, grasping the journalist's hand—which, like the rest of him, had grown almost entirely numb.

Suddenly, Smithback pricked up his ears. In the dark, he gradually became aware of a new sound.

"You hear that?" Smithback asked.

D'Agosta listened. "I hear something," he answered.

"It sounds to me like—" Smithback fell silent.

"A waterfall," D'Agosta said with finality. "But whatever it is must be a ways off. Sounds carry in this tunnel. Keep it to yourself."

The group slogged on in silence.

"Light," said D'Agosta.

Smithback turned it on, played it down the empty hall in front of them, then switched it off again. The sound was louder now; quite a bit louder, in fact. He felt a surge in the water.

"Shit!" said D'Agosta.

There was a sudden commotion behind them.

"Help!" came a feminine voice. "I've slipped! Don't let go!"

"Grab her, somebody!" the Mayor shouted.

Smithback snapped on the light and angled it quickly backward. A middle-aged woman was thrashing about in the water, her long evening dress billowing out across the inky water.

"Stand up!" the Mayor was shouting. "Anchor your feet!"

"Help me!" she screamed.

Smithback shoved the flashlight into his pocket and braced himself against the current. The woman was floating directly toward him. He saw her arm lash out and felt it wrap around his thigh in a viselike grip. He felt himself slipping.

"Wait!" he cried. "Stop struggling! I've got you!"

Her legs kicked out and wrapped around his knees. Smithback lost his grip on D'Agosta and staggered forward, marveling at her strength even as he was pulled off balance.

"You're dragging me under!" he said, toppling to his chest in the water and feeling the current sucking him downward. Out of the corner of his eye he saw D'Agosta wading in his direction. The woman clambered onto him in a blind panic, forcing his head under water. He rose up under her damp gown, and then it was clinging to his nose and chin, disorienting him, suffocating him. A great lassitude began to sweep over him. He went under a second time, a strange, hollow roaring in his ears.

Suddenly he was above the water again, choking and coughing. A dreadful shrieking was coming from the tunnel ahead of them. He was held in a powerful grip. D'Agosta's grip.

"We lost the woman," D'Agosta said. "Come on."

Her shrieks echoed toward them, growing fainter as she was swept farther downstream. Some of the guests were shouting and crying directions to her, others sobbing uncontrollably.

"Quick, everybody!" D'Agosta yelled. "Stay against the wall! Let's move forward, and, whatever you do, don't break the chain." Under his breath, he muttered to Smithback, "Tell me you've still got the flashlight."

"Here it is," Smithback said, testing it.

"We have to keep going, or we'll lose everybody," D'Agosta muttered. Then he laughed a short, mirthless laugh. "Looks like I saved *your* life this time. That makes us even, Smithback."

Smithback said nothing. He was trying to shut out the horrifying, anguished screams, fainter now and distorted by the tunnel. The sound of roaring water grew clearer and more menacing.

The event had demoralized the group. "We'll be all right if we just hold hands!" Smithback heard the Mayor shout. "Keep the chain intact!"

Smithback gripped D'Agosta's hand as hard as he could. They waded downstream in the darkness.

"Light," said D'Agosta.

Smithback switched on the beam. And the bottom dropped out of his world.

A hundred yards ahead, the high ceiling of the tunnel sloped downwards to a narrow semicircular funnel. Beneath it, the roiling water writhed and surged thunderously, then plummeted abruptly into a dark chasm. Heavy mist rose, bearding the mossy throat of the pit with dark spray. Smithback watched, slackjawed, as all his hopes for a best-seller, all his dreams—even his wish to stay alive—disappeared into the whirlpool.

Dimly, he realized that the screaming behind him wasn't screaming, but cheering. He looked back, and saw the bedraggled group staring upward, above his head. At the point where the curved brickwork of the ceiling met the wall of the tunnel, a dark hole yawned, perhaps three feet square. Poking out of it was the end of a rusty iron ladder, bolted to the ancient masonry.

The cheering rapidly died away as the awful truth dawned.

"It's too fucking far to reach," D'Agosta said.

= **58** =

They moved away from the Secure Area and stealthily climbed a stair-well. Pendergast turned to Margo, put a finger to his lips, then pointed to the crimson splashes of blood on the floor. She nodded: the beast had gone this way when it ran from their lights. She remembered that she'd been up this staircase just the day before with Smithback, evading the guard. She followed Pendergast as he flicked off the miner's lamp, cautiously opened the first floor door, and moved out into the darkness beyond, the bundle of fibers clasped over his shoulder.

The agent stopped a moment, inhaling. "I don't smell anything," he whispered. "Which way to Security Command and the Computer Room?"

"I think we go left from here," Margo said. "And then through the Hall of Early Mammals. It's not too far. Just around the corner from Security Command is the long hallway Dr. Frock told you about."

Pendergast switched on the flashlight briefly and shone it down the corridor. "No blood spoor," he murmured. "The creature headed straight upstairs from the Secure Area—past this landing and right toward Dr. Wright, I'm afraid." He turned toward Margo. "And how do you propose we lure it here?"

"Use the fibers again," she replied.

"It didn't fall for that trick last time."

"But this time we're not trying to trap it. All we want to do is lure it around the corner. You'll be at the other end of the hallway, ready to shoot. We'll just leave some fibers at one end of the hall. We'll make a—a what do you call it?—at the far end."

"A blind."

"Right, a blind. And we'll be hiding there, in the dark. When it comes, I'll train the miner's light onto it and you can start shooting."

"Indeed. And how will we know when the creature has arrived? If the hallway is as long as Dr. Frock says it is, we may not be able to smell it in time."

Margo was quiet. "That's tough," she finally admitted.

They stood for a moment in silence.

"There's a glass case at the end of the hall," Margo said. "It's meant to display new books written by the Museum staff, but Mrs. Rickman never bothered to have it filled. So it won't be locked. We can put the bundle in there. The creature may be out for blood, but I doubt it'll be able to resist *that*. It'll make some noise prying open the case. When you hear the noise, you shoot."

"Sorry," Pendergast said after a moment, "but I think it's too obvious. We have to ask the question again: If *I* came across a setup like this, would I know it was a trap? In this case, the answer is yes. We need to think of something a little more subtle. Any new trap that uses the fibers as bait is bound to arouse its suspicions."

Margo leaned against the cold marble wall of the corridor. "It has an acute sense of hearing as well as smell," she said.

"Yes?"

"Perhaps the simplest approach is best. We use ourselves as bait. We make some noise. Talk loudly. Sound like easy prey."

Pendergast nodded. "Like the ptarmigan, feigning a broken wing, drawing off the fox. And how will we know it's there?"

"We'll use the flashlight intermittently. Wave it about, shine it down the hall. We'll use the low setting; it may irritate the creature, but it won't rebuff it. But it will allow us to see it. The creature will think we're looking around, trying to find our way. Then, when it comes for us, I switch to the miner's light and you start shooting."

Pendergast thought for a moment. "What about the possibility of the creature coming from the other direction? From behind us?"

"The hall dead-ends in the staff entrance to the Hall of Pacific Peoples," Margo pointed out.

"So we'll be trapped at the end of a cul-de-sac," Pendergast protested. "I don't like it."

"Even if we weren't trapped," Margo said, "we wouldn't be able to escape if you miss your shots. According to the Extrapolator, the thing can move almost as fast as a greyhound."

Pendergast thought for a moment. "You know, Margo, this plan might work. It's deceptively simple and uncluttered, like a Zurbarán still life or a Bruckner symphony. If this creature devastated a SWAT team, it probably feels there isn't much more that human beings can do to it. It wouldn't be as cautious."

"And it's wounded, which may slow it down."

"Yes, it's wounded. I think D'Agosta shot it, and the SWAT team may have gotten one or two additional rounds into it. Maybe I hit it, as well; there's no way to be sure. But, Margo, being wounded makes it infinitely *more* dangerous. I would rather stalk ten healthy lions than one wounded one." He straightened his shoulders and felt for his gun. "Lead on, please. Standing here in the dark with this bundle on my back makes me very uneasy. From now on, we use only the flashlight. Be very careful."

"Why don't you give me the miner's light, so you'll be free to use the gun?" Margo suggested. "If we meet up with the beast unexpectedly, we'll have to drive it away with the light."

"If it's badly wounded, I doubt anything will drive it away," replied Pendergast. "But here it is."

They moved quietly down the corridor, around a corner, and through a service door leading into the Hall of Ancient Mammals. It seemed to Margo that her stealthy footsteps echoed like gunshots across the polished stone floor. Row upon row of glass cases gleamed dully in the glow of the flashlight: giant elk, saber-toothed cats, dire wolves. Mastodon and wooly mammoth skeletons reared in the center of the gallery. Margo and Pendergast moved cautiously toward the Hall's exit, Pendergast's gun at the ready.

"See that door at the far end, the one marked STAFF ONLY?" Margo whispered. "Beyond that is the corridor housing Security Command, Staff Services, and the Computer Room. Around the corner is the hallway where you can set up your blind." She hesitated. "If the creature is already there . . ."

". . . I'll wish I'd stayed in New Orleans, Ms. Green."

Stepping through the staff entrance into Section 18, they found themselves in a narrow hallway lined with doors. Pendergast swept the area with his flashlight: nothing.

"That's it," said Margo, indicating a door to their left. "Security Command." Margo could briefly hear the murmur of voices as they passed. They passed another door marked CENTRAL COMPUTER.

"They're sitting ducks in there," Margo said. "Should we—?"

"No," came the response. "No time."

They turned the corner and stopped. Pendergast played his light down the hallway.

"What's that doing there?" he asked.

Halfway down the hall, a massive steel security door flashed mockingly at them in the glow of the flashlight.

"The good Doctor was mistaken," Pendergast said. "Cell Two must cut this corridor in half. That's the edge of the perimeter, there."

"What's the distance?" Margo said in a monotone.

Pendergast pursed his lips. "I'd guess a hundred, a hundred and twenty-five feet, at the most."

She turned to the agent. "Is that enough room?"

Pendergast remained motionless. "No. But it'll have to do. Come on, Ms. Green, let's get into position."

The Mobile Command Unit was getting stuffier. Coffey unbuttoned his shirt and loosened his tie with a savage tug. The humidity had to be 110 percent. He hadn't seen rain like this in twenty years. The drains were bubbling like geysers, the tires of the emergency vehicles up to their hubcaps in water.

The rear door swung open, revealing a man wearing SWAT fatigues. "Sir?"

"What do you want?"

"The men would like to know when we're going back in."

"Going back *in?*" Coffey yelled. "Are you out of your mind? Six of your men were just killed in there, torn apart like frigging hamburger!"

"But sir, there are people still trapped in there. Maybe we could—"

Coffey rounded on the man, eyes blazing, mouth spewing saliva. "Don't you get it? We can't just go busting back in there. We sent men in not knowing what we were up against. We've got to get the power restored, get the systems back on line before we—"

A policeman stuck his head inside the door of the van. "Sir, we've just had a report of a dead body floating in the Hudson River. It was spotted down at the Boat Basin. Seems like it was flushed out of one of the big storm drains."

"Who the fuck cares about—"

"Sir, it's a woman wearing an evening gown, and it's been tentatively identified as one of the people missing from the party."

"What?" Coffey was confused. It wasn't possible. "Someone from the Mayor's group?"

"One of the people trapped inside. The only women still unaccounted for inside apparently went down into the basement two hours ago."

"You mean, with the *Mayor?*"

"I guess that would be right, sir."

Coffey felt his bladder weakening. It couldn't be true.

That fucking Pendergast. Fucking D'Agosta. It was all their fault. They disobeyed him, compromised his plan, sent all those people to their deaths. The Mayor, dead. They were going to have his ass for that.

"Sir?"

"Get out," Coffey whispered. "Both of you, get out." The door closed.

"This is Garcia, over. Does anyone copy?" the radio squawked. Coffey spun around and jabbed the radio with his finger.

"Garcia! What's going on?"

"Nothing, sir, except the power's still out. But I have Tom Allen here. He's been asking to speak with you."

"Put him on, then."

"This is Allen. We're getting a little concerned in here, Mr. Coffey. There's nothing we can do until power's restored. The batteries are failing on Garcia's transmitter, and we've been keeping it off to conserve juice. We'd like you to get us out."

Coffey laughed, suddenly, shrilly. The agents manning the consoles looked uneasily at one another. "You'd like *me* to get *you* out? Listen, Allen, you geniuses created this mess. You swore up and down the system would work, that everything had a backup. So you get your own asses out. The Mayor's dead, and I've already lost more men than I—hello?"

"This is Garcia again. Sir, it's pitch-black in here and we only have two flashlights. What happened to the SWAT team that was being sent in?"

Coffey's laughter stopped abruptly. "Garcia? They got themselves killed. You hear me? *Killed.* Got their guts hung up like birthday ribbons in there. And it's Pendergast's fault, and D'Agosta's fault, and fucking Allen's fault, and *your* fault, too, probably. Now, we've got men on this side working to restore the power. They say it can be done, it just may take a few hours. Okay? I'm gonna take that goddamn thing in there, but in *my* way, in my own sweet time. So you just sit tight. I'm not going to have more men killed to save your sorry asses."

There was a rap on the rear door. "Come in," he barked, switching off the radio.

An agent stepped inside and crouched beside Coffey, the glow of the monitors throwing his face into sharp relief. "Sir, I just got word that the Deputy Mayor is on his way over now. And the Governor's office is on the phone. They want an update."

Coffey closed his eyes.

Smithback looked up at the ladder, its rusty lower rung hanging a good four feet above his head. Maybe if there was no water he could have jumped it, but with the current nearing his chest it was impossible.

"See anything up there?" D'Agosta asked.

"Nope," replied Smithback. "This light's weak. I can't tell how far the thing extends."

"Turn off the light, then," D'Agosta gasped. "Give me a minute to think."

There was a long silence. Smithback felt another surge against his waist. The water was still rising fast. Another foot, and they would all be floating downstream toward—Smithback shook his head, angrily dispelling the thought.

"Where the hell is all this water coming from?" he moaned to no one in particular.

"This subbasement is built below the Hudson River water table," D'Agosta replied. "It leaks whenever there's a heavy rain."

"Leaks, sure—maybe it even floods a foot or two," Smithback panted. "But we're being inundated. They must be building arks out there."

D'Agosta didn't answer.

"The hell with this," a voice said. "Someone get on my shoulders. We'll go up one by one."

"Stow it!" D'Agosta snapped. "It's too damn high for that."

Smithback coughed, cleared his throat. "I've got an idea!" he said. There was a silence.

"Look, that steel ladder appears to be pretty strong," he urged. "If we can fasten our belts together and loop them over that ladder, we can wait for the water to rise enough so we can grab the lower rung."

"I can't wait that long!" someone cried.

D'Agosta glared. "Smithback, that's the fucking worst idea I ever heard," he growled. "Besides, half the men here are wearing cummerbunds."

"I noticed *you* have a belt on," Smithback retorted.

"So I do," D'Agosta replied defensively. "But what makes you think the water will rise enough for us to reach the rung?"

"Look up there," Smithback said, shining his flashlight along the wall near the bottom of the metal ladder. "See that band of discoloration? It looks like a high-water mark to me. At least once in the past, the water has risen that high. If this is half the storm you think it is, we ought to get fairly close."

D'Agosta shook his head. "Well, I still think it's crazy," he said, "but I suppose it's better than waiting here to die. You men back there!" he shouted. "Belts! Pass your belts up to me!"

As the belts reached D'Agosta, he knotted them together, buckle to end, starting with the widest buckle. Then he passed them to Smithback, who looped them over his shoulders. Swinging the heavier end, he braced himself against the current, leaned back, and tossed it up toward the lowest rung. The twelve feet of leather fell back into the water, missing by several feet. He tried again, missed again.

"Here, give me that," D'Agosta said. "Let a man do a man's job."

"The hell with that," Smithback said, rearing back dangerously and giving another toss. This time Smithback ducked as the heavy buckle came swinging down; then he slid the far end through and pulled the improvised rope tight around the lower ring.

"Okay, everyone," D'Agosta said. "This is it. I want you all to link arms. Don't let go. As the water rises, it'll carry us toward the ladder. We'll play this back to you in sections as we rise. I hope the son of a bitch holds," he muttered, eyeing the linked belts dubiously.

"And the water rises far enough," said Smithback.

"If it doesn't, you'll hear about it from me, mister."

Smithback turned to respond, but decided to save his breath. The current crept up around his chest, tugging at his armpits, and he felt a slow, inexorable pressure from below as his feet started to lose their hold on the smooth stone floor of the tunnel.

$= 59 =$

Garcia watched as the pool of light from Allen's flashlight moved slowly across a bank of dead controls, then back again. Nesbitt, the guard on monitoring duty, slouched at the coffee-stained "panic desk" in the middle of Security Command. Next to him sat Waters and the skinny, gawky-looking programmer from the Computer Room. They had knocked on the door of Security Command ten minutes earlier, scaring the three men inside half to death. Now the programmer was sitting quietly in the dark, chewing his cuticles and sniffling. Waters had placed his service revolver on the table and was nervously spinning it.

"What was that?" Waters said suddenly, stopping his pistol in mid-spin.

"What was what?" Garcia asked morosely.

"I thought I heard a noise in the hall just now," Waters said, swallowing hard. "Like feet going by."

"You're always hearing noises, Waters," Garcia said. "That's what got us here in the first place."

There was a brief, uncomfortable silence.

"Are you sure you read Coffey right?" Waters spoke up again. "If that thing destroyed a SWAT team, it could easily get to us."

"Stop thinking about it," said Garcia. "Stop *talking* about it. It happened three floors above us."

"I can't believe Coffey, just leaving us here to rot—"

"Waters? If you don't shut up I'm going to send you back to the Computer Room."

Waters fell silent.

"Radio Coffey again," Allen told Garcia. "We need to get the hell out of here, now."

Garcia slowly shook his head. "It ain't gonna work. Sounded to me like he was about five beers short of a six-pack. Maybe he's bent a bit under the pressure. We're stuck here for the duration."

"Who's his boss?" Allen insisted. "Give me the radio."

"No way. The emergency batteries are almost dead."

Allen started to protest, then stopped abruptly. "I smell something," he said.

Garcia sat up. "So do I." Then he picked up his shotgun, slowly, like a sleeper caught in a bad dream.

"It's the killer beast!" Waters cried loudly. All the men were on their feet in an instant. Chairs were thrown back, smashing against the floor. There was a thump and a curse as somebody struck the side of a desk, then a splintering crash as a monitor fell to the floor. Garcia grabbed the radio.

"Coffey! It's here!"

There was a scratching, then a low rattling at the doorknob. Garcia felt a gush of warmth on his legs and realized his bladder had given way. Suddenly, the door bent inward, wood cracking under a savage blow. In the close, listening darkness, he heard somebody behind him start to pray.

"Did you hear that?" whispered Pendergast.

Margo played the flashlight down the hall. "I heard something."

From down the hall and around the corner came the sound of splintering wood.

"It's breaking through one of the doors!" said Pendergast. "We need to attract its attention. *Hey!*" he shouted.

Margo grabbed Pendergast's arm. "Don't say anything you wouldn't want it to understand," she hissed.

"Ms. Green, this is no time for jokes," Pendergast snapped. "Surely it doesn't understand English."

"I don't know. We're taking a chance, anyway, just trusting the Extrapolator's data. But the thing has a highly developed brain, and it may well have been in the Museum for years, listening from dark places. It might understand certain words. We can't take the chance."

"As you wish," Pendergast whispered. Then, he said loudly: "Where are you? Can you hear me?"

"Yes!" Margo shouted. "But I'm lost! Help! Can anyone hear us?"

Pendergast lowered his voice. "It must have heard that. Now we can only wait." He dropped to one knee, right hand aiming the .45, left hand bracing right wrist. "Keep playing the light toward the bend in the hallway, move it around as if you're lost. When I see the creature, I'll give you the word. Turn on the miner's light, and keep it aimed on the creature, no matter what. If it's angry—if it's just hunting for revenge now—we have to use any means possible to slow it down. We only have a hundred feet of corridor in which to kill it. If it can run as quickly as you think it can, the beast can cover that distance in a couple of seconds. You can't hesitate, and you can't panic."

"A couple of seconds," Margo said. "I understand."

Garcia kneeled in front of the monitor bank, the butt of his shotgun snug against his cheek, the barrel pointing into the gloom. Before him, the outline of the door was faintly visible. Behind him stood Waters in a combat stance. "When it comes through, just start firing, and don't stop." Garcia said. "I've only got eight rounds. I'll try to space my shots so you can reload at least once before it reaches us. And turn off that flashlight. You trying to give us away?"

The others in Security Command—Allen, the programmer, and Nesbitt the guard—had retreated to the far wall and were crouched beneath the darkened schematic of the Museum's security grid.

Waters was shaking. "It blew away a SWAT team," he said, his voice breaking.

There was another crash, and the door groaned, its hinges popping. Waters screamed, jumped up and scrambled backward into the dark, his gun lying forgotten on the floor.

"Waters, you prick, get back here!"

Garcia heard the sickening thud of bone against metal as Waters stumbled under the desks toward the far wall, banging his skull. "Don't let it get me!" he screamed.

Garcia forced himself to turn back toward the door. He tried to steady the shotgun. The foul reek of the creature filled his nostrils as the door shuddered under another heavy blow. More than anything, he did not want to see what was about to force its way into the room. He cursed and wiped his forehead with the back of a hand. Except for Waters's sobbing, there was silence.

*   *   *

Margo shined the flashlight down the hall, trying to imitate the random motions of somebody searching for a way out. The light licked across the walls and floor, giving dim illumination to the display cabinets. Her heart was hammering, her breath coming in short gasps.

"Help!" she cried again. "We're lost!" Her voice sounded unnaturally hoarse in her ears.

There were no more sounds from around the corner. The creature was listening.

"Hello?" she called, willing herself to speak again. "Is anybody there?"

The voice echoed and died in the corridor. She waited, staring into the gloom, straining to see any movement.

A dark shape began to resolve itself against the far darkness, at a distance where the flashlight beam failed. The movement stopped. It seemed to have its head up. A strange, liquid snuffling sound came toward them.

"Not yet," Pendergast whispered.

It moved a little farther around the corner. The snuffling noise grew louder, and then the stench, wafting down the hall, violated her nostrils.

The beast took another step.

"Not yet," Pendergast whispered.

Garcia's hand was shaking so violently he could hardly press the transmit button.

"Coffey!" he hissed. "Coffey, for God's sake! Do you copy?"

"This is Agent Slade from the Forward Command Post. Who's speaking, please?"

"This is Security Command," Garcia said, breathing thick and fast. "Where's Coffey? *Where's Coffey?*"

"Special Agent Coffey is temporarily indisposed. As of now, I'm taking command of the operation, pending the arrival of the regional director. What's your status?"

"What's our status?" Garcia laughed raggedly. "Our status is, we're fucked. It's outside the door. It's breaking in. I'm begging you, send a team in."

"Hell!" came the voice of Slade. "Why wasn't I informed?" Garcia heard some muffled talk. "Garcia? Do you have your weapon?"

"What good's a shotgun?" Garcia whispered, almost in tears. "You need to get in here with a fucking bazooka. Help us, *please.*"

"Garcia, we're trying to pick up the pieces here. Command-and-control is all screwed up. Just hold tight a moment. It can't get through the Security Command door, right? It's metal, isn't it?"

"It's wood, Slade, it's just a goddamn institutional door!" Garcia said, the tears running freely down his face.

"Wood? What kind of place is this? Garcia, listen to me now. Even if we sent someone in, it'd take them twenty minutes to get to you."

"Please . . ."

"You've got to handle it yourself. I don't know what you're up against, Garcia, but get a grip on yourself. We'll be in as soon as we can. Just keep cool and aim—"

Garcia sank to the floor, his finger slipping from the button in despair. It was hopeless, they were all dead men.

= 60 =

Smithback gripped the belt, playing a few more inches back toward the group. If anything, he thought, the water was rising even faster than before; there were surges every few minutes now, and although the current didn't seem to be getting stronger, the roar at the end of the tunnel had grown deafening. The oldest, the weakest, and the poorest swimmers were directly behind Smithback, clutching to the rope of belts; behind them the others were clinging together, treading water desperately. Everyone was silent now; there was no energy left to weep, moan, or even speak. Smithback looked up: two more feet, and he'd be able to grab the ladder.

"Must be a mother of a storm out there," said D'Agosta. He was next to Smithback, supporting an older woman. "Sure rained on the Museum's party," he added with a weak laugh.

Smithback merely looked up, snapping on the light. Eighteen more inches.

"Smithback, quit switching the light on and off, all right?" D'Agosta said irritably. "*I'll* tell you when to check."

Smithback felt another surge, which buffeted him against the brick walls of the tunnel. There were some gasps among the group but no one cut loose. If the belt rope gave way, they'd all be drowned in thirty seconds. Smithback tried not to think about it.

In a shaky but determined voice, the Mayor started telling a story to the group. It involved several well-known people in City Hall. Smithback, despite scenting a scoop, felt sleepier and sleepier—a sign, he remembered, of hypothermia.

"Okay, Smithback. Check the ladder." The gruff voice of D'Agosta jerked him awake.

He shined the light upward, rattling it into life. In the past fifteen minutes the water had risen another foot, bringing the end of the ladder almost within reach. With a croak of delight, Smithback played more of the belts back to the group.

"Here's what we're gonna do," said D'Agosta. "You're gonna go up first. I'll help from down here, then I'll follow last. Okay?"

"Okay," Smithback said, shaking himself into consciousness.

D'Agosta pulled the belt taut, then grabbed Smithback by the waistband and heaved him upward. Smithback reached over his head, grabbing the lowest rung with his free hand.

"Give me the light," said D'Agosta.

Smithback handed it down, then grabbed the rung with the other hand. He pulled himself up a little, then fell back, the muscles in his arms and back jerking spasmodically. With a deep breath, he pulled himself up again, this time reaching the second rung.

"Now you grab the rung," D'Agosta said to someone. Smithback leaned against the rungs, gasping for breath. Then, looking upward again, he grasped the third rung, then the fourth. He felt around lightly with his feet to secure them on the first rung.

"Don't step on anyone's hands!" D'Agosta warned from below.

He felt a hand guide his foot, and he was able to put his weight on the lowest rung. The firmness felt like heaven. He reached down with one hand and helped the elderly woman. Then he turned back, feeling his strength returning, and moved upward.

The ladder ended at the mouth of a large pipe jutting out horizontally where the curved vault of the roof met the tunnel wall. Gingerly, he moved to the pipe and began crawling into the darkness.

Immediately, a putrid odor assaulted his nostrils. *Sewer,* he thought. He stopped involuntarily for a moment, then moved forward again.

The pipe ended, opening into blackness. Gingerly, he brought his feet outward and downward. A hard, firm dirt floor met his shoes a foot or so beneath the mouth of the pipe. He could hardly believe their luck: a chamber of unknown size, hung suspended here between the basement and subbasement. Probably some architectural palimpsest, a long-forgotten by-product of one of the Museum's many reconstructions. He clambered out and moved a few inches forward, then another few inches, sweeping his feet over the blackness of the floor. The stench around him was abominable, but it was not the smell of the beast, and for that he was profoundly grateful. Dry things—twigs?—crunched beneath his feet. Behind him, he could hear grunting, and the sound of others moving down the pipe toward him. The feeble light from D'Agosta's flashlight in the subbasement beyond could not penetrate the blackness.

He turned around, knelt down by the mouth of the pipe, and began helping the bedraggled group out, directing them off to the side, warning them not to stray too far into the dark.

One at a time, people emerged and spread out against the wall, feeling their way gingerly, collapsing in exhaustion. The room was quiet except for the sound of ragged breathing.

Finally, Smithback heard the voice of D'Agosta coming through the pipe. "Christ, what is that reek?" he muttered to Smithback. "That damned flashlight finally gave out. So I dropped it into the water. Okay, people," he said in a louder voice, standing up, "I want you to count off." The sound of dripping water started Smithback's heart racing until he realized it was simply D'Agosta, wringing out his sodden jacket.

One by one, in tired voices, the group gave their names. "Good," D'Agosta said. "Now to figure out where we are. We may need to look for higher ground, in case the water continues to rise."

"I'd like to look for higher ground anyway," came a voice from the darkness. "It stinks in here something awful."

"It'll be tough without light," Smithback said. "We'll need to go single file."

"I've got a lighter," one voice said. "Shall I see if it still works?"

"Careful," said someone else. "Smells like methane, if you ask me."

Smithback winced as a wavering yellow flame illuminated the chamber.

"*Oh, Jesus!*" somebody screamed.

The chamber was suddenly plunged into darkness again as the hand holding the lighter involuntarily jerked away—but not before Smithback got a single, devastating image of what lay around him.

Margo strained ahead in the dimness, slowly moving the flashlight around the hall, trying to keep from deliberately spotlighting the beast as it crouched at the corner, observing them.

"Not yet," Pendergast murmured. "Wait until it shows itself fully."

The creature seemed to pause for an eternity, unmoving, as silent and motionless as a stone gargoyle. Margo could see small red eyes watching her in the gloom. Every now and then the eyes disappeared, then reappeared, as the creature blinked.

The creature took another step, then froze again as if making up its mind, its low, powerful frame tensed and ready.

Then it started forward, coming down the hall toward them with a strange, terrifying lope.

"Now!" cried Pendergast.

Margo reached up and fumbled for the miner's helmet, and the hall was suddenly bathed in light. Almost immediately she heard a deafening WHANG! as Pendergast's powerful handgun barked next to her. The creature stopped briefly, and Margo could see it squinting, shaking its head against the light. It bent back as if to bite its haunch where the bullet had passed. Margo felt her mind receding from the reality: the low, pale head, horribly elongated, the crease of Pendergast's bullet a white stripe above the eyes; the powerful forequarters, covered with dense fur and ending in long, rending talons; the lower rear haunches, wrinkled skin descending to five-clawed toes. Its fur was matted with crusted blood, and fresh blood shone on the scales of the hindquarters.

WHANG! The creature's right foreleg was yanked behind it, and Margo heard a terrible roar of rage. It spun back to face them and sprang forward, ropes of saliva swinging madly from its jaws.

WHANG! went the gun—a miss—and the creature kept coming, accelerating with horrible deliberation.

WHANG!

She saw, as if in slow motion, the left hind leg jerk back, and the creature falter slightly. But it recovered, and, with a renewed howl, coarse hair bristling high on its haunches, it came for them again.

WHANG! went the gun, but the creature did not slow, and at that point Margo realized with great clarity that their plan had failed, that there was time for only one more shot and that the creature's charge could not be stopped. "Pendergast!" she cried, stumbling backward, her miner's light tilting crazily upward, scrambling away from the red eyes that stared straight into her own with a terrifyingly comprehensible blend of rage, lust, and triumph.

Garcia sat on the floor, ears straining, wondering if the voice he'd heard was real—if there was somebody else out there, trapped in this nightmare—or whether it had just been a trick of his overheated brain.

Suddenly, a very different sound boomed outside the door; then there was another, and another.

He scrambled to his feet. *It couldn't be true*. He fumbled with the radio.

"Do you hear that?" a voice behind him said.

Then the sound came again, twice; then, a short silence; then again.

"I swear to God, somebody's shooting in the hall!" Garcia cried.

There was a long, dreadful silence. "It's stopped," said Garcia in a whisper.

"Did they get it? Did they get it?" Waters whimpered.

The silence stretched on. Garcia clutched the shotgun, its pump and trigger guard slick from sweat. Five or six shots, that's all he'd heard. And the creature had killed a heavily armed SWAT team.

"Did they get it?" Waters asked again.

Garcia listened intently, but could hear nothing from the hall. This was the worst of all: the brief raising, then sudden dashing, of his hopes. He waited.

There was a rattling at the door.

"No," whispered Garcia. "It's back."

= **61** =

"Hand me that lighter!" D'Agosta barked. Smithback, falling blindly backward, saw the sudden spark of the flint and instinctively covered his eyes.

"Oh, Christ—" he heard D'Agosta groan. Then Smithback jerked as he felt something clutch his shoulder and drag him to his feet.

"Listen, Smithback," the voice of D'Agosta hissed in his ear, "you can't crap out on me now. I need you to help me keep these people together."

Smithback gagged as he forced his eyes open. The dirt floor ahead of him was awash in bones: small, large, some broken and brittle, others with gristle still clinging to their knobby ends.

"Not twigs," Smithback said, over and over again under his breath. "No, no, not twigs." The light flicked out again, D'Agosta conserving its flame.

Another yellow flash, and Smithback looked wildly around. What he had kicked aside was the remains of a dog—a terrier, by the looks of it—glassy, staring eyes, light fur, small brown teats descending in ordered rows to the torn-out belly. Scattered around the floor were other carcasses: cats, rats, other creatures too thoroughly mauled or too long dead to be recognizable. Behind him, someone was screaming relentlessly.

The light went out, then reappeared, farther ahead now as D'Agosta moved forward. "Smithback, come with me," came his voice. "Everybody, stare straight ahead. Let's go." As Smithback slowly placed one foot in front of the other, looking down just enough to avoid stepping on the loathesomeness beneath, something registered in his peripheral vision. He turned his head toward the wall to his right.

A pipe or duct had once run along the wall at shoulder height, but it had long since collapsed, its remains lying broken on the floor, half buried in offal. The heavy metal supports for the ductwork remained bolted to the wall, projecting outward like tines. Hung on the supports were a variety of human corpses, their forms seeming to waver in the dull glow of the flame. Smithback saw, but did not immediately comprehend, that all of the corpses had been decapitated. Scattered on the floor along the wall beneath were small ruined objects that he knew must be heads.

The bodies farthest from him had hung there the longest; they seemed more skeleton than flesh. He turned away, but not before his brain processed the final horror: on the meaty wrist of the nearest corpse was an unusual watch in the shape of a sundial. Moriarty's watch.

"Oh, my God . . . oh, my God," Smithback repeated over and over. "Poor George."

"You knew that guy?" D'Agosta said grimly. "Shit, this thing gets hot!"

The lighter flicked out again and Smithback immediately stopped moving.

"What kind of a place is this?" somebody behind them cried.

"I haven't the faintest," D'Agosta muttered.

"I do," Smithback said woodenly. "It's a *larder*."

The light came back on and he started forward again, more quickly now. Behind him, Smithback could hear the Mayor urging the people to keep moving in a dead, mechanical voice.

Suddenly, the light flicked out again, and the journalist froze in position. "We're at the far wall," he heard D'Agosta say in the darkness. "One of the passages here slopes down, the other slopes up. We're taking the high road."

D'Agosta flicked on the lighter again and continued forward, Smithback following. After several moments, the smell began to dissipate. The ground grew damp and soft beneath his feet. Smithback felt, or imagined he felt, the faintest hint of a cool breeze on his cheek.

D'Agosta laughed. "Christ, that feels fine."

The tunnel grew damp underfoot, then ended abruptly in another ladder. D'Agosta stepped towards it, reaching up with the lighter. Smithback moved forward eagerly, sniffing the freshening breeze.

There was a sudden rushing sound and then a thud-*thud!* above, and a bright light passed quickly above them, followed by a splash of viscous water.

"A manhole!" D'Agosta cried. "We made it, I can't believe it, we fucking made it!"

He scrambled up the ladder and heaved against the round plate.

"It's fastened down," he grunted. "Twenty men couldn't lift this. *Help!*" he started calling, clambering up the ladder and placing his mouth close to one of the pry-holes, *"Somebody help us, for Chrissake!"* And then he started to laugh, sinking against the metal ladder and dropping the lighter, and Smithback also collapsed to the floor of the passage, laughing, crying, unable to control himself.

"We made it," D'Agosta said through his laughter. "Smithback! We made it! Kiss me, Smithback—you fucking journalist, I love you and I hope you make a million on this."

Smithback heard a voice above them from the street.

"You hear somebody yelling?"

"Hey, you up there!" D'Agosta cried out. "Want to earn a reward?"

"Hear that? There *is* somebody down there. Yo!"

"Did you hear me? Get us out of here!"

"How much?" another voice asked.

"Twenty bucks! Call the fire department, get us out!"

"Fifty bucks, man, or we walk."

D'Agosta couldn't stop laughing. "Fifty dollars then! Now get us the hell out of here!"

He turned around and spread his arms. "Smithback, move everybody forward. Folks, Mayor Harper, welcome back to New York City!"

The door rattled once more. Garcia pressed the buttstock tight against his cheek, crying quietly. It was trying to get in again. He took a deep breath and tried to steady the shotgun.

Then he realized that the rattling had resolved itself into a knock.

It sounded again, louder, and Garcia heard a muffled voice.

"Is anyone in there?"

"Who is it?" Garcia answered thickly.

"Special Agent Pendergast, FBI."

Garcia could hardly believe it. As he opened the door he saw a tall, thin man looking placidly back at him, his pale hair and eyes ghostly in the dim hallway. He held a flashlight in one hand and a large pistol in the other. Blood trailed down one side of his face, and his shirt was soaked in crazy Rorschach patterns. A shortish young woman with mousy brown hair stood beside him, a yellow miner's lamp dwarfing her head, her face, hair, and sweater covered with more dark, wet stains.

Pendergast finally broke into a grin. "We did it," he said simply.

Only Pendergast's grin made Garcia realize that the blood covering the two was not their own. "How—?" he faltered.

They pushed their way past him as the others, lined up under the dark Museum schematic, stared, frozen by fear and disbelief.

Pendergast indicated a chair with the flashlight. "Have a seat, Ms. Green," he said.

"Thank you," said Margo, the miner's light on her forehead bobbing upward. "Such a gentleman."

Pendergast seated himself. "Does anyone have a handkerchief?" he asked.

Allen came forward, pulling one from his pocket.

Pendergast handed it to Margo, who wiped the blood from her face and handed it back. Pendergast carefully wiped his face and hands. "Much obliged, Mr.—?"

"Allen. Tom Allen."

"Mr. Allen." Pendergast handed the blood-soaked handkerchief to Allen, who started to return it to his pocket, froze, then dropped it quickly. He stared at Pendergast. "Is it dead?"

"Yes, Mr. Allen. It's quite dead."

"You killed it?"

"We killed it. Rather, Ms. Green here killed it."

"Call me Margo. And it was Mr. Pendergast who fired the shot."

"Ah, but Margo, you told me where to place the shot. I never would have thought of it. All big game—lion, water buffalo, elephant—have eyes on the *sides* of their head. If they're charging, you'd never consider the eye. It's just not a viable shot."

"But the creature," Margo explained to Allen, "had a primate's face. Eyes rotated to the front for stereoscopic vision. A direct path to the brain. And with that incredibly thick skull, once you put a bullet inside the brain, it would simply bounce around until it was spent."

"You killed the creature with a shot through the eye?" Garcia asked, incredulously.

"I'd hit it several times," Pendergast said, "but it was simply too strong and too angry. I haven't had a good look at the creature—I think I'll leave that until much later—but it's safe to say that no other shot could have stopped it in time."

Pendergast adjusted his tie knot with two slender fingers—unusually fastidious, Margo thought, considering the blood and bits of gray matter covering his white shirt. She would never forget the sight of the creature's brain exploding out of the ruined eye socket, at once a horrifying and beautiful sight. In fact, it was the eyes—the horrible, angry eyes—that had given her a sudden, desperate flash of an idea, even as she'd scrambled backward, away from the rotting stench and slaughterhouse breath.

Suddenly, she was clutching her sides, shivering.

In a moment, Pendergast had motioned to Garcia to give up his uniform jacket. He draped it over her shoulders. "Calm down, Margo," he said, kneeling at her side. "It's all over."

"We have to get Dr. Frock," she stammered through blue lips.

"In a minute, in a minute," Pendergast said soothingly.

"Shall we make a report?" Garcia asked. "This radio has just about enough juice left for one more broadcast."

"Yes, and we have to send a relief party for Lieutenant D'Agosta," Pendergast said. Then he frowned. "I suppose this means talking to Coffey."

"I don't think so," Garcia said. "Apparently, there's been a change of command."

Pendergast's eyebrows raised. "Indeed?"

"Indeed." Garcia handed the radio to Pendergast. "An agent named Slade is claiming to be in charge. Why don't you do the honors?"

"If you wish," Pendergast said. "I'm glad it's not Special Agent Coffey. Had it been, I'm afraid I would have taken him to task. I respond sharply to insults." He shook his head. "It's a very bad habit, but one I find hard to break."

= 62 =

Four Weeks Later

When Margo arrived, Pendergast and D'Agosta were already in Frock's office. Pendergast was examining something on a low table while Frock talked animatedly next to him. D'Agosta was walking restlessly around the office, looking bored, picking things up and putting them down again. The latex cast of the claw sat in the middle of Frock's desk like a nightmare paperweight. A large cake, purchased by Frock in celebration of Pendergast's imminent departure, sat in the middle of the warm sunlit room, the white icing already beginning to droop.

"Last time I was there, I had a crayfish gumbo that was truly magnificent," Frock was saying, gripping Pendergast's elbow. "Ah, Margo," he said, wheeling around. "Come in and take a look."

Margo crossed the room. Spring had finally taken hold of the city, and through the great bow windows she could see the blue expanse of the Hudson River flowing southward, sparkling in the sunlight. On the promenade below, joggers filed past in steady ranks.

A large re-creation of the creature's feet lay on the low table, next to the Cretaceous plaque of fossil footprints. Frock traced the tracks lovingly. "If not the same family, certainly the same order," he said. "And the creature did indeed have five toes on the hind feet. Yet another link to the Mbwun figurine."

Margo, looking closely, thought the two didn't seem all that similar. "Fractal evolution?" she suggested.

Frock looked at her. "It's possible. But it would take extensive cladistic analysis to know for sure." He grimaced. "Of course, that won't be possible, now that the government has whisked the remains away for God only knows what purpose."

In the month since the opening night disaster, public sentiment had gone from shock and incredulity, to fascination, to ultimate acceptance. For the first two weeks, the press had been abuzz with stories of the beast, but the conflicting accounts of the survivors created confusion and uncertainty. The only item that could settle the controversy—the corpse—was immediately removed from the scene in a large white van with government plates, never to be seen again. Even Pendergast claimed to be ignorant of its whereabouts. Publicity soon turned to the human cost of the disaster, and to the lawsuits that threatened the manufacturers of the security system and, to a lesser degree, the police department and the Museum itself. *Time* magazine had run a lead story entitled "How Safe Are Our National Institutions?" Now, weeks later, people had begun to view the creature as a one-of-a-kind phenomenon: a freak throwback, like the dinosaur fishes that occasionally showed up in the nets of deep-sea fishermen. Interest had started to wane: the opening-night survivors were no longer interviewed on talk shows, the projected Saturday morning cartoon series had been cancelled, and "Museum Beast" action figures were going unsold in toy stores.

Frock glanced around. "Forgive my lack of hospitality. Sherry, anyone?"

There were murmurs of "No, thanks."

"Not unless you've got a 7-Up chaser," D'Agosta said. Pendergast blanched and looked in his direction.

D'Agosta took the latex cast of the claw from Frock's desk and held it up. "Nasty," he said.

"Exceptionally nasty," Frock agreed. "It truly was part reptile, part primate. I won't go into the technical details—I'll leave that to Gregory Kawakita, who I've put to work analyzing what data we do have—but it appears that the reptilian genes are what gave the creature its strength, speed, and muscle mass. The primate genes contributed the intelligence and possibly made it endothermic. Warm-blooded. A formidable combination."

"Yeah, sure," D'Agosta said, laying the cast down. "But what the hell *was* it?"

Frock chuckled. "My dear fellow, we simply don't have enough data yet to say *exactly* what it was. And since it appears to have been the last of its kind, we may never know. We've just received an official survey of the *tepui* this creature came from. The devastation there has been complete. The plant this creature lived on, which by the way we have posthumously named *Liliceae mbwunensis*, appears to be totally extinct. Mining has poisoned the entire swamp surrounding the *tepui*. Not to mention the fact that the entire area was initially torched with napalm, to help clear the area for mining. There were no traces of any other similar creatures wandering about the forest anywhere. While I am normally horrified by such environmental destruction, in this case it appears to have rid the earth of a terrible menace." He sighed. "As a safety precaution—and against my advice, I might add—the FBI has destroyed all the packing fibers and plant specimens here in the Museum. So the plant, too, is truly extinct."

"How do we know it was the last of its kind?" Margo asked. "Couldn't there be another somewhere?"

"Not likely," said Frock. "That *tepui* was an ecological island—by all accounts, a unique place in which animals and plants had developed a singular interdependence over literally millions of years."

"And there certainly aren't any more creatures in the Museum," Pendergast said, coming forward. "With those ancient blueprints I found at the Historical Society, we were able to section off the sub-basement and comb every square inch. We found many things of interest to urban archaeologists, but no further sign of the creature."

"It looked so sad in death," Margo said. "So lonely. I almost feel sorry for it."

"It *was* lonely," said Frock, "lonely and lost. Traveling four thousand miles from its jungle home, following the trail of the last remaining specimens of the precious plants that kept it alive and free from pain. But it was very evil, and very fierce. I saw at least twelve bullet holes in the carcass before they took it away."

The door opened and Smithback walked in, theatrically waving a manila envelope in one hand and a magnum of champagne in the other. He whipped a sheaf of papers out of the envelope, holding them skyward with one long arm.

"A book contract, folks!" he said, grinning.

D'Agosta scowled and turned away, picking up the claw again.

"I got everything I wanted, and made my agent rich," Smithback crowed.

"And yourself rich, too," said D'Agosta, looking as if he'd like to use the claw on the writer.

Smithback cleared his throat dramatically. "I've decided to donate half the royalties to a fund set up in memory of Officer John Bailey. To benefit his family."

D'Agosta turned toward Smithback. "Get lost," he said.

"No, really," said Smithback. "Half the royalties. After the advance has earned out, of course," he added hastily.

D'Agosta started to step toward Smithback, then stopped abruptly. "You got my cooperation," he said in a low voice, his jaw working stiffly.

"Thanks, Lieutenant. I think I'll need it."

"That's Captain, as of yesterday," said Pendergast.

"Captain D'Agosta?" Margo asked. "You've been promoted?"

D'Agosta nodded. "Couldn't happen to a nicer guy, the Chief tells me." He pointed a finger at Smithback. "I get to read what you say about me *before* it goes to press, Smithback."

"Now wait a minute," Smithback said, "there are certain ethics that journalists have to follow—"

"Balls!" D'Agosta exploded.

Margo turned to Pendergast. "I can see this will be an exciting collaboration," she whispered. Pendergast nodded.

There was a light rapping, and the head of Greg Kawakita appeared from around the door to the outer office. "Oh, I'm sorry, Doctor Frock," he said, "your secretary didn't tell me you were busy. We can go over the results later."

"Nonsense!" cried Frock. "Come in, Gregory. Mr. Pendergast, Captain D'Agosta, this is Gregory Kawakita. He's the author of the G.S.E., the extrapolation program that allowed us to come up with such an accurate profile of the creature."

"You have my gratitude," Pendergast said. "Without that program, none of us would have been here today."

"Thanks very much, but the program was really Dr. Frock's brainchild," Kawakita said, eyeing the cake. "I just put the pieces together. Besides, there were a lot of things the Extrapolator *didn't* tell you. The forward placement of the eyes, for instance."

"Why, Greg, success has made you humble," Smithback said. "In any case," he continued, turning to Pendergast, "I've got a few questions for *you*. This vintage champagne doesn't come free, you know." He fixed the FBI agent with an expectant gaze. "Whose bodies did we discover in the lair, anyway?"

Pendergast raised his shoulders in a slight shrug. "I guess there's no harm in telling you—although this is not for publication until you receive official word. As it happens, five of the eight remains have been identified. Two were those of homeless street persons, who crept into the Old Basement, presumably looking for warmth on a winter's night. Another was that of a foreign tourist we found on Interpol's missing persons list. Another, as you know, was George Moriarty, the Assistant Curator under Ian Cuthbert."

"Poor George," Margo whispered. For weeks, she had avoided thinking about Moriarty's last moments, his final struggle with the beast. To die that way, then to be hung up like a side of beef . . .

Pendergast waited a moment before continuing. "The fifth body has been tentatively identified from dental records as a man named Montague, an employee of the Museum who vanished several years ago."

"Montague!" Frock said. "So the story was true."

"Yes," said Pendergast. "It seems that certain members of the Museum administration—Wright, Rickman, Cuthbert, and perhaps Ippolito—suspected there was something prowling the Museum. When a vast quantity of blood was found in the Old Basement, they had it washed away without notifying the police. When Montague's disappearance coincided with that discovery, the group did nothing to shed any light on the event. They also had reason to believe that the creature was somehow connected to the Whittlesey expedition. Those suspicions may have been behind the moving of the crates. In retrospect, it was a terribly unwise move: It was what precipitated the killings."

"You're right, of course," Frock said, wheeling himself back toward his desk. "We know the creature was highly intelligent. It realized it would be in danger if its existence in the Museum was discovered. I think it must have curbed its normally fierce nature as a means of self-preservation. When it first reached the Museum, it was desperate, perhaps feral, and it killed Montague when it saw him with the artifacts and the plants. But after that, it grew quickly cautious. It knew where the crates were, and it had a supply of the plant—or, at least, it would until the packing material gave out. It was parsimonious in its consumption. Of course, the hormones in the plant were highly concentrated. And the beast supplemented its diet occasionally, in stealthy ways. Rats living in the subbasement, cats escaped from the Animal Behavior department . . . once or twice, even luckless human beings that wandered too deep into the Museum's secret places. But it was always careful to conceal its kills, and several years passed in which it remained—for the most part—undetected." He shifted slightly, the wheelchair creaking.

"Then it happened. The crates were removed, put under lock and key in the Secure Area. The beast grew first hungry, then desperate.

Perhaps it grew murderous with rage at the beings who had deprived it of the plants—beings who themselves could be a substitute, though poor, for that which they'd taken away. The frenzy grew, and the beast killed, then killed again."

Frock withdrew his handkerchief and wiped his forehead. "But it didn't lose *all* rationality," he continued. "Remember how it hid the body of the policeman in the exhibition? Even though its blood lust had been aroused, even though it was mad with desire for the plants, it had the presence of mind to realize that the killings were attracting unwanted attention to itself. Perhaps it had planned on bringing the body of Beauregard back down to its lair. Chances are, it was unable to do so—the exhibition was far beyond its usual haunts—so it hid the body instead. After all, the hypothalamus was its primary objective; the rest was just meat."

Margo shuddered.

"I've wondered more than once just why the beast went into that exhibition," Pendergast said.

Frock raised his index finger. "So have I. And I think I know the reason. Remember, Mr. Pendergast, what *else* was in the exhibition."

Pendergast nodded slowly. "Of course. The figurine of Mbwun."

"Exactly," said Frock. "The figurine depicting the beast itself. The creature's one link with its home, the home that it had lost utterly."

"You seem to have it all figured out," Smithback said. "But if Wright and Cuthbert were aware of this thing, how did they know it was connected with the Whittlesey expedition?"

"I believe I can answer that," Pendergast said. "They knew, of course, why the ship carrying the crates from Belém to New Orleans was delayed so long—much the way you learned, I expect, Mr. Smithback."

Smithback suddenly looked nervous. "Well," he began, "I—"

"They also read Whittlesey's journal. And they knew the legends as well as anybody. Then, when Montague—the person assigned to curating the crates—disappeared, and a pool of blood was discovered near the location of the crates, it didn't take a savant to put everything together. And besides," he said, his expression clouding, "Cuthbert more or less confirmed it for me. As well as he was able, of course."

Frock nodded. "They paid a terrible price. Winston and Lavinia dead, Ian Cuthbert institutionalized . . . it's distressing beyond words."

"True," Kawakita said, "but it's no secret that it's made you top contender for the next Director of the Museum."

He would think of that, Margo thought.

Frock shook his head. "I doubt if it will be offered me, Gregory. Once the dust settles, rational heads will prevail. I'm too controversial. Besides, the Directorship doesn't interest me. I have too much new material here for me to delay my next book any longer."

"One thing that Dr. Wright and the rest didn't know," Pendergast went on—"in fact, something that nobody here knows—is that the killings didn't start in New Orleans. There was a very similar murder in Belém, in the warehouse where the crates had been housed while awaiting shipping. I learned about it when I was investigating the shipboard killings."

"That must have been the creature's first stop on the way to New York," Smithback said. "I guess it brings the story full circle." He guided Pendergast to the sofa. "Now, Mr. Pendergast, I suppose this also solves the mystery of what happened to Whittlesey."

"The creature killed him, that seems fairly certain," said Pendergast. "Say, you don't mind if I get a piece of that cake—"

Smithback placed a restraining hand on his arm. "How do you know?"

"That it killed Whittlesey? We found a souvenir in its lair."

"You did?" Smithback whipped out his microcassette recorder.

"Put that back in your pocket, if you please, Mr. Smithback. Yes, it was something Whittlesey wore around his neck, apparently. A medallion in the shape of a double arrow."

"That was embossed on his journal!" Smithback said.

"And on the letterhead of the note he sent Montague!" Margo chimed in.

"Apparently it was Whittlesey's family crest. We found it in the lair; a piece of it, anyway. Why the beast carried it from the Amazon we'll never know, but there it is."

"We found other artifacts in there, too," said D'Agosta, through a mouthful of cake. "Along with a pile of Maxwell's seed pods. The thing was a regular collector."

"Like what?" Margo asked, walking toward one of the bow windows and gazing out at the landscape beyond.

"Things you wouldn't expect. A set of car keys, a lot of coins and subway tokens, even a beautiful gold pocket watch. We looked up the guy whose name was inscribed inside the watch, and he told us he'd lost it three years ago. He'd visited the Museum, and been pickpocketed." D'Agosta shrugged. "Maybe that pickpocket is one of the unidentified bodies. Or maybe we'll never find him."

"The creature kept it hung by its chain from a nail in the wall of its lair," Pendergast said. "It liked beautiful things. Another sign of intelligence, I suppose."

"Was everything picked up from inside the Museum?" asked Smithback.

"As far as we can tell," Pendergast said. "There's no evidence the creature could—or wanted to—obtain egress from the Museum."

"No?" Smithback said. "Then what about the exit you were leading D'Agosta toward?"

"He found it," Pendergast said simply. "You were all very lucky."

Smithback turned to ask D'Agosta another question, and Pendergast took the opportunity to get up and head for the cake. "It was awfully nice of you to throw me this party, Dr. Frock," he said as he returned.

"You saved our lives," Frock said. "I thought a little cake might be in order as our way of wishing you bon voyage."

"I'm afraid, then," Pendergast continued, "that I may be at this party under false pretenses."

"Why is that?" Frock asked.

"I may not be leaving New York permanently. The directorship of the New York office is up for reassignment, you see."

"You mean it's not going to Coffey?" Smithback smirked.

Pendergast shook his head. "Poor Mr. Coffey," he said. "I hope he enjoys his position in the Waco field office. In any case, the Mayor, who has become a great fan of Captain D'Agosta here, seems to think I have a good shot at it."

"Congratulations!" cried Frock.

"It isn't certain yet," Pendergast said. "Nor am I certain I care to remain up here. Although the place does have its charms."

He got up and walked to the bow window, where Margo was standing, staring out at the Hudson River and the green hills of the Palisades beyond.

"What are your plans, Margo?" he asked.

She turned to face him. "I've decided to stay at the Museum until I've finished my dissertation."

Frock laughed. "The truth is, I refused to let her go," he said.

Margo smiled. "Actually, I've received an offer from Columbia. Tenure-track Assistant Professorship, starting next year. Columbia was my father's alma mater. So I've *got* to finish it, you see."

"Great news!" said Smithback. "We'll have to celebrate over dinner tonight."

"Dinner? Tonight?"

"Café des Artistes, seven o'clock," he said. "Listen, you've got to come. I'm a world-famous author, or about to become one. This champagne's getting warm," he continued, reaching for the bottle.

Everyone crowded round as Frock brought out glasses. Smithback angled the bottle toward the ceiling and fired off the cork with a satisfying *pop*.

"What'll we drink to?" asked D'Agosta, as the glasses were filled.

"To my book," said Smithback.

"To Special Agent Pendergast, and a safe journey home," Frock said.

"To the memory of George Moriarty," Margo said quietly.

"To George Moriarty."

There was a silence.

"God bless us, everyone," Smithback intoned. Margo punched him playfully.

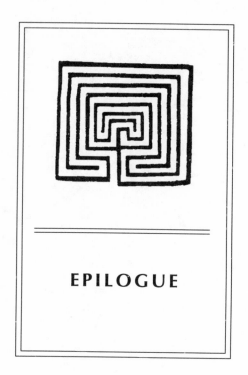

EPILOGUE

= **63** =

Long Island City, Six Months Later

The rabbit jerked as the needle sank into its haunch. Kawakita watched as the dark blood filled up the syringe.

He placed the rabbit carefully back in its hutch, then transferred the blood to three centrifugal test tubes. He opened the nearby centrifuge, slotted the tubes into the drum, and shut the lid. Flicking the switch, he listened to the hum slowly build to a whine as the force of the rotation separated the blood into its components.

He sat back in the wooden chair and let his eyes roam around the surroundings. The office was dusty and the lighting dim, but Kawakita preferred it that way. No sense in drawing attention to oneself.

It had been very difficult in the beginning: finding the right place, assembling the equipment, even paying the rent. It was unbelievable how much they wanted for rundown warehouses in Queens. The computer had been the hardest item to come by. Instead of buying one, he had finally managed to hack his way over the telephone long lines into a large mainframe at the Solokov College of Medicine. It was a relatively secure site from which to run his Genetic Extrapolation Program.

He peered through the dingy window to the shop floor below. The large space was dark and relatively vacant, the only light coming from aquariums sitting on metal racks along the far wall. He could hear the faint bubbling of the filtration systems. The lights from the tanks cast a dim greenish glow across the floor. Two dozen, give or take a few. Soon, he'd need more. But money was becoming less and less of a problem.

It was amazing, thought Kawakita, how the most elegant solutions were the simplest ones. Once you saw it, the answer was obvious. But it was *seeing* that answer for the first time that separated the timeless scientist from the merely great.

The Mbwun riddle was like that. He, Kawakita, had been the only one to suspect it, to see it, and—now—to prove it.

The whine of the centrifuge began to decrease in pitch, and soon the COMPLETED light began blinking a slow, monotonous red. Kawakita got up, opened the lid, and removed the tubes. The rabbit blood had been divided into its three constituents: clear serum on top, a thin layer of white blood cells in the middle, and a heavy layer of red blood cells at the bottom. He carefully suctioned off the serum, then placed drops of the cells into a series of watchglasses. Finally, he added various reagents and enzymes.

One of the watchglasses turned purple.

Kawakita smiled. It had been so simple.

After Frock and Margo had blundered up to him at the party, his initial skepticism had quickly changed to fascination. He had been on the periphery before, not really paying attention. But practically from the minute he'd hit Riverside Drive that evening—carried along in the stream of countless other hysterical guests who'd rushed from the opening—he began thinking. Then, in the aftermath, he began asking questions. When later he'd heard Frock pronounce the mystery solved, Kawakita's curiosity had only increased. Perhaps, to be fair, he'd had a little more objective distance than those who'd been inside the Museum that night, fighting the beast in the dark. But whatever the reason, there seemed to be small defects with the solution: little problems, minor contradictions that everyone had missed.

Everyone except Kawakita.

He'd always been a very cautious researcher; cautious, yet full of insatiable curiosity. It had helped him in the past: at Oxford, and in his early days at the Museum. And now, it helped him again. His caution had made him build a keystroke capture routine into the Extrapolator. For security reasons, of course—but also to learn what others might use his program for.

So it was only natural that he'd go back and examine what Frock and Margo had done.

All he'd had to do was press a few keys, and the program reeled off every question Frock and Margo had asked, every bit of data they had entered, and every result they had obtained.

That data had pointed him toward the *real* solution to the Mbwun mystery. It had been there under their noses the whole time, had they known what questions to ask. Kawakita learned to ask the right questions. And along with the answer came a stunning discovery.

A soft knock sounded at the warehouse door. Kawakita walked down the stairs to the main floor of the warehouse, moving without sound or hesitation through the gloom.

"Who is it?" he whispered, his voice hoarse.

"Tony," said the voice.

Kawakita effortlessly slid back the iron bar from the door and pulled it open. A figure stepped through.

"It's dark in here," the man said. He was small and wiry, and walked with a distinct roll to his shoulders. He looked around nervously.

"Keep the lights off," said Kawakita sharply. "Follow me."

They walked to the far end of the warehouse. There, a long table had been set up under dull infrared lamps. The table was covered with drying fibers. At the end of the table was a scale. Kawakita scooped up a small handful of fibers and weighed them, removing several, then dropping a few back on. Then he slid the fibers into a Ziploc bag.

He looked at his visitor expectantly. The man dug his hand into his pants pocket and extended a wad of crumpled bills. Kawakita counted them: five twenties. He nodded and handed over the small bag. The man grabbed it eagerly, and began to tear open the seam.

"Not here!" said Kawakita.

"Sorry," the man said. He moved toward the door as quickly as the dim light would allow.

"Try larger amounts," Kawakita suggested. "Steep it in boiling water, that increases the concentration. I think you'll find the results very gratifying."

The man nodded. "Gratifying," he said slowly, as if tasting the word.

"I will have more for you on Tuesday," Kawakita said.

"Thank you," the man whispered, and left.

Kawakita closed the door and slid the bolt back in place. It had been a long day, and he felt bone tired, but he was looking forward to nightfall, when the sounds of the city would subside and darkness would cover the land. Night was rapidly becoming his favorite time of the day.

Once he reconstructed what Frock and Margo had done with his program, everything else fell into place. All he'd needed was to find one of the fibers. But that proved a difficult task. The Secure Area had been painstakingly cleaned, and the crates had been emptied of their artifacts and burned, along with the packing material. The lab where

Margo had done the initial work was now spotless, the plant press destroyed. But nobody had remembered to clean out Margo's handbag, which was notorious throughout the Anthropology Department for its untidiness. Margo herself had thrown it in the Museum incinerator several days after the disaster, as a precaution. But not before Kawakita had found the fiber he needed.

Despite his other trials, the supreme challenge had been growing the plant from a single fiber. It had taxed all his abilities, his knowledge of botany and genetics. But he was channeling all his ferocious energies into one thing now—thoughts of tenure vanished, a leave of absence taken from the Museum. And he had finally achieved it, not five weeks earlier. He remembered the surge of triumph he felt when the little green node appeared on an agar-covered petri dish. And now he had a large and steady supply growing in the tanks, fully inoculated with the reovirus. The strange reovirus that dated back sixty-five million years.

It had proven to be a perversely attractive type of lily pad, blooming almost continuously, big deep purple blossoms with venous appendages and bright yellow stamens. The virus was concentrated in the tough, fibrous stem. He was harvesting two pounds a week, and poised to increase his yield exponentially.

The Kothoga knew all about this plant, thought Kawakita. What appeared to be a blessing turned out for them to be a curse. They had tried to control its power, but failed. The legend told it best: the devil failed to keep his bargain, and the child of the devil, the Mbwun, had run wild. It had turned on its masters. It could not be controlled.

But Kawakita would not fail. The rabbit serum tests proved that he would succeed.

The final piece of the puzzle fell into place when he remembered what that cop, D'Agosta, had mentioned at the going-away party for the FBI agent: that they had found a double-arrow pendant belonging to Julian Whittlesey in the creature's lair. Proof, they said, that the monster had killed Whittlesey. Proof. What a joke.

Proof, rather, that the monster **was** *Whittlesey.*

Kawakita remembered clearly the day everything came together for him. It was an apotheosis, a revelation. It explained everything. The creature, the Museum Beast, He Who Walks On All Fours, *was* Whittlesey. And the proof lay within his grasp: his extrapolation program. Kawakita had placed human DNA on one side and the reovirus DNA on the other. And then he had asked for the intermediate form.

The computer gave the creature: He Who Walks On All Fours.

The reovirus in the plant was astonishing. Chances are, it had existed relatively unchanged since the Mesozoic era. In sufficient quantities, it had the power to induce morphological change of an astonishing nature. Everyone knew that the darkest, most isolated areas of rain forest held undiscovered plants of almost inconceivable importance to science. But Kawakita had already discovered his miracle. By eating the fibers and becoming infected with the reovirus, Whittlesey had turned into Mbwun.

Mbwun—the word the Kothoga used for the wonderful, terrible plant, *and for the creatures those who ate it became*. Kawakita could now visualize parts of the Kothoga's secret religion. The plants were a curse that was simultaneously hated and needed. The creatures kept the enemies of the Kothoga at bay—yet they themselves were a constant threat to their masters. Chances are, the Kothoga only kept one of the creatures around at a time—more than that would be too dangerous. The cult would have centered around the plant itself, its cultivation and harvesting. The climax of their ceremonials was undoubtedly the induction of a new creature—the force-feeding of the plant to the unwilling human victim. Initially, large quantities of the plant would be needed to ensure sufficient reovirus to effect the bodily change. Once the transformation was complete, the plant need be consumed only in small quantities, supplemented of course by other proteins. But it was critical that the dose be maintained. Otherwise, intense pain, even madness, would result as the body tried to revert. Of course, death would intervene before that happened. And the desperate creature would, if at all possible, find a substitute for the plant—the human hypothalamus being by far the most satisfactory.

In the close, comforting darkness, listening to the tranquil humming of the aquaria, Kawakita could guess at the drama that had played itself out in the jungle. The Kothoga, laying eyes on a white man for the first time. Whittlesey's accomplice, Crocker, had no doubt been found first. Perhaps the creature had been old, or enfeebled. Perhaps Crocker had killed the creature with the expedition's gun as the creature disembowelled him. Or perhaps not. But when the Kothoga found Whittlesey, Kawakita knew there was only one possible outcome.

He wondered what Whittlesey must have felt: bound, perhaps ceremonially, being force-fed the reovirus from the strange plant he himself had collected just days earlier. Perhaps they brewed him a liquor from the plant's leaves, or perhaps they simply forced him to eat the dried fibers. They must have attempted to do with this white man what they had failed to do with their own kind: create a monster they could *control*. A monster that would keep out the road builders and the prospectors and the miners that were poised to invade the *tepui* from the south and destroy them. A monster that would terrorize the surrounding tribes *without* terrorizing its masters; that would ensure the security and isolation of the Kothoga forever.

But then civilization came anyway, with all its terrors. Kawakita imagined the day it happened: the Whittlesey-thing, crouched in the jungle, seeing the fire come falling from the sky, burning the *tepui*, the Kothoga, the precious plants. He alone escaped. And he alone knew where the life-giving fibers could still be found after the jungle was destroyed: He knew, because he had sent them there.

Or perhaps Whittlesey was already gone when the *tepui* was burned. Perhaps the Kothoga had been unable to control, once again, the creature they had created. Maybe Whittlesey, in his pitiful, terrible condition, had set his own agenda, which hadn't included sticking around as the Kothoga's avenging angel. Perhaps he'd simply wanted to go home. So he had abandoned the Kothoga, and the Kothoga had been destroyed by progress.

But, for the most part, Kawakita was indifferent to the anthropological details. He was interested in the power inherent in the plant, and the harnessing of such power.

You needed to control the source before you could control the creature.

And that, thought Kawakita, *is exactly why I'm going to succeed where the Kothoga failed.* He was controlling the source. Only he knew how to grow this difficult and delicate swamp lily from the depths of the Amazon jungle. Only he knew the proper pH of the water, the right temperature, the proper light, the correct mix of nutrients. Only he knew how to inoculate the plant with the reovirus.

They would be dependent on him. And, with the genetic splicing he had done through the rabbit serum, he'd been able to purify the essential strength of the virus, engineering it to be cleaner while diminishing some of the more unpleasant side effects.

At least, he was fairly sure he had.

These were revolutionary discoveries. Everyone knew that viruses inserted their own DNA into the cells of their victim. Normally, that DNA would simply instruct the victim's cells to make more viruses. That's what happened in every virus known to man: from the flu to AIDS.

This virus was different. It inserted a whole array of genes into its victim: *reptile* genes. Ancient reptile genes; sixty-five-million-year-old genes. Found today in the lowly gecko and a few other species. And it had apparently borrowed primate genes—no doubt human genes—over time, as well. A virus that stole genes from its host, and incorporated those genes into its victims.

Those genes, instead of making more viruses, remade the *victim*. Reshaped the victim, bit by bit, into a monster. The viruses instructed the body's own machinery to change the bone structure, the endocrine system, the limbs and skin and hair and internal organs. It changed the behavior, the weight, speed, and cunning of the victim. Gave the victim uncanny senses of smell and hearing, but diminished its eyesight and voice. Gave it immense power, and bulk, and speed, while leaving its wonderful hominid brain relatively intact. In short, the drug—the *virus*—turned a human victim into a terrible killing machine. No, the word *victim* did not fairly describe one infected with the virus. A better word might be *symbiont*. Because it was a privilege to receive the virus. A gift. A gift from Greg Kawakita.

It was beautiful. In fact, it was sublime.

The possibilities for genetic engineering were endless. And already, Kawakita had ideas for improvements. New genes the reovirus could insert into its host. Human genes as well as animal genes. He controlled what genes the reovirus would insert into its host. He controlled what the host would become. Unlike the primitive, superstitious Kothoga, he was in control—through science.

An interesting side effect of the plant was its narcotic effect: a wonderful, "clean" rush, without the unpleasant down of so many other drugs. Perhaps that was how the plant had originally ensured its own ingestion and, thus, its propagation. But for Kawakita, this side effect had provided cash from which to finance his research. He hadn't wanted to sell the drug originally, but the financial pressures he'd experienced had made it inevitable. He smiled as he thought of how easy it had been. The drug had already been given a name by the select coterie of eager users: *glaze*. The market was avid, and Kawakita could sell as much as he could make. Too bad it seemed to go so quickly.

Night had fallen. Kawakita removed his dark glasses and inhaled the rich fragrance of the warehouse, the subtle odor of the fibers, the smell of water and dust and internal combustion from the ambient air, mingled with mold and sulphur dioxide and a multitude of other smells. His chronic allergies had all but vanished. *Must be the clean Long Island air*, he thought wryly. He removed his tight shoes and curled his toes with pleasure.

He had made the most stunning advancement in genetics since the discovery of the double helix. It would have won him a Nobel Prize, he thought with an ironic smile.

Had he chosen that route.

But who needed a Nobel Prize, when the whole world was suddenly there for the plucking?

There came another knock at the door.